MURDER
ON THE BAY

by

Mark Ciccone

with illustrations by
Eileen Keeney

Riverhaven

Books

Printed in the United States of America

Paperback ISBN: 978-1-951854-50-8

Front cover by Erin Tilley Graphic Design,
https://erintilley.myportfolio.com

Edited by Christopher Blackman

Formatted by Riverhaven Books

To Eileen and all the girls
as well as
to the good folk of Duxbury—
past, present, and yet to come

"Halfway down a by-street of one of our New England towns stands a rusty wooden house…The aspect of the venerable mansion has always affected me like a human countenance, bearing the traces not merely of outward storm and sunshine, but expressive also, of the long lapse of mortal life, and accompanying vicissitudes that have passed within."

~The *House of* the *Seven Gables,* Nathaniel Hawthorne

"Here, said she, is your card, the drowned Phoenician Sailor,
(Those were pearls that were his eyes. Look!)…
Fear death by water."

~The *Waste Land,* T.S. Eliot

DUXBURY HARBOR AND BAY

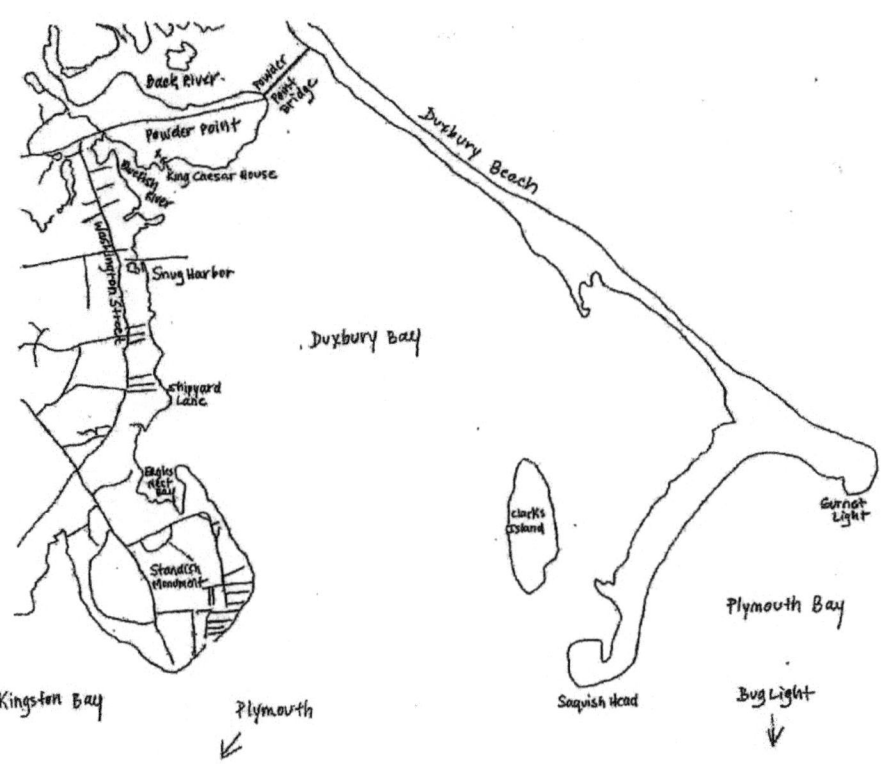

Back River

Powder Point Bridge

Powder Point

Bluefish River

King Caesar House

Duxbury Beach

Snug Harbor

Washington Street

Duxbury Bay

Shipyard Lane

Eagles Nest Bay

Clarks Island

Gurnet Light

Standish Monument

Plymouth Bay

Kingston Bay

Plymouth

Saquish Head

Bug Light

CHAPTER 1
THE DEATH

I'd been living in my late Uncle Fred's house for about a month when I began to suspect he may have been murdered.

That he'd died a few weeks previously had not been particularly surprising. After all, he'd been eighty years old. And the cause of his death due to a fall, though tragic, was not an uncommon one. Unfortunately, many otherwise healthy elderly people die that way. But aside from that, several puzzling things had occurred since then that had sent my head spinning.

The first was the very fact that I was living in his house in the first place. Not only was I living in it, but I now owned it because he'd left it to me in his will. Having not seen him for fifteen years nor having been particularly close to him for another fifteen years before that, his bequeathment had shocked me. I'd received a letter from a lawyer in Boston named Lyle Danforth, informing me of my inheritance and asking me to telephone him.

"I can assure you this is no mistake, Mr. Pavlik," Danforth had said as a reaction to my astonishment. "Your uncle's will clearly states his desire to leave you his house in Duxbury. There are some strings attached that you need to understand though."

"But where is Duxbury?" I asked. "I've not only never been there, I've never heard of the place. Last I knew he was living in Manhattan."

"It's a seaside community south of Boston, halfway to Cape Cod. He bought the place five years ago as kind of a vacation home. He had moved there full time about a year ago. You should come here and take a look. I can fill you in on a few things you need to know. Best done in person."

Two days later, I flew from my home in Toledo, Ohio to Boston and met Danforth in his office on Commonwealth Avenue in the Back Bay area of the city.

"I can't believe this whole inheritance thing," I said as I shook his hand. "I hadn't been in touch with my uncle for many years."

"True," said the lawyer with a smile. "But he liked you. He said he had many pleasant memories of you when you were a kid going to baseball games and such with him. And the fact is that he had no immediate family to leave his property to."

That much I remembered. Fred Peterson of Toledo had married Mary Kaminski, also of Toledo, and moved to New York City as a young couple. When Mary died years later of breast cancer, I went to the funeral with my mother Donna, who was Fred's sister. That funeral was fifteen years ago, and that was the last time I had seen my uncle Fred. Mary and Fred hadn't had children, and he had never remarried.

"Fred had done very well for himself financially," Danforth continued. "He had a very successful career in private equity in New York. He gave a big chunk of money to charity."

"He did have some family, though. He had another nephew and niece," I said, recalling my cousins Colin and Beth. They were the children of Fred's brother, my uncle Mike.

"Yes, but he told me he was not close to them."

I hadn't particularly cared for the two of them either. Uncle Mike was a widower living in St. Louis last I knew, and I hadn't seen him or my two cousins in twenty-five years. I'd never seen much of them before that either. I dimly remembered Colin as pretentious and Beth as a snob. I briefly thought of pressing Danforth for more information on them, but decided it was none of my business. Instead I asked him about the details of my uncle's death.

"It's very sad. He had paddled in his kayak out to an oyster farm just off shore in Duxbury Bay. He had been investing in the oyster business and wanted to learn more about it. He tried to climb out of his kayak onto one of the floating oyster sheds, fell on the platform, and knocked his head. He died of the blow."

"That's terrible," I said.

"Yes. Fred always thought of himself as a young man, even to the end. He took that kayak out somewhere every day in good weather, even

2

at his age. I'd warned him to slow down. Frankly I'd seen a change in him recently. Physically, he'd lost some energy. Mentally, he'd grown a bit scattered. And then he slipped on that platform."

The lawyer shook his head, then held up a document in front of me.

"This is your uncle's will." His voice had turned very serious. "Before you read it, I'll explain his thinking. You'll need this perspective."

"Sounds like it's going to be complicated."

"Your uncle was a complicated man. He gave most of his money away to causes and institutions that he felt strongly about. But he had great uncertainty about what to do with this house. He had me change his will several times in the last year regarding it. His mind was pulling him in two different directions."

"What do you mean?" I asked. The deeper I got into this, the more confused I was getting.

"Fred had developed a great love for history over the years. It became much more than a hobby. It was a central part of his life. He donated significant sums of money to various preservation projects around the country and even the world. Houses, churches, battlefields, museums — he had a broad range of historical interests. His style was to provide matching funds to various non-profits that were raising money. That way, he not only gave money, but he also encouraged others to do so."

"A real philanthropist, eh?" I said. "He's been the only one in the family, I guess. None of the rest of us have had a lot of money."

"But he was conflicted about this house," the lawyer continued, furrowing his brow. "He loved the history of it and initially wanted to give it to the local historical society. Then he changed his mind. Toward the end of his life, he became quite depressed that he'd never had a family of his own. In addition, he'd become estranged from your mother and his brother, Mike. He regretted he hadn't kept up with your mother. They'd always had a good relationship. But with Mike it was different. They had some sort of disagreement many years ago and never reconciled."

3

This was the first time in many years I'd heard any talk whatsoever about the three Peterson siblings. I knew they had grown apart but never knew why. I still didn't. Maybe it's just what families do over the years.

"But Fred did have fond memories of you, even if not recent ones," the lawyer continued. "This house had become very personal for him, and he began to think he should keep it in the family as a sort of legacy. And giving it to you was his solution. He'd only made his final decision a few weeks ago. He was planning on contacting you to explain it all, but he died so suddenly."

"And the complication is what?"

"I'll cut to the chase. He decided to leave you the house but under strict conditions. What he didn't want was for you to get a house that you didn't want and then just sell it on the open market. He said if you didn't want it, he'd give it to the town's historical society."

Danforth was getting at a key point I'd been considering from the very moment we'd first talked on the phone and I learned of the inheritance: I didn't know what I would do with this house. I'd gotten my own little place in Toledo that suited me fine. I'd moved there from LA when Melanie and I had divorced two years previously. Nothing was tying me to Southern California, and I figured I should be near my mother in Toledo who was in failing health. She probably didn't have much longer, and I figured I should be there. The small townhouse I had bought was more than enough for me. I didn't need a second house or its upkeep.

"So what are these strict conditions?" I asked.

"He spelled it out in this will. Let me summarize and then you can read it. He is giving you two options. First option: if you know for sure you don't want it, it goes to the town's historical society outright. He would leave you some cash instead."

Danforth mentioned an amount. It was what I'd call a very nice but modest sum for a man whom I'd just been told was wealthy. On the other hand, I'd been expecting nothing two days ago, and so anything he was leaving me was found money.

4

"What's the second option?" I asked.

"If you want the house—either as your primary residence or as a second home—it's yours. However, the requirement is that you need to keep it for at least two years—no selling, no renting it out. If you sell after that, the historical society has the right of first refusal to buy it from you at 25% of the assessed value at the time of sale. That way you get some money out of it, and the society gets the house at a price they can probably afford."

"That's very generous of him."

"It gets better. If after five years you decide to sell, you keep 100% of the sale price. By structuring the deal this way, he is showing that his clear hope is that you will want to keep the house in the family long term. That said, if you decide after two years it's just not working for you, he is giving you a very nice 'out.' I assure you that 25% of the appraised value of this place is a good chunk of money. Think of it as a sort of vesting process. The longer you keep the property, the better the value for you."

He gave me the will and I read it. I'm glad he'd explained this up front because it was written in a legalese. I'm not sure I would have totally comprehended had he not.

"Fair enough," I said when I'd finished. "I guess the ball is in my court now. I need to decide if I want to keep the house for at least two or five years or take his immediate cash offering instead. Can I have a few days to think this over? There's a lot to consider here."

"Yes. How about a week? Fred didn't want the fate of the house to be up in the air too long. A week should be enough. I am fully aware that this is highly unconventional. I told Fred that. I told him it was cleaner to give you a nice chunk of money outright and donate the house to the historical society. But he insisted on doing it this way. You'll want to start by checking out the property."

Checking the place out was precisely what I had intended to do even before I'd learned of this little bit of complexity. I had asked Danforth to set me up to meet with a local real estate broker at the house, which he had done. I wanted to spend the weekend there. I got up to leave, shook his hand, and thanked him

"I'll be in touch next week," I said.

"Fine. And one more thing you should know. Nobody, including the Duxbury historical society, knows the terms of this will. I am aware of the possibility that some members may know that Fred was thinking of giving the house to the society but had decided to leave it to a relative instead. But they definitely don't know that it would fall to them should you not want it. Fred didn't want to complicate things for you. Instead he left the society a significant cash donation in his will. They will be thrilled when they hear about it. It might even be a good start for them to purchase the house at the discounted price they'd get if you decide you don't want it after two years. They will know about the donation once you decide what you want to do."

"Boy, this is pretty complicated."

"Feel free to contact me if you have any questions. I might not have all the answers, but I might be able to steer you in the right direction. I was his personal attorney for many years, and I knew him as well as anybody at the end. And Brenda will be a big help."

"Brenda?'

"Oh yes. Sorry. That's the name of the real estate agent who's going to meet you at the house. She wants to show you around town too. She's a real charmer."

He handed me the keys, and I went to check into my hotel.

* * * * *

It later turned out I had several questions I would need to ask him. But I didn't know that yet as I drove my rental car the next day south toward the town on the Massachusetts coast that I'd never heard of. I had an appointment to meet real estate agent Brenda McCartney, owner of Be Coastal Properties.

CHAPTER 2
THE HOUSE

The drive took me a little over an hour. It was mostly all a heavily trafficked expressway until my GPS told me to take the Duxbury exit. From there I made my way several miles on a quiet road that led toward the coast. When I came to the water, I turned onto a peninsula and drove along a road that rimmed its coast. I passed many stately homes before ultimately turning onto a side street.

"You have arrived," said the GPS's computer voice when I was in front of the address I'd plugged in. 3 Spyglass Lane. I pulled into the driveway behind another car that was parked there. I got out and looked at my new house. To say I was impressed would be an understatement.

A white picket fence with a gate served as the entrance to a green lawn with a large tree in the middle. Clusters of well-manicured shrubs were tastefully scattered throughout the property. Off to one side stood a gazebo encircled by a garden with a riot of colorful flowers. It was a pleasant, very appealing scene made even more so by the smell of freshly mown grass on this warm sunny afternoon in mid-May.

The house itself was large but not overwhelmingly so. It was big enough to project great prosperity but designed in a way that conveyed a sense of warmth and intimacy. It had a white clapboard exterior, and had been built in the Colonial style with dark blue shutters. I counted seven windows across the second floor with six below it and a doorway with a portico in the middle. Above that was a widow's walk. It presented itself as a classically symmetrical, beautifully maintained antique structure. If I had to use one word to describe my first impression of it, I would say it had "character."

A woman got out of the car that was parked ahead of me in the driveway.

"John Pavlik, I presume?"

"Yes. Everybody calls me Jake. You're Brenda?"

"I am," she said with a smile, extending her hand. She was a perky woman in her early fifties I guessed. "Welcome to your new home."

"Thanks. I'm a bit overwhelmed at all this. I'm still processing."

"It's a wonderful property. Your uncle left you a gem. I'm here to answer your questions. I know the house well. I sold it to Fred when he bought it five years ago. Let's go in and sit down."

I unlocked the door and she went in first, then led me down a hallway, through a sitting room, and into a large living room. There were floor to ceiling windows on three sides, all with water views. I spotted several sailboats skimming along, tacking in the wind. While the core of the house was classical New England, this room and the wrap-around deck off it that faced the water must have been added fairly recently. It looked and felt new, almost resort-like, in quality.

"What do you think?" she asked with a smile.

"I think this is a slight improvement from my three-room townhouse in Toledo." Not a very elegant answer, to be sure, but totally honest because that's exactly what I was thinking.

"When Lyle Danforth called me to ask me to show you around, he told me something that surprised me."

"What?"

"That you had no idea that this house existed and that you never knew your uncle lived in Duxbury."

"That's right. This came out of the blue."

"So you weren't close to your uncle?"

I could tell she was genuinely surprised. "We were at one time, but that was many years ago. My mother and Fred were sister and brother. When I was a kid, he lived outside of New York City. My mother and I lived in Ohio, and I'd go visit him every summer for a week. He'd take me to Yankee Stadium. He'd never had kids. I guess I filled a need. And Fred did the same for me since my father had died when I was still in grade school. I didn't see Uncle Fred often enough for him to be a father figure, but I did enjoy my time with him."

"I gather you hadn't seen him in a while?"

"Only once in the last fifteen years. When Fred's wife died, my mother and I went to the funeral. But after that my mother rarely heard from him. Mainly Christmas card exchanges. At one point, he moved to London for a few years, and they fell out of touch completely."

"That's how it often goes. What was your mother's reaction when you told her he'd left you the house?"

"No reaction. Mom's been in memory care in Toledo for over a year. I moved there from LA because I thought I should be near her. She understands almost nothing that is said to her."

I had in fact visited her before my flight. I still tried to talk to her a bit even though she never showed any sign of recognition anymore. But you never know what the human mind can assimilate. You want to believe that at least a little gets through. I told her about the house and, sure enough, she'd stared at me blankly.

"Enough sad stories," Brenda said. "Let me show you the rest of the house."

We walked up a winding staircase with a beautiful curved banister of dark wood. The upstairs had six bedrooms, one of which was the master. It had a small sitting room with a fireplace just off of it. A sliding glass door opened onto a little balcony with a number of plants spaced throughout.

"They need attending to," said Brenda, glancing at a few potted flowers and grimacing. "Some people on Powder Point have gardeners. Fred did it all himself. Hope you have a green thumb."

"Not really. But I sure like the way this looks up here."

"Now follow me back down. This is pretty interesting. It's what Fred called his secret passage."

Rather than backtrack down the main stairs, she opened a door half-hidden in a corner of the hallway. It was another set of stairs, quite narrow and a bit twisty.

"Watch your footing," she said as she switched on a light. "This goes back to the original house."

"This almost has the feel of an escape route," I laughed, groping my way in the poor lighting. "I wonder if one of the owners had something to hide."

"You never know. All these old houses have their secrets."

We eventually ended up in what I would hesitate to call a basement. It was a large living area with a billiards table and bar. There was also a walk-in wine cellar with scores of bottles lining the walls.

Old Freddie liked his vino, I thought. I did too—way more than gardening.

She then opened a door that led to the back yard. We passed a little flower garden and a small potting shed. About fifty feet from the house was another building.

"This was a workshop built by the original owner," Brenda said. "He was a woodcarver. Wait until you see the second story. Your uncle remodeled it and converted it into a studio. Come in and take a look."

The first floor workshop had been beautifully restored by my uncle into a book-lined study. We walked up some steps to the second story. There were paintings and sketches scattered all about.

"Wow," I said looking around the cluttered room. "What's all this?"

"It's your uncle's work. He had become a serious painter. He devoted a lot of time to it."

In the center of the room were two easels. There were unfinished paintings on each. I examined them more closely. One was of a lighthouse at dusk with its beam shining on a small purple building nearby. The other was of a mermaid with her hair flying off wildly in all directions.

"She's very striking," I said.

"It looks like a figurehead of a ship. Fred loved nautical themes. Looks like these were the last two paintings he was working on when he died. As I said, nothing has been moved."

"He was really good. I had no idea."

"He was very good. He was well known in town for his work. He donated some to the art complex. You should see them some time. For now, let's go back to the house. I'll show you the view."

I followed her to the wrap-around deck off the main living room. We sat in two chairs and looked out over the water.

"Duxbury has a rich tradition," she said. "It has seen two eras historically important to the U.S. The first was the Pilgrim era. The town was founded in 1637 by members of the *Mayflower* who came over here from Plymouth, which is just a few miles across the bay from here."

She pointed out toward the water. I could make out a low-lying landmass in the distance and could vaguely discern some small buildings.

"A number of the Pilgrims sailed across the bay here to farm, and a few of the most important ones ended up living and dying here. They're buried in town in the oldest cemetery in the U.S. The second great era was just after the Revolutionary War, when the town became one of the centers of shipbuilding for the country. There are a number of homes owned by shipbuilders and ship captains here. And this is where your house comes in."

She explained to me that the original house on 3 Spyglass Lane dated back to 1790 when a man named Josiah Osborne built it. He was a sailor, as most men in the town were in those days.

"He rose to become a first mate and sailed the world," she said. "He appears in the records of voyages to South America off Chile, all across the Pacific, even to China. He was also a skilled wood carver, and at some point, he decided to settle down and establish his own ship figurehead business. His figures adorned the front of many a Duxbury merchant ship. He built this house and the workshop in the back yard. The core of the house remains essentially as he built it. Several additions have been made. And your uncle left his mark too. He added on this deck. He also had the workshop remodeled and turned into the studio."

"You really know your history," I said with a smile. "Very impressive."

"Don't forget: I'm in the real estate business. History helps sell these houses. I needed to learn all about them. Having that plaque on the front of this house that says 1790 is pretty meaningful to buyers. It was to your uncle."

"Tell me about his purchase. As I said, I knew nothing about him living here. How did it happen?"

"Since I was the one who sold him the house, I'm pretty familiar with most of the circumstances. Not all of them, but most. He came down about ten years ago and explained he was living in Manhattan and looking for a second home. This is a town with full-time residents. We don't have many vacation homes here. For that, people usually go an hour farther south onto the Cape or even Martha's Vineyard and Nantucket. He did say he'd probably become a full-time resident eventually because he was planning to retire in the next couple of years. And he wanted Duxbury specifically. He was looking for a place with some history to it, and he actually identified this house as one he'd love to buy if it ever came on the market. Five years ago it did, and he bought it the same day. Paid cash for it too."

"Do you know why he was looking specifically in Duxbury? I'm not aware of any connection he had to this area. He was originally from Toledo, as was his wife. They got married there after college. They ended up living in New York where he moved to begin his business career. That's where I got to know him when I was a kid."

"He told me he became familiar with this area when he got his MBA from Harvard. He lived in Cambridge for two years while going to school, and had a classmate who came from Duxbury. He'd visited him a few times and fell in love with the town and its history."

"Ah!" I exclaimed. "I forgot he'd gone to grad school at Harvard. It was always a source of pride for my mom. Here was a regular guy from Toledo whose father had worked in an automobile plant and ends up going to Harvard Business School and then becomes a partner in a big New York City private equity firm."

"That's interesting," she said. "I never knew all the specifics of his life. But I was struck that he carried himself as what you call a regular guy even though I knew he must have had a lot of money. At any rate, he told me that over the years he'd gotten to know the area even better. He did a lot of business in Boston and spent a lot of time here. Even became something of a Red Sox fan. For someone living in New York, that's a sure sign of affection for this area."

I was thinking that either my mother never knew he'd bought this house or, more probably, she just didn't think it was important enough to tell me.

"So, my uncle shows up here one day and wants to buy a house, possibly for his retirement. I'm curious. Who did he buy the house from?"

"The Phipps family. It was a family of four. The mother was a direct descendant of Josiah Osborne. They were very active in town, a very popular family. It was a pretty sad story. The father had been a very successful investor, particularly in real estate. But he made a few bad investments when the subprime mortgage market collapsed, and he had to declare bankruptcy. He died shortly thereafter, and his wife and two kids decided to sell. They didn't have the money to keep it in the family, so they asked my company to list it. So, after over two hundred years, it was available. Since he'd expressed an interest, I contacted him, and your uncle bought it. And now here you are."

"Yes, here I am," I smiled. "Coming in out of nowhere. Let me ask you a question. What do you think this house is worth?"

Her eyes widened as if she figured I'd be asking this question eventually. Getting in on the next sale is what any good real estate agent would be thinking, and I could already tell she was good at her job.

"This is a very desirable property in a very desirable part of town. This entire peninsula is called Powder Point. We get top dollar here. And our real estate market has appreciated significantly over the past few years."

I was expecting a pretty hefty price tag, but she gave me a number that exceeded my expectations. That made it worth maybe twenty times what my townhouse was worth. I tried to give a nonchalant reaction, but I'm afraid the startled expression on my face gave me away. I quickly did the math in my head and determined that the 25% I stood to make on any sale after two years of ownership was a damn nice addition to my nest egg in and of itself. If I hung onto it for five years and got 100% of the full market value, I'd be a real fat cat—at least by my standards—which was something that I never could have imagined given the current value of my 401k.

Noting my expression, she lowered her voice, as if speaking to me in the strictest confidence:

"Can I ask you a question? If I'm prying, please tell me to mind my own business."

"Fire away."

"Are you going to move into this house or are you intending to turn around and sell it? Are your circumstances such that you'll be able to move here and live in this house?"

Typical real estate agent question, I thought. She wants to know if I'm going to sell. She sees another commission on the near horizon. She didn't know the terms of the will, and I tried to answer ambiguously. I had no trouble in this because, as I stood there, I truly had no idea what I was going to do.

"I'm going to need to figure that out. As far as work is concerned, I'm pretty mobile. I work virtually, so I can live anywhere."

"And what do you do for a living if I might ask?"

I usually answer this question in one of two ways. To people within the show business community, I say I work in the field of animation. To outsiders, I give the most readily understandable answer, and since she was an outsider I said, "I do cartoon voices."

There are a variety of facial expressions that typically accompany people's initial reactions to this. Some show confusion, others delight, still others a "you're pulling my leg, right? What do you really do?" response.

"Seriously? That's SO interesting" she exclaimed, looking at me with a coquettish grin and touching me slightly on the arm. This reaction seemed to put her in the "delighted" camp, which made sense given she was in the business of connecting with clients. It came naturally to her.

"Sometimes it's interesting, sometimes it's not. It's like any job. I do some writing too. But the voices are my bread and butter. It's good steady work."

"That's wonderful! What kind of voices do you do?"

"I'm pretty versatile. I'm good with foreign accents. Old Japanese ladies, young Italian men, you name it. All kinds of animals too— dogs, cats, giraffes, monkeys. Talking objects are big too. Ever hear of Fluffo, the talking marshmallow?"

"Can't say that I have."

"Much of what I do is for kid shows for Disney and Nickelodeon. That's why I moved to LA in the first place years ago. I needed to get my foot in the door with the big studios. Now I've branched out into adult cartoons that are on the Cartoon Network out of Atlanta. My biggie now is the voice of Laszlo the Impaler—a rugby player in Budapest by day and a vampire stalker at night."

"My goodness."

"I know it sounds crazy to a lot of people, but there's a very solid market for these kinds of shows. And lots of smart people are fans. That particular Laszlo show is big in the Valley for example."

"Valley?"

"Oh, sorry. Silicon Valley. It's very popular with the unmarried twenty-something bro-techie demographic. They line up for autographs twenty deep at the animation conventions I sometimes attend. The best part is I can do my recording from anywhere as long as I have the proper recording equipment. The studios have given that to me, so between that and video calls, I can work through any script with the creative teams. If I can do it from Toledo, I can do it from here."

"That's wonderful to have so much freedom."

"But, as I said, I've been wanting to be near my mother, and I'm pretty settled where I am, so there's that to consider."

I'd also begun a relationship with a local Toledo woman who did my taxes, but I saw no reason to get into that. Nor did I feel the need to mention that my son was living with me. He was pursuing a PhD in something with a title that I didn't understand. I did understand, however, that his income was pretty close to zero. He needed free lodging, and I was happy to give it to him, although I did think at age twenty-three he should be a bit more independent.

"I can imagine it'll be a tough decision," she said, nodding that she understood. She really couldn't, though—at least not fully—because she had no idea of the complex terms of the will and how that might impact my decision. Frankly I didn't know yet either.

We spent a bit more time exploring the house and property which was appealing to me in every way. Particularly interesting was the little pier that was behind the house.

"Sorry to bring up a sad subject again," she said softly, "but this is the pier where your uncle tied his kayak. The day he died, he apparently paddled off from here into the bay toward Duxbury Harbor. It's only about a fifteen minute paddle."

She pointed in that direction.

"You can't quite see them from here, but some of the oyster farms are located just around the corner. The bay is dotted with wooden oyster platforms called floaters or sheds. That's where the workers clean up and shuck the oysters they've just dug up. He fell on one of those platforms apparently."

I made a mental note to try to understand that more as I wasn't totally sure I followed what she was saying. There weren't many oyster farms in Toledo. We walked back into the house. It was still in the exact condition it had been since the day he died. All the rooms were fully furnished—even the clothes were still in his closets.

"Lyle was down here yesterday. He took some papers and bills that needed attending to, but he said we should leave everything else as is," she said. "It'll be up to you to decide what should be done with all of this."

"This could be a big job. I'm going to have to think through how to do this."

"What are your plans now?" she said when we were finished touring the property.

"I'm going to spend the weekend here in the house, then go back to Toledo on Sunday evening. I have a few recording sessions next week, and I need to be near my equipment. After that, I'm not sure. I need to think this through then talk to Lyle."

"Of course. I'd love to show you around town tomorrow. Would you like that?"

I'd wondered if she might ask that, and I had my answer ready.

"That's very nice of you, Brenda. But given that I have limited time here to get my own impression of the place, I think it'll be better if I just knock about on my own."

This was mostly true, although I had another reason. I planned to look into a couple of things pertaining to my uncle's death that were better done alone.

"I'll try not to be offended," she said with a little pout. "But if anything comes up, please give me a ring. I live here in town and meeting up for coffee or lunch would be no problem. Here's my card."

"Thanks so much," I said.

"And rather than have you wander about aimlessly, at least let me give you this map. I've marked some of the places people new to town want to see."

She pulled a paper out of the folder she was carrying and unfolded it for me and began pointing things out.

"I've circled a couple of the best restaurants in town and our supermarket. It's a real gem. Here's the town beach. It's the best on the South Shore. You might want to go to the harbor area and town dock. It's in the center of town, which is sometimes called Snug Harbor. And maybe take a quick drive past some of the cranberry bogs too. Here's town hall. And here is the high school. But I guess you aren't interested in that. If you like history, we have some historic houses open to the public. They date from both the Pilgrim and shipbuilding eras. Some buyers are very into that sort of thing. I know your uncle was. And speaking of your uncle, let me leave you this copy of the local paper, he *Messenger*. It has a nice obituary in it about him. He'd been associated with the town for only a few years, but he touched many different people."

I shook her hand and thanked her yet again for her help. She was very nice and certainly was "a charmer," as Danforth had said. But I didn't need to be charmed. And she was just a little too talky for my taste. I was glad I'd decided to spend tomorrow on my own.

I went to my car, took out my suitcase, and began to settle in.

CHAPTER 3
THE TOWN

Because I'd planned all along on staying for just two nights, I'd only packed a small suitcase, and it didn't take long to unpack it. I decided that although my time was limited, I'd try to get as much of a feel for the house as possible, so I stayed in the master bedroom. Like the rest of the house, it had colonial decor. But the bathroom was huge and modern with a large step-in shower. From what I'd seen so far, everything about the house had been done first class, a good combination of historical preservation and modern creature comforts.

By now it was nearly six and beginning to get dark. It had been a long day filled with many conflicting emotions. I was drained, and so I thought I'd try to find a local restaurant. I looked at the map Brenda had left me and picked one of the places she had circled: The Shipyard Inn on Washington Street. I pulled out my phone and googled the menu. It looked good.

As I was walking through the house to get to the front door, The *Duxbury Messenger* caught my eye on the table where I'd left it. I remembered she'd mentioned my uncle's obituary was in it, so I sat down and leafed through the paper until I found it. It read as follows:

Fred Peterson tragically died in a fall he took on an oyster platform in Duxbury Bay last week. He had been a part-time resident for five years before moving here full time a year ago. A partner in the New York private equity firm LFP (Lancaster, Franklin, and Peterson), he had been living in Manhattan before moving to Duxbury. He remained on several boards after his retirement.

In his relatively short time in town, he made his presence felt. Not ready to fully retire, he helped launch several local startups, primarily in the food sector. He had also recently invested in Gurnet Oyster Farms in Duxbury Bay and had just helped the company create a three-year strategic plan.

A man of many parts, he was very active with the Duxbury Rural and Historical Society (DRHS) and was a sponsor of many of the society's events. His generosity was widely appreciated by DRHS. He also was an avid artist, and he took classes regularly at the Duxbury Art Complex Museum where he also was a benefactor. Some of his seascapes and pictures of historic houses hang in their gallery.

Mr. Peterson was born in Toledo, Ohio. He graduated from Kenyon College with a degree in history and later got his MBA at Harvard Business School. He is survived by his sister Donna Peterson Pavlik of Toledo, his nephews John "Jake" Pavlik, also of Toledo, and Colin Peterson of Philadelphia, Pennsylvania, and his niece Beth Peterson Fullerton of Short Hills, New Jersey. His wife of many years, Mary Kaminski Peterson, predeceased him. A short graveside service will be held in Mayflower Cemetery on May 6.

May 6. That was last week, just three days after he had died. I was very sorry I'd not been aware of his death and funeral as I would have attended. He apparently considered me as his only link to his family. But I'd been away at an animation convention in Chicago for five days during this period. The letter had been sent to my mother's old home address since neither Fred nor his lawyer had my email address or phone number. When my mother moved into the memory care facility, Mom had been aware enough to leave a forwarding address with the post office, and so Danforth's letter did ultimately catch up with me when I visited her on my return. But by then it was too late.

I got in my car and drove on the coastal road that circles the Powder Point peninsula until it intersects Washington Street, which is the main street that runs through the center of town. It too is lined with well-appointed captain's homes, primarily of the early nineteenth century. I saw a roadside sign I could barely make out in the fading daylight that said:

Entering Old Shipbuilding District, National Register of Historic Places

After a short drive I came upon a small cluster of shops and, just beyond them, a large building. In front of it was a large post with a wooden sign dangling from it that said The Shipyard Inn. I pulled into a very packed parking lot and got the last space.

"Sorry, we're fully booked," said the young hostess when I checked in at the front desk and asked for a table. "All we have is seating at the bar. You can order from the menu there."

I said that was fine and she pointed me in the right direction. It was swarming with customers. I squeezed myself into one of the empty seats.

"Is everybody in town here?" I commented to myself as I surveyed the bustling scene. I ordered a beer and quickly surveyed the place. It appeared to be yet another historic structure that had been remodeled and turned into a contemporary space. I picked up the menu which gave a quick history of the Inn.

Built in 1805, the Shipyard Inn was originally the home of Captain Chester Kent, who sailed the seas on many a ship owned by the Winsor family. Today it is owned by the Duxbury Oyster Farm Collective. Three oyster farms have joined forces to create a showcase eating space dedicated to life on the sea. Welcome one and all!"

As I looked around, the place indeed had many nautical references. Fish nets adorned the walls along with nautical paintings and a mural of a three-masted ship under sail. All were part of the decor. But it was the clientele which struck me most. While most were couples or families out to dinner, the bar area was filled with men who seemed to be connected to the sea. Sipping on my beer, I overheard the conversation of two young men who were speaking loudly. Both looked like they were in their late twenties or early thirties. They were both dressed casually.

"I wonder if Sam Larkin of Oceanview Oysters is still pissed over the Gurnet situation," one of them said. He was tall and rugged with a wind-blown complexion. "I know he wanted that lease."

"I know Bill Tidrow of Topnotch wanted that lease, too," said the

21

smaller of the two men. "He's been looking to expand and bring his son in some day. He said Len Barker had promised it to him. This blocks him for a while."

At this point a small cheer went up from one end of the bar where a TV screen was located. A group of four or five were watching a basketball game. I looked at it and noticed the score: Boston 102, LA 101. Seconds later, the cheering was followed by a group moan. Score: LA 103, Boston 102.

"Shit," I heard a man say.

"Play some defense!" a young woman exhorted.

I'd lived in LA long enough to become something of a Lakers fan, which I knew wouldn't go down well if I decided to live here in the center of Celtics Nation.

"Yeah, it might take a while for this to shake out," continued the big rugged man to my left. "The old man only died a week and a half ago. I wonder if that changes anything at Gurnet. Maybe Len will want to make a deal again."

My ears immediately pricked up. Gurnet. Where had I heard this strange word? It then dawned on me that Gurnet Oysters had been mentioned in my uncle's obituary. Were these two men talking about the same thing?

The background noise had become even louder as the score of the game seesawed back and forth, and I could no longer hear the two men. That was too bad because I'd grown curious about what they were saying. I considered leaning over and asking them what they were talking about. The obituary had reminded me that my uncle was not only an accomplished man of many parts, but he was also someone that I really didn't know all that much about. As the recipient of his great generosity as well as the person whom he was counting on to keep his treasured house in the family, I felt the obligation to learn more about him.

As I was about to engage them in conversation, a third man joined them, and they left the bar to go into the dining room for dinner. Casually asking a couple of strangers at a bar about the oyster business was one thing. Pursuing them to their dinner table was another. So I just ordered a hamburger and watched the rest of the game. When it was over, I paid my bill, grabbed a few items to have for breakfast at the local grocer, and drove back home.

It seems funny to use the word home to refer to a place I had never been to until a few hours previously. But figuring out if this really would be my home was what this was all about now. Was it really worth working through all the complexity to make it my home, or should I just to do the simple thing and cash out and move on? The potential payoff was enticing, but did I want to blow up my life in the process?

* * * * *

I slept well and woke up the next morning greatly refreshed. Although Brenda had cleared out the refrigerator of any perishables, the cupboards were still well stocked. I made myself a cup of coffee and toasted a bagel, contemplating how to best spend the day. A part of me wanted to start going through my uncle's things and assessing what, if anything, should be done with them. Apparently, it was going to be up to me to do that. But I only had one full day here, and I didn't want to get bogged down in a cleanup process. I needed to see if I wanted to keep the place. And that meant getting more familiar with the house and seeing more of the town. Would I fit in? Would I be comfortable here? That's why I had wanted to poke around alone for the day.

I took my cup of coffee and walked out the back door onto the deck. It was another warm spring day.

I could get used to starting my day with this view, I thought.

I decided to continue exploring my property and walked down the flight of twenty or so wooden steps to the pier. It was quite long—maybe fifty feet—and spanned a marshy area and ended at a small beach. At the end of it was a little deck with two Adirondack chairs. I sat in one of them and looked out across the water.

It was early—around 9:00—and very quiet. Not much activity yet on the bay. I saw a long wooden bridge in the distance that connected Powder Point to a strip of land on the other side. I could see a car driving across it. My attention was pulled off to my right by the sound of someone's voice. It was coming from the pier next to mine, about two hundred feet away. I saw a person standing at the end of it, waving at me. *It must be one of my neighbors*, I thought.

The woman motioned to me as if to meet, then walked back up her pier to what I assumed was her house. I walked back off my pier towards my back lawn. At that point, a small patch of woods separated the two houses, and I walked through it to her back yard.

"Are you the new owner?" she asked with a smile. She was a tall thin woman with grey hair who looked to be in her sixties.

Not wanting to get into the current status of my ownership, I simply said, "I am. My name is Jake Pavlik." I extended my hand.

"I'm Paula Spaulding. Nice to meet you. Am I right in saying you're a relative of Fred's?"

"He was my uncle."

"We figured he'd left the house to a relative."

"Really?" I was pretty astonished that he'd chosen to share this information with anyone, particularly since he hadn't even shared it with me.

"Yes," she continued. "First, let me offer our condolences. Such a terrible accident. It came as quite a shock here in town."

"Thank you. It came as a real shock to me as well." Given the circumstances, this was something of an understatement. "So word got out about a relative inheriting the place?"

"Yes, but it was only a rumor and not broadly circulated. It was mainly among the members of the local historical society. My husband Ed and I are members. Fred was too. He talked openly about possibly leaving the house to the society. But he recently told us he was leaving it to a relative and giving the society a donation instead. We didn't know if he'd followed through with those plans though."

I nodded.

"Listen," she said. "I've got to run. Can you come over tonight for a drink—say around 5:00? My husband and I have an event to go to later, but Ed would love to meet you."

"Sure. Very nice of you. See you then."

This, I thought, *was* the *perfect way for my due diligence this weekend to proceed.* Whoever the neighbors were wouldn't necessarily be the top element in my decision-making process. But knowing if I had good ones certainly wouldn't hurt either.

* * * * *

Returning to the house, I picked up Brenda's map of key spots in town. My first priority, however, was to close the loop on my uncle's death and visit the cemetery where he was buried. I knew from his obituary in the local paper that he was buried in Mayflower Cemetery, which I assumed was in town. Sure enough, there it was on the map, maybe two miles away on Tremont Street. I started off for there straightaway.

I drove through an entryway and then along a small, paved path, following the sign that pointed to the cemetery office. There was a woman seated in an office off the front lobby working at a computer. I stuck my head in and asked her if she could help me find a grave.

"Sure," she said. "All the locations are in our data base. What's the name?"

"Fred Peterson."

"Why that's easy. I don't even need to look that up. He was cremated and buried here just last week." She gave me a map of the cemetery, marking an x on it where the grave was.

"So he's buried in a plot with a tombstone even though he was cremated?" I said looking at the map.

"Yes. If the person is cremated, the remains are put in an urn, and we offer the option of an in ground or vault internment. Mr. Peterson specified in the ground next to his wife with a full tombstone. They haven't added his date of death to the stone yet though."

Map in hand, I walked along the path, turning in and out of several smaller pathways along the way. I saw some new graves with contemporary dates and some very old ones. Some of the latter dated back to the 1700s with barely discernible inscriptions, and others where the inscription was now totally obliterated. I later learned that, despite its antiquity, Mayflower is the modern one of Duxbury's two cemeteries. The other is even older and is where some of the Pilgrims were buried in the 1600s. It is no longer in use for burials.

At length I found my uncle's grave. The ground around it looked freshly dug, as indeed it had been only ten days since the internment. There were even two piles of dirt still on either side of the grave. The final landscaping hadn't been done yet. I approached the modest tombstone. It gave the birth dates of both Frederick Peterson and Mary Kaminski Peterson, as well as her death. Underneath was inscribed:

Two great lovers,
too long separated by time and space,
now reunited forever here and in eternity.
Ut Omnes Unum Sint

I knew from my aunt's funeral of fifteen or so years ago that she'd been buried in her hometown of Toledo—cremated just as my uncle had been and placed in a vault there. Based on the inscription here in Duxbury, I wondered if my uncle had arranged for her remains to be transferred here. What was clear, though, is that he wanted to be buried in Duxbury which, to me, spoke volumes regarding his affection for his adopted home.

I was now in the mood to push a little further into my uncle's death and this meant trying to get a glimpse of the place he died, which was somewhere out in Duxbury Bay. Referring to the map again, I located the town dockyard on Mattakeeset Court in Duxbury Harbor and was there in five minutes. Everything in this small town of fifteen thousand was close by.

I pulled into the parking lot and walked to the water to survey the scene. At this hour of the morning, the harbor had begun to come alive. A few men were in small rowboats moving from the dock to reach their motor boats anchored in the harbor.

Off to my right was a small building that had a sign that said "Harbormaster" on it.

As good as any place to begin, I thought. I knocked on the door and stepped into the small office. Sitting behind the desk was a familiar face: it was the tall, ruddy man that I had sat next to in the bar last night and whose conversation I had partially overheard.

"Can I help you?" he asked. He showed no sign of recognizing me.

"Yes," I said. "Are you the harbormaster?"

"No. I'm the assistant. Chip Gallagher is the harbormaster. How can I help you?"

"A relative of mine died in the harbor area a week ago, and I have a question."

The young man looked at me in surprise, maybe a bit suspiciously.

"You mean Mr. Peterson?"

"Yes. He was my uncle. I'm from out of town and just learned of his death, and I was curious to see where he died. I'm his closest relative."

"I wasn't on duty that day. Chip was. You'd have to ask him about it. You'll have to come back during the week. He's off on the weekends."

"I understand," I said. "Unfortunately, I'm going back home tomorrow. I was just looking for some general information, like where he died."

"That I know. He hit his head on the deck of one of these oyster sheds floating in the bay." He pointed to a cluster of sheds in the water not far in front of us. "It was one of those over there."

"What happens in one of those? I'm from the Midwest and know nothing about oysters."

"The workers bring the oysters they've harvested there to clean them up. They hose them down. They pull up in their boats, unload 'em, clean 'em, then bring 'em to shore."

27

"Was he alone when it happened?"

"I heard that he was. It was on the Bayside Oysters' shed which is owned by Bobby Atkinson. When Bobby showed up for work that morning, he saw the body. It was lying half in, half out of the shed. That's when he called Chip."

"How did it happen?"

"It was a rocky day on the water. He fell and hit his head. But that's all I know," he said, looking at his watch and standing up, indicating it was time to end this conversation. "Sorry for your loss."

"Thanks for your help. And if I have any more questions, I'll contact Chip."

I had no intention of doing so, however. I'd just wanted to know the basics of my uncle's death, and I'd gotten that. Why go around town asking unpleasant questions? That's the last thing a stranger should be doing. If I decided to live in town, I'd be a neighbor to these people, and nobody likes a snoopy neighbor.

* * * * *

I spent the rest of the afternoon wandering about, trying to get a feel for the town. Outside of the oyster business, I noted two other commercial entities within the harbor area. One was a yacht club. Rather than the opulence that you might expect in a town that has some money, the small compound was pleasantly rustic and cozy in appearance. Some workmen were painting one of the small buildings, getting the club spiffed up for the summer season when the harbor, now quite empty of pleasure boats, would likely be full of them.

Also right on the harbor was a large, impressive building called The Duxbury Bay Maritime School, or DBMS. I went in and picked up a brochure. It detailed a wide variety of classes on coastal fauna and flora for young people of all ages, as well as sailing, powerboating, and rowing lessons. It had a substantial boat shed too where I saw many sail boats and rowing shells stored. It mentioned that the facility was used as a training facility by high school students from all over the area. In addition, a number of students from around the country came to town during the summer for a variety of nautical programs.

Another of the town's main commercial activities that I noted is a very visible cranberry business. As I drove away from the water, I passed several large cranberry bogs. There wasn't much activity at this time of year. I knew enough to figure that would probably come mainly during the late summer when the bogs are flooded and turned into a sea of red berries, harvested with the help of a thrasher machine that separates the berries from their roots like an eggbeater. The berries would then be sold to the Ocean Spray company, a local cooperative. Most of the bog owners are members.

Other than oysters and cranberries, almost all other commercial activity in town consists of retail—some small locally owned shops, some restaurants, and a small upscale food market called Brothers. I'm a bit of a foodie and like to cook. If I moved here, I'd no doubt be a loyal customer at this store.

It was late afternoon by now. I had the 5:00 appointment with my neighbors and so I started back to Powder Point. As the road wound around the peninsula, I reached the wooden bridge I'd seen from my house the previous day. Several cars were driving across it. I still had time, so I did the same. It's an impressive structure, almost half a mile long and capable of handling the rather heavy summer traffic that comes across it to get to the long thin strip of land on the other side of it. I parked my car in the fairly large lot and got out to explore a bit.

Consulting my map once more, I could see that the sandy strip I was now on was actually another peninsula which served as a barrier beach between Duxbury Harbor and the open sea. It extended southward a good several miles, I guessed, with a lighthouse, Gurnet Light, at its very tip.

There's that funny word again, I thought.

A dirt road made it possible to drive all the way down to where the lighthouse was. I didn't have time to explore it now, but I did get out and took a short walk.

Looking back to my right toward town was Duxbury Bay and where all the oyster farms are located. I could make out the harbor in the distance and the maritime school. A good mile left of the harbor was a big hill with some sort of narrow structure atop it.

I consulted the map once more and read, "Myles Standish Monument." It was on the part of town identified as Standish Shores.

On the side of the island facing the sea was a thin sandy beach with an unmanned lifeguard stand in front. The map labeled this the town beach. A few people were walking along it, but it was not nearly beach season yet.

I looked back across the wooden bridge toward Powder Point, wondering if I could see my house. And sure enough, there it was in the distance, sitting on its little hill. I imagined it was looking at me, as if it were trying to tell me something from across the water.

Now you're getting silly, I chuckled to myself. *This place is playing tricks with my head.*

I looked at my watch: 4:45. I headed back down the road to my car. It was time to set aside this bit of idle daydreaming and go meet my potential neighbors. It felt like I was going to a business meeting, which it kind of was, now that I think about it.

Chapter 4

THE NEIGHBORS

At 5:00 exactly, I walked across my front lawn to the Spauldings' house, address 1 Spyglass Lane. But unlike my uncle's house, which had a simple address of 3 Spyglass, this one not only had a numerical address but a name as well. The wooden sign hanging from a post on the front lawn proudly proclaimed the property as Manderley.

Before ringing the doorbell, I took a moment to soak in the view. The house was bigger than my uncle's. It was in the Federalist style with yellow clapboards and green shutters. I counted four chimneys. It also had major additions on either side, one of which was in stone, which was strikingly different for this area. It was magnificent.

A man opened the door.

"Mr. Pavlik, right? I'm Ed Spaulding," he said as we shook hands.

"I'm John Pavlik," I said. "But everybody from high school on down has called me Jake."

Behind him stood his wife Paula.

"Right on time," she said. "Come on in and have a drink and some little snacks."

We walked through a series of rooms and into the stone addition, which consisted of a cathedral-ceilinged library lined with books. We seated ourselves in leather chairs in front of a big stone fireplace where a fire had been lit. On the table were a few plates of food—cheese, some cold cuts, and shrimp.

"What can I get you to drink?" said Spaulding. "I've got everything."

"I like Scotch if you have it."

"Ardbeg or Glenlivet?"

"I'd love the Ardbeg."

"My favorite too."

He walked over toward the wall of books across from the fireplace.

Built into the shelving was a liquor cabinet and little refrigerator. He mixed drinks for himself and me, poured a glass of wine for his wife, and brought them to the table with the food.

"First off, we offer our condolences on your loss," Paula said. "It's so awful the way it happened. He was such an energetic, robust man, even at his age—a picture of health, he was. We both went to the burial and service at the grave. It was a cold rainy day, but a number of people turned out. He'd made quite a few friends in the community."

"Thank you," I said. "That's comforting. I hadn't seen him in quite a while, and I'm happy he was at least surrounded by friends at the end. I didn't find out about this until after he was buried."

There was an awkward moment as there often is after talking about a terrible accidental death. Wanting to brighten the mood, I said, "I must say your house is beautiful," and I wasn't being merely polite.

"Thanks," she said. "It's too big for us now with the kids gone. But we find we just don't want to downsize."

"How long have you lived here?"

"Forty years now. We moved here from Virginia when Ed started working at Mass General."

"You're a doctor, then?" I asked turning to him.

"Yes. Neurosurgeon. Dealing with the human mind runs in the family. Paula does that too."

He looked the part—tall and slender with long white hair combed straight back. He was wearing a tweed sports coat and bow tie, and he spoke with the slight southern drawl of a native Virginian. Add it all up and he had the patrician look of a country squire whose favorite sport was fox hunting.

"So you're a doctor too?" I asked her.

"Yes. A psychiatrist. But I don't make a living that way. I'm a novelist."

"Really?" I exclaimed, becoming interested.

"Yes. I write mysteries, and always with a psychological angle. I never liked being a practicing psychiatrist. Too emotionally draining. I wanted to use my training somehow, though, and found writing more to my liking. Way better to deal with the problems of fictional people rather than real ones. And I can literally bump someone off as a character when they irk me."

We all laughed.

She'd spoken in a soft voice but with a definite twinkle in her eye. I had a hunch I'd enjoy her company more than her stolid husband's. He was probably a very nice guy, but very stiff and formal. I guess this is what you'd want in your neurosurgeon, though.

"Have you written anything I might have read?" I asked her.

"Maybe. Here, take a look." I followed her to the bookcase. "Here are some of them," she said, pointing to a row of about a dozen books.

I picked them up. They had titles like *Insanity is* the *Best Defense, A Slight Case of Paranoia,* and *Murder in* the *Asylum.*

"This one rings a bell," I said, holding one up to her. Its title was *Forecast for Death.* "Is it about a man with psychic powers and he predicts the deaths of wealthy people?"

"Yes, that's it," she smiled. "You read it?"

"No, but I saw the movie. It was pretty good."

"Read the book. It's better. Most authors are disappointed in the movie version of their books. I was reluctant to do the movie. I didn't like the screenplay. But, frankly, the money was good. In any event, I wanted to give it a try because I love movies. In fact, I named this house in honor of a movie."

"You mean Manderley? I saw the sign outside. It's the name of the big manor house in Hitchcock's *Rebecca* as I recall."

"You know that movie?" She was very engaged now. "It's my absolute favorite. Great psychological angles with the wife not understanding her husband. Based on the novel of a writer who has always been a model for me, Daphne DuMaurier. I'm impressed a young man like you has heard of this movie."

33

"I don't know if you'd call forty-eight young," I laughed. "But I love movies. They kind of gave me my start."

"In what way?" The enthusiasm in her voice was palpable. She'd become a different person than she'd been ten minutes ago.

"I was a journalism major at Northwestern in Chicago. I did some theater there, too. You took whatever job you could when you graduated. Journalism was a tough field even back then. There was a small newspaper that hired me to review movies. I did okay, and over time moved to a couple of larger papers in the Midwest. Not much money in it, but it was a fun job."

"Do you review now?"

"No. I've moved on."

"To what?"

"That's a story in itself. It came about in a crazy way. For about three or four years I'd been reviewing films for a newspaper in Peoria. I was also doing some improv at Second City in Chicago because I needed the money. Anyhow, it happened that there was a film festival in the city where some classic movies were being screened. Each movie was preceded by a talk from an expert or a panel discussion. A well-known critic who was supposed to be on a panel got sick the day before one of the movies was to be shown. The organizer of the event knew me and asked if I'd pinch hit. I knew the movie pretty well, so I agreed."

"What was the movie" she asked.

"The *Maltese Falcon*. I'd developed a special interest in film noir."

"I love film noir. Psychological undertones permeate the noir genre. It's right up my alley. Some of my books are very noirish."

I nodded then continued. "At one point, the panel moderator asked us something about the Humphrey Bogart role in the movie. I answered the question but, on a whim, I did it while impersonating Bogart. I got a lot of laughs with my answer."

"Here's looking at you, kid," said Paula, doing a pretty good female Bogie. She was beginning to fascinate me.

"Great impression, but a different movie," I said. "The line I used was 'this is the stuff dreams are made of.' Anyhow, I really brought the house down when I answered the next question doing my best Peter Lorre-as-Joel Cairo imitation. I'd always been good at voices. I used to crack the girls up in high school imitating the teachers."

"Quite a unique gift."

"And a profitable one as it turns out. After the panel discussion, a man in the audience approached me and said he was a voice agent, and asked me to do a little audition for him. On the spot I did a few of my favorites, including Porky Pig and Mr. Ed."

"My goodness. Peter Lorre, a pig, and a horse. A real renaissance man."

"I'd done them all at Second City, so it came easy. Anyhow, next thing I knew he'd become my agent. I did a few demo tapes, and I moved to LA. I made more money with my first animation job than I did in a year of reviewing films."

"So you do this full time now? Can you give us an example of one of your characters?"

I hesitated for a moment, not knowing how such an educated elderly couple working in very serious professions would react to my world. I am always reluctant to perform on command like this. But I decided to give them the full treatment. If they were going to be my neighbors, best to start off with my authentic self, which I am very comfortable with.

"Okay. This is from a current character of mine called Laszlo the Impaler. He's stalking a vampire and being threatened by a vicious dog." I launched into a few lines from the latest episode, doing my best Laszlo, vampire, and attacking dog voices.

"That's marvelous!" she said with a sweet, almost dainty, laugh, not at all what you'd expect from an ex-psychiatrist who writes murder mysteries. "And I detect some Peter Lorre in there too." She was almost like a schoolgirl now, albeit one who might be close to—or even past—seventy.

"Good ear," I smiled. "Coincidentally, they are both Hungarian. I had

35

Lorre in mind when I was developing this character."

I looked at Ed, and I could see that the usual binary reaction to people learning of my occupation was at play here. While Paula was "delighted," his expression was more "cut the nonsense. What do you really do for a living?" I could sense he wanted to change the subject. Refilling my drink, he asked me directly, "Where do you live now?"

"Toledo, Ohio."

"How will the house fit into your plans?"

Again, I needed to be vague here—but not dishonest either.

"I'm not sure yet. It's up in the air. Work is not a problem. I can live anywhere. I need to figure out some family things, though."

"I can imagine," she said sympathetically. "Ed and I talk about this all the time regarding our house. What will happen to it after we're gone?"

"And I'm almost fully retired now," he said. "At my age I don't do surgery anymore. I'm more of a teacher and mentor at Mass General. We have two married daughters. One lives in Dallas, the other in Denver. It would be disruptive to their families and careers to move here. They'll probably just sell it."

"Someone will love it. It's a wonderful house."

"And yours is too," said Paula. "Your uncle loved it, particularly the connection to the history of shipbuilding."

"Which is the thing our house doesn't have," her husband added. "It was originally built in 1890, well after that era. And when we bought it, we completely remodeled it. That's typical of many houses now on Powder Point—built in the late nineteenth or early twentieth century, then remodeled over time."

"They all seem so well done," I said.

"Yes, but only a few go as far back as yours. The most noteworthy historic house on the Point is The King Caesar House."

"That's the huge yellow house on the left as you come up the peninsula, right? I recall seeing a sign on the way past it earlier today and wondered what it was."

"King Caesar was the nickname of Ezra Weston who was one of the biggest ship builders in the entire United States in the early days of the country. His house is now a museum right where the Bluefish River meets the bay. But that's about it. Most of the interesting history of the town is found on Washington Street and in the Snug Harbor area near the town pier. That's where most of the historic captain's homes are. And also on Standish Shore. That's the other peninsula on the southern end of Washington Street on the far side of the harbor. You can see it from here across the bay."

"Is that the hill where the big monument is located?"

"Yes. That's the Myles Standish monument. He was the military leader of the Pilgrims. He made his homestead on that hill. We're still excavating it."

"By 'we' Ed means the Duxbury Rural and Historical Society," clarified Paula. "We've both been active members for years."

"I can tell."

"Your uncle was active in the society too," said Ed. "And he took great pride that his house was one of the most historic ones in this area from the shipbuilding era. Are you aware he was at one time thinking of giving his house to the historical society?"

Here was an example of someone knowing that my uncle had thought of leaving the house to the society at one time. Danforth had alerted me that some people might know of Fred's original intentions, and apparently, he was right. But he had also said that absolutely no one knew that the house could still go to the society if I decided to pass on it—or what the financial terms were depending on the length of my ownership.

"Yes, I'm aware of it," was all I felt comfortable in saying.

"But he did say he was going to pledge to the society a very generous donation instead," Paula added hastily. "He was a very big supporter. We're told that that should be announced soon."

I chose to remain silent and just nodded.

"Have you met the other neighbors yet?" asked Ed, changing the subject yet again.

"Not yet. I only ran into Paula this morning. I believe there are only two other houses on Spyglass?"

"Yes. A little farther down the lane are the Tsais. They are the babies of the neighborhood."

"They have two kids in school here," Paula laughed, "so that makes them the babies."

"Tommy has done well for himself," said Ed. "He's a smart young guy. He works for a company in Cambridge that does something in Artificial Intelligence. The stock has skyrocketed. They've lived here for only a few years. He told me he had to scrape the money together to buy the house. Now he's looking to buy a second place on Nantucket."

"And to complete the picture," said Paula, "the fourth house at the end of the street belongs to Max and Khatia Trevanian. They've been here about ten years. You can't see it from the street. It's behind a bunch of trees."

"What do they do?"

"He's an importer. Deals in all sorts of things, as I understand. Art, rare objects, jewelry. He has warehouses in Boston, Geneva, and Singapore. We don't know them well. You won't see them much if you come back. They keep to themselves. They travel a lot."

"So you and Paula have lived in the neighborhood the longest?"

"Yes," nodded Ed. "We became that when Henry Phipps died five years ago and your uncle bought the house."

"A sad story, as I understand it," I said, remembering Danforth telling me that my uncle had bought the house from a family that had gone into bankruptcy.

"Very sad," said Paula. "The Phippses were a nice couple. The house had been in the family for over two hundred years. But time marches on."

"It certainly does," said Ed, looking at his watch. "We need to be in

38

Cohasset for a dinner in thirty minutes. Sorry, but we need to be on our way."

"No problem. I appreciate your hospitality and all the background on the neighborhood."

"Hope to see you soon," said Paula shaking my hand.

"I hope so too," I said, and I left the house.

That night, I reviewed in my mind the conversation with the Spauldings. They had said something that had surprised me at the time, but I couldn't remember what it was now. Maybe I'd remember by the time I saw them next time.

But whether there would be a next time was still to be determined.

* * * * *

Nothing much happened the rest of my visit. I ate dinner that night at another local restaurant Brenda had circled on her map. It was a very rustic place a couple of miles inland and away from the water on a cranberry bog called, appropriately enough, Tavern on the Bog. It was an atmospheric place, formerly an old house, that was now a popular eatery in town. But I didn't overhear any interesting talk there as I had the previous evening. Just a quiet dinner to collect my thoughts.

The next morning, I spent a couple of hours walking around the house, getting more familiar with it. It was superb, a perfect blend of taste and comfort. Also, because of its history, it was a pretty fascinating place with many interesting touches—and none more so than the artist studio in the back. I spent a good thirty minutes in there, just soaking it in. I looked at some of the sketches more closely and examined in some detail the two unfinished paintings on the easels—one of the lighthouse and small purple building, the other the mermaid figurehead.

I was just living in the moment in these new surroundings, trying to assess how I felt about it all. Both pictures somehow brought me nearer to two people. One was my uncle for sure. He seemed to have been a man of considerable parts. I would have loved to have known him better.

The other was Josiah Osborne, the builder of this house. These were pictures that told his story to me—of his life as a sailor, a man of the sea, and his later career as a carver of figureheads. The mermaid and her wild unkempt hair really struck me. How much of her was Fred Peterson the twenty-first-century painter and how much was Josiah Osborne the nineteenth-century carver? I was daydreaming now, something I've been prone to do my whole life going all the way back to St. Jerome's elementary school in Toledo.

There were windows on all four sides of the space, providing a three-hundred-sixty-degree view of the peninsula with the water on three sides of it. You could see it all. From here, the Osbornes of old could watch all the Duxbury ships sail up the Bluefish River from the King Caesar Shipyards where they were built, then into the bay, then up the coast to Boston to be laden with cargo, then out to the open sea and on to various destinations around the world.

I saw a pair of binoculars lying on a table. I picked them up and looked through them. From here, I could see the other three houses on Spyglass. Most interesting was the one that wasn't visible from the street, the one owned by the importer, the Trevanians. It was a sprawling, modern-looking, single-story structure with a pool and tennis court. It was not at all in the character of the rest of Powder Point. It was clear these owners had different tastes than everyone else.

It was now noon, and I needed to get to the airport to catch a late afternoon flight back to Detroit, which is the nearest big city to Toledo. I wished I had more time, but I'd seen enough to give me a lot to think about.

And that's exactly how I spent the next week back in Toledo.

Chapter 5
THE DECISION

By the time I got back to my condo, it was after eight. My son Jocko wasn't home. But his dog Zarathustra was, who began barking with delight as I entered through the front door (I once did a demo dog tape that I entitled "Thus Barked Zarathustra." I didn't get the job). My son loves that mangy mutt and insists on keeping him despite my protestations. The last thing we need is a dog to tie us down, particularly one who, despite our best efforts, occasionally confuses the leg of the kitchen table with a fire hydrant. But as has been the case with the vast majority of my other domestic kerfuffles over the years, I lost this one. And so The Big Z (who weighs little more than fifteen pounds) remains a fixture at chez Pavlik.

I was tired, so I had a quick bite to eat and went to bed.

The next morning at breakfast I was looking over the scripts of the two recordings I was scheduled to do that day. The first was in about two hours and was for a relatively minor character I portrayed for a cartoon show produced by PBS called *Bobby Goes to the Zoo*. In it, I did the voice not of Bobby but of a giraffe. For some reason, giraffes are in vogue these days. But this was only a few lines and not much prep was needed.

The other recording would be in the afternoon, and it was for an episode of my bread and butter, *Laszlo the Impaler*. I'd need to be on my game for that. I hadn't looked at the script in any great detail yet, and so I began to dig into my lines.

But I couldn't focus on them. My mind was full of the Duxbury house and the decision I had to make. It had dominated my thoughts on the plane ride back to Detroit, then the forty-five minute drive to Toledo, and it was doing so now.

With the benefit of a good night's sleep and some coffee, how did I feel about things? I had broken down the situation into four aspects. The first two favored me taking the house, the other two gave me reason to pause.

First there was the property itself. It was really fantastic in every way. The house itself was beautiful—unique and luxurious in its own way, yet homey and livable. Powder Point was a desirable neighborhood, and the accompanying views of the water were something out of a travel magazine. I found there was nothing I didn't like about 3 Spyglass Lane. I could never hope to afford a property like it on my own.

Which brought me to the second element: the finances. They strongly argued I should accept this property short and long term. True, I could get some decent money up front if I turned it down. But the way my uncle had structured his will made it an overwhelmingly better deal for me to accept ownership. It would give me a financial benefit I couldn't come close to achieving in any other way at this stage in my life. As a general rule, I never consider money as the number one factor in any decision I have ever made. But if ever there would be an exception to this rule, this might be it.

However, things got murkier from here because the next thing to consider was the town of Duxbury. It certainly was a prosperous and by all accounts a desirable place to live. Moreover, it seemed to be filled with interesting sorts of people. And although I wasn't all that much into history, I judged I might be over time. I did wonder, however, what the lifestyle would be like there. I would be a single middle-aged guy in a small town surrounded by families. True, I was only an hour from Boston, but my daily life would be characterized by trips to the supermarket or puttering around the house. How would I respond to that? My condo in Toledo was in a much more urban setting near movie theaters, many restaurants, and other forms of diversion. I even had season tickets for the Toledo Mud Hens. Not much, you might say, but I had developed my own routines.

And finally, and maybe the most important thing to consider, was my personal situation. I had three important people in my life: my mother, my son, and my paramour Gloria (or was I her paramour? I love the word but can never get straight who is who). Our relationship was only six months old, and things were still in a state of flux. Each of these three would be impacted by my decision, and I hoped the next week in Toledo would clarify things with all three. I intended to spend time with each, fully laying out the choice I had to make. The first such encounter would begin when Jocko, who was still asleep in his room upstairs, would wake up. Since this rarely took place before 10:00, I had time to assess how things stood with him.

First off, he has a lot going for him. IQ wise he is quite smart. He's always gotten top grades, and he graduated cum laude from the University of Michigan. He's very likable with a nice, easy-going, and engaging personality. He's honest and loyal too.

What he is not is pragmatic. He can't focus his attention for long, which, while not uncommon for young people in this unfocused era of social media, he takes to extreme levels. For example, he changed majors four different times as an undergrad, moving from Computer Science to Mathematics to Philosophy to Anthropology. I'm actually not sure what he ended up getting his degree in. Further, what he seems to be pursuing now for his PhD at the University of Toledo was some multidisciplinary combination of all of the above, with Italian being thrown into the mix recently too for some unfathomable reason. I had no idea what his dissertation was all about even though he'd been writing it for two years.

His lack of focus spilled over into his employment track record. Aside from an on-again, off-again part-time position as a barista at a local coffee house, he'd never had a job that remotely interested him. And even now he had no income as a grad assistant because the professors at the university had trouble assigning him to a class because they couldn't pinpoint his field. Academically he existed in some interdisciplinary limbo, able to continue to pursue the PhD but without any financial assistance to do so.

I've often wondered how this happened. Although I am not necessarily a role model for pragmatism myself, I mostly blame his mother (my ex-wife) Melanie for the majority of his problems. Instead of allowing me to give our son an occasional kick in the ass as every good father has done since the beginning of time, Melanie insisted we cater to his every whim because he was "special." It started with his name, which is something I don't believe he has ever totally overcome. I wanted to call him James. Both Melanie's and my father were named James. Jim Pavlik was just fine with me.

However, Melanie insisted on naming him Giacomo, the Italian version of James. She was an artsy sort when we got married, way too pretentious for me in retrospect, and she thought that naming him after the Italian opera composer Giacomo Puccini was impressively highbrow. She thought it would encourage him to think of himself as different. I thought it sounded silly—Giacomo Pavlik—and the other boys would tease him. As I usually did with her, though, I ultimately gave up and gave in.

But I had my own form of quiet rebellion. I started calling him Jocko, a real down-to-earth nickname in my opinion. Melanie was aghast when she first heard it, but I told her I was using the Italian derivative of the name—Giaco—which is pronounced exactly the same. Although there is no such Italian derivative, she bought it, not realizing that I was using the "j" spelling in my head, as in a baseball umpire of that era named Jocko Conlin. Melanie always thought of our son as a Giaco, which is how he viewed himself too—much to his disadvantage in my view. But we were where we were on this.

I was musing along these lines when Jocko appeared in the kitchen, pajama bottoms on and wearing a T shirt that had an image of Maslow's hierarchy of needs pyramid on it. The pinnacle of the pyramid said "self-actualization," which I totally get. I'm all for it. People are free to self-actualize their tushes off in my opinion. I just wished I had seen the word "employment" somewhere on the pyramid too.

"Ciao, Papa," he said pouring himself a cup of coffee and sitting down at the table. "How was the trip?"

Before I flew to Boston, I had told him about Danforth's letter and my subsequent phone call with the lawyer informing me that I stood to inherit a house in Massachusetts from my uncle. My son had never met Fred. I hadn't even mentioned him much over the years, and so Jocko had found the house inheritance news as surprising as I had.

"The trip was interesting. It's a beautiful house. Your great uncle was a man of means."

"What are you going to do with it?"

"That's the question I'm asking myself. I don't need it."

"Then maybe sell it? Or you could rent it out?"

"I can't rent it out. For one thing, the town is totally residential and has been taking a hard stance against owners who have listed their houses for short-term rental on Airbnb and the like. It's causing a lot of tension between neighbors in parts of town. I don't want to cause problems. Besides, my uncle's will prohibits me from renting it out. There are some conditions he left me in the will."

"Like what?" he asked idly, then listened while making himself a bowl of Cheerios.

I then took ten minutes to explain the terms of the will.

"Mama Mia," he said after his last bite. "What do you suppose Uncle Fred was thinking?"

"He obviously hoped I'd take it and give it a shot to live there. The financial incentive is pretty compelling."

"Would you seriously consider picking up and leaving here?" I had his attention now. There would be no more faux Italiano from him.

"My job would allow it, so that's not a problem. But I don't know. There's a lot to consider. How would you feel if I did?"

He hesitated. "Would you keep this place?"

I'd thought about this angle. "Yes, I would. I've paid off the mortgage, and the taxes and utilities are very low, so the expenses are doable. Of course I'd have taxes and utilities on the new house, and they'd be higher than here. But I think I could afford to keep both places, at least for a while. So you could stay here."

"I'm probably two years from completing my dissertation and getting the PhD. Hopefully after that I could handle any expenses on my own."

My initial reaction was that getting a PhD and then "hopefully" being able to pay taxes and utilities on a small already-paid-for condo in Toledo, Ohio was setting a pretty low bar. On the other hand, this was as close as he'd ever come to conveying to me any semblance of a financial plan, and I took it as progress.

"Don't worry about that. I'd never leave you high and dry, son."

"I'm not going to lie, Dad. I'd be in trouble without this place. But you should do what you want."

"I appreciate your sentiment. Now all I have to do is figure out what I want. Let's loop back on this later. I'm here all week."

I patted him on the shoulder as I passed by on my way to my bedroom upstairs where my recording equipment was set up. It was time for me to go to work.

* * * * *

That evening I took Gloria out to dinner. I had just described the house to her.

"That sounds like quite a place. Certainly a step or three up from your little place here."

Her assessment was very accurate, although more blunt than I would have expected from a woman I was trying to figure out if I loved.

"Yes, it is. I'm just not sure what to do with it." I then explained the terms of the will.

"Hmmm," she said. "The accountant in me says this is a no brainer finance-wise."

"How about the woman in you?" That was the question I'd been dying to ask her.

She paused, then said, "What does the man in you say?"

46

There was a short awkward silence between us, then we both laughed. We were too old to behave like young lovers. We were both divorced, and we had met when I had moved to Toledo from LA two years previously. My divorce from Melanie had just been finalized as had Gloria's from her husband of twenty years. For years, I had gotten my taxes done at Deloitte in LA and asked to be assigned one of their CPA's in Toledo when I moved there and, voila, there was Gloria. What was at first a business relationship had gradually grown into something more. How much more was the question.

"I'll go first," she finally said. "A part of me has thought from the start that our relationship doesn't need to 'go anywhere' as they say. Just some good times and companionship would be enough. Now I'm not so sure. Time marches on, and I wonder what the future looks like."

"I'm in the same place. You get to the point where you wonder if the future is now."

Gloria and I had both met when our confidences were low. Our respective spouses were the ones who had initiated divorce procedures against each of us. In my case, Melanie had announced one day that she had fallen in love with the director of a well-known museum in LA. I was surprised, but in retrospect I should have seen it coming. Our relationship had become stale, our lifestyle sedentary and unexciting. We'd both put on a few pounds and suddenly she started taking some weight loss drug. She slimmed down and looked great, if I must say. Unfortunately, it was all for her new beau. His name, ironically, was Jim, and I wondered if she called him Giacomo. At any rate, they had married and were living in Pasadena.

"Yes," said Gloria, taking my hand. "We seem to be running in place."

One of the signs of this was the fact that, despite numerous conversations, we hadn't moved in together. We couldn't move into my place because there was no space since Jocko was there. Gloria had a big house with plenty of room, but she had a teenage daughter still living with her—a senior in high school—and having me move in there felt awkward to both of us. Maybe it could happen when the daughter went away to college the following year. So there were reasonable excuses for putting off any domicile-related next steps. But the thought had crossed my mind that maybe I really didn't want to wake up every morning next to the person who did my taxes. And maybe she wasn't all that thrilled with the prospect of hearing the voice of Laszlo whispering sweet nothings in her ear at night. At any rate, cohabitation had not happened yet.

We talked through all the options over dinner and at her place afterwards. Maybe she could move in with me in Duxbury. Or maybe I could maintain two homes and still see her relatively frequently back in Toledo. Or maybe I could turn down the Duxbury house outright. One option we never mentioned, however, was getting married. That was the elephant in the room.

We agreed that each of us would think about it for the week, and that's how we left it that evening.

* * * * *

Then there was my mother. I visited her at the memory care facility— The Homestead—every day that week, spending at least an hour there each time. I primarily just talked to her or watched television with her, trying to stimulate her. I would also escort her into a common area where family members often sat with their loved ones or onto the patio in the back and then a stroll in the garden. I was still hoping for any sign of recognition from her, any sign she knew what was happening.

But there was nothing positive I could cling to. She was fully conscious and was even able to say some words. But she talked in half-formed sentences and random unconnected thoughts that made no sense. Every now and then she smiled at me, as if she knew who I was. But it was more likely wishful thinking on my part. The nurses told me she was probably totally oblivious to her surroundings, and she had been like that for months now. There would be no turning back of the clock. At least she was comfortable and in no pain.

My conversations throughout the rest of the week with Jocko had become very interesting. It seemed that he was sparking to the idea of living alone. He thought it would do him good to be his own man, and I did too. What was most important to him was having a paid-up place to live. My presence in it was not necessary. I wouldn't say we'd grown tired of living together, but the prospect of not doing so didn't seem to bother either of us. It actually felt normal.

Gloria was another matter. I spent most nights that week at her place, going round and round with her, talking through various scenarios. In the end, she said she couldn't uproot her entire life and follow me east, at least at this time because of her daughter and her job. She wasn't sure she could work it virtually. Deloitte might give her a transfer, but she wouldn't even ask until her daughter was off to college and I was sure I wanted to stick it out in Duxbury. On the other hand, we both still felt that we might have a future together, and a long-distance romance wasn't the worst thing in the world as we continued to work through our feelings. I said I could come back to Toledo occasionally, and she said she'd visit me too. Despite these promises, I think we both were wondering if we were splitting up but afraid to call it that.

And how was I processing this? As the week wore on, the idea of accepting the Duxbury house seemed more and more doable, even attractive. I liked the idea of Jocko being more independent. It was about time. Also, my mother seemed totally unaware of my presence when I visited her. I was in effect useless. She was safe and well attended to in her facility, and Jocko said he'd visit her regularly. Furthermore, I'd only be a few hours away if I absolutely needed to get back. I said to myself I'd be returning fairly often anyway to see Gloria.

I'd also come to think that a change of scenery might be refreshing. After many years in LA, Toledo was beginning to feel awfully small and boring. I'd grown up there, and there is a lot of truth in the saying that you can't go home again—at least some people can't. It kind of implies you couldn't cut it elsewhere, and I was too young to think that.

True, Duxbury was a very small town, and I was unsure how I'd react to that. On the other hand, living in such a place would be new and different from any place I'd ever lived before. It began to feel like it all might be a growth opportunity for me. And Boston was only an hour away. It was a terrific and accessible city and had always been one of my favorites to visit. The Red Sox and Fenway seemed an upgrade compared to the Mud Hens. You could throw in the Celtics, Bruins, and Patriots too.

And then of course there was the financial part. I wanted to think that money wasn't driving this decision. But in all honesty, if a tie-breaker was needed, this was clearly it. I concluded that I had to give this a shot. The worst-case scenario was that if after two years I wasn't happy there, I'd just move back to Toledo since I wasn't selling my condo, I'd give the Duxbury Rural and Historical Society the Powder Point house, and I'd get the 25% of the assessed value. No harm, no foul.

On Friday I called Danforth and told him I wanted the house. I would leave on Sunday and drive to Duxbury, bringing my recording equipment with me, ready to move in.

"Okay," he said. "I can meet you at your house Monday morning. I'll bring all the necessary paperwork for you to sign."

"Thanks," I said.

So early Sunday morning I set off in my SUV, my equipment, clothes, and a few miscellaneous items packed in tightly. It felt like I was making a new start, but one not without some risk.

As it turned out, my instincts were correct.

Chapter 6
SETTLING IN

It is a long drive from Toledo to Duxbury—about twelve hours with no traffic. The entire trip is almost all on one road, Interstate 90. And it is very flat and thoroughly boring. At one point in western Massachusetts there is a sign off to the side that reads, *Elevation five hundred twenty meters: Next Highest Elevation on I-90 is at Oacoma, South Dakota.*

That's 1716 miles of relative flatness. Although Toledo to Duxbury is "only" eight hundred of those miles, that's still a lot of boredom, and I had real trouble keeping my eyes open for the last third of the drive. When I finally arrived at the house late that Sunday evening, I vowed I'd never make that drive again. I'd fly from now on. I had only done it this one time in order to get my car and recording equipment to Duxbury.

Danforth pulled into my driveway the next day at our prearranged time of 10:00.

"Thanks for coming out here," I said, shaking his hand and leading him into the house. "Saves me a trip into Boston."

"No problem. My wife and I live a couple towns north of here in Hingham, but we have a second house on the Vineyard. When the good weather in May comes around, we start spending our weekends on the island and all through the summer. I usually come back to my Boston office Monday morning. The ferry at Woods Hole is only an hour from your house, so stopping here is on my way back to work. I stopped here all the time to handle business with Fred."

"I'm looking forward to getting more familiar with the geography," I said leading him into the kitchen where I had brewed some coffee. I poured him a cup, and we sat at the table. He opened his briefcase

"First of all, congratulations," he said unpacking from his briefcase a stack of papers that he put on the table. "You have a terrific place here."

"Yes, I know. I couldn't pass it up."

"We'll need to go over some papers and have you sign off."

We spent half an hour reviewing the will again. It included a couple of items I hadn't been aware of. It was more good news. For one thing, my uncle had left me a small motorboat.

"Fred liked to kayak," said Danforth, "but he liked to cruise around the bay in his Grady White powerboat too. He kept it in the Bayside Marina near the harbor where they have a put-in service. It's there now."

Even more interesting was that my uncle had left me two very small additional pieces of land about three miles from the house. The first was a quarter acre of land with a shack on it near the Gurnet Point Lighthouse.

"Fred mostly used it for storage. The key to the front door is somewhere on the ring with all the other keys I'm going to give you before I leave. You'll just have to find the right one."

"Explain to me exactly what the Gurnet is," I said. "I've heard the word a couple of times."

"It's an area at the southern edge of the peninsula where the town beach is. Technically it's in the town of Plymouth. You can access it either by boat or by driving over the Powder Point bridge, then following the dirt road that parallels the beach. There's a lighthouse and a little community at the end. It's about a four-mile drive to get there by land. I've never been out there myself."

The other property was an acre of empty land on a place in the bay called Clark's Island.

"You can only get there by boat. His property is just a bunch of trees I believe. I've never been there either."

After he'd reviewed everything with me, I signed the necessary papers.

"We're done?" I said.

"Yes. It's all yours. Good luck."

"Now I just need to start going through everything in the house and deciding what needs to go. He must have some personal items lying around. But everything looks so neat and in order."

"One thing you won't have to worry about is your uncle's business and personal affairs. After the funeral, I spent some time going through Fred's mail and desk files, and I've attended to all outstanding items. I was very aware of all of his dealings. As his executor, I'll continue to handle those things as they come up. I'm sure there will be some loose ends. I think it's easier to have all his mail forwarded to me for a while. I'll send you back anything you'll need to handle personally, and you can start converting things like utilities to your name."

"Sounds good. I've been very worried about that. It's a huge relief to me to know someone is on top of all those details. How long were you his lawyer? Did you two go way back?"

"We met about five or six years ago. He was living in New York, but he was doing a lot of business in Boston. I was representing a company his firm was acquiring. He saw me as a tough but fair negotiator, and I felt the same way about him too. We immediately hit it off, so when he bought the Duxbury house and started spending time up here, he asked me to become his personal attorney. His lawyer in New York had just retired, and he wanted someone local as his legal advisor."

"It was good he had someone he could depend on."

"Particularly at the end. He could become muddled and overwhelmed at times. He was as sharp a guy as you'd ever meet, but he had started to age pretty quickly. He was on some medications, as you'd expect for someone his age. I gradually noticed some differences in him."

I remembered that when we first met, Danforth had mentioned that my uncle had started to decline. This gave his remark more context.

"But he never slowed down it seems," I said. "You have to admire him for that."

"Fred certainly played to the final whistle. That was his style."

We'd completed our business and Danforth said he needed to shove off. "Oh, one final thing before I go," he said. "Now that you've accepted the house, according to Fred's will, his monetary gift to the Duxbury Rural and Historical Society will kick in. I'm going to inform them of it. They will be very pleased."

"I'm glad you brought that up. Just so I'm clear, they don't know the conditions of the will regarding me owning the house, correct?"

"Correct. They will not know that."

"But it seems some members do know that my uncle was thinking of leaving the house to the society at one time. My next door neighbors belong to the society, and they mentioned that to me."

"I have no specific knowledge of that, but it wouldn't surprise me. I suspected that Fred may have shared his thinking with a few people he was particularly close to. I told him that worried me because when that happens, rumors can spread. But as for the terms of your ownership, once he decided on that, he kept mum about it. Again, if any questions come up, you know how to reach me. I'll get all of this recorded at the registries of probate and deeds."

I walked him to the door, shook his hand one last time, then watched as he got in his car and drove off leaving me alone in the house. It was now officially mine.

* * * * *

I spent the next week settling in. The moving-in part was easy. Since the house was totally furnished, I had brought nothing with me other than my clothes, my laptop, and my recording equipment. I set the latter up in the converted workshop out back. I had three recordings that week, and they all went just fine. I could do these things from anywhere that was quiet and had a good internet connection. The workshop had both of these.

I was also able to do an inventory of the contents of the house. All the furnishings were better than anything I would have chosen, and it was an easy decision to leave everything as is. I gave all of my uncle's clothes to a local charity. I also went through all the drawers of his desk in his backyard office. It was pretty empty, as I assumed Danforth had taken out all relevant files pertaining to Fred's business affairs. All that was left in there were supplies like stationary, pens, and the like. There was nothing personal that pertained to my uncle other than one old album that contained pictures primarily of his wife Mary and himself. I did notice there were a couple old photos of my mother and one even of me in my Little League baseball uniform standing next to my father. He had died of an aneurysm a year later. He had been only forty-two years old—six years younger than I was now.

In town, I attended to practical details such as opening an account at the local bank. And in order to operate my new Grady White, I would need a license. Knowing absolutely nothing about boating, I began the on-line safety course the state required, then signed up for lessons at the Maritime School which was next to the marina where Fred kept the boat. At the town hall, I bought car stickers for the town dump and town beach, as well as an over the sand permit which would enable me to drive out to the Gurnet. I'd made progress—at least on the surface—in becoming a member of "Deluxe-bury" as the town is often called in both admiration and sarcasm. Whether I "fit in" was still TBD.

One morning when I was standing in my front yard, a man in running gear came jogging by me.

"Are you the new owner?" he asked. He was young—probably in his thirties.

"I am. I'm Jake Pavlik."

"And I'm Tommy Tsai. I live next door. Welcome to the neighborhood." He had a big smile and shook my hand firmly.

"Thanks, nice to meet you,"

"You'll find it's pretty quiet around here. Everybody keeps to themselves. Except us, I guess. With our two kids, we always seem to be coming or going. How about joining us for dinner some time."

"I'd love to."

"How about tonight? I'll throw some burgers on the grill."

I agreed and we set a time.

So that night I went to the Tsai house and met the family, which consisted of Tommy's wife and two kids.

"You're a relative of Mr. Peterson, right?" his wife said. Her name was Sarah and, like her husband, looked to be in her mid-thirties. "We'd heard that he'd left his house to a family member, but that's all we knew."

"He was my uncle."

"He was a nice, friendly guy," said Tommy. "Very active for someone his age. Seemed to be in great shape. We saw him just a couple days before the accident. He was so energetic."

This didn't totally jive with the picture Danforth had painted of my uncle as an old man in rapid decline. I then remembered that this is what had confused me about my conversation with the Spauldings the week previously. They too had called Fred healthy, even using the word robust. But Danforth knew more about my uncle than the neighbors would have, I reasoned. He had known Fred longer and any slippage from his former self would have been more apparent to him, his lawyer. Danforth would have dealt with my uncle more on a business than social basis, where cognitive ability or lack thereof would be more in the spotlight.

"It's all so tragic," I said in what was now my standard line.

"Come out to the grill while I flip the burgers and tell me what you do," he said, and we both moved outside.

When I told him my profession and then some of the characters I portrayed, he let out a shout. "You are the voice of Laszlo the Impaler? You're kidding me! I've loved that show since my college days. That's awesome, bro."

He's about the *right age*, I thought. That show has run for fifteen years now. College guys loved it when it first came out, and many have stuck with it as they have gotten older. I'm always amazed at the staying power that show has with young men as they move from college frat boys to middle-age dads. Mentally, I was outgrowing the part sooner than my audience did, which is way better than the alternative.

"Hey, Sarah!" he yelled. "Jake is the voice of Laszlo the Impaler."

"Who?" she called back in a voice definitely less enthusiastic than her husband's. But this is par for the course as my fan base is heavily skewed to young men that call me bro and dude.

"Wait till I tell the guys at work," he gushed.

"And, if I remember correctly, you work in AI?"

"Yeah, I'm the CMO of a company called Procuria. We build AI-powered supply chain platforms and solutions. Very topical in this era of tariffs, rising costs, and political sanctions. We can't keep up with the demand. I'll be honest, homie. I stepped in shit when I got this job. The stock's gone wild."

"Good for you," I said, momentarily thinking of sarcastically adding the word "sonny" at the end. I guess I should be glad when younger people think I'm enough of a contemporary to call me dude, bro, or homie. But for some reason, the older I get, the more it irritates me. It feels like I'm being put in a box I no longer belong in.

During the course of the evening when Tommy and I drank a bit too much beer, I learned a bit about him. His parents had emigrated from Hong Kong to Palo Alto where his father ended up teaching Electrical Engineering at Stanford. Tommy majored in EE himself at the school and that's where he met Sarah. After starting with HP in the Bay Area, he took a chance and joined a startup in Boston named Procuria. He had worked there for five years now and made a lot of money.

"I was employee number friggin' four, dude!"

His eleven-year-old daughter Brianna played tennis, taking after her mother who had been a co-captain of the Stanford tennis team. His eight-year-old son Brendon, however, was his pride and joy. He was a defenseman on South Shore's traveling midget hockey team.

"The kid is incredible. He watches every Bruins game and models his game on various NHL tough guy enforcers. Boy, can he hit. He practices all the time all year round."

I could well believe this as Brendon was on roller skates the entire evening, intent on delivering forechecks on his parents, his sister, and even me. Tommy looked on with adoring eyes while I contemplated taking a penalty for tripping. It would have been worth it.

He knew my uncle a little bit, and they recently had a very friendly conversation instigated by my uncle about whether Procuria could address some sourcing issues he was having with a couple of the startups he'd invested in.

"Your uncle was aces, bro. Too bad it ended the way it did for him. But I'm looking forward to hanging with you too. I'd love to introduce you to my co-workers. They'll go nuts!"

And so my first week ended with a bit of a hangover the next morning. It had been a good week—productive and quiet. The next couple of weeks were also productive, but they were not as quiet.

Chapter 7
THE GURNET

The next week I made a business trip to Atlanta for a couple of days. That's where the headquarters of The Cartoon Network is. I'd been working with them on developing a new show—this time as a writer, not as a voice actor. The producer of the show wanted to meet with me and my writing partner, Ben Kapler, who flew in from his home in New York.

Bennie and I went way back to our college days at Northwestern. We were in a couple of shows together on campus and had even written one together. It was a spoof of the *Book of Genesis* in which I played the serpent that tempts Eve. After that, he began calling me Jake the Snake, a nickname that caught on throughout my college years and one he still calls me. He came from a nice Jewish family, and I visited the Kaplers a number of times at their home on Long Island during school breaks. He'd been the best man at my wedding. Our friendship had outlasted the marriage.

We had co-written a couple of other shows for the network over the years. While neither of them were big hits, each had enough success to last a couple of seasons, which encouraged us to keep plugging away as a team. He had lots of other writing credits to his name, and while I didn't, I'd grown less interested in performing and more in writing. After all, I had started out as a journalist and had a pretty good way with words. As I grew older, I aspired to do more writing—and not only for animation programming. I thought I might even have a book or two in me, if I could only get into a regular writing rhythm. I'm a very disorganized person, and putting some order into my writing has always been my weakness. That's Bennie's strength and why we work well together.

He was very interested when I told him over lunch of my move east. I explained everything about the house, including the specific terms of my ownership. Besides Danforth, only Gloria and Jocko knew about that. Since Ben was maybe my best friend, I felt comfortable confiding in him too. But that would be it. No one else needed to know.

"I can't say I'm totally surprised," he said. "I always thought you'd grow tired of Toledo."

"This certainly is way different than Toledo. Boston is great, but Duxbury is really small. I'll need to fill the time."

"You can always pop down to see us on Long Island. This is the closest you've ever lived to Judy and me. There's a ferry that leaves from New London, Connecticut to Orient Point on the eastern tip of Long Island. From there you can be at our place in Sag Harbor in no time."

"Or you could come up my way too. The ferry goes both ways they tell me."

"Sure, a home and away series. And maybe your new lifestyle will give you a chance to do more writing. You've always said you need more time to do it. Maybe this will be the catalyst."

"Maybe so. And maybe I'll start carrying around a notebook with me like a REAL writer." I had long teased him for carrying one around, jotting down ideas and phrases as they came to him for possible usage later in something he'd be writing. Keeping such notebooks or journals, I found out, is common practice for many professional writers.

"Laugh at me if you will," he said, and he pulled out his own well-worn notebook. "I never go anywhere without it. It's a good discipline if you're serious about writing. It's also a useful personal outlet to say what's on your mind when you're not ready to go public with your thinking yet. You need this more than I do."

I smiled.

Two days later I flew back home. Not long after that, I made a little trip that led me to remember his last words to me.

* * * * *

The next couple of weeks flew by. I had several recordings and a couple of video calls with Bennie and our producer regarding our fledgling show. It was coming together nicely. In addition, my agent Becky Cartwright—specifically, she is my "voice agent" —sent me a contract for a new Disney movie she'd lined up for me. I only do minor characters for Disney, but the royalties are significant because those movies get global distribution. To sum it all up, the business part of my new situation was working out just fine.

On the personal front, nothing much was happening in Toledo. I talked or emailed with Gloria and Jocko every day. He saw my mother regularly and reported back that she didn't recognize him.

"She is totally out of it," he emailed me. "But her vital signs are good and she seems at peace, so don't worry about her."

Gloria and I said we missed each other, which was largely true, at least on my end. She seemed to mean it too, as she threw out the idea of coming to visit me. I said the same about me popping back to Toledo soon. But we hadn't scheduled anything firm yet, so we carried on in our romantic limbo.

My Duxbury leisure activities were picking up too. I'd begun boating classes and would soon earn my license. I also signed up for the film noir class Paula Spaulding had mentioned. She was taking it too. The teacher was a retired legendary history teacher at Duxbury High School. He really knew his noir, and he dressed the part too, wearing his homburg to class. I wished my history teacher at Toledo Central High had been as stylish—and interesting.

"Fred took this class too," she said. "Frankly, I had to drag him to it. He wasn't a fan of old movies, but I thought he'd enjoy the group. He did."

It was now June and the weather was fine enough to go to the town beach, and one warm sunny Saturday I decided to check it out. Although I lived close enough to have walked or jogged over the wooden bridge, I took my car. It was easier that way because I was bringing a beach chair, a cooler with some lunch, and a book. I had begun to read *Mildred Pierce* by James Cain. In my noir class, we'd just seen the movie version of it, and I wanted to read the source novel. Some think the story, although set in California in both the novel and movie, was inspired by a trip Cain may have made through Duxbury. The thought of a noir classic set in such a quiet idyllic town was a prospect too delicious to resist, and so I borrowed Paula's copy from the Spauldings' well-stocked library.

Because school hadn't let out yet, the town beach wasn't too busy. I parked myself on the beginning of the four-mile-long peninsula across the wooden Powder Point bridge. While learning more about the area, I found out one side of this narrow spit of land—no more than one hundred yards in width—is Duxbury Bay and the Snug Harbor area with the maritime school, the yacht club, and the Bayside Marina where my boat was. On the other side is the open sea. At first, I had mistakenly thought this body of water was the ocean, but it is not. It is actually Cape Cod Bay—at least for the first twenty miles. After that it becomes the Atlantic.

The few people that were there had the same idea I did to enjoy the sand and surf and were seated in low beach chairs or lying on blankets. No one was in the water. When I waded in up to my shins, I found out why. It was freezing. I ended up sitting in my chair reading.

Having grown bored after an hour or so, it dawned on me that I had yet to see my uncle's little plot out on the Gurnet on the tip of the peninsula. The other day I'd been in his studio and had glanced at his unfinished painting called *Gurnet Light and the Purple Shack at Dusk* which was still on its easel. I'd made a mental note to get out there and check out the scene. Since I had my car with me now, I took my chair and book, put them in the back seat, then drove out that way on the long dirt road. It was in bad shape with many potholes. But it was drivable, and after fifteen minutes of bumps and rattles, I saw the lighthouse and got out.

It sits on a little mound within an old, earthen work fort originally built in 1776 and known as Gurnet Fort. It was later rebuilt and renamed Fort Andrew during the Civil War. There was signage explaining that this is the oldest wooden lighthouse in the United States. At one time there were actually two lighthouses standing side by side, but the second structure had been destroyed in a storm. The surviving lighthouse stands on land that is managed by a nonprofit.

Just across from the lighthouse was a small flight of wooden steps that lead to the top of the earth walls of the fort. I climbed up and looked out. From here you get a really spectacular three-hundred-sixty-degree view of the Gurnet and surrounding area. In one direction was the road I'd just driven up. I could see the entire length of the peninsula back to the wooden bridge and the water on either side. In the opposite direction and across several miles of water was a land mass where the town of Plymouth is located. In this water, which is where Duxbury Bay meets Kingston Bay and Plymouth Bay, stands another lighthouse called Duxbury Pier Light, or Bug Light as it is more familiarly known. It, like Gurnet Light, is maintained by a nonprofit organization. The expansive watery view was breathtaking.

But what most caught my eye was the view inland and into the small Gurnet community just outside the lighthouse area. I saw several short dirt streets lined with houses. This was the scene depicted on the canvas on the easel in my uncle's studio. From here I could see a dozen or so houses, one of which stood out among the others. While most of the houses were white, one was not. It was a deep purple. *This*, I thought, *must be* the *shack my uncle—and now I—owned and which had given its name to his painting.*

I exited the fort and walked toward the little community of a couple dozen houses. I found the shack easily. It was made of cinder block and was very humble in appearance. As Danforth had said, it stood on a very small lot, much of which was sandy, although patches of overgrown grass were scattered here and there. A small, badly rusted, dilapidated metal shed stood off to the side. A few old buoys were nailed to the door. A kayak covered partially in sand and mud was on the ground next to it.

The place didn't look abandoned, but it did not appear as well maintained as the other houses near it. They were all much bigger wooden structures, most with grey cedar shingles and very tidy with green lawns. I had my key ring with me, and I finally found the one that fit the lock in the front door.

As I walked in, I saw a single large room which had been subdivided into a living room with a sofa bed, a kitchenette with two chairs and a table, and a curtain behind which was a toilet and shower. It was primitive and had the feeling of a storage space but without much being stored there. There was a large life-size dilapidated wooden statue in one corner and several boxes stacked in another, but that was it. On the table were a few books and some papers.

The defining image of the entire space, however, was the wall across from the table. About a dozen black line illustrations on sketching paper had been taped to the sheet rock. They were arranged in a rough circle, in the middle of which was a poster. Written on it in capital letters was:

MY COMPLICATED LIFE IN DUXBURY: NEW WORK IN PROGRESS

While the rest of the room looked haphazard, the circle looked purposefully organized, although its full meaning was not apparent.

I moved closer to examine the sketches. Some were of people, places or scenes, a few of which I was familiar with. One was of an oyster shed in the harbor, another of my house, still another of The Shipyard Inn. There was also a portrait of a woman, two of lighthouses, a couple more that depicted old two-masted ships, and several other miscellaneous scenes. I assumed my uncle had drawn these sketches. Individually they were very well done and clearly identified by titles and captions on the bottom of each. Collectively, they presented themselves as new work he seemed to have been contemplating.

I went over to the table and looked at the books on it. One was a history of sailing ships built in Duxbury. Another was a facsimile of the logbook of a certain Seth Sprague, the captain of a nineteenth-century merchant ship called the *Smyrna*. Another was on the early history of the

New England China trade. Another was called *Essential Writings in Transcendentalism*. Also on the table was a big blotter-sized calendar of the current year with brief handwritten notes by many of the dates. Finally, there was a box of cards—tarot cards to be precise.

It was a curious space, and I wasn't entirely sure what to make of it. Danforth had called it a place my uncle used to get away to every now and then just for the day. It had an isolated Robinson Crusoe feeling to it, very different than that of the house on Spyglass Lane even though it was only a few miles away. I took out my iPhone and made a video of the room. I then decided to take the sketches, books, and the materials on the table back with me to examine them in more depth. I put them all in a small empty box I found in the corner and carried it to my car.

I went back into the shack. I figured I would eventually clean the place out completely and wondered if anything else was worth taking with me. It seemed unlikely. I looked around the room again. Leaning in the corner against the wall was the wooden statue of a woman. It was in very bad shape. It had a bit of color to it, so it had evidently been painted at one time. But much of the paint had faded or was gone completely. Some of the wood had rotted away and the right arm was missing. There was something familiar about it, though. It was the hair, flying wildly in all directions.

Then it dawned on me. It looked like Fred's unfinished painting of the mermaid I'd seen in his studio. Brenda had said it was a painting of a ship's figurehead. So, this old rotting thing was no statue. It was an old figurehead. Maybe it was even the model Fred was using for his painting. Despite its poor condition, I decided I'd take it back with me. It was a little taller than I was and made of pine. It was surprisingly light, and I was able to get it into my SUV easily.

Before going, I went to the rusty shed and turned the handle. It opened right up. It wasn't even locked, and I could see why. There was nothing in there but junk. I moved around some of the debris to see if there was anything worth keeping. There was not. It was all refuse and nothing more. Just some stuff that had been idly thrown into it over the years. I did uncover something lying underneath some old blankets that caught my eye, though. It was a wooden arm two or three feet long. I picked it up and realized it was the missing right arm of the mermaid I'd just put in my car.

What the *heck*, I thought. *I'm taking* the *mermaid back. Might as well take her arm back too. Maybe I can get her restored. Not everybody can own an authentic figurehead!*

As I was closing the house door and locking it, a man came up to me. He looked like a workman of some sort.

"Is this your house?" He was a husky young man, maybe 6'2".

"Yes."

"What happened to the old guy?"

"He died. He was my uncle. Did you know him?"

"Not really. I once talked to him about doing some work."

"What kind of work?"

"I do odd jobs around here. I'm out here now doing some landscaping. Some of the owners ask me to watch their houses in the off season too. Like this guy right next to you. Been doing it for him for a couple years. I fix things too. They call me Mr. Fixit as a matter of fact. I talked to your uncle about repairing his shed. It's falling apart."

"I see that. I was just looking at it."

"Yeah, I saw you carrying some stuff out. If you want to sell this place, I'd be interested. I live in Plymouth, and it's a pain in the ass to get here. I wouldn't mind having a little place like this to crash."

"No plans to sell, but if I ever do…"

"In the meantime, I fix anything, believe me. Give me a call if you want the shed done. Here's my number." He told it to me as I entered the number into my phone.

"I'm Jake Pavlik. What's your name?"

"I'm Joey. Joey Fixit. They don't call me Mr. Fixit for nothing."

He laughed and lumbered off, presumably to his next job in the neighborhood.

I got back in my car and made the slow bone-rattling ride back. Next time, I vowed, I'd take my boat now that I had my license. But it probably wouldn't be that often, I figured. I didn't see the point in making the effort of coming out all this way to such a ramshackle little place—or at least not nearly as often as my uncle apparently had. Maybe I'd even sell it to Mr. Fixit.

Chapter 8
SUSPICION

At about this time, Danforth informed me that he'd made the Duxbury Rural and Historical Society aware of my uncle's donation to it.

"They are very happy, and they are going to reach out to you," he emailed me.

A few days later, I received a letter from Caroline Hawksmoor, Executive Director of DRHS. It was an invitation to a reception at which my uncle's donation was to be announced. The venue was one of the group's historic properties: the Nathaniel Winsor House on Washington Street near the harbor. Apparently it also serves as the business headquarters and occasional function space for the society. I was happy to attend, knowing the affection my uncle had for the organization. I was also curious to see the reaction to his donation.

The Spauldings were there when I walked in, and they immediately made their way to me. I'd had a couple of nice conversations with Paula at my film noir class, and she was eager to introduce me to the other members. Her first line was always, "This is the nephew of Fred Peterson." At a certain point, a very professionally looking woman came up to me.

"I'm Caroline Hawksmoor. I am so happy you were able to join us today. Paula and Ed have told me all about you. Sorry it's taken so long to meet you. And sorry for the loss of your uncle. He was a wonderful friend of the society. Very generous."

I was interested to see how generous myself. I still didn't know.

After some conversation and cocktails, an announcement was made to grab a glass of champagne and move to another room where folding chairs had been set up. With everyone seated, Caroline began.

"Good evening. I'd like to say just a few words. PJ Parsons, the chairman of our fundraising committee, is in bed with a fever and couldn't be here tonight else he would have joined me up here for this announcement.

"Last month the society lost a great friend, Fred Peterson. He began attending some of our events when he bought his house here five years ago and immediately became fascinated with Duxbury's history. He had a special interest in this very house where we are tonight. As you know, Nathaniel Winsor made his living creating figureheads. Although lesser known, so too did Josiah Osborne, the man who built Fred's house. Fred became increasingly interested in both men and spent many hours in our archives here and in our Drew collection on St. George Street doing research. He took so many notes that I jokingly asked him if he was writing a book, and he said maybe he would. Now that can never happen. Maybe someone else in his family can take up the work."

She looked at me and smiled. I didn't think she was being serious—that she was just using this as a way to introduce me—because her next words were, "And that someone is here tonight. As some of you know, Jake Pavlik is Fred's nephew and has just moved into the Osborne house. Welcome, Mr. Pavlik. We hope to see more of you."

I acknowledged this with a wave of my hand which was followed by a polite applause from the group.

"Fred did more than show interest in our history," she continued. "He supported it. And it is with great gratitude that I announce that he left us a fine donation."

She mentioned the amount, which drew a very loud applause. It was a nice sum. She then raised her glass. "Here's to Fred Peterson, a patron and friend."

This was followed by a couple of "here here's."

More informal conversations followed this with people coming up to me saying nice things about my uncle. Eventually the proceedings began to wind down, and I was about to leave when a middle-aged woman wearing glasses came up to me.

"I'm Sheila Compton," she said. "Quite an evening for your uncle."

"Yes. I'm glad I could be here. Did you know him well?"

"I didn't know him personally. I'm a reporter for The *Duxbury Messenger*. I'm actually here covering this event for the paper. Over the years I've written a few stories on some things he was involved with around town. I met him a few times in the process. I wrote the article about his accident and obituary too. Did you read them?"

"Only the obit. It was very nice."

"The article appeared a week before the obit. I can email it to you if you want. It includes a few more details of the accident. Were you close to your uncle?"

"In my younger days, yes. But I hadn't seen him recently. Seems like he was well liked in town."

She hesitated a moment.

It was a moment I recalled later.

Her smile looked forced when she continued. "He was. But anybody as active as he was in a town so small is bound to stir the pot, even if unintentionally. That's particularly true for an outsider."

I was slightly taken aback by this cryptic comment. I wanted her to elaborate.

"Really? Anything specific?"

Was she again slightly hesitant in responding or was it my imagination?

"You know what? This is probably a longer discussion. Why don't you drop by the *Messenger* office tomorrow. I can explain. You might find it interesting."

* * * * *

The *Duxbury Messenger* is a very good small-town newspaper. Published every Wednesday, it is family owned and community minded. All of its stories are devoted to happenings about town, including alerts for upcoming events, reviews of past ones, and the various accomplishments of residents—from senior citizens to high school students. Most of what can be considered serious news deals with issues such as land usage, taxes, business development, and benign dog-bites-man-type stories. There is a police log where readers see short references to an occasional DWI or petty crime, but rarely anything more than that. The writing is very polite and neighborly.

My uncle's death was a very atypical story for the town and paper. Sheila had emailed me her article about the accident which, for such a tragic event, was very restrained. It simply provided some additional facts that were not in the obituary.

A man was found dead on a floating oyster shed in Duxbury Bay on Tuesday. The body of 80-year-old Fred Peterson of Duxbury was discovered by Bob Atkinson, 45, also of Duxbury.

Atkinson, who owns Bayside Oysters, arrived by boat at his shed on Tuesday afternoon.

"As I climbed onto the platform, I suddenly noticed a body half in, half out of the shed," he said. "The door was partly closed, and I hadn't seen it lying there till I got out of my boat."

Atkinson immediately notified Harbormaster Chip Gallagher who contacted Duxbury Police, and they arrived at the shed minutes later.

"The deceased suffered a blow to the head due to an apparent fall," said Police Sergeant Phil Banks. "The water was rough and the surface of the platform was wet and slippery. It looks like he fell into the shed where he hit his head on the floor. As was his habit, he had apparently paddled out to the shed in his kayak. We found it drifting, empty, a couple of hundred feet away." The probable time of death was placed at anywhere from 10 to 12 hours previously.

Peterson was an investor in several oyster farms in Duxbury, including this one.

"He was often out by the sheds in his kayak talking to oystermen," said Len Barker, owner of Gurnet Oysters. "He was trying to learn the ropes. He was a big investor in my business, and he had an open invitation to come out to my shed any time he wanted to. He'd paddle out a few times a week from his home, which was only about ten minutes

71

away. He usually brought with him a thermos of coffee for the guys. He'd be wearing a windbreaker, khaki workpants, and sneakers. We kidded him and called him the Wall Street Oysterman. He loved it. He'd tie his kayak up to one of the shed decks, shoot the breeze for a few minutes, and then head back home and go about his regular business. He was totally into the scene. He told me it had become a part of his morning routine."

"I knew him pretty well," said Atkinson. "My shed is near the Gurnet Oysters shed, and he'd pass me when he went out there. He'd come on the deck sometimes, and we'd talk. He was always asking questions about the business."

It is believed Peterson was on his way to the Gurnet shed and stopped at the Bayside shed first when he fell.

"We talked most every week," said Atkinson. "I guess he was going to wait to see if I was working that morning, or maybe he mistook my shed for the Gurnet shed. They are the same color and model and are adjacent to each other in the same part of the bay. It was a little hazy that morning too, and visibility wasn't great."

The result was a terrible accident and one of the most tragic events in the recent history of Duxbury Harbor.

I met her later that day in the office of the *Messenger*, which is in a small brick building on a side street near the center of town. We spent an hour together, and I learned a little about her. She'd been a reporter for The *Boston Globe* in her younger days and moved to Duxbury when she married her husband Stu, who had recently retired from the Duxbury Police Department and was running for the selectboard. Her son Jordan was getting his master's from BU and tended bar at The Shipyard Inn on weekends. Her daughter Jessica was a teacher at Duxbury High.

"Thanks for sending me your article," I said. "It gives me more context on what happened,"

"It's pretty barebones I admit. Since there were no eyewitnesses that saw him fall, we just have to assume he slipped somehow either standing on the platform or climbing on to it. The water was choppy, and waves likely rocked the floater while he was on it. Those sheds can be a bit unstable in rough waters. Your uncle should not have been out in his kayak."

"I guess we'll never know exactly how it happened."

"Probably not. You know, this is the only story I've ever covered in my ten years with the *Messenger* that comes close to the kind of stuff that I used to cover for The *Globe*. It's the sort of story they'd have wanted me to follow up on and keep alive back in the day. Tragic deaths of wealthy people attract eyeballs. If it bleeds, it leads as they say. Here, it's the opposite. Something like this is unsettling and people don't want their little corner of paradise disturbed. So we move on quickly. If any more details came to light, though, I'd do a follow up."

"Speaking of following up, I'm interested in your comment last night about my uncle having ruffled a few feathers in town. What did you mean?"

She paused for a moment, then said in a very serious tone of voice, "Before going on, Mr. Pavlik, we need to agree on our rules of engagement."

"Rules of engagement? What do you mean?"

"Often, someone talking to the media will say they want to speak off the record. This is the reverse. This is the media—me—wanting to speak off the record to you."

"I once worked for newspapers. I never did any news stories, but I fully respect what off the record is. So, okay. Off the record it is. But I'm confused about how it applies here."

"Let me go on and you'll see. Between my husband, my son, my daughter, and my work at the paper, we pick up just about everything that happens around town. Most of it is gossip, and we keep it to ourselves. And I'd never consider putting any of it into the paper. My editor would never allow it anyway. He's a good local guy."

"So is what you have to tell me about my uncle gossip?"

"Call it what you will. I tell you this only for your benefit as his closest relative and heir."

"Please go on," I said warily. *What is she getting at?*

"Your uncle became very interested in helping some local businesses be more successful."

"He had made a career in investing in them."

"Yes. But the ones I'm referring to here are very small and all locally owned, nothing remotely approaching in scale the businesses he invested in during his career. I interviewed him one time, and he said he wasn't in it for the money. He just wanted to keep active in business and help the community in the process."

"His longtime lawyer told me the same thing."

"Most of these businesses were local food companies. Two sisters that make baked goods, a man who produces honey, a family that owns an apple orchard. He approached Blaise Rogers, the manager of Brothers Market here in town, and asked if the store would promote these products. He wanted to do some consumer testing to help these companies expand into other stores around the area. He called it a test store for local products, and he'd pay for the space. Blaise told me he loved the idea because that's what the store wants to be. Farm to table, think local—that kind of branding. Things the big chains can't do well."

"I'm a bit of a foodie, and I love finding local products. I've been in that store, and I love it."

"You should tell Blaise. He'll want to meet you. Anyhow, Fred was particularly interested in the oyster business. We have over thirty farms in the bay operating on leases and permits issued by the town. Several of the very small farmers were struggling and were talking about giving up their leases. Fred approached all three, convinced them to consolidate into a cooperative agreement, gave them some money, and helped them create a business plan. They went to market as Gurnet Oysters and were becoming quite successful."

"Sounds like a good story."

"For Gurnet, yes. But not good for everybody."

"What do you mean?"

"Those three struggling farms had other owners just waiting to take over their leases. The number of farms that the town allows to exist is frozen at current levels. No new ones have been allowed to open for many years. If a current farm wants to expand, or someone new wants to come in, you have to wait until the owner of one of the existing farms wants out. Turnover is very low and waits can be long. When something becomes available, it gets everyone's attention. With your uncle investing in the three failing ones, it took them off the market."

"Sounds all above board to me."

"It was. But that didn't stop a couple of the other owners from getting upset. My son hears all kinds of things tending bar, and he's heard at least two other owners say some very nasty things about your uncle. One of them called him a disruptive force coming in from the outside at the last minute and blowing up deals that were already in place. He said your uncle would end up regretting it."

"What does that mean?"

"Who knows? My son said it sounded like a threat. But the guy was drunk, and soon after one of his friends helped him home."

"Did my uncle know about this?"

"I don't know. Nor do I know if he was aware of a detractor he had in the historical society."

"What? I didn't see that last night. They all seemed to love him. And why not? He was one heck of a benefactor."

"That he was. But Caroline Hawksmoor told me that he had one vocal detractor."

"Who and why?"

"She didn't tell me. She said one of the members was upset Fred wasn't leaving his house to the society although he promised he would."

"But he left them money."

"True, although nobody knew for sure that he would do so until they received the official notice after he died. All anybody knew was that he had changed his mind about the house. The historical society members are some of the finest people in town and no one had a problem with that."

"Except one irrational jerk it seems."

"Yes. And there seems to have been another irrational jerk in your uncle's life. Do you know who the Phippses are?"

"My uncle bought the house from a family with the name of Phipps as I recall."

"Yes. It's the same family. My daughter Jessica was a high school classmate of their daughter Olivia. They're still friends. Olivia is the last remaining Phipps left in town. She's a curator at the art complex. Olivia told my daughter that one of her family members was full of resentment at your uncle for buying the house."

"But it was for sale. What's the problem?"

"That family member didn't want to sell the house. It had been in the family for two hundred years. This member has had some drug problems too. It doesn't take much to set him off."

"Terrific. My uncle rescues a couple of failing oyster farms, gives money to the historical society, and buys a house at full market value from a family that goes bankrupt and, in doing so, he pisses some people off in the process. Sounds like he should be thanked."

"And he was. People loved him—except for a few bad apples."

"Why are you telling me this?"

"Good question. I debated whether I should. But the way your uncle died didn't sit well with me."

"In what way?"

"Too many unanswered questions, like why did no one see him fall? There were a few oyster sheds nearby. And why didn't anybody spot the body earlier. It seems your uncle had been dead for hours when Bob Atkinson found him. The body must have been lying for hours in an area of the bay that other boats passed by fairly regularly. It seems strange no one noticed it. There wasn't that much blood either. And why was he on Atkinsons' shed alone? Maybe he was waiting for Bobby, or maybe he mistook the Bayside shed for the Gurnet shed where he often went alone.

76

They are the same color and very near each other. But still…"

"What are you suggesting?" My voice rose. "Foul play?"

"Given what I knew about the grudges held against your uncle, I must say the thought crossed my mind. In retrospect, it's too bad an autopsy wasn't done. It might have turned up something."

"Should one have been done?"

"It's always a judgment call. With my husband having been on the police force, he knows the protocol. One is done only when the cause of death is suspicious. The fact that the Boston Medical Examiner chose not to do one mildly surprised my husband. But it was well known that Fred had taken a bad fall the past winter outside the post office and had suffered a concussion. The EMT's had to rush him to the hospital. After all, he was eighty. So you can see why there wasn't an autopsy."

"This doesn't seem all that concerning to me, frankly."

"By itself, maybe not. But add to that the fact that I got a very strange email from him two days before he died."

"Email? What did it say?"

"He said he wanted to see me, and it was urgent. He was very worried about something, and he thought I could help him."

"What did he want to talk about?"

"He didn't say. My husband and I were out of town, so we made an appointment to meet when I got back a few days later. The meeting never happened, so I don't know what was worrying him. It was surprising to me that he sent me an email like this. I didn't know him that well."

"Again I ask why are you telling me this, Sheila? I find this conjecturing very disturbing."

"I'm very sorry for that," she said almost apologetically. "I just thought you should know."

I was about to say I understood, but I stopped short of doing so because I still didn't quite understand her motive.

"Have you voiced any of this to the police?"

"No. They know nothing about the people your uncle had rankled.

And I'm not in the business of spreading rumors about things I've picked up around town. That's not what the *Messenger* stands for. It's crossed my mind that all of this is probably just the overactive imagination of a former beat reporter for a big city newspaper who has seen a lot of crazy things done for crazy reasons. Bad stuff can happen anywhere—even here. But I have no proof, and I'm not going to pursue this any further. This paper doesn't want me to go around trying to dig up dirt about local people who are probably innocent. I can't—and won't—be visibly associated with any of that."

"I can appreciate that."

"But that doesn't mean that the truth shouldn't be pursued by someone."

"By whom?"

"I don't know. Maybe you?"

"What are you getting at?" I was growing impatient.

"I'm proposing an alliance."

"What kind of an alliance?"

"I tell you what I know, and you dig around and see where it leads you. I can't be associated with this in any way, so you'll have to do this on your own and not allude in any way whatsoever to my giving you any leads."

"What do you mean by leads? This sounds a lot like police work, frankly."

"There are three people I think you should talk to that might lead you to more information. They are three people that you could easily approach without arousing any suspicion because you'd have reason to want to meet them anyway given your uncle's activities. If you were subtle about it, you might draw them out a bit without them knowing what you are poking at. If I do it, it looks like the *Messenger* is doing some unwanted and maybe libelous investigative journalism."

"Who are these three people?"

"Len Barker. He's the managing director of the Gurnet Oyster cooperative. He knows the names of the two other bidders who lost out to your uncle."

"Who else?"

"Caroline Hawksmoor. She never told me which society member was upset. I can guess, but you should see if you can get it from her."

"And who's the third?"

"It's the trickiest one of all. Olivia Phipps. She obviously knows the family member who was threatening your uncle. You can find her at work in the art complex. Your uncle has some of his paintings on display there, and you should see them anyway."

I mulled this over for a minute. It didn't sit well with me.

"So in the name of what you think might be the truth, I should poke around for you and probably make enemies in a town where I'm trying to make friends? Sorry. It doesn't sound like a good way to win friends and influence people. I'm going to take a pass."

"Just think it over. If your uncle's death was not an accident, that should be known. Some proof needs to come out before the police—or I—go on a fishing expedition. If you find something concrete, I'll take it to the Duxbury Police and, if they find it credible, they'll get the state police involved. They are the ones who would conduct any formal investigation."

"I'll think about it," I said. "But frankly I'm a little upset that you want to get me involved at all. If what you suspect is true, this could be dangerous. I'm concerned you think I'm dispensable."

"I'm sorry you feel that way," she shot back. She was definitely being defensive now. "You are his closest living relative and his heir. I thought you should know."

"Okay, now I know. Consider your mission accomplished, and let's leave it like that. I'll have nothing more to say."

I left the office without a goodbye, my mind already made up. I had no intention of ruining my reputation in town going on a wild goose chase on behalf of a woman who was after a story but was afraid to go get it herself. At least that was what I told myself then.

But something happened a few days later that made me reevaluate my position.

Chapter 9
THE PHIPPS FAMILY

In the ensuing days, I tried to put my conversation with Sheila Compton out of my mind. I had no intention of following up on any of her "leads." In fact, my initial reaction was to resent her for putting her disturbing and unsubstantiated notions in my head. It almost felt irresponsible for her to have done so since she had no proof of any wrongdoing.

On the other hand, I had to admit that she might actually be doing me a favor. Because she had legitimate questions about the nature of my uncle's death, she had felt an obligation to tell someone about it. The police had found nothing untoward, and the *Messenger* would not have encouraged her to roil the town over mere hunches on her part. But she seemed genuinely interested in finding the truth about the matter, and quietly informing a family member of her concerns did not seem irresponsible in that light.

In fact, some might say it was compassionate. She was putting the entire matter in my hands and allowing me to determine how much—or little—I wanted to pursue this. It was far better than a high-profile person in town such as herself snooping around and drawing attention to an event that I'd sooner forget. If I had a sense of unfulfilled justice, I could pursue it to whatever extent I wanted. If I stumbled across anything that proved her hunch, she'd then help me. The ball was in my court.

My conversation with Sheila had another impact on me as well. She had mentioned that Olivia Phipps worked at the Duxbury Art Complex Museum where my uncle had some of his paintings. I hadn't visited the complex yet to see them. Doing so would afford me a very natural way to meet Olivia. I was very curious to do so and learn more about the family that had lived in my house for so long.

I went on the art complex website to find opening hours and noticed there were several events there in the next few weeks. Most notably there was a lecture on New England seascape painters the following week. The presenter was assistant curator Olivia Phipps. It was perfect for my purposes.

* * * * *

I arrived at the complex a few minutes before the lecture and found a seat in the back row of the room next to the exhibition space. The room was full—maybe forty people in total—which included a group from the senior center and some students from a class at the local high school. Eventually a woman went to the podium and introduced herself as Olivia Phipps. She was very young, in her mid-twenties. She was blonde and very fair. She was wearing a black dress which contrasted so sharply with the whiteness of her face and arms that I almost felt like I was looking at a negative photo. Although she was not beautiful per se, she had an ethereal presence that was riveting.

She began her presentation which consisted of PowerPoint slides of seascapes from various Masters with names such as Winslow Homer, John Frederick Kensett, Fitz Henry Lane, William Trost Richards, and a few others. It was a topic I knew absolutely nothing about. Her presentation style was very formal, her voice soft and serious. She was very articulate and knowledgeable, but I thought her delivery could benefit from an occasional smile or witticism.

She talked for about thirty minutes then offered a question and answer session.

A man asked. "Are there any New England locations that were particularly favored by painters of the sea?"

"Indeed," Olivia answered. "Gloucester on the North Shore has a strong artist seaside community. The coast of Maine too. Oak Bluffs on Martha's Vineyard has been an inspiring site for African American painters for a century."

"Anybody famous from Duxbury?" asked a student from the high school.

"Nobody super famous. At least not yet. Maybe one of you." She said this with a slight smile which, even though small, lit up her face. She had untapped potential, this one did. "But we do have some talented painters in this town. If there are no other questions, I can show anybody interested a few current examples in our gallery now."

About a dozen people, including myself, followed her over to a room where a number of paintings were on display.

"This is a new exhibition of local artists I've helped to curate," she said. "It will last all summer. Many of these works were created in some of the classes we offer here at the museum. There's good talent in town. And you'll notice that many of these paintings depict scenes right here in Duxbury. There's no reason we couldn't develop our own little artist colony here. These are some of my favorites."

She began pointing out a few.

"We have some great locations here," she continued. "Old historic houses, beaches and sand dunes, and of course, the water. Bays, rivers, coves, islands. Boats of all sorts. We have such variety. Here's an artist who loved lighthouses. Take a look."

She was standing in front of two paintings, one called *Gurnet Light at Twilight*, the other *Bug Light during a Tempest*. I looked more closely at them. Each bore the signature of Fred Peterson. They were similar to the paintings I had seen in the backyard studio of his house.

"This artist painted these lighthouses repeatedly," she said. "But they are all different. You can paint the same object dozens of times and, through variations in lighting, angles, time of the day, weather conditions, each says something different. The great French artist Monet painted the same cathedrals many times and each has a life of its own."

She made a few more points and the group began to break up. As she was walking away, I called out, "Ms. Phipps. May I have a word?"

"Yes, of course," she said.

"It's about these two lighthouse paintings you mentioned. I'm interested in them."

"They are quite good. The artist was a gentleman who started painting late in life. He was very talented. Unfortunately, he just died."

"I know. He was my uncle."

I studied her reaction. She was obviously startled and at a loss for words. An awkward pause followed. I had sprung this on her so suddenly. It was not my intention to make her feel uncomfortable, which she obviously was.

"So you are his nephew," she said.

"Yes, I am. I'm very sorry to have surprised you. I should have introduced myself in a better way."

"I was wondering when we'd meet. I'd heard you moved into our old house."

"I didn't know until a few days ago that you were living in town. Did you know my uncle well?"

"Yes. He was my mentor."

Now it was my turn to be startled. Sheila had led me to believe there was friction between the Phipps family and my uncle.

"Do you have a moment to talk? I'd like to know more. You probably knew him better than I did."

"I knew him very well. I'm done for today. Let's go for a walk so we can be alone. I'll show you around too."

We exited the building and walked down a path. Presently we came to a structure that had an exotic Asian look.

"This is the Japanese Tea House. It was brought here from Kyoto. We have functions in there."

Further down the path was another structure, this one more in the colonial style of the rest of the town.

"This belonged to the Alden family," she said. "Do you know them?"

"I'm afraid not," I smiled. "I'm going to need to bone up on my history if I'm going to be a true Duxburian. By the way, is that what you all call yourselves?"

"Not that I'm aware of," she responded with a slight smile. "We're just residents of Duxbury. Anyhow, the Aldens came over on the

Mayflower in 1620 and settled here. Longfellow wrote a poem about them. They literally have millions of descendants all over the world. Marilyn Monroe and Orson Welles are even descendants."

"I can't believe it! Orson Welles is one of my heroes. Next you'll tell me Peter Lorre is a descendant."

"Who's that?"

"My goodness, I feel so old," I grinned. I was enjoying this conversation immensely. I couldn't imagine her ever calling me dude or bro, even though she was the right age to do so.

"Back to this house. An Alden descendant built this in 1790, and the art complex bought it when it opened in 1971. It's now a studio. Classes are held in here. Your uncle took quite a few here himself. Come take a look."

We walked in. The room was filled with easels with paintings on them. There were no people in it.

"We're having a class here this month on oil painting," she explained. "Your uncle spent a lot of time here. He had become obsessed with his painting. He said it helped him make sense of what was going on in his life. He told me he liked to tell stories with his paintings. 'I'm an amateur version of Norman Rockwell,' he would joke with me. And he was that, although he was much better than an amateur."

"So my eighty-year-old wealthy uncle whose life was a total success was still trying to make sense of his life. I love it! Gives me hope for myself. And he seems to have been quite a prolific painter. His studio in the house is filled with his work in various stages of completion. Have you been there to see it?"

"Yes, several times. He told me this studio inspired his."

She then grew silent as if collecting her emotions. I felt a bit uneasy over this last exchange and wondered if my reference to her old house had touched a nerve. I decided to address this head on.

"Does it upset you to visit the house? I know it was in your family for centuries."

"If I'm being honest, sure. At first it did. I had so many happy memories in that wonderful house. And then it all ended. Have you been told the story?"

"I heard that your father died and that you all decided to sell."

"Yes. We decided to sell because we needed to. My father went bankrupt. He died soon after that and my mother needed the money, and she sold and moved to Vermont. I have an older brother Donald who didn't want to sell. He became very upset, and he made life very difficult for us. He has some serious problems that he can't seem to overcome and it worries my mother…"

She stopped for a moment. I could see she was on the verge of tears.

"Excuse me," she said, collecting herself. "As I was about to say, my brother took some of his frustration out on your uncle I'm afraid. He was very unfair and said some very nasty things to your uncle. And then he left town and moved to Vermont with my mother."

"So now you're the only Phipps left in Duxbury."

"Yes. I had left too. I was going to college at Middlebury in Vermont and stayed up there after graduation. I had a serious boyfriend. But when that ended, I decided to move back here. I was given some money from the sale of the house which allowed me to buy a little place a few miles from here in Marshfield. And that's where your uncle came into my life."

"In what way?"

"I didn't have a job when I moved back, and I was doing some volunteer work at the art complex. I was an art history major at Middlebury, and I did an internship here for a couple of summers. I loved the place and wanted to keep busy until I found something, which isn't always easy for an art history major."

"I can believe it," I said. I was thinking of Jocko's nomadic wanderings through four majors as an undergraduate, and now his incomprehensible dissertation at the graduate level on a topic absolutely nobody understood, including himself. Headhunters would not be knocking on his door anytime soon—if ever.

"One day I was in the studio here helping to set up a class that your uncle was taking. We got to talking and he discovered who I was. He became very interested in me because of the house. He knew the story of my family's problems, and he was very sympathetic. He was so gracious, particularly since my brother Donald had been so unpleasant and unfair toward him. I felt very guilty about that and apologized for the bad behavior. Between his graciousness and my apologies, we hit it off. We kind of bonded, which you'd think unlikely given the differences in our ages. He always sought me out when he took a class here to ask how I was doing. He once asked me if he could help me in any way."

"You know," I said, "he never had children, and I heard that made him sadder and sadder as the years went by." I remembered that Danforth had said this was one of the reasons Fred had left me the house, but I didn't say anything to her about that.

"I guessed the same thing too," she continued. "But I think it was something else too. I think we felt sorry for each other."

"Really? I'm a bit confused. Why would you feel sorry for a rich successful old man? Because he never had kids?"

"Maybe that was a part of it. But I think it ran deeper. He was very lonely. With all his success and wealth, he didn't seem to have anybody to confide in. He was very friendly, but he had no close friends. He even told me he thought some people in town didn't like him. It really concerned him, especially over the last month or two. He seemed kind of worried about it."

Here was Sheila Compton's hunch surfacing again. I didn't know exactly how to respond to this, but Olivia continued before I could.

"Anyhow, he eventually did help me—and in a way I never could have dreamed of. He gave the art complex a substantial donation to fund a new position of assistant curator for special exhibits, and he strongly recommended that I get the job. He had enough credibility, and I guess I had enough of a track record here, and I got the position. I've been here a couple of years now."

"I'm so glad it worked out. Thanks for sharing this about my uncle. I owe him a lot too."

Her cell phone rang, and she looked at the caller ID.

"Oh, I've got to go now," she said. "I hope you will be happy here. It's a wonderful town."

* * * * *

I thought about Olivia later that evening as I was having a scotch on my deck, looking out across the bay. Our meeting had produced a strange effect on me. This girl—she struck me as no more than that—conveyed a sweet sincerity that was so genuine. There was an element of fragility too, a sadness in her. It made me a little sad too—because I realized she reminded me of Melanie when I first met her. They even resembled one another. Melanie had been interested in art too. But she didn't have the authenticity this girl had, nor the same softness either.

There was one other thing that struck me about our meeting. Although I had not been conscious of it at the time, I had done exactly what Sheila Compton had suggested I do and that I said I would not. I had gotten information about the Phipps family and their relationship with my uncle. What I learned was that one of them, Donald, had an open animosity toward him. Olivia had said her brother had problems that he couldn't overcome and it worried the family. She hadn't been more specific, but I knew from Paula Spaulding that one of the Phipps children had a drug problem. This guy didn't sound like a person you'd want as an enemy, but it seemed he viewed my uncle as one. And maybe others did too based on Olivia's comments on my uncle's concerns in his last months.

If this was the kind of fact finding Sheila was suggesting, I had been successful. It didn't feel like success though. I went to bed with that thought in mind, and I slept poorly.

Chapter 10
THE SKETCHES OF A DEAD MAN

I finally made a trip to Toledo. I hadn't been there since I'd moved out six weeks previously. Jocko and Zarathustra were doing just fine. His class work was finished for the summer. He would continue to bang away on his train wreck of a dissertation (he seemed to be narrowing his focus though), and he was now free to come visit me. We made a date for him to come for July 4th. I saw my mother and talked to the nurses. Nothing had changed with her. Vital signs fine, cognitive ability very poor.

I also saw Gloria. Her daughter was away in Detroit visiting her father, and I was able to stay at her place. We'd picked that weekend for me to visit for that very reason. We said we missed each other but had no heart-to-hearts. We were still trying to determine where all this was going but had reached no conclusions. We discussed her coming to visit me, but we didn't pick a date. Same old, same old. And then it was back to Boston on Monday

Back in Duxbury, I was doing my best to establish a routine. I had my work. It was no different than it had been in Toledo. It had the usual rhythm of deadlines, recordings, and rehearsals.

I also had developed a little bit of a social life. I had my weekly noir class, and while most of the people were older than me, we were all film buffs, and I enjoyed the conversations. And one night I invited the Tsais and Spauldings over for a barbecue. I'd also left an invitation in the mailbox for the Trevanians, but they didn't respond. They seemed to be away much of the time.

It was now summer and therefore prime beach season. The crowds were becoming substantial and the parking lot full. The water was still cold—apparently it never got warm, but I enjoyed walking along the shore or just lazing in a beach chair reading. I began to take my boat out too. I stayed within the calm waters of Duxbury Bay, but I was feeling more and more confident with my nautical skills and planned to make some short excursions along the coastline soon. I even took Tommy Tsai and two of his buddies from Procuria out once, and we had a few beers on board.

I ate out several times a week, usually at The Shipyard Inn. I became recognized as a regular and would small talk with some of the others. I went into Boston at least once a week too. There was always a game in town or a movie or play to see. One evening I had dinner with Danforth in the North End, the Italian section of Boston. Although we exchanged emails occasionally, we hadn't met in person since I'd moved in. He wanted to know how I was doing.

"I'm doing well," I said. "Although I find it exhausting to be living two lives."

"Two lives? What do you mean?"

"I'm living my own life and also living—or re-living—my uncle's. Everywhere I go, whenever I tell people who I am, they always seem to have a story about him. I feel like I'm living alongside of a ghost—and a very popular one."

"Old Freddie did get around. Too much so in my opinion. Find anything surprising?"

"A couple of things. Nothing major. I ran into one of the Phippses."

"Must have been the daughter. She's the only one left in town."

"Yes. She told me some of the history of the family."

"Did she tell you about her brother? He's a bad sort."

"So you know him?"

"I know of him. He sent Fred some crazy letters back when he bought the house from the family. Fred showed them to me. Rambling crazy stuff like the house had some sort of ancient curse on it, and Fred needed to move out. The kid has had emotional issues in the past. Drugs too. Luckily the whole family moved away except the girl."

"I was surprised how close Fred was to her. He confided in her. Oh, and I finally made it out to his shack on the Gurnet."

"Really?" he said, eyebrows arched. "I've heard it's not much of a place, eh? I've never been out there."

"Not much at all. It's kind of run down. I ran into a guy who watches some of the houses nearby."

"Who's that?" Danforth seemed to be surprised at this.

"Just some local guy who does odd jobs for folks. The outside was a mess. All that was on the inside were some sketches and a few books on the sea. I got the impression the place was an artist's retreat house for him—a place to go and think and do some sketching. There were some random papers scattered about, a few boxes, a calendar with appointments. That kind of thing."

"Anything I should know about? I'll attend to any loose ends that you trip across." Danforth had proven to be a very meticulous executor, emailing me every couple of weeks to ask if I had found anything that needed his attention. The more I knew about all of the things my uncle had dabbled in, the more I appreciated Danforth's conscientiousness.

"I really haven't looked at any of it," I said. "I'll let you know if I find anything that needs to be handled."

"Yes, please take a look. I'm here to help."

* * * * *

Dinner with Danforth reminded me that I hadn't gone through the things I'd brought back from the Gurnet. There was of course the battered old mermaid figurehead. I managed to get it into the downstairs room in the backyard workshop where I thought I'd keep it until I could move it to the art complex and let them find somebody to restore it there. They had expertise and connections I didn't have. There were also a few books, the pack of tarot cards, and his appointment calendar.

Of much more immediate interest were the dozen or so sketches that had been tacked to the hut's wall in the form of a circle. I did an inventory of them and listed them in the notebook I had started to keep. On the bottom of each sketch was its title as well as the brief notes my uncle had written to himself.

1. Title: Gurnet Light and Purple Shack at Dusk
Note: the view from atop the rampart of the fort. Light shines on purple shack. Is it here?

2. Title: Gurnet Light and Clark's Island at Nightfall
Note: the view from Saquish Head. Light shines on left corner of island. Is it here?

3. House with a Past
Note: 3 Spyglass Lane today. Two figures standing on lawn— one a Pilgrim, one a seaman. Is there a curse on it? Alternate title: The House of Conflict.

4. Title: Market Day in Duxbury
Note: Front of Brothers with vegetable stands in sidewalk out front. Sunny, festive. For mural?

5. Title: Aerial view of Spyglass neighborhood
Note: thin out trees a bit, focus on 5 Spyglass eyesore. Alternate title: Strange Bedfellows

6. Title: Brig sailing into the Black Sea, 1830
Note: minarets along the Bosporus in background.
Must have "vague" object in there. Must be gold.

7. Title: Brig unloading cargo, East Boston (1830)
Note: 3 crates—one marked figs, another dates, third with an X on it. Banners of Weston Shipyard and Perkins Shipping hanging from a flag post on the pier. Add in a third banner? Alternate title: Unfortunate Partnerships

8. Title: Figurehead of the Sad Mermaid (carved by Josiah Osborne)
Note: mermaid with a sad face, tear on cheek

9. Title: First love

Note: Coco today with an enigmatic Mona Lisa-like smile on her face. Need to schedule sittings in May.

10. Title: The *Oyster Wars*
Note: three oyster farmers at work, one in a shed, two on boats, dark clouds

11. Title: A Fight at the *Inn*
Note: involves three men in the *bar*

12 Title: The *Face of Evil*
Note: scene of bustling harbor area, boats (sail and motor), three oyster floaters. A human face hovering in sky above it all (a question mark where the features should be), menacing. Who is this and how to depict? As The *Hangman?* The *Merchant?* The *Fool?*

I deduced that these rough sketches were concepts for future paintings. Fred's creative process seemed to involve him coming out to the Gurnet to sketch a prototype and then do the actual painting back in the studio.

Some of the titles were self-explanatory. Numbers 1 and 2 were literally depictions of the two respective scenes in question. 4 was the Duxbury Brothers store. I recognized 5 as the view from the window in the studio in my back yard, only with fewer trees in the picture than in reality. The ship of 6 was named the *Smyrna*, and it was passing what was clearly Constantinople. And I recognized The Shipyard Inn bar in number 11.

Other sketches or their titles were a bit mysterious and begged various questions. For example, the house in number 3 was my house. Who were the two figures, and why did the note have a reference to a curse? The brig in 7 was the *Smyrna* (as it was in 6). Why was he interested in this ship and why was there an X on one of the crates? Why did the mermaid have a tear in 8? Who was the woman in 9? What was the "war" in 10? It just appeared to be a normal work scene in the bay.

93

And what on earth was the ghost in 12 all about?

But the biggest mystery was why they had been organized in the Gurnet shack in a circle with the words "My Complex Life in Duxbury" in the middle? It implied my uncle viewed the twelve as a collection or a series that was meant to tell a story. But because of their remote location in the purple shack, no one would ever have seen them organized this way except Fred. Was he telling a story to himself?

I then looked at the other contents from the box. It included the blotter sized calendar for the months of April and May. The calendar was big and the square for each date was large enough to show appointment dates and also a remark or two. There were some repetitive entries. Every Tuesday and Thursday "Sketching day at Gurnet" was written in. Every Wednesday was the film noir class. The other dates contained the names of people. A few names occurred several times, including Danforth, Len Barker, Caroline Hawksmoor, Blaise Rogers, Olivia Phipps, and someone named Coco. There were several names that appeared only once.

Every date before May 3 had a name, check mark, plus a short comment. It was obvious he was using this calendar as a sort of mini-journal as well. I noted these in particular:

April 8
Len Barker
Says yield is good
Larkin a pain

April 12
Caroline H
Says PJ is making waves
Let me see Smyrna logbook

April 15
Noir class
Séance on a Wet Afternoon

Hits close to home. Painfully relevant.

April 22
Lunch with Coco
Such great memories

April 23
Julie and Nancy
Saw them in Brothers. Blaise says sales are good

April 24
Went to Gurnet
Sketched all day

April 25
Emma called me. Emailed me newspaper article
Very concerned

April 26
Called Garrett (stonewalling me)
Left message for Ken to call me. No response yet
Probably need to fly down to meet in person

April 30
Call PMU at 508-777-4333 about Clark's Island complaint
Result: Good call. I'm sure I understand what's happening

May 1
Colin—out of the blue!
Dinner at Saraceno in Boston
Very surprising
Need to reevaluate things

May 2
Another Trevanian dust up, this one at my house.
Discussed options with Danforth on the phone. Getting serious.

After May 3 were the appointments he never kept because of his death on that day. The dates that stuck out for me were:

May 4
Meet with Sheila Compton. Ask her to connect me to Derek Parker of The *Globe regarding* the *article I read.*

May 5
Delta flight 4 Boston to JFK

May 6
Delta flight 43 JFK to Boston

May 8
Meet Danforth <u>in person.</u> Show him documents and get his reaction!

The rest of the dates included just familiar names like Coco, the Spauldings, Len Barker, and Olivia Phipps. There were no clarifying notes.

All of this served the purpose of me continuing to be dragged into my uncle's life. And although some of it aroused my curiosity, I probably would have done my best to ignore it all. I didn't particularly relish living with his ghost, much as I owed him my gratitude. But then Dana Andrews came into my life and I had no choice.

* * * * *

It happened in my noir class. The movie that week featured Dana Andrews as a hard-boiled detective trying to solve a murder. He had pinned various photos, newspaper headlines, and various clues on his office wall. It helped him to see links in the evidence, to connect a person to the clues. Afterwards, during our group discussion, our class instructor mentioned that this was the earliest example he could remember of seeing this concept in a police procedural.

"Now you see it all the time," said a woman who was always dropping in nuggets of interesting information. Last class she had told us she knew for a fact that Meryl Streep was staying in Duxbury at the home of her best friend from her Vassar days. The class before that she mentioned that her nephew had been the college roommate at Tufts of Ben Mankiewicz, the Turner Classic Movie host, and that "Mank" had visited Duxbury many times.

"My goodness," said a man who had worked as a film editor for several movies. "You can't watch an episode of *Shetland* or The *Unforgotten* without the police creating these displays."

"I agree," said Paula. "We call it the Evidence Wall, or the Murder Wall. It's overdone, frankly. The new thing is to connect the clues with thread too. It's sometimes referred to as a link chart. I must confess I've used it in a couple of my books."

"Which ones, Paula?" a man asked. She was the star pupil in the class, and everyone was always eager to get her point of view. Having written a dozen mysteries plus two movies gave her that deserved place of honor. I'd reviewed films for a living for five years, and she knew way more than I did.

"Most notably The *Case of* the *Obsessive Detective*. People with OCD go off the deep end with these kinds of puzzles, and this detective had it. He cluttered up the walls so obsessively with clues that it became obvious he was not a well human being. He was the killer. It worked, though. It was one of my best sellers."

"Baloney. I bet the police never use this at all," said a small, extremely frail looking man who had a nervous twitch and a voice that quivered when he talked; he reminded me a bit of Don Knotts in The *Incredible Mr. Limpet*. Despite his Casper Milquetoast appearance, he aggressively nitpicked every single movie we saw. "They'd use computers to do this today. This is old school."

It was at that moment that it struck me like a bolt of lightning what my uncle might have been up to. Had he created a sort of evidence wall with the twelve sketches in the Gurnet Shack? I wouldn't go as far as saying it was a murder wall, but he was obviously trying to connect certain things in his head.

The film inspired me to take a deeper look at the sketches. I even remembered I'd taken a video of the interior of the shack. And so, asking myself WWDAD (What Would Dana Andrews Do?), I spread them out on the floor in the order my uncle had. For the better part of an afternoon, I tried to make some sense of it, but to no avail. Some of the references in the sketches were too obscure.

I debated if it was worth putting any more time into this. Maybe there was nothing to this at all—that this was no wall of evidence but just a little game my uncle was playing. Maybe it was just a normal part of his creative process.

What argued against this were Sheila's ongoing suspicions. She had said that there were several people that had issues with my uncle. My conversation with Olivia confirmed that there was at least one—her volatile brother Donald, though it sounded like he wasn't in the area. Sheila had implied there might be another in the historical society and another in the oyster business. Also, Olivia had said my uncle seemed to be worried. Maybe it was regarding Donald, but maybe it was wider than that.

All of this convinced me that I should indeed continue to poke at this. Clarifying what these sketches might mean seemed a logical next step, so I picked three I knew absolutely nothing about: the two that had a brig called the *Smyrna* as their subject and the one with the figurehead of the mermaid that was apparently carved by Josiah Osborne. The person who might have the best insight into them was Caroline Hawksmoor. Since she was one of Sheila's "leads" as well, I made an appointment for later that week to meet her at the society's archives on St. George Street.

Chapter 11
A PICTURE IS WORTH A THOUSAND WORDS

"Of course I've heard of the *Smyrna*," said Caroline as if she were mildly offended. "I assume you mean the most well-known one."

"There's more than one?

"Yes. There were three *Smyrnas.*"

"Shouldn't that be three *Smyrnae?*"

This little witticism of mine produced not even the trace of a smile from her. I have to constantly remind myself that what is found humorous in my little corner of the comedy world often doesn't play well outside of it, particularly with serious scholars.

"Here, take a look," she said.

She'd gone into a cabinet of books in the historical society archive and had set one of them in front of me. It listed all the merchant ships built on the south coast of Massachusetts in the first half of the nineteenth century. It included a short description of the ship, the owner, the captain, and sometimes a crew member or two.

"I see the entry for the three *Smyrnas*," I said, adopting her form of the plural. "Which is the famous one?"

"The middle one. The first was owned by the Winsors of Duxbury and built here in 1822. The last was owned by Ezra Weston—King Caesar—and was built in Duxbury in 1839. The middle one was also owned by Weston and built in 1825 in Marshfield for some reason."

"Why is the middle one the best known?"

"Because it was the first American ship in history to be given permission to sail into the Black Sea. Why are you asking?"

"Because my uncle seemed to have been interested in that ship for some reason."

"I do recall him asking me for information about it not long before he died. I gave him a facsimile of the captain's logbook and an old rendering of the ship. I can find it for you."

She went to a file cabinet and, after a brief search, pulled out the rendering. It was a simple line illustration.

BRIG SMYRNA, 1830
(from Duxbury Archives – Illustrator Unknown)

Built by Ezra Weston 1825
Two Decks, Two Masts, Square Stern
Seth Sprague – Captain
Eight Man Crew

"He never told me why he was interested," she said.

"Looks like he was using this illustration as a model for his own work," I said examining it. "I found two sketches of his that include the *Smyrna*, and they each look just like this sketch. I believe he was going to eventually turn them into oil paintings. In one sketch, the ship is sailing into Constantinople. You can see minarets in the background. That makes sense given that voyage is an historical fact. But the other sketch is a bit baffling."

"In what way?"

"It depicts the ship at a dock in East Boston as its cargo is being unloaded. It consists of three crates—one is marked dates, another figs, and the third has a big X on it. What is that all about?"

She thought for a moment, then got up and searched in the file cabinet yet again. She found something and said, "Here's the ship's logbook. It lists the cargo. Looks like there were dates and figs from Greece but most of it was opium from Turkey."

"Opium? Really?"

"Oh, yes. It was legal for Boston ships coming back from certain foreign ports to bring back opium. They would take out certain goods from the colonies, trade them to the Turks for opium, and bring it back to Boston. Then other ships would turn right around and take the opium to China and trade it for tea and silk."

"And it was all legal you say?"

"Legal in the US but illegal in China. Have you ever heard of the Opium Wars? It was between Britain and China. The English were shipping in all kinds of opium against the wishes of the Chinese government. The US was doing the same thing on a lesser scale. Most of the US trade was done by Boston ships, and opium money built a lot of the old Boston. The pressure grew here to stop this practice because it created a massive addiction problem for the Chinese. Eventually we did stop."

"Does it sully Ezra Weston's reputation?"

"Not really. Although he owned the ships, he didn't participate in the trading. He leased ships like the *Smyrna* to the big traders in Boston, like R.T Perkins. They are the ones that did business with the Turks and Chinese."

"Would the X on the one crate be referring to the opium?"

"It might. Although it was legal to ship it to the Chinese, an 'X' implies something sinister."

"Maybe because the traders were knowingly contributing to massive addiction problems for profit? Or maybe it was some other product he had in mind?"

She thought for a minute. "Could well be. But there is one other possibility. Maybe it is opium, but it isn't all going out to China. What if it is staying in the US."

"Did that happen?"

"It's not written much about, but it undoubtedly did. There was too much money in it for someone not to. Opium was not illegal yet in this country and was used for medicinal purposes. But trafficking in Turkish opium was often a very dirty business and ruined lives here too. The government tried to control it, but some got smuggled in by profiteers. If this were true with the *Smyrna*, where would your uncle have gotten this information? I've never heard about this before."

"No idea. But let's move on. What do you make of this?"

I showed her a piece of paper I had brought with me. It was Fred's curious sketch of the figurehead of the mermaid with the sad face and wild hair.

"The title makes clear it was carved by Josiah Osborne, the builder of your house," she said, looking at the sketch with great interest. "It's strange that the figure is crying. It can't be a literal depiction."

"Why is that?"

"Having such a figurehead would be a sign of bad luck for the ship and crew. I know your uncle didn't get any figurehead renderings from me. We don't have any in the archives. It must be his own interpretation of something. What could it be?"

Figurehead of the Sad Mermaid
(Carved by Josiah Osborne)
Note: Mermaid with a Sad Face, Tear on cheek

"How much do we know of Josiah Osborne?" I asked.

"Not much. We know his grandfather was a sailor who came from England. His father was a sailor too. He was loyal to the English crown during the Revolution. Some of the locals here were. Josiah started off as a sailor but eventually became a woodcarver and built your house in 1790. But that's about all we know. He wasn't nearly as well known as the major woodcarver in town, Nathanial Winsor Jr. He overshadowed Josiah and came from a prominent family. The Osbornes before and after Josiah were all commoners. They all left town except for the branch that continued to live in your house until your uncle bought it. Olivia Phipps' mother was an Osborne."

"I've met Olivia. I like her."

At this point a woman walked in.

"Oh, hello, Colleen," smiled Caroline. "I'll be right with you. We're just finishing up here."

"Take your time," said the woman. "I'm a little early."

"Have you two met?"

We both said no and Caroline introduced us.

"This is Jake Pavlik, Colleen. He's Fred Peterson's nephew. Jake, this is Colleen Parsons. She's a member of Duxbury Rural & Historical Society. Her husband PJ is the head of our fundraising efforts."

"We haven't met," she said with a smile. "I wasn't able to attend the reception that announced your uncle's donation. My husband and I were both out of town. I'm very glad to meet you."

"Likewise," I said, extending my hand. Although she was elderly, she had a very pretty, youthful-looking face. She also looked vaguely familiar. I stared at her trying to place her, but I couldn't. I must have seen her somewhere about town.

"I was good friends with your uncle. We went way back. I hope to see you again."

"Excuse us, Jake," said Caroline while moving toward the door. "We have a luncheon appointment. Feel free to stay."

"I've got to leave myself," I said. "Bye."

I took my sketches and returned home.

* * * * *

My conversation with Caroline had helped clarify partially—although not entirely—the meaning of three of my uncle's sketches. In addition, some light was shed on a fourth almost immediately thereafter, and it was extremely interesting.

At my next film noir class, I mentioned to Paula that I had met another member of the Duxbury Rural and Historical Society.

"Who?" she said.

"Colleen Parsons."

"One of my favorite people," she said. "We're good friends."

"She said she was good friends with my uncle too."

"Yes. She mentioned him to me on a number of occasions. They went way back. They knew each other even before Fred bought the house."

"Really? How is that?" I asked with surprise.

"It's very sweet. When Fred was getting his MBA at Harvard, one of his classmates was Colleen's brother Larry Connors. They got to be friends, and Larry invited Fred a number of times to Duxbury. It's actually how Fred got exposed to the town for the first time."

"Fred's lawyer told me he'd first been down here as a student and became captivated by the town. He kept it in mind all those years, and that's why he decided he wanted to retire here."

"Fred explained that to me too. He got to know all the members of the family, including Colleen. They even went on a couple of dates together. I used to kid them both about it all the time. After graduation, he moved to New York, and she met her husband PJ when she was going to Wellesley. Funny how they were able to reconnect all these years later through the society. Too bad her husband didn't like Fred. It was obvious, and it began to play itself out in public. It embarrassed her."

"How so?"

"Well, there was a recent little incident at the Rotary Club. Fred and

PJ were both members. Fred had proposed some sort of an idea. PJ disagreed with it and started to attack Fred personally. Fred tried to ignore him, but PJ wouldn't let up. I wasn't there, but those who were said they'd never seen anything like it at a club meeting. That group is super collegial. Everyone was surprised at how emotional PJ got. He seemed to have some deeper grudge against Fred."

"Any idea what it was?" I asked. This was getting interesting.

"Yes. PJ felt Fred had lied about giving the house to the society. He said they had a signed agreement to that effect, but your uncle voided it. It was completely unreasonable by PJ. Keeping the house in the family was understandable, and your uncle left the society a generous donation. Do you remember that PJ wasn't at the reception when your uncle's gift was announced?"

"Yes. Caroline said he had a fever and couldn't make it. But Colleen wasn't there either. She had a different reason. She said they were out of town."

"Hogwash. PJ had no fever. He was boycotting the event. Everyone knew it. Colleen was mortified to attend alone under those circumstances, so she said they were going to be at their place in Maine. Just between us, Colleen and PJ have been having difficulties for a while. It's a bit awkward within the society to be honest. I feel sorry for Coco."

"Who's Coco?"

"Sorry. That's the nickname Colleen had as a kid. Short for Colleen Connors. Her oldest and dearest friends still call her that. I've known her for forty years now, so that's what she'd prefer me to call her. Fred called her that too. He knew her even longer."

This immediately triggered a thought, and I couldn't wait to get home.

* * * * *

That night I laid the sketches out in front of me. In particular, I was looking at the one with the title *First Love,* which was the image of a woman. It was the face of Colleen. Fred's note underneath the title made things even more explicit. He had written: "Coco today." Colleen had looked vaguely familiar when I'd first met her at the archives the other day, and now I knew why.

I pondered the sketch's title as well as Paula's comment that Colleen and her husband had been having difficulties. It made me wonder if PJ Parsons' dislike for my uncle went deeper than a disagreement at the Rotary Club or a disappointment over the fate of a house.

Chapter 12
STRANGE CARGO

I had now lived in Duxbury for a couple of months, and I thought I'd seen just about everything you could see there. Boy was I wrong. Around this time, somebody gave me some information that knocked me for a complete loop. Initially, I had a good laugh over it because my first reaction was that my leg was being severely pulled. But I soon saw that this person was very serious. Here's how it happened.

One morning I found a note in my mailbox.

Greetings
If you are available, please come to my house for lunch this
Saturday. My wife Khatia and I are available at 1:00. Hope to
see you.
Your neighbor,
Max Trevanian

I was more than curious to do this. Even though they literally lived next door, I hadn't met the Trevanians yet. They never seemed to be around, although I did notice a small motorboat going out and coming in to their pier a couple of times. But I couldn't make out who was on board.

The next day I showed up at their house at the appointed hour and rang the bell. The door opened and a man answered, smiled, and immediately extended his hand.

"Mr. Pavlik, I presume? Please come in. I'm Max Trevanian."

I was very surprised by his appearance. I don't know what I'd been expecting—maybe somebody mysterious looking, given that I was told he was an importer and a man of the world, rarely home. Instead, I was greeted by an enormously heavy man wearing a Hawaiian shirt, swim trunks, and sandals. On his head was a Panama hat.

"Pleased to meet you, Max. And call me Jake," I said, trying not to burst out laughing. There was something very comical in his appearance.

"Excuse my appearance," he said ushering me into the house. "When we are home in the summer, Khatia and I live poolside. It is such a short season here in these northern climes that we take advantage of every nice day. Come outside."

I followed him through several large rooms that left me open-mouthed. One had a dozen Persian rugs hanging from the walls. Another was filled with Asian art. I'm no expert, but there was definitely a Chinese influence. There was a statue of Buddha and other figures of the Far East. The wallpaper depicted scenes from the Chinese countryside. A back room just off the patio was filled with Roman and Greek statues and artifacts. The place looked more like the Museum of Fine Arts in Boston than a house on Spyglass Lane.

We passed through open double doors onto a patio which led down to a fairly large infinity pool. Music was playing softly in the background. It was a bosa nova. There was a woman on the patio, swaying to it. Standing next to her was a very tall man with a beard.

"Say hello to our neighbor Mr. Jake Pavlik, my dear," he said to the woman. "This is my wife Khatia, Jake."

"A pleasure," she said with a smile. She was dressed in slacks, a New England Patriots tee shirt, and was wearing a straw hat. She was, like her husband, about my age. Although she was a tad on the plump side, she looked like a peanut standing alongside her enormous husband. She had the quirky look of Ruth Gordon playing Mia Farrow's "witch next door" in *Rosemary's Baby*. (Ironically, I later learned in my noir class that Ruth Gordon was cremated at the Duxbury crematorium).

"Forgive our lack of neighborliness at not having you over sooner," she said motioning for us all to sit down on some lounge chairs. "Max and I travel a lot."

"And when we are in town, we tend to keep to ourselves," he said. "But we are not anti-social, although we may have that reputation. We're just an average quiet couple finding our own little amusements."

I looked at the two of them, so eccentrically dressed. Living in a lavishly decorated house and speaking in foreign accents that I couldn't quite place, they didn't strike me as my idea of an average quiet couple.

"And this fine-looking gentleman is Sidney Garber," Max said, nodding to the tall man who was dressed in a coat and tie. "He manages our gallery in Cambridge. He was just giving me his opinion of some new artwork I've purchased."

"A pleasure to meet you," said the man, shaking my hand. "I was just leaving. Ciao, Max, ciao, Khatia. See you soon. I'll see my own way out."

"So how do you find our little hamlet?" Max said, pouring me a glass of wine.

"Very nice. Everyone has been very welcoming."

"Good to hear. Many of these small historic New England towns can sometimes be so caught up in their own tradition, and it takes an outsider time to get their footing."

"I can see that. How long have you lived here?"

"Seven years. We moved in a couple of years before your uncle bought his house. We bought it from a family that had lived here many years. We created quite a stir when we completely tore down their old house and built a new one with such a contemporary design. We wanted something different because, as you can see, we are a bit different."

"Where did you move from?"

"Switzerland. We still have our house in Geneva. We lived there full-time for twenty years. And we still spend a lot of time there looking to our interests. Technically my business is headquartered there."

"Are you Swiss?"

"We are Swiss citizens but not Swiss by birth."

"We're Caucasians," Khatia said with a straight face.

"I-I don't understand," I said, not knowing what she meant by this answer. People usually don't refer to their race when asked about their background.

"This is what we sometimes say just to have fun with people," laughed Max. "It's amusing to watch their reaction. But it's technically accurate. We're from the Caucuses. Do you know that name?"

"It rings a bell."

"They're a mountain range south of Russia and north of Iran. They are unspeakably beautiful and largely unknown to Americans. There are three countries in the area, including Armenia, which is where I'm from."

"And Georgia, where I'm from," said Khatia. "Azerbaijan is the other one. Max and I met in Georgia. That's another thing we say to people: 'We met in Georgia.' When they ask 'Atlanta?' we say 'No, Tbilisi.' Most people don't quite get it. But again, it's true."

"I'm going to have to look at a map I'm afraid."

"A not uncommon reaction," he said. He had a constant smile on his face. I could tell he was enjoying the banter. "I went there a lot on business. I still do. Khatia worked for a company in Batumi that I dealt with from time to time. The first time I saw her, I was swept off my feet. And as you can see, that's not easy to do!"

I chuckled at his self-effacing answer. I'm attracted to people who don't take themselves too seriously. I'm told I have this attribute myself, which is essential when you do what I do for a living. This provided a good lead-in to tell them all about myself, which I proceeded to do at some length.

"Bravo, Jake," said Max. "We'll get along great. I can feel it."

At this point the doorbell rang and a woman carrying food in some boxes appeared on the patio.

"Delivery from Brothers," she said.

"Our favorite food store," said Khatia and motioned for the woman to spread the food out on the table.

"We love that place," said Max. "We use their home delivery app several times a week."

I'm in the voice business, and I found his fascinating. His speech was clearly foreign but with a faint British accent. His vocabulary was eclectic—colorfully Dickensian sometimes, slang the next. The more he talked, the more he reminded me of someone near and dear to my heart.

"Did anyone ever say you resemble Sidney Greenstreet?" I asked.

"Why no. Who's that?"

"An old-time actor. He played in some of the greatest movies of all times, like *Casablanca* and The *Maltese Falcon*. He was often cast alongside Peter Lorre, one of my heroes. They were a great team."

"Really! We don't know much about old American movies I'm afraid," he said while reaching for at least his third lobster roll in the last ten minutes.

"I'll tell you more sometime if you're interested. Lorre and Greenstreet were totally unalike, but they were a great team."

"How appropriate in our case. I think we can be a great team too."

I was confused by his answer. He had an uncanny ability to present himself as totally open and then interject a little comment that threw you off. It seemed to come naturally to him.

"I can see I've taken you aback by my comment, Jake. Sorry. Just trying to be amusing in my own way. I believe in teamwork and kindness. There's so little kindness in the world."

"That's what I said to my ex-wife when she told me she was leaving me for another man," I said. I often resort to some glibness when I'm at a loss for words—although in this case I think I actually did say those words to Melanie.

"Ah, life has its ups and downs," he said, reaching over and slapping me on my knee. "If I may, I'd like to talk about a potential 'up' in your case. May I take the liberty of doing so? We barely know each other, but I can tell we can be very transparent. May I continue in that vein?"

"I'm not sure I follow but, sure, go ahead."

"You have praised the way our house is furnished. Thank you. It is a byproduct of the business we are in, which is buying and selling special items of artistic, cultural, and sometimes historical significance. Our sources to obtain these items are varied and global, our clients refined—

112

from very wealthy individuals to museums. The MFA in Boston, the Metropolitan Museum in New York, and the Getty in LA are all clients, for example. Khatia and I sometimes keep a few objects for our own too. Call us amateur collectors."

"You seem more than amateurs."

"We are devoted, if nothing else. And we have passion, particularly for certain types of objects and artifacts. And that's where you come in."

"Me? I'm afraid I don't understand Max."

"I'll explain. Take another glass of wine and follow me."

I noticed his wife had disappeared. Apparently, this was now some sort of business discussion.

We entered the room with the Persian rugs. In it was an elaborately carved wooden bureau.

"This is a fine piece of furniture," I marveled.

"It's from my old stomping grounds in Armenia. It belonged to a seventeenth-century king. Reminds me of home. Such a beautiful land. So troubled too, alas. But it's what's inside that I want to show you."

He took out a box. Out of it he took an old ledger and several folded maps. He opened one of them and spread it out on a nearby table.

"This is a story of long ago that takes place in the area shown on this ancient map. Are you familiar with the story of Jason and the Argonauts? It was first told in the *Argonautica* written by Apollonius of Rhodes in the third century BC." As he said this, he reached in the box and pulled out a paperback copy of this epic poem, which he gave me.

"Actually, I am a little bit," I said, quickly rifling through some pages. "I did an audition for an animated film of it once. The part was for some animal—a dragon I think. But I never got the part though. I wasn't scary enough. I don't remember anything about it."

"Happy to fill you in, and so interesting you almost played the dragon! Jason was the son of a Greek king and heir apparent to the throne. But for various reasons we need not get into, he was ordered to complete certain tasks before he could take over the throne. One of them was to sail to a

113

faraway land called Colchis. It was at the eastern coast of the sea then known as Pontos Axenios. It's now called the Black Sea. Here is his path of sail."

He traced with his finger a sea route on the map.

"I never heard of any of these places," I said. "It's all Greek to me." Even I groaned over this poor and obvious witticism.

"This map shows the modern names of these places," he said unfolding another map. "Jason started here in Greece, went up the Aegean over here, through the Dardanelles, and into the Sea of Marmara and past the area that is now Istanbul. Then, through the Bosporus and into the Black Sea, ending on the coast of Georgia, then called Colchis. The big city there is called Batumi today. That's where I met Khatia and where Jason met Medea. But my love life turned out better than his."

"Oh?"

"Jason betrayed Medea and she murdered their two children. Had our Supreme Creator blessed us with children, my beloved Khatia never would have done that." He laughed. "Then again, I never would have betrayed my little Bati."

"Bati?"

"It means 'goose' in Georgian. I must tell you I had to win her hand from many other suitors. What a beauty—she still is. But she chose little old me!"

The last thing I wanted to hear about was Max's wooing of Khatia. Luckily, he moved on.

"It was in Colchis where Jason was to perform his final task: to capture a golden fleece that was hidden in a cave guarded by a dragon. Sorry to remind you of a past professional failure—it's essential to the story."

"I absolve you completely."

"Jason slew the dragon, captured the golden fleece, brought it back to Greece, and became king."

"A happy ending for everybody but Medea."

"There's another happy ending out there too—if you choose to partner with me."

"I enjoyed your story, Max. But you've woven this partner thing into it a couple of times and you're confusing the hell out of me, frankly."

"I'll get to the point. I like people who get to the point, Jake. You may not think I am at the moment, but I am. There are those historians who believe this Jason myth—like many myths—is based on facts. They believe that archaeological evidence—which is something I base many decisions on and where I have some expertise—shows that although Jason himself may not be a historical figure or based on one, the Golden Fleece may well have been based on a real artifact. We know there were several gold mines within the confines of ancient Colchis. In fact, we believe the one in nearby Sakdrisi is the oldest in the entire world. Golden objects of all kinds were produced there. Many people in Batumi believe that that Golden Fleece existed and that it never was removed by any Greek. Colchis was too far away for the ancient Greeks to get there, and that the author Apollonius was just trying to tell his fellow Greeks a story of Greek heroism. The Georgians believe that fleece never left Colchis, and even if it did, that there was probably more than one."

"Very interesting, Max. Again I ask, how does this involve me?"

"I come to that now. First, I must show you yet another map—not of as great antiquity as the one of Colchis and Pontos Axeinos, but old nonetheless, at least in the standards of our young and dynamic country."

He reached back in the bureau and pulled a third map out and unfolded it. "Do you see what it says?"

"Yes. It's a map of Duxbury and the bay in 1830. So?"

"I refer you to the Powder Point area here, near the tip. A plot of land is traced out and there's an X in the middle of it. It's entitled PROPERTY OF JOSIAH OSBORNE. Do you see what this property represents?"

"No. The map is nearly two hundred years old. Things have changed."

"But look at the shape of Powder Point. That hasn't changed. Do you see where this property is?"

"Ah, I see. Are you saying this is where my house stands today?"

"Let me be more specific. It is where OUR houses stand today. And that is of critical importance."

"I don't follow."

"Let me continue. Do you know anything about the Osborne family?"

"Caroline Hawksmoor of the historical society told me a little. She said Josiah was a seaman until he became a woodcarver. Nothing more is known about him. There's nobody in the rest of the family that is noteworthy." I almost added that maybe Olivia Phipps' troubled brother was somewhat noteworthy, but I let that pass.

"Partially correct," he said. "But I know much more about the Osbornes than Miss Hawksmoor and the historical society do. That's because I have some information that they don't have, and I haven't shown them. I tell you this in complete confidence, you understand."

"I understand. Go on."

"Josiah Osborne had two sons, the older was Samuel, the younger Matthew. Matthew became a minister here in Duxbury. Samuel became a seaman like his father. When Josiah died in 1827, Samuel as the eldest took over the house. But then Samuel died of typhus suddenly in 1831. The house was then taken over by Matthew who sold half the property—the half that my house represents. While your land and house remained in the Osborne family, my land and the house that was eventually built on it has changed hands numerous times over the years. Although various owners made improvements, the whole place was antiquated and in desperate need of repair when I bought it. I decided it was better to just tear it down and start over. The result is my little pleasure dome that you see today!"

He made a grand gesture toward the house. Even if the inside of it was lavish with more than a touch of magic, the one-story modern exterior was quite garish.

"That's an interesting story, but where is it all leading?"

"It's leading, Jake, to an unbelievable discovery I made six years ago.

116

Some information was literally—LITERALLY—unearthed that changed my life. When my old house was torn down and the new foundation was being dug, the workers discovered an old vault buried underneath the house. In it was a chest containing various papers explaining some of what I have just told you. Most importantly, though, was this ledger. It was written by Josiah's son Samuel. Here, take a look."

He extended the book toward me. Thinking he was giving it to me to look at, I reached for it. But he quickly pulled it back.

"Only look at the cover of it!" he exclaimed.

For the first time I detected an edge to his voice.

"Once we have come to an agreement in principle, I'll be glad to let you look inside."

"What exactly are you getting at, Max?" I snapped back, putting an edge to my voice too. "You seem to be playing a game with me."

"No game at all, Jake. Not in the least. In this ledger, which Samuel Osborne wrote in 1830 and which I also emphasize was found on my property, is fantastic information. In the ledger are notes Samuel made from several voyages. It is mostly short, uninteresting entries such as daily nautical conditions and ports of call, but there are also more detailed entries where he gives information on his state of mind, his thinking, his future plans and intentions. Quite a complicated and ambitious man. He aspired to be a captain some day, unlike his father who never rose beyond first mate before he retired to be a carver. Anyhow, of most interest in this ledger are his notes he made when he was a mate on a voyage on a ship called the *Smyrna*. It was the first American ship to sail into the Black Sea."

"I know that ship. My uncle painted a couple of pictures of it."

"I've seen them, Jake. I've seen them. He knew about the *Smyrna* because I told him about it. Based on that, he began his own research."

"Caroline Hawksmoor told me about it. She says my uncle sat in the historical society's archives and read the captain's log of its voyages several times, particularly the one into the Black Sea."

"I've read that captain's log too before Fred did and before Caroline Hawksmoor was the executive director. It is accurate but very incomplete. It does not contain the most interesting aspects of that voyage. That's because the captain who wrote the official logbook of the voyage—Seth Sprague Jr. —knew nothing about certain things that occurred on that journey. But Samuel Osborne did, and it's in this ledger."

"So what was this mysterious thing that happened?"

"It seems that Samuel was not an entirely transparent man. His writings in his journal show him to have a propensity to obtain articles on these voyages that he kept for himself. Nothing major and not always illegally obtained. But sometimes he crossed the line. He did on the *Smyrna*'s Black Sea voyage."

"And what did he do?"

"He had developed a system to bring his own secretly obtained goods into the U.S. and sell them. We need not get into that now—nor is it particularly interesting. In my business you see all kinds of importing schemes. All that is important is to say what he brought back aboard the *Smyrna*."

"Let me guess. Opium?"

"Good guess, and not entirely wrong. But I'm referring to something else. His acquisition on this occasion was far more than a little hooch. He brought back with him Jason's Golden Fleece."

I burst out laughing. If I had given this wild story any credence, all of that went out the window when I heard this.

"You're kidding, right, Max? Just some neighborly joking around."

"I am not surprised by your reaction," he said soberly. "It's basically what your uncle did, much to his regret."

"Okay, I'll play along. How did he get this thing?"

"Let's go back to the map of the Black Sea. The modern map of today is best because we must deal with the current, not ancient, names. I've made some notes on it, just to make things clearer. Here, take a look."

"The ship stopped at Smyrna, now called Izmir, next at Istanbul, then called Constantinople, to pick up the opium." He traced the route with his finger as he spoke. "That was on July 9, 1830. But that was not the final destination. The ship continued on all the way to the north coast of the Black Sea to this point here. Take a look."

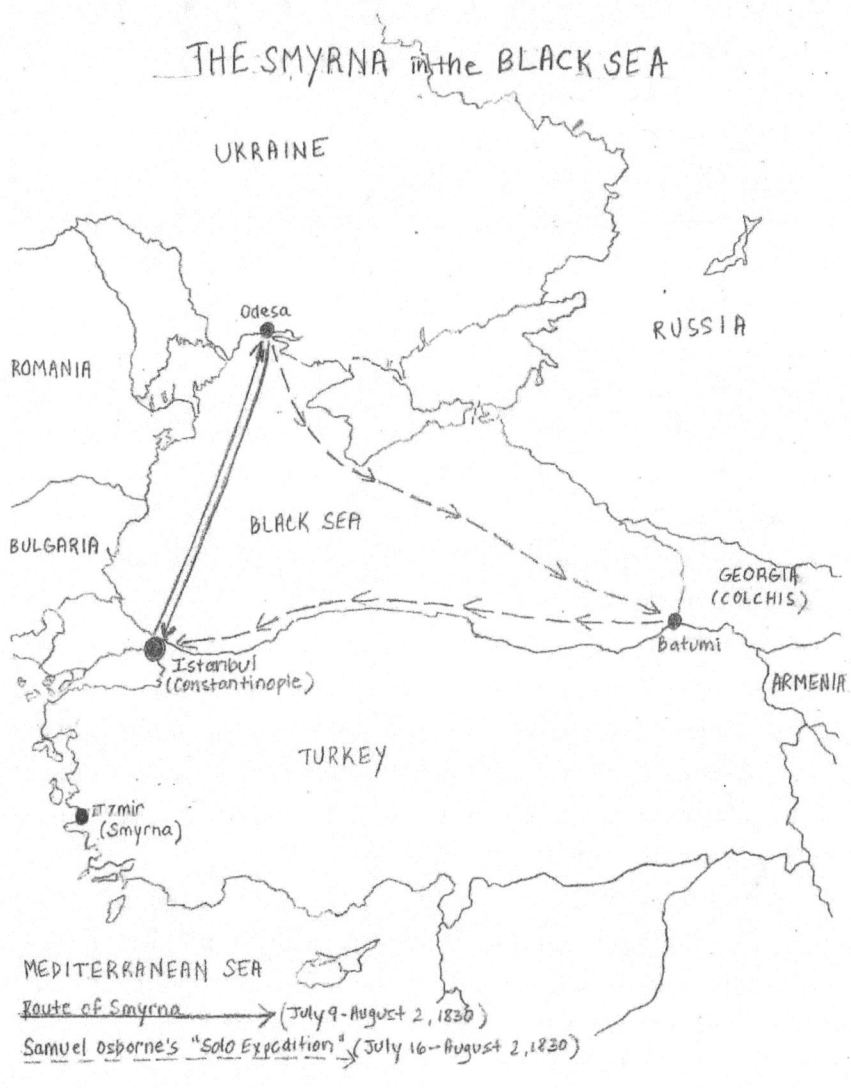

THE SMYRNA in the BLACK SEA

UKRAINE

Odesa

RUSSIA

ROMANIA

BLACK SEA

BULGARIA

GEORGIA
(COLCHIS)

Batumi

Istanbul
(Constantinople)

ARMENIA

TURKEY

Izmir
(Smyrna)

MEDITERRANEAN SEA

Route of Smyrna ——→ (July 9 - August 2, 1830)
Samuel Osborne's "Solo Expedition" (July 16 - August 2, 1830)

"It's Odesa in Russia?"

"Close. Ukraine. Surprisingly, the *Smyrna* stopped there for quite some time."

"To pick up more cargo?"

"Possibly. Captain Sprague's logbook of the voyage isn't clear. But the ship arrived there on July 16, and the next entry is on July 30 when it is leaving Odesa to pass through Constantinople and then on to Trieste. That ship was in the Black Sea for fourteen days."

"Why?"

"Captain Sprague makes no mention in the ship log. They most likely were in quarantine for a few days. Possibly they lingered in Odesa to enjoy this fine city. Possibly to visit other ports too. But that would need to have been mentioned in the ship log. Perhaps, though, Sprague was waiting for a member of his crew to return."

"I don't follow."

"The answer is here in Samuel Osborne's ledger," he said, waving the book at me again. "Samuel writes that on July 17, with the captain's permission, he caught a Turkish ship from Odesa to Batumi on the Georgian coast, former home of my beloved Khatia and me."

"Why did he do that?"

"He said that Sprague had instructions from the shipping company of J&T Perkins back in Boston to gather information and make connections in other ports on the Black Sea as long as it didn't delay the return. After all, no other American ship had ever sailed into the Black Sea, and American shippers and traders were eager to understand these markets for potential opportunities."

"So Samuel Osborne went on a reconnaissance mission?"

"Yes. Samuel's journal said he left the *Smyrna* in Odesa on July 17, got to Batumi on July 22, and then relooped with Sprague and crew in Constantinople on August 1. Again, no mention is made of this in Captain Sprague's log entries that are found in the archives of the Duxbury Rural and Historical Society. I encourage you to go to the archives and ask Miss Hawksmoor if you can look at it. Everything I've mentioned is in there—except the Batumi excursion by Samuel."

"And I presume that in your ledger Samuel tells what he did?"

"He does, and in some depth. If we become partners, I'll let you see his entire account. But for now, it suits our purposes for me to tell you that Samuel, while in Batumi, heard the legend of the Golden Fleece and that a sort of self-styled Georgian archaeologist had found it a year previously. Whether through some tough negotiations or, as is far more probable, some sleight of hand, Samuel ended up with it and brought it back to Boston on the *Smyrna*. He makes it quite clear that he told no one on board of his find and that he hid it in his gear."

"What happened to it?"

"This is the most amazing part of all. When he got back to Duxbury, he hid it in his house—your house! His last entry includes that he was in the process of trying to figure out what to do with it, but he died of typhus shortly after. He was not married and told no one of his treasure, not even his brother. Samuel figured Matthew the preacher would not have approved of this little freebooting escapade. That fleece is still somewhere in your house!"

"Does Samuel say where in his journal?"

"Not directly. He was not only a man of shall we say slippery morals. He was also paranoid. Many times in his journal he says that he trusts no one. So I'm guessing he didn't want to put too much in writing in case the journal fell into the wrong hands. But he says enough that I think I can figure it out if I were able to closely examine your house. It might involve some digging, though. But maybe not."

"This just sounds too wild, Max." I still wasn't sure if this was a joke. "This journal could be the ravings of a madman."

"Yes, there is that possibility," he said nodding. "But I can say without a scintilla of false modesty that I am very knowledgeable about this part of the world and trade there regularly. I have lived there and have a major network there. A number of things have long been known

121

on that corner of the Black Sea, or at least been fervently believed. First, that although the individuals in *Jason and* the *Argonauts* are mainly mythological figures, a Golden Fleece really existed and is the factual basis of the story. Second, that the fleece never left Colchis in ancient times. Apollinaire invented that out of Greek pride. Third, that an amateur Georgian archaeologist did find it in the nineteenth century in a necropolis near the ancient gold mines. And, finally, and this is key, that someone from abroad either stole the fleece or tricked the archaeologist. I've heard that rumor over the years."

"And now it's somewhere in my house?" Again I laughed.

"This is exactly how your uncle received this news at first. But I know that over time he did his own research, and he began to put more and more credence in it. Do you know why I'm sure he did, Jake?"

"No idea. Seems hard to believe he would have."

"I know he began to believe it because he refused to accept a partnership with me. He thought he could find it on his own and not need to split anything with me."

"What kind of partnership?"

"The simplest of all, Jake. And the same one I offer you. We agree up front that if we find the fleece, we will upon its sale split the proceeds equally. You have the fleece somewhere on your property but won't ever find it because you have no information as to where it is. I on the other hand have this information. I also have access to individuals and institutions that will want to buy such an unbelievable object for various reasons. This fleece is worth an extraordinary amount of money if made available to the right people. Frankly, it's priceless."

"So what does this mean? That you will traipse around my house, examining everything in it?"

"Or even under it. There are several possible locations based on Samuel's journal."

"This sounds pretty disruptive, Max. And all to find something that I still don't believe existed."

"I can see you're skeptical. I don't blame you. I've hit you with a lot. I didn't expect you today to become a partner with someone you've never met. So let's do this. Khatia and I will be gone on business for the next few weeks. Think about my proposition while we are gone. Do research of your own. And look yourself in the mirror and say why you wouldn't at least give this a try? Your uncle kept dragging his feet on this whole thing and finally said no. He made a big mistake. I know what I'm doing, Jake. I know how to find and sell stuff. I've made my living doing this sort of thing for thirty years all over the world—in Italy, Greece, the Middle East, China. I just never thought I'd be doing this in Duxbury!"

I sat there looking at this ridiculous looking man in a Hawaiian shirt, Panama Hat, and swim trunks, listening to him spinning this incredible yarn, alternately smiling, laughing, scowling, lecturing. I didn't believe any of it, and I couldn't believe my uncle had either. But I was convinced Max did.

"Okay," I finally said. "I'll think about. I'm not favorably inclined at the moment. But I'll think about it."

"Splendid, Jake. That's very kind, and I repeat there is so little kindness in the world. I hope for a favorable response when I get back. But don't overthink it. Your uncle did and look at how that turned out for him."

This seemed like an awkward way to sum things up. And was he giving me a subtle warning at the end? But I didn't ask for a clarification. All I wanted to do was get back home. I'd heard enough weird things for one day, maybe the weirdest I'd ever heard and trust me when I say I've heard a lot of very weird stuff over the years.

Chapter 13
OYSTERS

I began to frequently examine my uncle's sketches and calendar of appointments that I'd brought back from the Gurnet. I was looking for clues that would shed light on what was going on in his life—and inside his head—at the time of death. I had already talked to a number of people with whom he'd had recent appointments. Olivia Phipps, Colleen "Coco" Parsons, Max Trevanian, Caroline Hawksmoor. From them I had learned that at least three people had an issue with him, and all of them because of his house: the troubled Donald Osborne for an irrational hatred of my uncle for buying it, PJ Parsons for him not bequeathing it to the historical society as promised, and Max Trevanian for him not forming a partnership over the supposed treasure found somewhere within it.

It might also be possible that PJ Parsons was jealous of my uncle's longstanding relationship with his wife. Maybe there was something there too—although I must say that the prospect of such elderly people being in a romantic triangle brought a smile to my face. All of these seemed very foolish spats, none of them my uncle's fault. Yet from such things maybe trouble could have followed.

Sheila Compton had emailed me, asking if I'd found anything interesting. I said no, not wanting to spread gossip on unsubstantiated hearsay. Since her intention was to involve the police if I found anything, I decided it would have to be a smoking gun for me to pass anything on to her. I would keep her at arm's length and not dial up my efforts to find such proof. I had my own life to live. Yet if something overly suspicious fell in my lap, I felt I owed it to my uncle to pass it along. So I continued a very low-key investigation into his life.

The name Len Barker of Gurnet Oysters had been penciled into Fred's calendar a couple of times, so I thought I'd look him up. The oyster business clearly had been of interest to my uncle as an investor, and he met his end on an oyster floater. Both seemed good reasons for me to contact the Gurnet Oysters CEO. His name, like the other names on the calendar, had a phone number next to it.

"I'd be delighted to get together," Barker said. "I owe a lot to your uncle. He saved my business. How can I help?"

"I'd love to ask you a few questions on the oyster business. I know it interested my uncle."

"How about if we meet for a quick coffee at Brothers tomorrow? They have a nice little eating area. Then I'll take you out around the harbor in my boat and show you a few things. That's the best way to learn the oyster business."

I thought this was a fabulous plan, and so we met at Brothers the next day. I went to the eating area within the store and saw two men and a woman sitting together. One of the men called out, "Are you Jake by any chance?"

"I am."

"I'm Len. Have a seat."

I approached, nodded a greeting to everyone, then sat down.

Len introduced the others. "Meet Blaise Rogers, manager of Brothers. And this is Julie Hawthorne. We're going over a food event that the store is hosting here and we're participating in."

"Pleased to meet you," said the manager. "Your uncle was a great friend of this store."

"I've heard that about a thousand times before. He made a lot of friends."

"He was a big supporter of local food businesses. We're having a showcase for a few of them here on Saturday. Julie here will be one of the participants."

"I sure will," said the woman. "I have a small baked goods company here in town. My sister actually does the baking, but I create most of the recipes. Your uncle helped us finance a huge new oven. He was wonderful."

"Let's leave you to your oysters," said the manager. "Hope to see you at the showcase."

"You can sample our new eclairs," said the woman. "I call them Julie's Guilty Pleasures."

"With a name like that, how can I resist?" I said.

"I've been meaning to ask you, Julie," said Barker, "how do your students relate to their Algebra teacher having guilty pleasures? Julie's day job is teaching in the high school here, Jake."

"I've no idea," she said. "But if it keeps the little darlings guessing, so much the better. Eleventh graders rarely think of their teachers as human beings, which we occasionally are."

"Perish the thought," joked the manager. "Let's take a look at your product over in the bakery department."

"See you at the showcase Saturday," she called over her shoulder as they left. "I'll give you a sample of some pastry that will change your life. Where are you from?"

"Toledo, Ohio."

"I guarantee I'll show you some things you've never seen in Toledo. See you."

I saw instantly that she had a very engaging way about her that I bet held her in good stead with both customers and students. I also thought it delightfully quirky that a high school math teacher was moonlighting as a roguish baker, or was it vice versa?

"So, what can I tell you about the oyster business?" asked Barker when we were alone.

"Tell me the story of Gurnet Oysters and how my uncle saved you."

"Sure. Let me give you the big picture on the way the oyster business works in Duxbury. To own an oyster farm, you need to lease a section of the bay from the town. It's usually a three-year lease that you can keep renewing. This entire bay is totally tapped out with leased farms. Every square foot is leased out and no other new leases will be granted. The town does not have the onshore facilities to handle more. We're already the largest oyster town in all of Massachusetts. We just passed Wellfleet on the Cape."

"How many leases are there?"

"There are thirty farms. Each can be up to three acres."

"Can an owner have more than one farm?"

"The rules get tweaked every now and then, but the bottom line is, as of now, you can for a child or another family member, as long as they live in Duxbury. And if you list yourself as a wholesaler, other farms can sell their product to you. Take Island Creek Oysters. They're the biggest oyster business in Duxbury and are known globally. ICO not only owns several farms, but they are wholesalers and dealers too. I've sold to them in the past. They actually launched the oyster business in Duxbury, and not that long ago. It was 2000 when Skip Bennett and a couple buddies started their farms. Other owners came in one by one until the town put a freeze on new leases in 2004."

"So how can a new owner enter the market?"

"Only when someone drops their lease. Maybe an owner gets tired of the business. It can be demanding physically. It's a lifestyle, not just a job. Or if they can't make a go of it financially, they get out."

"Okay, give me an example. I have a farm and I want out. What happens?"

"You can transfer the lease to another person as long as they are a Duxbury resident. Or you can make a deal with someone to buy you out to include your equipment like the boat, oyster cages, the shed. You agree on a price. Or you can let the town take back the lease and they grant it to the next in line. There's a waiting list to get a new lease. Again, you have to prove to the town that you are a full-time resident."

"So how did you get in the business?"

"I got in twenty years ago. Leases weren't hard to get then. I did okay but then my costs went up and I had trouble finding a good wholesaler. What really hurt me was two years ago when we had to shut down for a while because of algae. It can happen if the water temperature gets too warm. It hurt the yield. Two other farms were struggling too, and the three of us decided to end our leases. Me, Bluefish Oysters, and Snug Harbor Oysters. But we stayed in because of your uncle. We three owners became partners, thanks to him."

"What did he do?"

"He wanted to become active in the business community here, and he heard I was in trouble and approached me and the other two owners. He gave all three of us a substantial sum of money to tide us over. In return we gave him some shares of our businesses. He then helped us find a good agency he knew in New York to put together a marketing plan for us. The first thing they convinced us to do was go to market under one name. So we chose the name of my farm, Gurnet."

"And it's worked out I gather?"

"In spades. Sales and profits are way up. The other two owners and I split the profits three ways. Your uncle got a share too. But he never cashed in. He invested back into the business. He said we were now big enough to become wholesalers too. Other farms would sell to us, making us even bigger. Maybe even open a restaurant or store too. We were exploring that with him when he died."

I now needed to steer this conversation in a slightly different direction. Sheila had said her bartender son had heard that other owners were upset that my uncle had saved some oyster farms because they wanted to take over the leases themselves. Who were these disappointed owners? And how could I find out without Barker becoming suspicious? I didn't want him to think I was pumping him for information because I suspected foul play from other owners. I decided I could subtly lead the witness by referring to the conversation I'd overheard my very first night in Duxbury. I had a much greater appreciation for that conversation now than I did then.

"I get the impression there were hard feelings over those leases not coming on the market," I said. "I overheard some conversation to that effect at The Shipyard Inn bar a while back."

128

Barker hesitated a moment, then said, "Maybe a little. I don't want to spread gossip, but it's common knowledge that two other owners had been talking to me and the owners of Bluefish and Snug Harbor Oysters, trying to convince us to transfer over our leases. I even had an informal verbal agreement in place with one of them. One evening, your uncle and I were having a beer at The Shipyard. We were talking about Gurnet expanding into the wholesale business. Fred knew how to think big and was ready to spend to help us. Billy Tidrow of Topnotch Oysters overheard and came up to us. He started calling me a double dealer. He accused me of doing some last-minute backroom deal with slick outsiders, and he laid into your uncle. Said he wasn't really a resident and should stop interfering in a local business built by hard working oyster lifers. He was aggressive, told your uncle to back off if he knew what was good for him. A few people at the bar heard it. Billy had had a couple of drinks too many, and the bartender had to settle him down."

I remembered that Sheila Compton's son, the bartender, had told her about this too.

"Sounds like my uncle was helping the locals like you out, not hurting them," I said shaking my head. "And he WAS a full-time resident, at least for the year prior."

"Sure. Billy was wrong about that. And Fred wasn't even the owner and never took a nickel out of the business even though he could have. Billy was acting on raw emotion. He's been frustrated he hasn't been able to grow his business and is always blaming it on one thing or another. Anyhow, he's not a bad guy, just a hothead."

"You said there was another owner upset with my uncle."

"Yes, that was Sam Larkin of Oceanview Oysters. He's been trying to get a lease for his son for a long time now, and he was next in line to get one. That would have been Bluefish Oysters' lease. But that didn't happen because your uncle gave Bluefish some cash which allowed them to join forces with me. Just as well. Sam's son isn't even a resident. Games would have to be played with his residency to get him qualified.

That's happened before, and the town's Shellfish Committee can usually sniff it out. But the son's been a problem in other ways. He had a run-in with a couple of owners who accused him of poaching. Sam denied it."

I'd pushed this about as far as I could—or wanted to—for the moment, so I said, "Are you still okay timewise to take me out on the water for a bit? I'd like to see the oyster operation up close."

"Sure, let's head out," and we grabbed our coffees and left.

We drove two minutes down to the harbor and took a rowboat to his motorboat which was at its mooring. For the next hour, he sped from one end of the bay to the other giving me a running commentary. Some of it related to oyster farming (which he knew a lot about) and some of it more historical (where his knowledge was more limited—he wasn't in the tour guide business). I had brought with me a map of the bay for reference. I was still trying to make sense of the rather complicated series of peninsulas, rivers, inlets, bays, and beaches that form this intricate little coastal corner of Massachusetts.

It was high tide, and we were able to go into Eagle's Nest Bay and around the hilly Standish Shores peninsula with the Myles Standish monument atop it—the highest point in town and visible for miles. Then it was into Kingston Bay all the way across to where the Jones River empties into it.

"It was named after Jones, the captain of the Mayflower," he said.

Then we turned up the bay all the way to Gurnet Point.

"Gurnet's a funny name. Where'd it come from?"

"It's a fish off the coast of England. The Pilgrims named this area after them."

He pointed to a long strip of beach that extended off Gurnet Point at a ninety-degree angle back into the bay.

"This is Saquish Head," he said. "Although it's attached to the Gurnet now, it probably used to be an island. It's a fragile ecosystem here. It keeps evolving. It needs to be watched and cared for best we can."

"Saquish. Doesn't sound very Pilgrim-my."

"It's not. Let's not forget this was initially the Wampanoag's land. In their language, Saquish meant 'abundance of clams.' They were a key source of food for both the tribe and the Pilgrims. Clams were actually the first shellfish business in Duxbury—way before oysters, which is a pretty new business here. Not much clamming done anymore, though. Just a very few small one-man operations now."

"What's that," I asked pointing to a small island only a few hundred feet away.

"Clark's Island. It was named after a mate on the *Mayflower*. The Pilgrims spent a night anchored off the island before they landed in Plymouth in 1620. They had a church service on the island thanking God for surviving the crossing. A service is still held there on Pulpit Rock every year for whoever can get out to it."

"Is the island inhabited?"

"There's about a dozen houses with seasonal residents," he said. "All electricity comes from generators, and water needs to be shipped in. It's a different world. I own a property out there. So does the historical society. It's been rented out over the years. A famous writer lived out there one summer."

"Really? Who was that?"

"The name escapes me. A couple of his books were made into movies. What's the one with the song *Moon River*?"

"That's *Breakfast at Tiffany's*. That novel was written by Truman Capote."

"That's the one."

"I'll be damned," I said. I do a pretty damn good Capote impression, but I decided to forego it. This was a day for me to be serious.

Bug Light and the town of Plymouth were further out, and we didn't go that far. We turned and hugged the bay side, keeping the town's barrier beach to our right. As we went, Barker continued to add color commentary. He was a hearty, swaggering man of the sea and spoke in a heavy New England accent. Physically he reminded me a little of Robert Shaw in *Jaws*.

"Some historians think a Viking named Thorvald landed here on this beach way before Columbus. There's a debate about it."

We then made our way underneath the Powder Point Bridge and into the small Back River, then turned back under the bridge and up the Bluefish River past the King Caesar house and near to a low bridge that crosses it on Washington Street. There was a group of boys jumping off the bridge and into the river.

"That's the Bluefish River Bridge," he said. "I jumped off like that as a kid. Kind of a rite of passage in the town. You can only do it around high tide, though. When it's low, it's almost bone dry."

Indeed, the amount of navigable water in these rivers and parts of the bay varies greatly depending on the tides, which are quite dramatic. I'd read an article in the *Messenger* recently that the famous transcendentalist and essayist Henry David Thoreau of *On Walden Pond* fame sailed in Duxbury Bay several times in the 1850s. Once he was on Clark's Island at low tide and thought he could walk all the way to the mainland. He made it halfway when the tide started coming in. Luckily a fisherman was in the area and saved his life. So while the tides are very tricky for a novice, I learned they are part of an ecosystem that is perfect for oyster farming. The constant influx of new water keeps the bay fresh.

As we circled around, we passed through many oyster farms, some delineated by buoys. There was much activity on the water, and Barker was able to explain the details of how an oyster farm works, from the planting of millions of microscopic seeds then through their various stages of growth until their harvesting one to two years later. We ended up back near the central Snug Harbor area and near to what was of most interest to me: the floating oyster sheds. There were maybe a dozen of them anchored across the harbor.

"This blue one here is the Gurnet shed," he said as we approached one. "No one's there now. Later in the day my guys will pull up with bags of oysters and cull them, then wash the shells down with that hose you see there, then bring them on shore. We have to immediately put them on ice."

"Can we get out and onto your shed for a minute?" I asked. "I'd like to look inside."

"Okay, but be careful. It can be tricky if you haven't done it before."

Barker maneuvered the boat to the edge of the platform, and I stepped onto it.

"Watch your footing on that upweller," he warned.

"What's an upweller?"

"It's the platform attached to the front of some these floating sheds and is designed to be an incubator for shellfish. It has a tank circulating water constantly through the baby oysters underneath. The circulation provides food and nutrients to grow the oysters to full size."

This was now the time and place for me to address my uncle's death. I hoped me raising it would flow as a natural part of our conversation given where we were located.

"So, my uncle died on one of these sheds, right?" I said. "Which one?"

"Over there," he said, pointing to a shed about twenty yards off to the right. "Bobby Atkinson owns it."

"I'm still trying to piece together how it all happened. I read the *Messenger* account, but I still have trouble visualizing it."

"He was discovered by Bobby himself. He was climbing onto the shed deck to begin work. The door was half closed but he could see into it. And there was Fred's body. The way Bobby explained it to the police was that the upper half of the body was inside the shed with blood on the side of the head and on the floor. The lower half extended out of the shed and onto the upweller. Fred must have slipped trying to move around and fell into the shed and hit his head on the floor. There was some bad weather the night before, and it was still raining earlier that morning. The water was a little choppy when he got here. It can be a bit tricky to move around that floater if it gets a bit rocky. He probably shouldn't have been out here. But he was so eager to learn the business."

I spent another hour with Barker talking about the oyster business. I liked him a lot. He was a hearty outdoorsy sort—just the sort of hail fellow well met you'd expect in his profession. When he dropped me back at the harbor, we shook hands warmly.

"Call me any time with questions. As I said, I owe your uncle a lot."

Somehow, I knew those would be the very words he'd leave me with.

* * * * *

The day on the water had given me more food for thought, and that evening I again spread out the twelve sketches. I was possibly reading too much into Barker's comments, but a couple things he said potentially shed light on two of those drawings. One was entitled *Fight at the Inn*. It depicted a fracas among three men at a bar. Barker had mentioned that angry oyster farm owner Bill Tidrow had confronted my uncle and himself at the Inn. Was this a portrayal of that?

Then there was the sketch of the oyster farmers at work on the bay named The *Oyster Wars*. That had seemed a strange title for such a folksy scene. Was it a reference to the competition that existed among farmers for leases? By all accounts the Duxbury oyster community was a collaborative one, but all it took was just one inebriated outlier to cause trouble. Had one done so for my uncle?

One thing seemed to be for certain. He had carefully and purposefully arranged these drawings in a circle in his hut on the Gurnet, in the middle of which was a poster with the words MY COMPLICATED LIFE IN DUXBURY: POTENTIAL NEW WORK. That told me that these drawings were a collection of scenes, events, and observations that involved him in some way. Writers kept notebooks to record biographic details and personal musings. Painters kept sketch books. These drawings were a visualization of what was on his mind right before he died.

As interesting as it might be to know that, there was a much larger question beginning to form in my mind—one that had very serious and pragmatic implications. Did any of this relate to how and why he died?

Chapter 14
THE HOUSE GUESTS

That weekend, I hosted several out-of-town guests at my house. I'd invited each weeks previously, and they had finally gotten back to me saying they were available for the upcoming weekend. The first guest was Gloria. She'd had trouble working around her daughter's schedule but now she had this short window to get away. So, she was a given.

Then I heard from Bennie Kapler saying he and his wife Judy could come up the same weekend. At first I thought to put them off. Gloria and I could use some time alone. At the last minute, I changed my mind. I had this hunch that we'd have a better time if we all got together. The house had plenty of room and so I thought, what the hell, let's make it a couple's weekend.

Everyone got to my place late afternoon on Friday. After they'd settled in, I gave them a walk around the house and property. The general consensus was that the place was amazing.

"On a scale of one to ten, this is a twenty," marveled Bennie. "I had no idea. What a location. The view off your deck is world class."

"And the furnishings. They're out of *Better Homes and Gardens*," gushed Judy.

"My uncle had great taste," I said humbly but accurately.

"He must have," teased Bennie. "No offense, but your sense of style has always been a mixture of Jack Klugman in The *Odd Couple* and the college frat in *Animal House*."

"Oh, Ben, lay off," said Judy. "He just took a while to find himself."

"It's not that he found himself, it's more that his uncle found him. I can't believe your luck."

"I am very lucky," I said.

I looked at Gloria, waiting for her assessment. She hadn't said a thing.

"What do you think, my dear?" I finally asked.

"It's wonderful, Jake," she answered very softly. "Quite a step up from your place in Toledo. Congratulations." And she kissed me lightly on the cheek.

I'd planned a barbecue that night so that we could just sit around and catch up. Ben and I talked a little shop. The Cartoon Network had picked up our latest collaboration. It was about four guys—a Slovak, a Mongolian, an Italian, and a cowboy from Montana who join forces every now and then to save the world from various disasters. We'd co-write each episode, and I'd do all four voices. That's more than I'll typically do in a show, but three of them were easy for me, the Montana cowboy being the exception. I am not convincing as a cowboy. I don't relate to it. I don't like country music either. It all sounds the same to me.

"It's based on a video game called *Team Badass*," Bennie told the ladies. "Somehow that doesn't capture the diverse nature of our foursome though, so Snake and I are still spit balling titles."

"Oh, stop the cartoon talk for God's sake," said Judy, rolling her eyes. "And knock off the Snake thing, okay? It's so sophomoric. Tell us how you're doing, Jake. This is quite a change."

"Yes, it is," I said.

"For the better, right?" said Bennie. "I mean what's not to like?"

"Well, it has its pluses but also its minuses," I said, looking at Gloria who had remained quite subdued.

"Like what?" pursued Ben. "You can't use your Mud Hen season tickets?"

Sensing I needed to choose my words very carefully, I said, "No. For one thing it's sometimes lonely. I'm new here and New England has a reputation of being rather cool to newcomers."

"I've heard that too," said Judy. "Have you found that?"

"Well, a little bit," I lied. I hadn't found this at all. But it seemed I should say it. "There's a lot about Toledo I miss. Some of the people."

Gloria gave a little smile at the inference here and said in what I interpreted as a gentle probe, "I'm sure you're making friends, though. You are a very friendly guy after all."

"Yes, but let me tell you how it was with my uncle," I said, trying to stay somewhat on the topic of assimilation into new surroundings but changing to a more neutral example. "He owned this house for five years. Far as I can tell, he made lots of good acquaintances. On the one hand, it's rather humbling to be sort of stepping into his shoes. On the other hand, I've run across a few people that weren't great admirers of his."

"Oh? In what way?" asked Gloria, suddenly more engaged.

I'd vowed that I wouldn't get deeply into my uncle's life this weekend, so I answered in vague generalities. "Nothing all that dramatic. Just the predictable little kerfuffles you'd find in most small towns. It's an environment that takes some getting used to is what I'm trying to say. School's still out as to whether I can feel fully at home here."

We spent the rest of the evening in small talk. Gloria was doing fine. Her daughter had decided she'd go to college next year at Bowling Green State University which was only twenty minutes from Gloria's house in a suburb just south of Toledo. The daughter had been accepted to several schools in other parts of the country but wanted to stay local and commute. She was a homebody and wanted to get a semester or two under her belt living at home before deciding if she wanted to move on campus. This, I immediately realized, would impact Gloria's mobility short term.

Everyone was tired and the night ended early. As we walked upstairs, I grabbed Gloria's hand and said I missed her, which was true. She said the same, and I believed her. By an unspoken mutual consent, we agreed to put off what the future might hold for at least one night.

* * * * *

The next day was spent tooling around town. Everyone was keen to understand what my new life was like. In the morning, I drove to some of the historical spots, pontificating as if I had deep knowledge to impart when the truth was I'd only lived in town eight weeks and had barely scratched the surface of what there was to know.

In the afternoon, I called ahead to the marina and asked them to pop my boat in the water, then I loaded everybody into it for a cruise around the bay. The Gurnet, Clark's Island, the beach, the wooden bridge, the Bluefish River, the harbor with the oyster sheds—I showed it all to them. Having brought our swimsuits and it being a hot late-June day, we even took a dip in Eagles Nest Bay, one of the shallowest and therefore one of the warmest bodies of water in town. A few water skiers sped by us. At one point, several boats came close together to form a little flotilla at anchor, and people—obviously neighbors—moved from one craft to another, exchanging food and drinks. They waved at us and signaled to join them, but we decided we'd move on.

It was the Saturday of the local product showcase at Brothers, and I thought I'd stop in with our group after our little boat tour of the bay. We needed to buy food for dinner anyway. We'd decided eating at home and enjoying the property was more fun than eating out. Judy is one heck of a cook and had volunteered her services to do something simple. I enjoy cooking too and said I'd help her.

We walked into the cafe portion of the store. The tables and chairs had been pulled out and about a dozen sampling stations for various local products had been set up, each with their owner standing alongside. On the walls were signs that said things like "Eat, Drink, and Be Local" and "Brothers Supports Local Businesses." A number of customers were moving station to station.

Blaise Rogers noticed me and shook my hand. He, like all the store employees, was wearing a black tee shirt that said "Butcher, Baker, Farmer, Roaster."

"Meet some good friends visiting from Ohio and New York," I said.

"Wish we had a store like this where we live," said Judy, looking around. Bennie had already gone on ahead and had started sampling some of the goodies.

"Half the owners here for the showcase were supported by your uncle," Rogers said. "Let me introduce you to them."

139

For the next fifteen minutes, the two women accompanied me as I met the owners of a cranberry bog, a honey business, a sauce company, a microbrewery, and a salt company, all heaping the usual praise on my uncle. The owner of Snug Harbor Oysters was there too, and I explained to Judy and Gloria that this was one of three oyster farms my uncle had supported financially.

Julie Hawthorne was there as well. She was standing at her booth next to a sign that read "Julie's Guilty Pleasures." She was in an animated discussion with Bennie. We walked over.

"I'm on my second eclair and third apple tart," said Bennie between bites. "I hope you haven't planned too much for dinner, Jake. I'm full already."

"Hello," she said to me with a big smile. "Glad you stopped in. Please give a try to some of these."

On a table in front of her were a number of cakes and pastries. In a wheelchair next to the table sat a woman.

"Hello," she said to the three of us. "I'm Julie's sister Nancy."

"She does all the baking," said Julie, putting a hand on her sister's shoulder. "She's so talented."

"So, it really should be Nancy's Guilty Pleasures?" I teased.

"That's what I wanted to call it. But Nancy insists on staying in the background."

"Good decision," whispered Bennie to me. "This Julie is a looker. After being with her for the last five minutes, I'd buy this on the name alone."

"Yum! This is to die for," gushed Judy, taking a bite out of cupcake. "If I lived here, I'd lose my girlish figure."

"You lost that years ago after the twins, Jud," laughed Bennie.

"Not funny," said Judy curtly. "Remember: You can be replaced."

"Where do you do your baking?" asked Gloria, surveying the spread.

"Until last year, at home," said Nancy. "Julie and I live together here in Duxbury. Then a year ago, Fred invested some money in us, and we were able to open a little bakery in town with really good equipment. We now have the capacity to do a lot more baking. I've even hired a woman to manage the store and another to help in the baking. We're in all six Brothers stores south of Boston now. We can't keep up with the demand."

"And it's all because of your uncle," Julie said to me. "We owe your family a huge debt of gratitude."

"Let's do some shopping for tonight," Judy broke in. "Being surrounded by all this food has made me hungry."

After we had checked out and were leaving the store, Julie tracked us down at the door and said to me:

"Again, I want to say how much we owe your uncle. He was a beautiful man. It's meant the world to Nancy to build this business. It's made a difference in her life."

* * * * *

"This has been quite a day," said Gloria with a weary little sigh after we'd cleaned up and were having a nightcap.

"I'll say," said Judy. "I'll sleep well tonight."

"The town seems like a great place," said Ben. He didn't look tired at all. "I could get used to it pretty quickly— particularly that woman with the baked goods."

"Oh, stop it," said Judy. "No one enjoys your little adolescent jokes."

Judging by the scowling expression on her face, Gloria certainly didn't seem to be enjoying his attempt at humor either.

"No, she's intriguing," persisted Ben. "Seriously. I wonder what happened with her sister and why the two are living together."

"Knowing my uncle, he seems to have been attracted to underdogs. Maybe there's a story there."

"If I were you, I'd find out my friend."

"You're a real Neanderthal, Ben," snapped Judy. "Grow up."

I did not appreciate Ben's remarks either. His repeated references to the attractiveness of Duxbury—and Julie—struck me as tone deaf, considering that he knew the barriers facing Gloria to move here. As we went up to bed, I said to her, "Penny for your thoughts. You look pensive."

"I was just thinking how good your life is becoming here. You'll never come back to Toledo."

"I don't know that for sure. There's a lot to think through. On your part too. Could you see yourself living here?"

"It's a moot point, short term at least. My daughter continuing to live at home means I'm not exactly footloose and fancy free. And there's my work."

"But Deloitte would move you, right?"

"I'd have to look deeper into it. They probably need help here. And I could keep some of my old clients working from here."

"You'd be a lot closer to one of them," I smiled.

"Which reminds me, I have some tax questions I need to ask you."

"Can it wait until tomorrow? We could use our time now more productively."

That was certainly true. But we never did have that tax discussion the next day. Something significant happened that put that topic very far on the back burner.

* * * * *

It was about 9:00 next morning, and we were sitting around lazily with our coffees. Gloria and Judy were in the living room chatting. Bennie and I were sitting in our swim trunks on the back deck reading the papers. Since Gloria had an afternoon flight back, all we'd have time to do would be to squeeze in a couple hours at the beach before I'd need to drive her up to the airport.

Suddenly, my iPhone rang. It was lying on a table off to the side and I rose to get it.

"Who would call so early on a Sunday?" I muttered.

"Probably a scam," said Bennie. "That's all 80% of my calls are anymore."

I picked up the phone and saw Jocko's name. I immediately knew what it was, and it wasn't good.

"Grandma just died, Dad," he said in a very somber voice. "I just got a call from The Homestead. It was a stroke. I'm going to go over now to get more details."

I was not surprised. This had been a long time coming and probably the best thing for my mother. Still, it took a minute to sink in, and I had to fight off the tears, which I did not totally succeed in doing.

"I'll get the first plane back" was all I said and hung up.

"Bad news from Toledo, Jake?" said Ben.

"Yes. Mom died. I'm going to need to head back immediately I'm afraid."

"Of course. Judy and I will shove off as soon as we can."

I went in and told the girls the news. Gloria got up and hugged me.

"What can I do?" she said and squeezed my hand.

"Nothing much," I said. "I'm going to try to get on your flight to Detroit. It's 2:00, right?"

"Yes. Delta."

I sat down to search on my phone online for a ticket.

"Shit," I said. "That Delta is sold out. But there's a 5:00 on Jet Blue. Let me get on that. I'll drive you up and try to go standby on your flight. If it doesn't clear, I'll just wait at the airport. There's nothing else to do."

The trip to the beach now didn't seem appropriate, and I wanted to be alone for a bit. I called The Homestead and talked to the nurses. One of the attendants had gone in to wake mom up to give her a bath before breakfast and found her lying in bed with no pulse. They had called the doctor on duty who had come in and said it appeared to be a massive stroke.

I called Jocko back. He was about to head to the facility to do any necessary paperwork. Then he offered to drop into the local funeral home to see if anyone was available to talk next steps. I told him of my flight plans, and he said he'd pick me up at the airport regardless of which flight I took.

I packed, preparing myself for a stay of a week if need be. By the time I finished, it was time for me to drive to the airport. The Kaplers said goodbye and drove off, and Gloria and I headed up to Logan. We avoided any talk about us as a couple. Neither of us was up for that given the circumstances. And I didn't know what I'd say anyway. I still didn't know how I felt about our relationship. Gloria had said something significant when she informed me her daughter would continue to live at home while going to college. So, nothing seemed to have changed— unless I decided to give up the house and move back. But I knew I wouldn't do that, at least short term.

It turned out I didn't clear the wait list onto Gloria's flight, so we parted at the gate and said the predictable things.

"I'll call you when the dust clears," I told her.

"If there's anything I can do, let me know," she said.

We kissed, and I sat to wait for my later flight out.

Chapter 15
THE LETTER

Most of the next week was filled with the funeral and the details leading up to it. The service itself was a very small affair, held at the Catholic Church we had belonged to in the old neighborhood when I was a kid. I hadn't been there in thirty years.

There weren't many of my mother's friends who were still alive, but a few attended. A couple of the employees of the foundry where she had been a bookkeeper for most of her career had seen the little obit in the paper, and they came too. I saw several of my boyhood friends who knew her from the old neighborhood. Three or four of Jocko's friends came too. Aside from a few people I didn't recognize, that was it. My mother had known the parish priest quite well, but he had died, and a younger priest who really didn't know her performed the service and gave a pretty generic, impersonal eulogy.

From the church our small caravan of about ten cars made its way to the cemetery for a short internment ceremony. A blessing, a few tears from Jocko and me, and a hug from Gloria for both of us, and then we adjourned to a nearby restaurant for a luncheon for whoever had wanted to stay for a bite. About fifteen people showed up. At a certain point, a stranger came up to me and took me aside.

"It's too bad about your mother. I know she had not been well."

"No. The last few years she was not herself."

"It's a pity. I hadn't seen her for years."

He was a short bald headed elderly man with wire-rimmed glasses and stooped shoulders. I had noticed him at the funeral and cemetery but couldn't place him.

"Did you work with her at the foundry?" I asked.

"No, I'm your uncle, Mike."

I stood there thunderstruck. I hadn't seen him since my teenage years, and the only image I had of him was that of a spry energetic man with jet black hair in the prime of life. The old man who stood in front of me looked like no one I had ever seen before.

"I-I'm sorry," I stammered. "I didn't..."

"You didn't recognize me, eh?" he said with a wry smile. "The black sheep of the family at the funeral of the sister he hadn't seen in years. We all change physically as the years go by. But most of us remain the same person inside. You look very well by the way. And you've had some luck, eh?"

"Luck?" I asked. I wasn't sure what he meant by this remark, particularly since I had just buried my mother.

"Yes, you getting Fred's house."

"So, you heard about that?" I was taken aback by his directness.

"Yes. Fred told me about that shortly before he died. He had reestablished contact with me after many years. He said he wanted to get some things off his chest."

"What things?"

"About the split in the family. He'd been thinking a lot about it as he got older. He also told me he was going to leave his property to you and not my kids. He wanted to keep the house in the family, and he felt closest to you. I'm sure you know there wasn't a lot of brotherly love between us."

It was an awkward conversation because I knew Uncle Mike had never gotten along well with his brother and my mother, even when they were kids. Although Fred and my mother had talked very seldomly over recent years, they had been close at one time. My father, Jim, and Fred had been best friends—inseparable as boys—and it was through Fred that my father met my mother. Mike as the youngest of the three siblings was odd man out and always resented it.

Things had gotten much worse when Mike married my aunt Eleanor, a pretentious woman from St. Louis whose father owned a chain of department stores. Eleanor thought she was too good for the Petersons and convinced Mike he was too. Eventually he took over the business from Eleanor's father and acted like a captain of industry. Fred was a nobody then. Mike's relationship with his two siblings had totally fallen apart after that. My father died and my mother became a sort of depressed loner for many years. Ironically, Fred's career took off and Mike's collapsed when the department store business began to deteriorate. The circumstances had flipped and what were once petty jealousies had turned into animosity. At least that was the story I heard from my mother.

"Look," he said. "I didn't come here to drag up family history. It's no secret my brother and I never hit it off from day one. Water and vinegar. But your mother and I—I regret we fell out of touch. In fact, I had reached out to her after my wife died a couple of years ago. She'd said some nasty things to your mother over the years, and I wanted to apologize. I even visited her when she first entered the assisted living facility. She told me you were living in Los Angeles at the time."

This jogged my memory.

"Now that you mention it, I remember she told me something to that effect," I said. "That was around the time when they moved her to the memory care wing, right before I moved back. She still had occasional spurts of clarity then. But she quickly went downhill."

"Yes, I know. I called the facility every so often to check in. I even called last week. That's how I learned of her death. Listen. This isn't the time or place to get into the Peterson grudges. I just wanted to pay my last respects to your mother. I had nothing personal against her, although she probably held some things against Eleanor and me. It was way more complicated between Fred and me. Colin wanted to better understand that, and it made him angry. But that's a totally different story that doesn't matter anymore now."

He wished me good luck and left without shaking my hand. As I was watching this fragile old man walk out the door, Gloria came up to me.

"Who was that talking your ear off?" she asked.

"My long-lost Uncle Mike. I can't believe he was here."

"I've heard you mention him. Just paying his condolences?"

"Probably. That was nice. But I'm not sure if that was entirely it. He hinted at a couple of things that confused me. The Petersons of St. Louis were always difficult for me to understand. My cousins Colin and Beth never had much use for my mother or me. Or for my uncle Fred either. But it seems Colin and Fred had recently met in Duxbury."

"Any idea why?"

"None. I just know they did because I saw it noted in his appointment calendar. Now we'll never know."

* * * * *

The next day I went to The Homestead to collect my mother's things. She didn't have much. She had gotten rid of almost all of her stuff two years previously when she had sold our old house and moved in here. What little she had left I was going to give to charity or, as was more likely, throw away. It was very sad. All that was left of her life that I wanted to keep were a few small personal objects like her wedding ring and some photo albums.

Her affairs were simple. She had almost no money other than an annuity to help pay for her room at The Homestead, and even that wasn't enough. I had to chip in, which I willingly did. The only other business-related paperwork I found was in two boxes underneath her bed. Her will was there as well as a very small insurance policy and a few years of tax returns I had done for her. There were also some miscellaneous papers, bills, receipts, and a half dozen or so letters she'd never opened. I proceeded to open all of the latter. None were of any importance—except one which was dated four months previously.

She had entered The Homestead reluctantly; she had not wanted to live there. Although in a state of cognitive decline obvious even to herself, she still had enough of her wits about her to argue—sometimes angrily—that she did not need to go into any facility yet. I resisted until she took a bad fall on the bathroom floor of her old house. She lay there all night, unable to move, until she had been discovered the next morning by the woman I'd hired to spend mornings with her and help her bathe. That was enough for me, and I had insisted she give up the house and get the care she needed.

For her first few months there, she insisted on continuing to read and answer her own mail. She even did a little email. Even after I moved back, I let her do that, thinking it would ease the transition. But her further decline was rapid. I began to notice she wasn't on top of her affairs anymore and that she sometimes threw away her mail, lost it, or didn't open it. From then on, I looked at all her mail first. But this unopened letter must have been stashed away before I saw it or perhaps it was just lost in the shuffle.

This particular letter bore no return address. I opened it. It was from my uncle Fred. It was long and rambling.

My dear Donna,

I hope this finds you well in your new surroundings. I know it was difficult to leave the house behind after so many years there—so many memories I'm sure, both good and not so good. Such is life.

I'm glad you wrote me a couple of months ago telling me where you are. I've called The Homestead a couple of times and left messages, but you haven't returned my calls. I don't know where Jake is these days (did he move from LA?). So, I thought I'd write you. If you have trouble reading it, maybe somebody could read it to you and respond for you. Maybe I'll fly out to see you too if you are up to it.

I hope we can now stay in more frequent touch. With Mary gone these many years, you and Jake are the only meaningful link I have back to the happy days in Toledo long ago. I think of the past more and more as the years go by—some with deep regret, some with joy. Your husband Jim falls into the latter category, and I was thinking of him just last night. I never had a friend to replace him. He was such a funny guy. So full of life. I know a part of you died when he did. A part of me did too. But I've been thinking lately that he still lives on in Jake. It's got me thinking about something, and I need your perspective.

I have been reevaluating my life these days. I wonder, what do I have to show for it? A few business deals? Some didn't go my way, but many did. I was lucky. But what good did it do? I sit in this big house by the sea and am trying to make sense of things. I've tried to be active in the community in several ways. For example, I've been supporting some small businesses around here. I feel I can take some of what I've learned over the years and help out the little guy trying to get started. I'm through with the big corporate types. Those days are gone for me. They probably went on for too long. I'm afraid I've ruffled a few feathers along the way though, and I must admit it's put some tension in my life at a time when I don't need any. And there's one deal I did many years ago that I deeply regret. Private equity can be a very cold-hearted business. I'm trying to see if there's any corrective action I can take. My lawyer thinks I'm a fool to revisit this and that it'll just open a can of worms. More tension...

On the plus side, the house and community are wonderful. I love living here. And I've got my painting to fall back on. I'm devoting more and more time to it. It settles me down and helps me think through things. I've developed a couple of confidants I can confide in which really helps. Above all, I'm trying to see if I can leave any sort of positive legacy behind. Or is it too late for that?

In that regard, you may be surprised to know that I have developed a huge sense of history living around here. Preserving what's good about the past is important to me, and I'm donating some money to that effect. And it's becoming very personal for me. Since I don't have any children and our own immediate family has splintered, I feel some sort of need to connect the past—my past—to the future. I want to leave something behind, and I'm debating what that should be. Let me tell you a story.

When we were growing up, do you remember Dad saying that his grandfather told him that there was a family legend that the Peterson family went way back to the early days of the country? He said that not much was known, but there had been a persistent rumor in the family that our early American ancestors came from somewhere in New England—maybe even as far back as the Pilgrim times—before some members moved west. I never thought a second about it. It felt like it was the wishful thinking of our grandfather, a modest shoemaker from Toledo trying to embellish the history of his family.

I remember our brother Mike looked into it once. When he got married to Eleanor and she and her family were looking down their noses at the Petersons, he thought proving that we had blue-blood ancestry would impress her. But he found that we descended from a Peterson that came to Toledo from England in the early 1800s. He was a shoemaker.

But the legend resurfaced years later. I was going to grad school at Harvard. One of my classmates was from a small town south of Boston named Duxbury, and we became good friends. He invited me to his parents' house one semester break, and I hit it off with the family. My friend had a very cute sister, and we went out a few times. Eventually, she said she was too young to get serious and we both moved on. And we did. She married a local man some years later, and I relooped with Mary back in Toledo after graduation and we married. I couldn't have loved her more. I miss her every day.

Anyhow, the mother of this Duxbury family, like many others in this small town, was very active in the historical society. Her own people had come to the area in the 1700s. When I told her we had a family legend that the Petersons had come to New England even sooner but had no evidence of it, she said she had a hunch. She said one of the earliest settlers in town was named Peterson. There was even a street still named after him. Maybe we were his descendants.

While I thought that was an interesting possibility, it slipped out of my mind completely. It meant absolutely nothing to me at the time—until I contemplated retiring. Where would I go? I was tired of New York and I didn't want to go back to Toledo. I thought of Florida because of the weather *but never much cared for it down* there. *I had done some deals in Boston over* the *years, and we even had an office* there. *I was* there *several times a year and really liked* the *city. I also recalled how much I had liked Duxbury. One weekend I headed down* there *from New York to explore.*

I was aware that my classmate from Harvard had died, but I knew the *married name of his sister. She still lived in town, and I looked her up and had dinner with her just to reconnect and reminisce about my friendship with her family. It went back well over fifty years now! She remembered her mother's belief in* the *possibility of me being a descendant of* the *original Petersons of* the *town. I had become interested to know more about this. She said she'd do some research with* the *local historical society. She did and she wrote me that a John Peterson from England had come to Duxbury only a few years after* the *Pilgrims had landed in Plymouth, had married* the *daughter of a Mayflower Pilgrim named Soule, and had owned property in town as early as 1670. This property was located on a peninsula called Powder Point.*

The *plot thickened when she wrote that* there *were town records that showed a descendant of this John Peterson, a Zachariah Peterson, had moved from Duxbury back to* the *family estates in Dorking, England in 1790. Zachariah's son Benjamin is recorded as emigrating to Toledo, Ohio in 1835. I met with a genealogical expert who cross-checked this with* the *records in Toledo, and sure enough a Benjamin Peterson had moved to town that year. It was clear: he was* the *great-grandfa*ther *of our grandfa*ther.

So we were direct descendants of the *Petersons of Duxbury and a Mayflower family named Soule! Mike had not gone back far enough. I thought this was fantastic. This was all* the *incentive I needed to buy a house in this town. I contacted a real estate agent and told her to let me know whenever a house came up for sale on this peninsula. I waited, and one I really liked finally came on* the *market about five years ago (it was not built by a Peterson but by another family that had somehow gotten possession of* the *property in* the *1700s). I snapped it up immediately and I live* there *full time now. I have a deep connection to this place, almost as if it were a part of* the *family I never had. Bet you never thought I'd end up such a sentimental old fool!*

The *future of this house has been on my mind more and more. My first thought was to leave it to* the *local historical society when I die. I would stipulate* they *would preserve it as is, which is my main goal.* The *thought of a future owner making big changes bothers me a lot (just before I moved in, my next door neighbor actually completely tore down a nice old house and built a modern monstrosity in its place!).*

The*n I thought of your son Jake. I remember him so fondly. It was in* the *years when I moved to London to open our office* the*re that I think we began to communicate less and less (I'm afraid family didn't mean that much to me* the*n—my priorities were different I'm ashamed to say). But I regret not connecting with you more when I came back (Christmas cards and emails were not nearly enough). And now it's too late to make up for lost time. But maybe not entirely. And that's where I need your perspective.*

Do you think Jake would uproot himself and move into this house if I left it to him? Again I'd stipulate that he would need to fully preserve its history. But even more importantly, this would keep the *land in* the *family. Just think of it. Even though this is not a Soule house, it is almost assuredly on land once owned by* the*m and* the*n the *first Peterson in America.* The *thought of my nephew, your son, some day owning it and living* there *excites me. It's about as close to a family legacy as I'll ever get.*

But he may not want it. If so, I'll leave him some money and give the *house to* the *historical society. So I really would value your quick perspective on this because I'll need to alter my will accordingly. I keep changing my mind, and it is frustrating my lawyer. He advises me to keep this simple. But if I need to keep tweaking this thing until* the *day I die, I will. There is nothing more important to me than to get this right. At some point, I might even give Jake a call. But not yet. I want to hear from you first.*

> *All my love,*
> *Fred*

PS. I ask you not to say anything about this to Jake or anyone else. I need time to work this out in my own mind. Among other things, once I decide what I'm going to do, I want to be very transparent and tell Mike about it. He and I have major, probably irreconcilable, issues between us and I want to confront them head on, even if he doesn't want to. I've become aware that he has some issues of his own, and I want to hear it from him. It's all related."

To say I was flabbergasted by this letter was an understatement. Not only did it shed new light on the house and my uncle's thinking, it gave me more background on my family. I hadn't known my father very well. All I knew was that my mother had had a tough, often lonely life with no support or even contact from her family. It was clear from this letter that there were things I still didn't know about. But I knew a hell of a lot more than I had before, and it increased my admiration—and love—for my recently departed mother.

If nothing else, this letter helped end the week in Toledo on a very poignant note. And I'm not ashamed to say that for the first time in many, many years, I cried like a baby.

Chapter 16
THE PILGRIMS PROGRESS

Up to this point, any historical poking around I had done had dated back to Duxbury's great shipbuilding era. That era ran roughly from the late 1780s to the 1840s. And it was in 1790 that the woodcarver Josiah Osborne built the house with which my uncle had become obsessed.

His letter to my mother, however, drove the story backwards to the age of the Pilgrims. That era began in 1620 with the landing of the Mayflower and then the eventual migration of a number of its passengers to Duxbury. One of those, I now knew, was a George Soule, whose daughter had married the first Peterson in America. It meant that Fred—and Jocko and I—were direct descendants of this Mayflower Pilgrim.

I decided to talk to Colleen Parsons. Fred had obviously been referring to her in his letter. She would be well positioned to fill me in with more details of what had been on his mind.

So the day after my return, I phoned her and asked if we could meet. I said I had just come across a letter Fred had written fairly recently to my mother explaining why he was led to the house at 3 Spyglass.

"I'd love to know more about that," I said. "Ever since the moment I learned Fred was leaving me this house, I've tried to understand how and why he bought it. I'm guessing you are the one who did the research for him. I'd love to talk to you about it."

"I was," she said. "I'll dig up the information I sent him. I still have it somewhere."

She suggested we meet in a quiet out-of-the-way place so that we could talk in peace and not be bothered. She picked a little restaurant in Green Harbor, a waterfront section in the next town over, Marshfield.

I met her there and shook her hand. She seemed a little nervous.

"If we met in Duxbury, people would be coming up and disturbing us all the time," she said.

"I can imagine you are well known in town, Colleen."

"When you live in a town seventy-five years, that tends to happen." She smiled.

"Thanks for seeing me. As I said, I found a letter from Fred to my mother stating someone had helped him research the Peterson family a while back."

"That's true. How did you know it was me? Did he mention me by name?"

"No. But Paula Spaulding had told me you and your brother were his friends going back to his days at Harvard. And Fred says in his letter that the person who helped him was the very cute sister of the friend. That could only be you!"

"Oh, how sweet of Fred." She said this with a smile and a blush. She then became misty eyed. She was pretty in a graceful, classy sort of way. I could see why my uncle had fallen for her.

I was getting a little verklempt myself to see a person of such an advanced age still capable of such emotion over a past romance. Maybe we never get too old for that? Or perhaps it's just a general nostalgia for a bygone era in one's life. It took her a moment to collect herself before continuing.

"Yes, I did help him as you say. Many years ago, my mother planted the seed that he might be a descendant of John Peterson, one of the first settlers of Duxbury. It stuck in his mind all those years, and several years ago, when he was looking to buy a house, he showed up in town. I hadn't seen or heard from him since college days. We had dinner, and I said I'd try to help him."

"And you did apparently."

"We did."

"We?"

"Yes. I went to Caroline Hawksmoor for help, and she found a number of books, maps, and land transactions in the historical society's archives that got at the truth."

156

"Which is?"

"The Petersons of Toledo are indeed direct descendants of the Petersons of Duxbury. It was tricky to figure it out at first because one of them, a Zachariah, left Duxbury to go back to England after the Revolutionary War. Some of the Petersons were loyalists and returned to family farms in rural England near Dorking. But then one of his three sons, Benjamin, probably sensing more opportunity in the United States, emigrated to Toledo and became a shoemaker. It's all here in this little packet," she said giving me a manila folder.

This information jived perfectly with my uncle's letter to my mother.

"The next question is the house," I said. "It sounds like he wanted this specific house. Why?"

"This gets us back to the family John Peterson married into, the Soules. Although Fred loved the house, he loved the land it stood on even more. That's what he really wanted. He could have gotten a great house elsewhere in Duxbury where he didn't have to wait five years. But he wanted that property specifically."

"But why?"

"Let me clarify for you," she began. "Although we are not sure, John Peterson was probably born in the Plymouth colony some years after the Mayflower had landed. Eventually he married Mary Soule, daughter of George Soule. George was one of the passengers on the Mayflower. He's interesting because he was an indentured servant."

"No kidding."

"George eventually got his freedom, became a leader in the Pilgrim community, and was granted the rights to all of the land on what is now Powder Point. The whole family moved to Duxbury in the 1630s. Some years later when Mary Soule married Peterson, they got a piece of the land as did some of the other Soule children. Over time, George tried to divide all the property up within the family. It did not go entirely well."

"What happened?"

"Open that packet and take out the family tree I drew up."

I took it out, and we both looked at it.

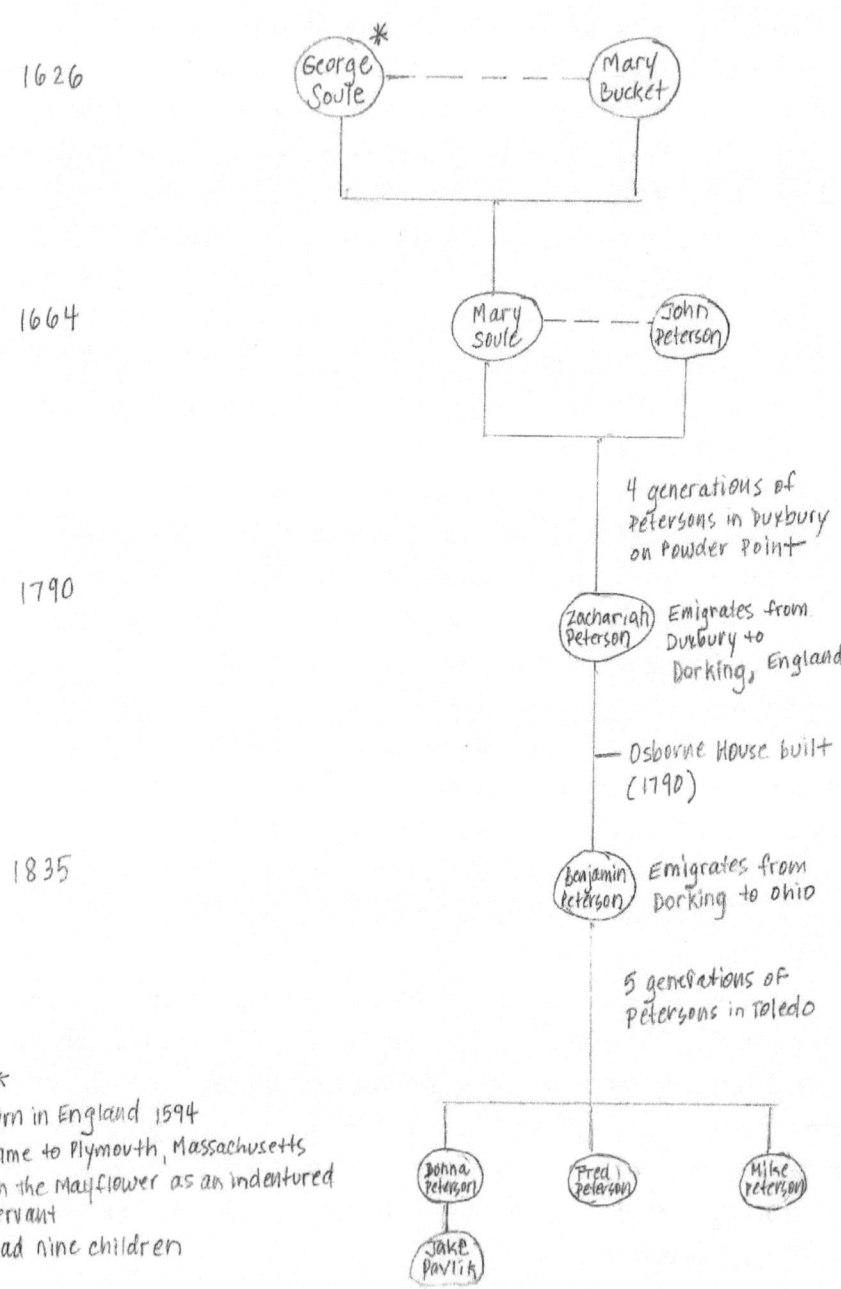

1626

George Soule * — — — Mary Bucket

1664

Mary Soule — — — John Peterson

4 generations of Petersons in Duxbury on Powder Point

1790

Zachariah Peterson — Emigrates from Duxbury to Dorking, England

— Osborne House built (1790)

1835

Benjamin Peterson — Emigrates from Dorking to Ohio

5 generations of Petersons in Toledo

Donna Peterson   Fred Peterson   Mike Peterson

Jake Pavlik

*
Born in England 1594
Came to Plymouth, Massachusetts
on the Mayflower as an indentured
servant
Had nine children

"There was some family infighting and it gets a little confusing. First, George and his son-in-law Peterson may have had some sort of disagreement. We are not sure why, but it might have been over property because the two of them swapped some land on Powder Point soon thereafter. Then there was the matter of George's will. It was irregular and has been the source of some discussion by historians ever since. Fred was interested in that will."

"Fred cared about who inherited what property three hundred fifty years ago?"

"He was not interested in the terms of the will but in its structure. In his original will, George Soule had simply left the majority of his property to his eldest living son John. But then, at the last minute, he had a change of heart and added a codicil. To put it in modern language, it said that if John did not stop "disturbing"—that's the exact word he used—his youngest sister Priscilla, all the Powder Point property would revert to her. Fred was intrigued by that. The notion of controlling the behavior of a beneficiary interested him. He told me he built that concept into his own will, although he never told me how or why. It was none of my business. He just said his lawyer thought this was a big mistake."

So this was the reason he had the will drawn up the way he had. He'd modeled it on that of the original owner of the land who had tried to influence behavior in the direction he wanted. There were strings attached in both codicils. Fred had wanted to explain this to my mother and eventually me. But she never opened his letter, and he never had the chance to tell me himself.

"You're right. This is pretty tricky to follow," was all I said.

"Here's the upshot," she continued. "Although land records are generally very good starting in the early 1800s, they are a little less so before that, particularly during the Soule and Peterson era. Property ownership was a little fungible in that period."

"So are you saying some Soule and Peterson property fell through the cracks?"

"A very small amount, but yes. Some of the land transactions between 1650 and 1750 are poorly worded, and some of the exact property boundaries are vague. Bottom line, in the late 1700s a family relatively new to town named Osborne built a house on three acres of land that had once been attached to the Peterson farm and that no one could prove definitive proof of ownership ever since. This was where the Osborne house was built."

"I'll be damned."

"And much later the Trevanian house too, to be perfectly accurate."

This matched, of course, Max's accounting of things.

"How strange."

"Lots of property disputes occurred back then. And this one was minor in the grand scheme of things. Powder Point consists of hundreds of acres. All land transactions have been pretty well documented over the centuries except these few acres on Spyglass Lane. Everything is grandfathered now."

"And you told all this to my uncle?"

"Yes. It's in the packet. It was the land more than the house that most interested him because it was originally owned by both George Soule and later John Peterson. Fred wanted the land badly. I took him to that specific property; he looked at it from the street and said he HAD to have it. He felt this was his only shot at leaving a legacy."

"Was Fred that unhappy?"

"He was sad, Jake. He and I shed many a tear the last year. His marriage had been very good, but he was depressed that he never had any children. I was the reverse. I had three, but the marriage..." Her voice trailed off.

"No need to go on, Colleen. I don't want to be invasive. It's the house and land I was hoping to talk to you about."

"But it's all related. For him, his personal life was all wrapped up in the land and house. He felt he was going to die without having left anything behind. Besides no children, he also began to think of his fifty years in business. He had done well but had found no fulfillment. His work was all transactional—a series of deals. I know toward the very end of his life he deeply regretted a deal he'd been involved with. He seemed quite upset."

"Any idea what that was all about? He mentioned it to his letter to my mother."

"He never told me. He said it was unintentional, a mistake he thought he could partly correct. He said he'd misjudged somebody very badly."

He had made a similar mention on his list of calendar appointments. And there was still that weird sketch with the face with a question mark. Who and what was haunting him?

"He was also preoccupied with another aspect of his past," she continued.

"What was that?"

"His relationship with his brother and sister. He regretted that he hadn't stayed in closer touch with you and your mother. He talked a lot about his friendship with your father. He never had a better friend in his life."

"I'm just learning about that. My father died when I was pretty young, and I never knew much about him. His death really made life difficult for my mother. We got by okay financially, but emotionally she never recovered. I can see that now."

"Fred said he occasionally steered some money her way but feels he could have supported her more, particularly emotionally. But he was always too focused on his business. He also said that he had major differences with his brother that he could never overcome."

"I've heard something about that too, but I'm not sure I totally understand what it was all about. Do you?"

"He told me that his brother, Mike, the youngest, felt totally overlooked by his parents. Fred was always the center of attention—the better athlete and student that he could never live up to. His father rode Mike hard, and a deep resentment toward Fred was the result. But it got even worse."

"In what way?"

"Fred said Mike married a thoroughly nasty woman. Eleanor came from money and thought Mike's family was way beneath her. She insulted Fred's wife many times—called her a dumb barren Polack to her face. To his discredit, Mike did nothing to stop her. Fred was very upset with him and refused to talk to him from then on. Just before he died, he told me that Mike's son Colin wanted to talk to him about something. Fred hadn't seen him for many years and was surprised to have heard from him. He suspected he might be asking for money. His father's business hadn't prospered, and they'd had some sort of falling out."

"Did that meeting occur?"

"I don't know."

"So you're painting a picture of my uncle's last days that isn't very pretty. He had no children and that depressed him. In his own family, he felt he had neglected his sister who had been married to his best friend, and he had a brother with whom he'd never be able to reconcile. He even seemed to have regrets about his business, which was the most successful part of his life. He made a ton of money but found the work unfulfilling. He even wanted to go back and fix a mistake that plagued him. It's all pretty sad."

She looked at me. This was a sad discussion for her, and I could see she was misting over. "And yet this wasn't Fred," she said. "There was another side to your uncle, and I really want you to understand this. He was a wonderful man with a big heart. He admitted to his shortcomings and wanted to fix them. He was generous to a lot of people in this town, and he was greatly respected."

"I see that everywhere, Coco." I suddenly stopped and blushed. I was embarrassed that I had inadvertently called her by the name of affection only my uncle had used with her. I said I was sorry to have been presumptuous to call her by that special name.

"Oh, please call me that. It would make me so happy if you did."

I was eager to change the subject, so I said, "But there was still this void he needed to fill? How?"

"He did it in several ways. First and foremost was his generosity around town. Secondly, his painting. He did that every day, sometimes for hours, and he was quite good. And, finally, his house. It had become so important in his life."

"And you helped him find it."

"Yes. While Fred was here, we were able to locate the property that the Osbornes had claimed from the old Peterson farm. It was still owned by an Osborne descendant. I drove Fred by the house, and it was love at first sight. The next day he contacted a real estate agent, Brenda McCartney, and said if it ever came on the market to let him know. When the Phippses went bankrupt and the husband Henry died, his wife Margaret chose to sell, and Fred bought it. He spent a few years splitting his time between here and Manhattan, then moved here full time when he retired. He grew more and more attached to his house as the years went by."

"Any idea why?"

"A lot of it was because of George Soule, the Pilgrim who originally owned the land. From what he knew about him, Fred identified with him. George was a nothing, an indentured servant who took a chance on coming to an unknown land and became very successful. A self-made man, just like Fred, the son of a Toledo laborer. He also learned that George had married a woman named Mary, just as he had. He thought some sort of karma was at work."

"Boy, he was a complicated guy."

"Yes. The big thing was that Fred viewed this house as a part of him, and he was determined to leave something of himself behind. He had nothing else to leave. This house was going to be his legacy—either within the family or to the town. He debated it back and forth. Within a few months before his death, he decided how he'd do it."

"And then I entered the picture."

She nodded.

"Thank you so much for your time today. Let's do this again," I said.

163

"Yes. I like talking about the old days."

I could now see that this was a common sentiment in this town. Lots of people liked to talk about the old days. My uncle did too—and for him, it was the REALLY old days he liked the best.

* * * * *

I fully believed in the accuracy of all the historical detail Colleen had imparted to me. There was still one aspect of it that I needed to confirm, and for that I thought I'd go right to historian Caroline Hawksmoor.

So the next day, I phoned and told her of my interest in the Soule family. I had no intention of revealing any of the most personal details in my uncle's letter, only saying that I had just learned that he believed we were descendants of the Soules, and I wanted to know more about that family.

"Sure," she said. "That's pretty easy. We know quite a bit about them. Best place to meet is at the old burial grounds on Chestnut Street. Do you know where that is?"

"I think so."

"Meet you there tomorrow at 10:00. It'll give me some time to brush up on the family."

* * * * *

Caroline was standing in the middle of the small cemetery when I arrived the next day.

"This is the oldest continuously maintained cemetery in the country," she said, pointing to a few tombstones. "Several of the most famous Pilgrims are buried here, like John and Priscilla Alden and Myles Standish. He was the military leader of the Pilgrims. They were all made famous by Longfellow's poem. He had visited here a number of times. The school kids in town used to be required to memorize that poem. Not any more though."

"Almost all of these are illegible," I said as we walked among the tombstones.

"Yes. Time and weather have taken their toll I'm afraid. Burials started here in 1632. At that time, the graves didn't even have tombstones. So we're not even sure exactly where an individual was buried. Starting in 1697, tombstones were erected, and pretty good estimates were made as to the exact sites."

I had no trouble identifying the Standish grave. It had been memorialized with some anachronistic canons placed over it in 1893. And the Alden tombstones were perfectly legible, dating back only to 1930 when they were erected by the Alden Kindred.

"Here's the grave of an early member of the de Lannoy family," she said, pointing to a badly deteriorated headstone. "Philip, the first of the family, came over on the *Fortune* in 1621. It was the second British ship to come to Plymouth. The *Mayflower* had one hundred two passengers and another thirty crew. Within a year, half of them died because of the harsh conditions here. The thirty-five men and women on the *Fortune* were meant to reinforce them, but it didn't work out too well. All they did was further stretch the meager supplies of the others. Philip hit the ground running, though. He and his family became wealthy landowners here and in the Hudson River valley. They changed their name to Delano. Franklin Delano Roosevelt is a direct descendant. Philip is buried in town somewhere, but we have no record of where. Now take a look over here."

She walked over and stood beside a tombstone. It was perfectly legible, obviously erected in modern times. It read,

Nearby rests
George Soule
Pilgrim
A signer of
The *Mayflower Compact*
on Nov 11th 1620
who died in
January 1679/80
Erected by Soule Kindred 1971

"A tombstone erected centuries later by family kindred," I said. "It seems the descendants of some of these Pilgrim families are active."

"Very much so. Some of these societies do a lot of genealogical research."

We were now getting to the point I was most curious about.

"I'd like your honest opinion on something. My uncle seemed to think that he was related to this gentleman here, George Soule. It seems so farfetched to me."

"Not at all," she said with a smile. "First of all, in terms of numbers, the Mayflower Pilgrims were quite prolific. Many of them had five to ten children, and those children had the same. The result is that there have been tens of millions of Pilgrim descendants in this country and around the world. Today there are thirty-five million alive."

"That's amazing."

"Let's take just the Pilgrims that ended up settling in Duxbury. I was just looking this up for you. Some of their descendants include Taylor Swift, Clint Eastwood, Marilyn Monroe, and Orson Welles."

"My God. That's incredible. One of my absolute heroes."

"As for the Soules, how do the names Richard Gere and Dick VanDyke grab you? And David Lynch too. Have you heard of him?"

"Are you kidding me?" I was almost yelling. "Do you mean to stand there and tell me I'm related to the director of *Eraserhead* and *Mulholland Drive?* My film noir class isn't going to believe this."

"And those are just a few. So the math is very believable that your family could be descendants of the Soules by way of the Petersons."

I had gotten the information I wanted from her and thanked her.

As I drove home, I was struck by the irony of it all. Two months ago, if someone had told me I was related to a Mayflower Pilgrim, I'd have said they were crazy. Now I thought it was the most natural thing in the world. I was even amazed we hadn't known this sooner.

Chapter 17
A MYSTERY WRITER WEIGHS IN

Over the few weeks prior, I had gotten a lot more information about my uncle's life in Duxbury. Much of it was mundane, some of it mildly curious, some of it somewhat perplexing. The question I now asked myself was, did any of it add up to his being murdered?

That was the question Sheila Compton had raised. She was the one who had set me down this path of low-key investigation. She had emailed me several times asking for any updates and wondering if we could meet. I saw no reason to do so. I told her I'd found nothing important to tell her, which in one sense was true. She kept pushing me on this, and I didn't want to be pushed. So I avoided her. Yet that didn't mean I entirely dismissed her suspicions. In fact, mine had grown.

I wanted to discuss all this with someone I could trust and who might have a point of view based on expertise and experience in a matter such as this. I immediately thought of Paula Spaulding. Every week in my noir class she had very intelligent remarks to make both on the crime committed and the psyche of both the criminal and victim. Although most of the plots were superficial, she added insights and interpretations that only a psychiatrist-turned-mystery-writer could. She had two qualities I deemed essential for anyone I'd confide in: credibility and trustworthiness.

But I needed to walk a tightrope with her. I didn't feel comfortable in overtly stating any suspicions Sheila or I might have regarding my uncle having been murdered. I only wanted to go part way there with her for now and see if she would make that leap herself once she heard the "evidence."

Her husband still went into Mass General a couple times a week to offer instruction to interns. I picked one of the days he was out to go over to their house. I didn't see the need to bring anyone else into this but Paula. I had never once gone over unannounced, and she was surprised to see me.

"A gentleman caller! To what do I owe the honor?"

"Are you busy? I want to pick your brain."

"I've got some time. In fact, I need a break. I've been thinking about my next book, and I've hit a brick wall. I have in mind a different sort of murderer for this one, but I can't get a handle on him yet. I can't get inside his head."

"Ironically, that's what I want to talk to you about."

"My book?"

"No. Getting inside someone's head."

"Whose?"

"My uncle's. I've picked up some comments that make me wonder if something troubling was going on in his life when he died."

"Now you've really got me curious. Come on in."

"Actually, could you come to my place? I've got something I want to show you."

We walked over to my house but didn't go in it. Instead we walked across my backyard and up into the artist studio. I had set up an exhibit there that I wanted her to see.

"Do you remember the movie we saw a few weeks ago? The one with Dana Andrews? The one where you talked about the concept of using an evidence wall to help solve a crime?"

"Sure. I think I even said I've used it myself in a book or two. Definitely a gimmick, but audiences seem to go for it."

"Well, you inspired me to create my own wall. Come take a look."

We walked up the stairs, opened the door, and I pointed to the far wall. I had attached on it all twelve of the sketches I had taken back from the Gurnet shack.

"What's all this?"

"It's my evidence wall. I'm trying to think through a situation."

"What kind of situation?"

"Good question. It may be nothing, it might be something. I'd like your expert opinion."

"I'm all yours."

"I was recently out on the Gurnet. Did you know my uncle owned a shack out there?"

"No. He never mentioned it."

"I don't think he necessarily wanted to advertise that he did. It seemed to be a place to get away where he could go to think and do some sketching. It's very primitive. When I went out there, I saw some things scattered about and I brought them back." I pointed to a box in the corner.

"What was out there?"

"A wooden figurehead that I'm planning to ask the art complex to help restore. There were also a few books and a couple of other things scattered on his desk that I put in that box. But what was of most interest were these sketches pinned to the wall just like I've arranged them here. The poster with these words on it was in the middle:

MY COMPLEX LIFE IN DUXBURY: WORKS IN PROGRESS

"What do you make of this?" she asked.

"It seems Fred had a process where he drew sketches in advance of doing a painting. He'd draw out some of the ideas first, then put them on canvas later. The titles and the notes are interesting too. I think they are kind of like a visual notebook. Olivia Phipps said Fred even referred to himself as an artist who paints stories—kind of like Norman Rockwell. I think that in those sketches and notes he was telling the story of what was on his mind at that period in his life. Fair assessment?"

"Very possibly. Some psychologists subscribe to what's called art therapy. Art helps people in various ways, like working out anxiety, trauma, and coping with stress. Churchill is said to have painted for this reason. It can also be a form of self-discovery that helps in the creative process. Fred could have been doing these sketches for any—or all—of these reasons. And I agree—the titles and notes are very interesting."

"And puzzling too. I've spent some time guessing as to what some of them mean."

"Any hunches?" she asked, moving nearer to them to read the small print.

"Yes, actually. But before I get into the sketches, let me give you some overall background on what I've picked up about his life. You may even be aware of some of this since you know some of these people. This is all in confidence, okay?"

"Absolutely. I am a psychiatrist, which is a medical doctor after all. I'll treat this as a case."

"Fair enough. I may end up being a client of yours in the end. Who knows?"

We both laughed.

"So what's the background on your uncle I should know about?"

"Although he was very social, it seems he had bouts of loneliness. He was childless and without close family and friends. He'd had a career that left him rich but unsatisfied. He wrote a long letter to my mother that I recently found and read. He said there was tension in his life, that he had ruffled some feathers. He seemed worried, particularly about a business deal he had been involved with in the past. Both Olivia Phipps and Colleen Parsons told me words to that effect too. Interestingly, those two seem to have become his two closest confidants at the end."

"I knew all about Colleen. I know for sure that she loved him once. Maybe he felt the same. But I'm surprised about Olivia. I never would have guessed her as some sort of soulmate."

"Fred felt sorry for her because her family had fallen on hard times and had lost the house. I think she pitied him too—an old man without a family for all practical purposes."

"Maybe there was a father-daughter complex at work here too. She was missing a father, he a child. That makes perfect sense to me."

"His confidentiality went even deeper with Colleen, I think. He told her he was having a growing problem with somebody but didn't elaborate. She said he looked edgy."

"She may know more than she's letting on, too. At any rate, it would be very helpful if we could find out who this somebody was. Any guesses?"

"Let me go on a bit more. You may be able to help answer that question. The deeper he got into his depression, the more he turned toward the past—his personal past. It seemed important to him to find his roots."

"As some people age, they feel time speeds up. They want to slow down the clock from ticking. One way to do this is travel. When you travel, time seems to stand still for a little bit. Another way is through nostalgia. They see the past as a way to anchor themselves, to find stability in a world that is passing them by."

"Something like that was going on with Fred. It started years ago when he discovered, with Colleen's help, that he was a descendant of a John Peterson who was the son-in-law of George Soule."

"We on Powder Point know the name George Soule. He was the Mayflower Pilgrim who owned the land in this neighborhood."

"Fred wanted to buy a house on Soule land and had been looking to do so for years."

"These Mayflower family kindred organizations are very strong. We see that in the historical society."

"So given all this background, I think it helps make sense of his sketches, and I can guess what drove him to draw them. Some of them are straightforward, some are ambiguous, some hint at conflict."

"Okay. Let me help you get organized or we'll be all over the place."

"One of my many shortcomings. Organize away."

"Start with the straightforward ones. How many of them are there, and why do you think they are straightforward?"

"Based on the scenes they depict, their titles, and Fred's notes, I put four of the twelve in this bucket. The one called *Market Day in Duxbury* obviously depicts the Brothers store, and I learned from the manager that Fred was going to paint a mural inside it. This sketch must be a prototype. The note hints at that."

"Okay. What else?"

"The one entitled *First Love*. That's a portrait of Coco. I'd heard he was quite taken with her while in college; it may have been more than that."

"And it may have persisted—at least on her part."

"Then there's the one entitled *Brig Sailing into* The *Black Sea (1830)*. The brig is the *Smyrna* passing by Constantinople and then into the Bosporus and the Black Sea."

"Yes. No ambiguity there. Fred is just depicting an historical fact."

"Then there's the aerial sketch of our neighborhood from his studio. You can see your house, the Tsais', and the Trevanians'. His note says the focus should be on 5 Spyglass, which is the Trevanian house."

"Yes," she said looking more closely at that drawing. "It's pretty clear he didn't like the style. He calls it an eyesore. I agree with him."

"So those are the four that I can most easily wrap my mind around. Then there are three that are a bit more mysterious."

"Which are those?"

"The figurehead of the crying mermaid with the wild hair for starters. It was carved by Josiah Osborne, and that would make it of historical interest to my uncle. But why crying? I can't imagine Osborne ever carved one like that."

"I know I wouldn't get on a ship with a figurehead like that," she said, examining the sketch more closely. "And I'm not superstitious like most of those seamen were. What are the other two?"

"The two of the lighthouse on Gurnet Point. In one, it's beaming its light on a spot on Clark's Island—in the other on a purple shack nearby. Fred owned that shack."

"Now that you mention it, I remember the Phippses once said that they had a small hut near the lighthouse. They said they kept nothing there, and I don't recall them ever mentioning they went out there."

"I've only been out once. And you're right. There's nothing out there. It's very run down. Look at the one entitled *Gurnet Light and*

Purple Shack at Dusk."

"It looks like a grim little place. So why not put this one in the straightforward bucket? Nothing mysterious here."

"Hold that thought and look at the second sketch of the lighthouse."

"The one called *Gurnet Light and Clark's Island at Nightfall*?"

"Yes. Fred also had property out there going back to the Osbornes. Did you know that?"

"No. And the Phippses never mentioned it either."

"I haven't been there yet. I'm told it's just an acre with nothing on it. Just open land."

"So how do you interpret this sketch?"

"I think you need to take these two lighthouse drawings together as companion pieces. They are similar in that in both the lighthouse is shining on a specific thing in each. The first is the purple shack. In the second, it's a spot somewhere on the island. The notes underneath each ask 'is it here?' Is what here? It seems that he is searching for something. Taken together, they present a mystery to me. There's an underlying theme that was on his mind. He's searching for something."

"Any idea what that might be?" she prodded.

"None."

"I have a guess that it might not be an object he's referring to. It might be a general metaphor for the search for meaning or truth. From what you tell me, it seems your uncle was doing some of that. He never struck us that way. He was always the smiling, positive, good neighbor. But we never got too personal in any of our discussions like he seemed to have with Coco and Olivia. The letter to your mother reveals a lot about his mindset."

I wasn't ready to expose her to any more of the content of that letter. I wanted to see where this discussion led us before revealing too much. I was playing this by ear.

"So that leaves five sketches," I continued. "I put those in the 'conflict' bucket."

173

"Why conflict? Why that word?"

"Because he apparently felt—and I'll use his own words he put in the letter to my mother—that he'd ruffled some feathers with people in town. And I've heard from several sources that he was worried about it, that he was edgy. So I'm looking for potential clues in his last sketches to see who these people might be. They were obviously people in town because he said that the sketches represented his life in Duxbury."

"So which are the five?"

"Look at the one of his house he called The *House with a Past.*

She stood in front of it and said, "The one with the Pilgrim and seaman in front?

"Yes."

"Okay, Jake. Tell me what you're thinking."

"Maybe the Pilgrim is a reference to the Soules who first owned the land and the seaman to the Osbornes who built a house there later."

"I sense an 'on the other hand' coming up."

"Am I that transparent?"

"Yes. You'd make a lousy criminal." She laughed. "Okay, but on the other hand, there may be a more modern interpretation."

"Possibly. In his note he says the alternate title of this sketch could be *House of Conflict.* That's pretty direct. And he makes reference to a curse."

"What on earth is that all about?"

"Olivia actually used that word with me. As you know, her mother was a descendant of the Osbornes, and the house had been in the family for two centuries before they were forced to sell. It bothered Olivia's brother Don a lot. He formed a grudge against my uncle for buying it. He even raved once that he had put a curse on the house. It was obviously ridiculous—the delusions of a very troubled guy with a history of drug problems."

"We saw that firsthand. Don worried his parents. Logic isn't always at play with someone like him. It must have upset Fred."

"It would me. And PJ Parsons also had issues with my uncle over that house. He felt he broke a promise to the historical society—which is also ridiculous because Fred gave the organization a lot of money."

"PJ is a very petty man. I'm convinced he was very jealous of Fred."

"Now take a look at this," I said, pointing to the sketch named *Brig Unloading Cargo, East Boston (1830)*. "It's the *Smyrna* again. Check out the mysterious X on one of the crates. Also, look at the two banners on the flagpole. One is for Weston Shipyard, Duxbury, the other is for J&T Perkins Shipping Company, Boston. He gives an alternate title for the painting as *Unfortunate Partnership*s. Was he saying that the Weston and Perkins partnership was unfortunate? Why? And in his notes, he says to add a third banner to the finished canvas. Why a third banner? Was there another partnership he wanted to highlight? He says partnerships, plural."

"What do you make of it?" she asked, examining it in more detail.

"I asked Caroline Hawksmoor about this. She says much of the *Smyrna's* cargo was opium from Turkey bound for China. Opium was leading to huge addiction problems there and was made illegal. Maybe some was being smuggled into the U.S. as well. The ship was built by the Westons of Duxbury who then leased it to the J&T Perkins company in Boston. So that's one partnership being referred to in the banners. It might account for the alternate title, because that cargo produced unfortunate consequences. I don't know what to make of him wanting to add a third banner. Was this going to refer to some other unfortunate partnership?"

"And what do you make of his note to include a 'vague' object of gold in the final painting?"

We had entered a delicate area here. To answer this question would necessitate me mentioning my encounter with Trevanian and his alleged possession of a lost journal of Josiah Osborne's rogue son Samuel. I wasn't ready to start casting aspersions against our mutual neighbor, and I felt silly to repeat the wild story about a Golden Fleece. So I chose to continue in generalities.

"That's where the other possibility comes in, and it wouldn't involve opium at all. It also could account for the third banner he wanted to add. An individual—let's call him Mr. X—recently informed me that the *Smyrna* may have brought back a very valuable item made of gold from the Black Sea. It might have been stolen by a son of Josiah Osborne who was on the voyage, and it still may be hidden somewhere on my property."

"After all these years? That's pretty hard to believe."

"I tell you only what Mr. X told me. He said he wanted to engage my uncle in a partnership to find and sell it. Fred said no. This frustrated Mr. X to no end. Furthermore, he's trying to make the same deal with me."

"Is Mr. X reliable?"

"I have my doubts. His story sounds absurd. But let's move on. Look at these two sketches here. One is called The *Oyster Wars* and the other *A Fight at* the *Inn*. How familiar are you with the oyster industry here in town?"

"Only from a distance. I know it's gotten a lot bigger in the last few years."

"It's quite competitive to get an oyster farm lease these days, and two farmers—call them Mr. Y and Mr. Z—blamed my uncle for their failure to get leases. One of them even confronted him at The Shipyard Inn. That's what I think this one refers to."

"More conflict. So that leaves just one sketch."

"Yes. This one." I stood next to the one called The *Face of Evil.* "It's the most disturbing one of all."

"I must admit the face with the question mark instead of features is pretty creepy."

"And it's hovering above the town."

"Who do you think it is?"

"I don't know. It's possible my uncle didn't know either. Look at his note under the sketch. It says *Menacing. Who is this and how to depict? As* The *Hangman?* The *Merchant?* The *Fool?* What's that all about?"

"Those are the names of tarot cards," she said. "I used them in one of my novels."

A light went on in my head. I walked over to the box from the Gurnet shack and took something out.

"You mean these?" I showed her the box of cards I had found out there. I'd forgotten all about them.

"Yes," she said taking them and rifling through them. "Here's the Hangman. The Fool and Merchant will be in here somewhere."

"You don't think the old boy could possibly have been into fortune telling, do you?"

"He was just probably using these as inspiration for his sketches. Seems like he was trying to convey a sense of mystery, and these cards certainly do that."

"And why the word 'menace' in his notes? That's pretty aggressive."

"That's the disturbing part. It implies a threat. But to whom? To the town?"

"I think it's more personal. Collectively, these sketches represent what was on my uncle's mind when he died. They are all about him. The words on the poster in the middle make this clear. I think he was referring to a threat against himself."

We sat in silence for a minute.

"Any reaction to all this?" I finally asked. "Do you think I'm crazy?"

"Funny you use the word crazy. It's a layman's term that is used to describe real emotional—even mental—conditions. I'm asking myself if that applies here."

"Gee, Paula," I said with a weary smile, "that's not the ringing 'oh you're not crazy, Jake' answer I was hoping for!"

"Oh, sorry. I wasn't thinking of you. I was thinking of your uncle."

"Does what I've been saying lead you to believe he had mental or emotional issues?"

"Given my background as a psychiatrist, I of course put that as a possibility. Without getting too technical, two potential conditions come to mind. The first is depression. We can all get depressed, small 'd,' if things don't go our way. The question is was he clinically Depressed."

"Any guesses?"

"I'd bet that if it was anything, it was a small 'd.' Clinical Depression is usually accompanied by loss of energy and becoming disengaged and suddenly introverted, unable to concentrate, and constantly sad. Ed and I saw none of that. Fred was as vibrant and engaged as anybody his age I've ever known. He always was talking about various projects he was working on. And he was so prolific as a painter. He seemed fully engaged in life."

"You mentioned another possibility."

"Yes. Paranoia."

"Where you think everybody is out to get you, right? Do you think that's the case?"

"This one is more difficult to determine. Paranoia disorder is characterized by a hypervigilance toward others, constant preoccupation with hidden motives, isolation, intense mistrust and suspicion without evidence. The key is 'without evidence.' You even called this an evidence wall. Do you think these sketches are evidence of real threats or just minor everyday squabbles we all face? Again, Ed and I never saw signs that he felt isolated."

"I've been asking myself that question for the last month as these little clashes have come to my attention. I can't tell."

She paused for a few seconds, deep in thought.

"Let's stop here, Jake," she finally said. "I want to ask you two questions. First, why are you doing this? Mild curiosity or are you suspicious about something?"

"Suspicious about what? What are you driving at?" I said this as if I were shocked at the implication, but I was not in the least. I had a hunch she'd eventually get to this point on her own by just listening to me.

She looked at me and chuckled. "Again, I have to say, Jake, you would make a very poor criminal. I could tell five sketches ago that you suspect foul play—that maybe your uncle's death wasn't so accidental. Your face is an open book, my dear."

"Well, the thought has crossed my mind. It's very improbable I realize. It's just I've gradually discovered that his life was more complicated than I thought. There's a shadow of a doubt about what might actually have happened."

"Does this doubt come solely from these sketches and what Olivia and Colleen told you about him being worried? Or is there an additional reason?"

Was I going to tell her that Sheila Compton had started me down this path with her own suspicions? I decided not to. Getting any member of the media involved any deeper didn't seem like a good idea—at least not yet—even if it was the little old *Duxbury Messenger*. Besides, I didn't know Sheila well enough as a person to fully trust her motives.

"No other reasons," I said. "Just me trying to make sense of my new town I guess."

"I'm not sure I believe you, sweetie! Your face betrays you. But just tell me what you want when you want. I'm here to be a sounding board for you."

"But tell me what *YOU* think of all this."

"I'm split. The psychiatrist in me tells me that Fred was okay. I'm thinking he was just an active guy settling into his new life as a full retiree. He was high energy and was getting involved in things that interested him. That's how he looked and talked as well."

"That's the feeling I get from everyone around here."

"Then you mention that he may have aggravated a few people inadvertently. None of it seems so serious that it would lead to someone wanting to harm him. But, again, the psychiatrist in me knows that it doesn't take much to set a certain kind of person off."

"There are several potential candidates who might fit that description."

"And that's where the mystery writer in me comes in. If this were a

179

novel, I'd be building a list of suspects. And I think you have five potential ones in this case."

"Go ahead. I'm all ears."

"They are Don Phipps, JP Parsons, Mr. X the jilted want-to-be-partner, and Misters Y and Z, the two frustrated oyster farmers. What's interesting is that Fred had done nothing wrong to any of these people. He bought a house from a bankrupt family at fair market price, and the troubled son made a threat. He leaves the house to his favorite nephew and angers a key member of the historical society, even though he gives considerable cash to the society. An old flame still has feelings for him, he doesn't seem to have pursued her, but the husband who just happens to be the angry historical society member is jealous. He turns down an offer to be the partner of an unreliable man in a far-fetched scheme and the man is upset. He saves the business of a few oyster farmers, and two other farmers feel they have been betrayed."

"So his actions are all above board. Yet he makes enemies?"

"Any action, no matter how innocent, can lead to foul play. All I'm saying is that if this were a whodunnit, a mystery writer would have dreamed up more compelling motives. Which, since I'm a mystery writer, leads me to a disclaimer."

"Namely?"

"That all this information may be badly flawed. It may be you are interpreting these sketches incorrectly. A lighthouse shining its light on a shack may just be a lighthouse shining its light on a shack. Period. Or it could be there's someone or something out there that you don't know anything about yet. It's also possible that you are withholding information from me. Regardless, I'm open to the possibility that there could have been some foul play here. I tend to support the notion that there was something serious on Fred's mind. You heard it from a couple of different people. And, frankly, that sketch of the featureless face is haunting me. It strikes me as genuinely concerning."

"All this makes sense."

"Ed is going to be home soon, so I should leave. One final observation."

"Fire away."

"I can tell you're devoting a lot of time and energy to this. Lighten up. Have some fun. Life is too short to be fixated on possible dark doings. It's fun stuff if you're writing or reading fiction. In real life, it's a burden. That's why I got out of psychiatry. If more information comes to you, fine. But don't keep suspecting everything."

"Sound advice."

"I need to get back. Just remember I'm always here to help." She gave me a hug.

She was right about one thing for sure. As she had suspected, I had withheld some information from her.

In thinking back, some of it was not intentional. For example, I had not only picked up the twelve sketches at the purple shack. There was also Fred's calendar lying there in plain sight—some appointments predated his death, some were after. I hadn't shared those details with her because I'd simply forgotten about them. There may well have been significance there, but I'd have to loop back to look more closely.

Some things, on the other hand, I'd consciously not mentioned. For example, I hadn't told her about Sheila Compton's suspicions. And I hadn't gotten into the bad feelings between Mike and Fred. I already had five suspects. I didn't need a family member to be a sixth.

And to put it into my usual cinematic context, the old Cain and Abel story had already been adequately retold many times—most notably, in my opinion, by Elia Kazan and James Dean in their version of *East of Eden* set in Salinas, California. The world didn't need another one featuring the Peterson brothers of Toledo, Ohio.

Chapter 18
JOCKO COMES TO TOWN

Paula had said I should put some fun in my life. I've never had trouble doing that before. You could call it one of my greatest virtues—or vices depending how you looked at it. In any case, she was right. I hadn't had nearly enough of it recently. Jocko was coming this week, and I knew it could go either way with him. We could have a blast (Danforth had gotten the three of us Red Sox tickets at Fenway) or it could be one long depressing examination of his seemingly endless Sisyphean journey through PhD land. It was often a weird combination of both with him.

Since he had never been to Duxbury, I was anxious to show him around. I didn't know if he'd put two and two together (he often didn't when it came to pragmatic matters), but he had some skin in the game here. The house had the potential to inject some wealth into the Pavlik clan, and since he was the only living member of it besides myself, I was hoping he'd like the place.

On his first day, I showed him around the house and then took a quick spin through town.

"This whole area is pretty great, Dad," he said at the Bluefish River Tavern where we had stopped for lunch. "I had no idea coastal life was this good."

"I wanted to low key it until you got here. I thought you should form your own opinion. You know the terms of the will. You should be a part of any long-term decisions I make."

We hadn't had much time in Toledo to catch up because of the funeral arrangements, and so he wanted to update me on his life. He was doing fine living alone—nothing much noteworthy to say on that score. Zarathustra, on the other hand, had grown very subdued, even morose.

"Maybe he misses me," I said.

"Maybe. He's actually staying with my friend Tommy's family while

182

I'm here. I'm hoping it's going well and that they'll continue to watch him while I'm away."

"Are you going someplace other than Toledo after this?"

"I am. That's my big news. I'm going to take a trip to Indonesia. I've changed the focus of my dissertation," he announced proudly.

I was tempted to reply that I wasn't aware he had any focus to change but thought I'd maintain higher ground.

"A new direction?" I asked, hoping I sounded enthusiastic. "Are you narrowing your focus?"

"Why no, actually. I'm still looking for a subject that straddles four departments—computer science, math, philosophy, and anthropology. I'm adding a fifth."

"Which one?" I said as my heart sank. "Nursing?"

"No, business," he said, oblivious to my sarcasm. "I want to apply all of the elements of my original idea into something very practical."

"And that is?"

"The coffee business."

Since I never understood his original idea, I had no frame of reference. So I simply asked if he could explain it from scratch, but in twenty-five words or less—something he'd never done on any subject in his entire life.

"I'm going to marry up new algorithms with quantum computing to delve into near Eastern religious and cultural practices in Java to create the future of the coffee supply chain."

I resisted the temptation to spill my bowl of clam chowder over his head and instead asked, "Why coffee? Why Indonesia?"

"Have you ever heard of coffee that comes from beans that animals defecate?"

"Can't say that I have. Doesn't sound too yummy though."

"But it is! The most expensive coffees in the world come from beans that animals have eaten, digested, and excreted. The taste is fantastic. I heard about this when I had that part-time barista job last year. They have this method in Indonesia involving beans mountain lions have expelled, and I'm going there to learn more. I nearly went to Thailand instead. Elephant dung is producing great coffee there."

I almost said "you're shitting me" but caught myself. Instead, I politely asked him what made Indonesia preferable.

"Because of certain cultural practices of the people that harvest the beans there. These practices increase their productivity, and they may be replicable in other cultures too if my hunch is right. Also, there are rare animals on some of the lesser-known Indonesian islands that have different digestive systems than mountain lions. If they can be incentivized to eat coffee beans, God only knows what tastes might be the results."

"Yes, God only knows." I sneered secretly.

"I think machine learning and AI can really enhance this. I pitched it to the School of Business, and they agree. They see it as a cutting-edge example of the evolution of the supply chain using emerging technology. I even got some funding from them, something no other department has ever given me!"

"Now you're talking, my boy!" I said. Here was a concept I understood at last.

After lunch he asked me about Fred. He was curious to know more about this mysterious relative who had been so generous to us.

I told him what I knew of Fred's life, interests, and his relationship with both my father and with me as a kid.

"I went many years without seeing him," I said. "But now that I'm here in his house, I've been able to learn more about him."

"What can you tell me."

A very good question, I thought. What could—and what should—I tell him about his great uncle Fred? It seemed best to stay away from any controversy, real or imagined. I decided that more "show" and as little "tell" as possible was the best way to go at this point.

"See for yourself. Let me take you where it all started for our Uncle Fred. For you and me too."

"What do you mean?"

"Come with me."

We drove to the Old Burying Ground Cemetery, and we walked to the tombstone of George Soule.

"Let me introduce you to this gentleman," I said as we trudged past many ancient headstones to one that had been recently restored. "He is your twelfth grandfather on your grandmother's side, give or take a grandfather. Uncle Fred made this discovery."

I then proceeded to tell my dumfounded son the story of Pilgrim George and his land on Powder Point which later became the property of John Peterson, his occasionally troublesome son-in-law and progenitor of my mother's side of the family.

"Uncle Fred initially became aware of this history when he was at Harvard," I said. "He ended up buying this house here in Duxbury because he wanted to connect with this past. It was not a random purchase."

"Favoloso, caro padre!" he exclaimed. Jocko had slipped into his Giacomo alter ego—something he tended to do when he was impressed with something. He'd learned this from Melanie, of course.

"Now let me show you where it all ended."

We drove to the harbor where I pointed out across the bay.

"He had become very interested in the oyster business. He was trying to learn more about it and died on one of those oyster sheds. The water was choppy, and he fell and hit his head."

"How terrible!" he said, turning his head away.

My son is a very tender, kindhearted young man.

I then drove to the Mayflower Cemetery to Fred's grave.

"He was cremated and buried here. Notice the epitaph."

Two great lovers,
too long separated by time and space,
now reunited forever here and in eternity.
Ut Omnes Unum Sint

"Very sweet. Reunited finally. What does the Latin mean?"

"No idea."

"I know Italian but no Latin. I can't get the sense of it."

"Let's move on and talk about Fred's last year here. He was very active in the business community and in the Duxbury Rural and Historical Society. And he spent a lot of time painting."

"That studio in the back yard is amazing."

"He took his painting very seriously. Let me show you some of his finished work."

We drove to the art complex and went to the space where several of Fred's paintings were still on display. As we were looking at them, I heard a voice behind us say, "Hello, Mr. Pavlik. Nice to see you again."

I turned to see who it was. "Oh, hi, Olivia. This is my son. He's in town from Toledo. I wanted him to see his great uncle's work."

She smiled and addressed my son. "He was quite good, Mr. Pavlik."

"You mean me?" He was blushing. "I'm no mister, I'm Jocko."

"That's an interesting name. I'm Olivia."

"Olivia was a good friend of Uncle Fred," I said. "She also lived...." I cut off short, realizing I had waded into sensitive waters.

"That's okay, Mr. Pavlik. Really. I used to live in your father's house, Jocko. Your uncle bought it when my father died. Your father can tell you all about it later."

I wanted to hug her for rescuing me. She had a soft, innocent look about her. If I'm going to roll out one of my old movie comparisons, she reminded me of a young Yvette Mimieux.

Suddenly my cell phone rang. I saw it was Danforth, and I stepped away to answer it. He had gotten a bug and couldn't go to the game. He said he'd email me the three tickets. I could give his to someone if I wanted.

When I returned, Jocko and Olivia were in an animated conversation. She had asked him about his name, and he explained the Jocko/Giaco thing.

"How unique! So you're named after both a composer of opera and a baseball umpire? Which do you prefer?"

"Depends on how I feel. Right now, I think I'm Giaco with a 'g.'"

"Too bad. If it were me, I'd want to be more of a Jocko with a 'j.'"

"Why?"

"Because I love baseball so much. I like opera, but I LOVE baseball. *La Boheme* is okay, but I'll take a Red Sox game any day over it."

I'll be damned, I thought. *I like this kid more and more.*

We talked for a while about Fred and the art complex. At a certain point, I looked at my watch and said we needed to get moving to Fenway. A sudden inspiration came over me and I said, "We have an extra ticket. Would you like to join us? We can all drive up in my car, but you'd have to leave now."

"Are you kidding? I'd love to go. We close in five minutes. We can leave from here."

* * * * *

Paula Spaulding would have been proud of me because that evening I had the most fun since I'd left Toledo, and for many reasons.

A lot of it was as simple as a father and son enjoying a ball game. Baseball was the favorite sport of both Jocko and me. I was a pretty damn good pitcher in high school and even pitched a little college ball. Jocko was okay too. Although he had a fastball that couldn't break a pane of glass, I worked with him constantly and helped him develop a knuckleball—that quirkiest of all pitches that somehow fit his personality (he also played the bassoon, the orchestral version of a knuckleball). That pitch got him on the high school team, but the knuckler didn't dance enough to fool hitters at the college level. Above all, the two of us spent many happy hours playing catch and watching the Mud Hens, with an occasional trip up the interstate to Detroit to see the Tigers.

Most remarkable was Olivia. I barely knew her, and my first impression of her was that she was rather quiet, shy, and introverted.

That may still have been true, but I saw another side of her that night. From the moment we three started up the expressway to Fenway, she was a different person. Her first line when we got in the car was, "How special is it that the Dodgers and Mookie Betts are in town tonight! He's my all-time favorite player. I cried when the Sox traded him to LA. What a stupid move."

All night long, she rattled off the statistics of various players— batting averages, RBI's, Earned Run Averages. I kept up with her at first, but when she launched into the new stats based on data analytics, she began to lose me. Spin rate, exit velocity, wins above replacement value—all the nomenclature that has entered the game in the Moneyball era—has made me something of a stats dinosaur (and happily so I might add). But there was Jocko going head-to-head with her all evening.

It wasn't all baseball talk, though. I could hear them discussing each other's lives. He was very interested in her job at the art complex, she in his dissertation. Unbelievably, she even showed signs of understanding what he was talking about. She was saying things like "that's what I've always thought, too" and "have you read the book by such and such." She was particularly informed on the anthropological aspects of his project. She had been an Anthropology minor at Middlebury and had even heard of one of the native tribes on the smaller Indonesian islands. She liked coffee too.

I was particularly pleased that my son was Jocko with a "j" throughout the evening, which surprised me. You would have thought that sitting next to a curator of an art museum would bring out the Puccini in him, but he stayed on the "j" side all night. It didn't look like he was forcing it either. As complicated a person as he occasionally is, he is 100% authentic.

Above all, I was really happy to be with two energetic young people. I'd spent the last couple of months burying a mother who had wasted away in memory care and researching the life and final days of an 80-year-old man I didn't really know. It was a breath of fresh air to hear the banter of two people with their whole lives in front of them rather than confronting the issues facing old people at the end of theirs.

* * * * *

The next day I took Jocko out on the boat. It was a clear and hot July day. We took our swim trunks, and I anchored us for an hour in Eagles Nest Bay where we took a dip, then drank a beer. From there, I made for the Gurnet, anchored at the cove there and walked to the lighthouse and the purple shack. I hadn't been there since I'd removed the twelve sketches. The exterior was as rundown as I remembered it, and the grass hadn't been cut.

"This beautiful place is ours too," I said. "The Osbornes got it at about the same time they took possession of the Soule land from the Petersons on Powder Point in the mid 1700s. Some latter-day Osborne built this little shack in the early twentieth century. Fred used to come here to think and sketch out future concepts to paint."

I unlocked the door, and we walked in.

"Phew," said Jocko. "Could use a good spring cleaning."

"It's way beyond that. I probably should tear it down and start from scratch. Nothing much worth saving here. I took out a few things when I was here a month or so ago. I met a guy who said he'd buy it. Maybe I should sell. But let's move on."

We walked back to the boat and set off for the next stop on my little itinerary, Clark's Island. We dropped anchor again literally three minutes later, the access point to the island being only a few hundred yards from the Gurnet. On the shore waiting for us was the young man the DRHS hired as caretaker for the peak summer months. The society owns seventeen acres, including a historic home called Cedarfield and a huge boulder called Pulpit Rock, or Election Rock, where, legend had it, the Pilgrims held their first service in the new world. Access to Clark's Island is difficult. Aside from Cedarfield, the entire island is private property and consists of only eleven homes.

I had requested from the society to have someone meet us. I had a

189

map that marked the spot of the location of my acre, but I wanted someone who knew the island to help me find it. Also, I was told that my Grady White was too big to pull right up to shore and it would be easier if we were shuttled there by dinghy. Once I'd anchored my boat, a man on shore started rowing out to us.

"Hi, I'm Jason Carpenter," he said as we climbed in the dinghy. "I'm the caretaker of Cedarfield. So you've never been out here, eh?"

"Never. I understand my acre has nothing on it."

"I've never seen the property actually. I've walked past it, but some trees block the view. It's kind of in a little gully. I'll show you."

We helped pull the dinghy ashore then followed him past the DRHS house called Cedarfield.

"This is where I live until September. It was built in 1836 and eventually owned by a woman named Sarah Wingate Taylor. She operated it as a school for a couple of years and later as a retreat for writers. Thoreau, Emerson, Louisa May Alcott, and others have stayed here. Her descendants gave it to the historical society in the 1960s. Now, if we walk up this way, we'll get to Pulpit Rock. Stay on this path. This is all private property along here."

We followed a narrow trail through woods and in short order we came to an open field. In the middle of it was a huge boulder.

"Here's where a group of Pilgrims held their first religious service," he said. "The *Mayflower* had been in Cape Cod Bay for a few weeks, and they were trying to decide where to establish their settlement. They sent out various exploratory parties in search of a place they could farm and have access to fresh water. They stumbled across this island. The first person to set foot on it was the first mate Clark. They then had a service here. It came down to either settling here or Plymouth. They liked this place a lot, but after a vote, they narrowly chose Plymouth because it had more open land to farm. That's why it's sometimes called Election Rock."

"So we came within a gnat's eyelash of this little place being the site of the first Thanksgiving, eh?"

"You could say that. Not much goes on here today other than once a year in July the society holds a picnic for those who can get out here."

"Very cool," said Jocko. Among his many interests, the kid has a keen sense of history too. I knew he could really get into that aspect of living here.

"Now let me walk you to your property," said Jason. "I need to look at your map. It's over on this path to the right. Stay on it. There are a couple of owners that abut it, and one is a crusty old guy."

We walked for a few minutes until we saw a house in the distance.

"That's old man Crawford's house. He's a real complainer—goes crazy when anyone gets even two feet off this path and on his property."

"How many houses are on the island?" I asked,

"Only eleven. Five are still owned by the Watson family or their descendants. That family has owned most of this island since they first got here in 1690. In the 1800s, the Taylor family owned most of the other half. But over the years, they sold off some of their land. Crawford is one of the newer owners."

Between the house and us was a slight dip in the terrain—it was little more than an indentation in the earth. It was mostly covered with trees.

"Based on your map, this is where your acre is," said Carpenter.

We made our way down to the indentation. We passed through the trees that rimmed the space and into the center. This spot was a fifty-yard strip of flat uncultivated land, grass knee high. From there you could not see beyond the trees.

"Nothing here," I said, turning completely around.

"I thought all this land in this area of the island was owned by either the historical society or the Crawford family," said Jason. "I wasn't even aware your uncle owned it until the society told me just recently."

"This acre was a part of the estate of Josiah Osborne," I clarified. "As I understand it, there's some confusion when and how he got it. The records are unclear. But I don't think my uncle came here much. Why would he? There's nothing here."

191

Suddenly we heard a yell. A man was standing up by the tree line looking down on us, waving a stick.

"What's going on over there?" he shouted as he scrambled down to where we were.

"Meet Henry Crawford," said Carpenter. It sounded like a warning more than an introduction.

"Please to meet you, sir," I said. I offered my hand, but he did not take it. "I am exploring my property."

"Your property, eh? I thought somebody my age owned it."

"He did. But he died and gave it to me. I'm his nephew."

Without so much as an "I'm sorry for your loss," he spat out, "Well, I'll tell you what I told him. Trespassing on my land has increased a lot recently. I've complained to the historical society."

"I'm well aware of that, Mr. Crawford," said Jason. I could tell this old goat intimidated him. "We do what we can to ask our members to respect the property of others when they visit Cedarfield."

"Well try harder," he rasped and then turned to me. "And I told your uncle the same. I said that somebody with a metal detector had been on his property recently and had wandered onto mine. The guy said he had permission from your uncle."

"Why the metal detector?" I asked.

"He said there were Wampanoag arrowheads and trinkets still lying around. Big goddamn deal! I told him to stay the hell away from my property or I'd call the police. I did in fact. They said if it continued to happen, let them know. And look at this."

We followed him to a corner of the flat, grassy area where a hole seemed to have been dug and filled in with dirt.

"This is freshly overturned earth," he growled. "If I start seeing people traipsing around here and causing a racket, watch out. I'm warning you both just the way I warned him!"

With that, he turned and stomped back to the trees and beyond.

"What a friendly chap," I said.

"He's a lot of trouble for the DRHS."

And maybe a lot for my uncle, I thought. Just another one to join the list of people who had made his life difficult.

I'd seen enough for the day, and we walked back to the dinghy. As we did, I could see lurking in the distance across the water the top of Gurnet Light. I thought of my uncle's sketch of its light illuminating a corner of this island with his cryptic note "is it here?" What was my uncle meaning by this? Or was it, as Paula had suggested, just as simple as a picture of a lighthouse and an island at night?

I kept this all to myself. I was more convinced than ever it was best to leave Jocko out of all of this. Why clutter anybody else's brain but my own with questions that more than likely had no answers.

* * * * *

The week flew by. I had quite a bit of business to attend to—recordings, video calls about the new show, a couple of podcasts, and working with my voice agent Becky to set up a few appearances for me at upcoming Comicon conventions. I was fast losing my interest in these in-person events, but I thought I had one more season of them left in me before I hung up my autograph pen.

Jocko was happy to fend for himself when I was busy. I gave him the car and, after his usual late starts in the morning, he was on the go the rest of the day. He loved the beach. One day he drove into Boston and met a professor at BU who knew something about Indonesian tribes. His evenings were full too. He'd eat at home with me, then head off somewhere, usually with Olivia.

He did have one setback, however. One day, feeling in an exploratory mood, he launched Fred's kayak that I kept tied to our pier and set off down the Bluefish River and past the King Caesar House. Ahead of him was the former town bank and telegraph office, now a private residence called the Cable House, which was the terminus in 1869 of the first transatlantic cable (it was French) ever to touch the United States. In front of it is a little ten-foot-long bridge on Washington Street that spans the river. Some boys were jumping over the railing into the river. He paddled his way underneath and continued downstream to where the river ended near the town golf course.

After resting, he paddled his way back to pass underneath the bridge again. But being a rookie, he had misread the notorious Duxbury tides. The water level had risen two feet from when he'd first passed through. It was now only a foot and a half from beneath the underside of the concrete bridge. He briefly wondered if he could even fit back through but decided if he lay totally flat on his back in the kayak he could eek his way through. He did make it through, but not before he'd scraped his nose badly on the underside of the bridge. When he got to the house, it was bleeding pretty badly.

"You idiot!" I said. "I can only imagine how high that water must have been to produce a scrape like that. You could have decapitated yourself."

Olivia had arrived at the house to meet him and was horrified at the way he looked.

"You poor boy!" she exclaimed. She spent the next ten minutes cleaning up his face and putting a band-aid on his nose. While I thought he looked like a ridiculous version of Jack Nicholson in *Chinatown*, she was treating him as if he'd been wounded in combat protecting the nation.

Finally, it was time for his flight back. I dropped him off at Logan and wished him well in Indonesia.

"Happy coffee bean hunting," I said.

"Thanks for the great week, Dad. I'll be back soon."

"So you think you'll find time to spend time with your good old dad?"

"Sure. But honestly it helps that Olivia is here. I'm crazy about her."

As I watched him walk into the terminal, I thought this could be a wonderful thing for Jocko. There was a part of me, though, that suspected that a romance involving families where one had supplanted the other in their ancestral home might add a little complexity somewhere down the road.

Chapter 19
MOTIVES

At the risk of interjecting a possibly profound and certainly uncharacteristically poetic thought into this little brew, I will assert that we do not always know what lurks deep inside the hearts and minds of our fellow humans. What motivates a person to take a certain action is often incomprehensible to others, even to the person themselves. This little bit of very serious bloviation is best appreciated when applied to very serious situations, such as my uncle's death. If anybody did wish him harm, understanding the possible motives out there in town would, theoretically, help lead me to a Mr. or Ms. X (if there was one). In such a case, the process of digging for motive is essential, even if it is accompanied by some personal anxiety.

But most of what we encounter in life is trivial and not worth delving deeply into possible motivation. A driver tailgates us, a salesclerk is not attentive, a dog owner casually allows Fido to sniff the butts of passersby, parents beam adoringly at their precious three year old as he screams bloody murder in a crowded restaurant. Why over-worry about any of this? Why wonder "what on earth is this guy thinking?" The juice isn't worth the squeeze.

This thought crossed my mind as I pulled into Hawthorne's Bakery. It was located on St. George Street in a small cluster of stores. Why had I come here unannounced? I told myself I was always in the market for baked goods. I loved the stuff, much to the detriment of my waistline—something Melanie had conquered through her weight loss drug but I had not.

Or perhaps I was curious to see another business my uncle had bankrolled. I'd sought out and gotten to better know people in other enterprises he'd helped: Len Barker and his partners at Gurnet Oysters, Blaise Rogers at Brothers, Olivia Phipps at the art complex, Caroline

Hawksmoor at DRHS. Why not the Hawthorne Bakery too?

Or maybe it was because I was interested to learn more about Nancy. She had interested me from the moment I'd met her. Why was she in a wheelchair? What was her backstory?

Or maybe it was something else altogether, not known by even myself. At any rate, why a person enters a bakery definitely falls into the "trivial activity" category—not worth overanalyzing. The simple fact was that I was standing in front of a small building with a sign over the door that read "Hawthorne Bakery" and I was about to walk into it.

"Hello," said the clerk, a middle-aged woman. "Can I help you?"

"Hi. I'm Jake Pavlik. I was wondering if Nancy or Julie is here?"

"Julie's not here. Nancy's in the back. I'll let her know you're here."

The fact that I was slightly disappointed in this response perhaps hints at a subconscious motive for me to have visited the place. But, again, it was only a visit to a bakery, so why dwell on it?

The clerk told me that Nancy was in the back, and she'd see me there. I went behind the counter and into a kitchen area with a huge oven where Nancy and a baker were working. The smell of baked goods filled the air. She was stationed in front of a table. A huge wedding cake was on it. She saw me and said, "Hi there! Welcome to world headquarters of Hawthorne Bakery. See what your uncle's investment has produced." She motioned to the oven and wedding cake.

"Greetings. Just thought I'd drop by and say hello. Looks like you're busy though. I can come back another time…"

"Nonsense. I'm glad you came. Julie's at a summer camp where she helps out. Let's go back to my office."

She wheeled herself into an adjoining room with a desk. Papers were scattered all over it. She motioned for me to sit down in a chair in front of it.

"Looks like business is good," I said.

"Very. I'm bringing on another baker and installing another oven. It's all because of your uncle."

"How long have you been in business?"

"I started about ten years ago when Julie and I moved down here. I had been a grade school teacher and wanted to do something else. I've always loved to bake, and so I opened a small bakery in Marshfield and did okay. Then your uncle came along. He'd heard about me from Brothers where they had given me some space to sell some things. He was interested in helping small local businesses and offered to invest in expanding the operation. As a result, I relocated to this bigger building about a year ago, bought some new equipment, hired a couple of people, and here we are. Julie only does this part time. Helps out with the paperwork and customer relations in addition to creating and tweaking recipes."

"So you and Julie moved here ten years ago?"

"Yes. We were living in Salem on the North Shore. We came to Duxbury a few years after the accident."

"Accident?" I asked this haltingly, afraid where this might be going.

"Yes. I'm guessing you haven't heard about it. People feel awkward talking about it. Julie's husband and I were in a car accident. I was the lucky one."

"I...I'm sorry," I stammered as the implications of what she was saying sunk in.

"Greg and Julie had been married a few years. They were great skiers. Me too. We grew up in Salem and our parents had a condo up near Waterville Valley in New Hampshire. It was only two hours from our house, and we went skiing almost every weekend in the winter. We were both on the ski team at Dartmouth. Julie was two years ahead of me. That's where she met Greg who was on the team too. They'd bought a house in Salem after they got married, and I was living in an apartment nearby in Danvers where my school was.

"Our plan was for the three of us to go skiing at Waterville one weekend, but Julie wasn't feeling well. She was three months pregnant, and she cancelled and said Greg and I should go alone. On our way up, the weather turned bad and the roads were icy. We were on a steep two-lane mountain road near Franconia Notch when a car on the other side of the road skidded and crossed into our lane. We flipped over a guard rail and rolled over. Greg died. As I said, I'm the lucky one."

I sat there looking at her in her wheelchair. She had spoken calmly but with great impact. I was at a loss for words, then finally said, "What a terrible tragedy, Nancy. I'm so sorry."

"It's always been a tough story to tell. It was even tougher when we lived in Salem after the accident. I moved into Julie's house there. She was devastated, and she miscarried. I couldn't manage by myself in those days, so we needed each other. But we were surrounded by people who knew us and felt such pity for us. It was painful for everybody—we were reminded daily of the way things used to be. Julie got into a very dark place—even more than me. We wanted new surroundings. Our mother had passed, and our father had moved to Florida. We didn't want to live down there. But we wanted to move on together and get a fresh start somewhere else. She applied for several teaching jobs, got an offer here, and so we bought our place here. We didn't know anyone, which is how we both wanted it. Now we've found our niche. At least I have."

"But not Julie?"

She gave a small smile and said, "Actually, I'm glad we are talking this. I was hoping we'd do so eventually, and without Julie present. It gives me the opportunity to tell the story the way it needs to be told with regards to her situation."

"Her situation?"

"It's been over ten years, and she still hasn't fully recovered from Greg's death. They were very much in love and were thrilled when she finally got pregnant. They'd had trouble doing so. And with her miscarriage, even the idea of his child being his legacy ended. She became bitter. To this day, she refuses to have an active social life, although she's had lots of chances. For one thing, I think I'm holding her back."

"What do you mean?"

"She's giving too much of her life to me. She needs to be her own person. I told her it would be better if we lived separately. Lots of men don't want to be saddled with a woman who insists on living with a helpless sister. I'm not helpless though. One of the reasons I bought this place was that it's got two small apartments attached out back. I'm subletting them now, but I'd be happy to live in one. I'd rent the other one out at a reduced price to someone who could run errands for me and drive me around. It would be snapped up in a minute. There's a huge shortage of affordable housing in this town. It's discussed all the time."

"But she won't do it?"

"No. Frankly, I think she needs me more than I need her. That's why I haven't moved out already. I might do it anyway, though. It would be for her own good. We'd still see each other all the time. And we do work together. I do need her for that."

I thought it was ironic that Nancy, the badly injured one, had adjusted to life better than her sister. I've heard it said that happiness is a choice, and it seemed that Julie had refused to choose it. It reminded me of my mother who I suspect was never truly happy a day of her life after my father died. *How sad*, I thought. *What a waste of a life.*

"But let's change the subject. Tell me about yourself and what you do for a living."

For the next half hour, I told her the story of my life. She was really intrigued about my profession and laughed out loud as I launched into some of my voices and impressions. I used to do a standup routine at conventions in my younger days—something I've long since abandoned. But I roll out portions of it every now and then, and I felt this was a time when some levity was needed. I even tried out a new voice I'd been thinking about since moving into town: an Italian who had stowed away on the *Mayflower*. I saw him as a cross between Myles Standish and Father Guido Sarducci, the old Saturday Night Live character. In fact, that's what I called him: Milo Sarducci. On the spot, I improvised a scene where Milo opens the first pizza place in America right where Hawthorne's Bakery now stands.

Nancy laughed so hard she had tears in her eyes. "That's hilarious! You're like a comedy version of the Plimoth Patuxet outdoor museum."

"What's that?"

"It's a re-creation of the original Plimoth settlement in 1620."

"Kind of like Williamsburg and the Colonial era?"

"Yes. But what makes this different is that the reenactors are portraying real people and never step out of character. They speak the old English of the Pilgrim era. They never make a reference to anything that has happened after 1620. It's awfully good. You might get a kick out of meeting other people who do voices. Seems like you'd be kindred spirits."

"This sounds very interesting. I guarantee I'm going to make a trip down there."

"And how about making another trip?"

"Where?"

"Back here to do your Italian Pilgrim routine for Julie. She could use a good laugh."

The clerk out front had come in to ask a question about an order, and I thought I should shove off.

"Give me your email address, Jake. I'd like to stay in touch."

After we'd exchanged contact information, I shook her hand and drove home.

* * * * *

Two days later I got an email from Julie.

Hi Jake,

I got your email address from Nancy. She mentioned to me your profession. I do volunteer work at Camp Wing here in Duxbury. It's a summer camp for kids from around the Boston area. It's mostly outdoor activity like hiking and boating, but we are experimenting this year by doing a workshop for some of the kids who are interested in theater. I talked to a colleague of mine and he thinks they'd be interested to hear from someone who makes their living in "show biz." Would you be willing to come here some afternoon and talk to them? I'll be here too.

I responded immediately.

I'd be delighted to do this. I'm always happy to help young kids.

While it is true that I don't mind helping kids, I found the fact that she was going to be there even more of an incentive. But of course I didn't say this, or even admit it to myself. We agreed on a date, and I showed up at the camp a few days later.

Camp Wing is located in a forested area in the westernmost part of Duxbury bordering on the town of Pembroke. It is about five miles inland from the bay, which is about as far away from the water as you can get while still being in Duxbury. Located in a section of town called Ashdod, it had little direct role in seafaring history and was always a community of farms and sawmills in bygone times.

I met up with Julie at the camp director's office. She was dressed in jeans and a tee shirt that said *Crossroad*s. She greeted me with a big smile and a handshake.

"Thanks for doing this. Let me show you around."

We walked the property, which is quite extensive, consisting of a series of cabins where campers live, dining facilities, and various playing fields. Although in the woods, it has a strong aquatic theme to it because it spreads out on the shore of a fairly big body of water called Keene Pond and has two large outdoor swimming pools.

"There's been a boys and girls camp here for almost one hundred years," she explained. "Today it's operated by a non-profit called Crossroads. The goal is to give kids a summer of outdoor activity where they can have fun, build self-confidence, and make relationships they normally wouldn't. They come from all over the Boston area. Very few are from Duxbury. And about half are low income."

"How long have you been involved?"

201

"Since a couple of years after we moved to Duxbury. Our house is on this side of town. I used to drive past and stopped in one day. I talked to a director and liked what I heard. I saw a chance to help kids from backgrounds different than the ones I teach in the high school. So every summer I help direct some activities here. I was a swimmer in college, so I spend a lot of my time supervising the water sports activities."

As she said this, I couldn't help but recall that she and her sister had participated in another sport in college too: skiing. It was a troubling reminder of the ongoing challenge in their lives.

"So you live near here?" I found myself quickly saying.

"Yes. We're a ten-minute walk away. I sleep here a couple nights a week too. Gives me more time with the kids."

Our tour ended at a platform on the shore of the pond. Sitting on the grass in front of it were about twenty-five kids in their teens.

"This is your audience," she said. "They all have an interest in singing or acting. Some are in their school drama clubs. This is our little stage. We put on skits here. There's a big talent show at the end of camp too. Some of these kids are really good. Ah, I see my colleague Walter over there. He's the camp director. Let me introduce you to him."

A tall, extremely good-looking man came up to me and shook my hand. He bore a resemblance to Brad Pitt.

"Hi, I'm Walt Conforto. So pleased to meet you. Can't thank you enough for doing this. When Julie told me about you, I was thrilled you agreed to come. She can be very persuasive, trust me!" He smiled and winked at her when he said this.

"I can imagine she is," I said, briefly wondering if the wink and smile portended something deeper.

"Here let me introduce you to the kids."

I accompanied him onto the stage where he introduced me in very flattering terms. I then gave about a twenty-minute overview of my background, how I got started, and offered some advice on careers in entertainment.

This was followed by a Q&A. One of the campers asked me to do a couple of my characters. I'd anticipated this and prepared for it. This was a far younger crowd than I usually talk to. My fandom definitely skews older, primarily between the ages of twenty and thirty-five, and it was safe for me to assume that very few of them would know any of my characters on The Cartoon Network. The fans of those shows—who are mainly guys—respond to satire and irreverence, which I am more than happy to give them. But with this younger group, I thought it best to play it safe and stick with Disney-type material.

I figured animals and talking objects would go over well with them, so I launched into some of the more traditional old school cartoon characters I'd done. For the boys, I did the likes of Harry the Hamburger and Stretch the Giraffe. For the girls I did Tonya the Teacup and Daisy the Dandelion. I got a pretty good response—a smattering of polite laughter. I noticed a few of the older boys looking bored and whispering among themselves. One wearing a Boston Celtics cap in particular was scowling and looked like he could turn into a heckler.

Sensing I needed to spice things up, I rolled out a new bit I'd been working on. It involved Milo Sarducci putting some moves on a few Pilgrim women. Although I never attempt to do female voices with total accuracy, I can get the essence of a woman using a kind of falsetto voice. And I'm really good with exaggerated mannerisms. So my Priscilla Alden had shades of Taylor Swift in her (I hoped) and my Susanna Winslow hinted at Beyoncé. My John Alden and Elder Brewster were closer to home in echoing Snoop Dog and Tom Brady respectively. The reaction was immediate. The laughter was much louder, the bored boys suddenly engaged. That was all the encouragement I needed to go on in that vein.

Several of the adult counselors had heard the laughter and had come over to investigate. I could see they were laughing the loudest of all. Encouragingly, I saw that Julie was too. I almost threw in some adult material but decided against it. That was best kept for another crowd on another day.

I finished to loud applause and cheering. A few of the counselors came up to me and shook my hand.

"You had them in the palm of your hands," said one. "That's not easy to do with some of these kids."

Another said, "I was watching Billy Tidrow. Even he was into it. He can be a troublemaker. Runs in the family," and she nodded in the direction of the surly kid in the Celtics cap. He was off to the side staring at me. The name sounded familiar, but I couldn't place it.

"That was wonderful!" said Julie. "These are good kids, but some of the boys can be a tough crowd to please."

"Who is that boy they said was a troublemaker?" I asked.

"That's Billy Tidrow. He's a local kid. The word is his father's hard on him. He can cause us trouble too. Both father and son have a temper."

Then it dawned on me where I'd heard the name. Billy Tidrow senior was one of the oyster farmers who had an issue with my uncle.

"Bravo," said Walter Conforto shaking my hand. "Congratulations. And thank you so much for reaching out to him, Julie. I've got to go. This is one of your nights to stay here, right?"

"Right."

"Then I'll see you later at the usual spot. Ciao."

"I've got to go too," she said to me. "Thanks again for doing this."

She said goodbye to me in the same way she had greeted me: with a smile and a handshake.

I was now alone with my thoughts which, despite an overall very pleasant day, included two concerns. The first was that I'd heard yet another troubling confirmation that Tidrow, one of the oyster farmers who had picked a fight with my uncle, was widely known to have a bad temper. And his son, who had been glaring at me, had one too. Could it possibly be that he saw me as a part of some problem between our two families?

The second was either nothing at all or potentially far more serious. I was a bit suspicious of the wink a Hollywood-handsome Brad Pitt look-alike had given to Julie. Even worse, I was downright depressed over his remark that they'd meet later "at the usual spot." I hoped I was wrong, but I suspected that to a lothario-in-the-woods, it wouldn't be her bakery.

In this town, if it wasn't one thing, it was another.

Chapter 20
DISAPPEARING ACT

A few days after Jocko returned to Toledo, I rehung the twelve sketches in the backyard studio. I was tempted not to. Maybe it was time to forget the whole thing. But the trip to Clark's Island with Crawford's attack on my uncle plus the encounter with Billy Tidrow's son at Camp Wing kept me pressing forward. New information on the little contretemps involving my uncle's last days kept coming my way whether I liked it or not. It felt that there might still be more out there.

As I reached into the box with the sketches, I noticed that Fred's calendar of appointments was in there too. I hadn't really given it much of a look when I'd first found it in the Gurnet shack. But I knew much more now than I did then, and so I examined the appointments for April and May more closely. Most of them included familiar names where the reasons for the meeting seemed obvious: a couple of "sittings" with Coco (he was painting her portrait), Len Barker (they were reviewing business plans), the Spauldings for dinner, Olivia Phipps for lunch. Others were not so obvious and piqued my curiosity. I divided these into two groups: those before his death on May 3 and those after.

Looking at things with a fresh pair of eyes now, the ones before his death that intrigued me were:

April 25
Emma called me.
Emailed me newspaper article.
Very concerned

April 26
Called Garrett (stonewalling me)
Left message for Ken to call me. No response yet
Probably need to fly down and meet in person

April 30
Call PMU at 508-777-4333 about Clark's Island complaint
Result: Good call. I'm sure I understand what is happening.

May 1
Colin—out of the blue!
Dinner at Saraceno in Boston
Very surprising
Need to reevaluate things

May 2
Another Trevanian dust up, this one at my house. Discussed options with Danforth on the phone. Getting serious.

Then after May 3, those that caught my eye were:

May 4
Meet Sheila Compton. Ask her to connect me to Derek Parker of The Globe regarding the article I read.

May 5
Delta Flight 4 Boston to JFK

May 6
Delta flight 43 JFK to Boston

May 8
Meet Danforth in person
Show him new documents and get his reaction!

All of these bore looking into. Since the encounter with Crawford on Clark's Island had occurred quite recently, it was the freshest in my mind, so I addressed that one first. He had called someone with the initials PMU to discuss Crawford's complaint on April 30 and had written "I'm sure I understand what happened."

What DID happen? I wondered. I called the number by the

appointment date to find out, having no idea who PMU was.

"Plymouth Marine Unit, can I help you?"

"I'm sorry. I may have dialed the wrong number. I'm afraid I don't know what the Plymouth Marine Unit is."

"We're a division of the Plymouth Police Department."

It then dawned on me that Clark's Island was in Plymouth, not Duxbury, and so of course that's who Fred would have called to learn more about Crawford's complaint.

"Actually, this is the right number. Sorry. I'm calling to investigate a complaint."

"What do you mean? You want to make one?"

"No. It was made against my uncle a couple of months ago on Clark's Island. He has since died, and I now own the land involved in the complaint."

"What do you want to know?"

"Can you tell me how the complaint reads?"

He told me it was not policy to discuss this over the phone with an outsider, which he said I was. But he'd be glad to discuss it if I came down to the station. I was happy to do this, and so the next day I met the officer who my uncle had talked to.

"I'm Sergeant Forbes. I handled that complaint. What do you want to know?"

I explained I now owned the property and wanted to know exactly what had transpired.

"I remember talking to your uncle," he said. "Clark's Island is an oddball location and the meeting with your uncle sticks in my mind. There's one owner out there—this man Crawford—who has complained many times about people trespassing. When we check it out, it's nothing we can follow up on. It's small stuff like someone passing a few feet on his property. This was more of the same, although there was a little more to it this time. Here are my notes from his calls to me a couple of months ago."

He took out his notebook and read:

April 25. Mr. Henry Crawford, resident of Newton, Massachusetts and seasonal resident of Clark's Island says that two men had trespassed on his land twice in the last week. He has security cameras on his house that show a large man with a metal detector and a tall, bearded man with a shovel straying onto his property. He notified his caretaker Gordy Garrison who later was able to confront the men. The man with the detector told Garrison that he was a friend of the owner who had authorized him to do some work on his property. He said he was sorry if he wandered onto a different private property by mistake. Garrison told Crawford that the man had a foreign accent.

April 29. Crawford called to complain again. His camera picked up the same two men trespassing. Officer Jenkins researched with Plymouth town hall, and they found the name, address, and phone number of the owner of the property on the island abutting Crawford's. It is a Fred Peterson of Duxbury.

April 30. I notified Peterson of the complaint, and he came to the station where I talked to him. He was very sympathetic and said he thinks he can put a stop to any problem.

"That's it," said the sergeant. "That's all we know. I haven't heard from Crawford since. And I know your uncle passed away. Hopefully everything was settled before he passed."

"Let's hope. If there are any more problems, please contact me."

He offered me a notebook and pen so I could write down my information.

My uncle's note said he understood what had happened. I had a hunch I did too.

* * * * *

Later that week, as I was pulling into my driveway, I heard a voice from behind call me. It was Khatia Trevanian. She was walking briskly across my lawn toward me. She was with a man.

"Oh, Mr. Pavlik. Can we talk?" She had been walking to me quickly and was out of breath. I detected some stress in her voice. "It's about our conversation a few weeks ago."

I had been expecting something like this. The last time I talked to Max, he had said he was going abroad and would follow up with me regarding his wild partnership offer when he returned. That was four weeks ago. Was this the follow up?

"Where's Max?" I said, eyeing the man. He looked vaguely familiar.

"He isn't available. This is Sidney Garber who manages our Cambridge gallery. You met him briefly at our house last month. He speaks for Max. It's easiest if he and I handle this for us. Can we come in?"

If nothing else, I thought, the*se Trevanians were pushy*. Under normal circumstances, I would have told them to get lost. But these circumstances were far from normal. I was curious to see what was on their mind. I too had something on mine, and I wanted to say it. I invited them in, and they followed me into my living room.

"I need to bring you up to date," she said. "Max is in Geneva. He had to stay there longer than anticipated to attend to an important matter. I came back alone, some of it because of you."

"Me? What do you mean?"

"We didn't want any more time to go by without formalizing our agreement with you."

"What agreement? If you mean that partnership idea you mentioned, I'm not interested. It sounds crazy. And I don't feel like giving anybody access to my house to search through it."

"Max thought you might say that," said Garber. He spoke in a cultured accent (think Clifton Webb in *Laura*). With his trim beard, he looked like the quintessential art gallery curator, right out of central casting. "You are making a very big mistake, sir. There is an immensely important artifact ready to be re-discovered right under our noses. It's worth a good deal of money and is of immense cultural importance. You must listen to reason."

"I am listening to my reason, and it is telling me to laugh this whole thing off."

"This is no laughing matter, Jake," said Khatia. This quirky Ruth Gordon look-alike was now a very aggressive Bette Davis. "Why do you not believe us?"

"For one thing, why should I believe you've found some lost logbook? You haven't shown it to me. Why?"

"Frankly, because it's our leverage, Mr. Pavlik," said Garber pointedly. "If we showed it to you, you'd have no incentive to partner with us."

"You have a strange idea of partnership," I said. "Why complicate things by hiding information? Just tell me what you know, and I'll see if I can find it. No offense, but we don't know each other very well, and I don't fancy strangers going through the contents of my house. Let's look at the logbook together—if you even have it. After all, you say your purpose is to restore a piece of cultural importance to the world. Why not be open with me?"

"You are half right, Mr. Pavlik" said Garber coldly. "Our purpose would be to restore it to the world—but at a price."

"What price?"

"At the highest price possible!" Khatia almost screamed this. There was venom in her voice now. "Don't you understand our business? Don't you? Don't you?"

She said this with such force that it startled me. She'd grown so frustrated that she was becoming unhinged. I looked at her and saw something that scared me. I saw the face of unbridled greed—a greed that would stop at nothing to achieve its goal. I'd seen the same look on her husband's face, but I hadn't recognized it at the time.

"Now settle down, Khatia," said Garber more calmly. I guessed his role tonight was to be the calm negotiator. It was probably his ongoing role with Max too. "We can maybe start with a partial agreement to show we are both acting in good faith. Samuel Osborne's logbook of the

211

Smyrna voyage is our source of information. It very much exists. We are sure it has all the information we need to find this object, but in general its wording is vague and imprecise. It can lead down blind alleys."

This was my opportunity to play the card I'd been waiting to play.

"Like you and Max trespassing on my property on Clark's Island to do a little digging and what not? How's that for going down a blind alley?"

"What do you mean?" cried Khatia. "How dare you say such lies?"

"Because I can put two and two together. And because I have video footage of their two little trips there in April. Oh, and an eyewitness too. The island is seasonal. No one goes there at that time of year. You thought you and Max could sneak there unobserved off season, Garber, but you were wrong. It's pretty amateurish for a couple of guys like you, frankly. I have a mind to call the police and tell them all about it if you continue to harass me."

Garber was looking at me thoughtfully, sizing up the situation. He was obviously the cooler head of the two.

"Mr. Pavlik has a point, Khatia," he finally said. "And I can see he is not above using a little leverage of his own when he has it. Potential partners need to be transparent. It is true, Jake—if I can be allowed to call you by your familiar name—Max and I did make those trips out there. I was against it to be honest, but I went along because he's my boss. Samuel Osborne's notes identify several possible locations on his property where he regularly hid little prizes acquired on his voyages. One is clearly identified as a small piece of land he owned on Clark's Island. Max and I researched land ownership, and we were able to identify the approximate location. We thought we'd start there because it was a remote unobserved place—or so we thought. And you are right. It was so amateurish. It's embarrassing. But think about how valuable this object must be to have reduced Max and I to such a low level as common trespassers."

"If this is supposed to be a point in your favor, the logic escapes me. But go on."

"In the interest of trying to find common ground, I'll accept your little shot at me. I find it sometimes comes with the territory in this business. But let's move on. Yes, we came up empty on Clark's Island. There are, however, three more spots Samuel Osborne mentions where he hid things of value, and they are all on what is today your property on 3 Spyglass Lane. Two of those spots are described very vaguely. This notebook was for his eyes only, and he didn't need to clearly describe places he already knew. It appears that both these spots will involve some digging, just as the construction of the Trevanian house was necessary to unearth Samuel's logbook and notebook. But the third spot is clearly described and it involves no digging. No traipsing through your things. Let's focus on that and see where it takes us."

It was against my better judgment to encourage this line of thinking. I'd determined about five minutes into this encounter that I wanted nothing more to do with these people. But I had to admit I was intrigued to see where their delusion was taking them. More importantly, I was wondering if any of this was related to my uncle's death. That was the showstopper for me.

"Go on," I said. "But please get to the point. What is this 'clearly described hiding place' in the logbook?"

"It's not a place. It's a thing—a figurehead."

"What?"

"I'll explain. As Josiah got deeper into the carving business, his ambitions began to grow. His rival in the figurehead business was Nathanial Winsor Jr., who was far more successful and wealthier. The Winsors built their vast wealth around shipping and not carving. Josiah was jealous and realized he wasn't going to get rich woodcarving, so he turned to smuggling. While he was a seaman, he developed his own little ecosystem at various ports of call—a collection of individuals of questionable repute who could help him find and remove objects and products of interest for him to take back with him. But because he had no ships of his own, his haul was minimal. He was limited to what he could hide in his personal possessions.

"He then had another idea. He was a gifted woodcarver, and he retired to pursue that trade. When he began to carve figureheads, it became his practice to hollow out a portion of some of them to allow secretive stashing of goods. Above all, he needed someone on the ship to obtain these objects and bring them back to Boston. That someone was his son Samuel who, by all accounts, was outwardly a respectable seaman himself, but in reality a smuggler. Much of his illegal trading was based on offloading opium bound for China and selling it in the US. To do this, he found a willing custom official in Boston to be his collaborator in "losing" crates or sacks of opium, chiefly from Turkey.

"His hauls extended beyond drugs, though. His network began to obtain for him antiquities that interested wealthy collectors. Small statues from Greece, pottery from Italy, coins from the old Phoenician coast—all made their way back to Boston hidden in those figureheads. Sometimes other crewmen would help him. Getting the stash into the figurehead unnoticed was key, and having a co-conspirator on board was helpful. The ship's carpenter or sailmaker were obvious targets. They were charged with ship repairs during voyages and had access to all parts of it at all hours."

"So the people that built my house were thieves."

"You could say that. But if it's any consolation, they weren't very successful at it, and it didn't last long. Samuel had three daughters and they all married upstanding citizens. Osborne roguery only lasted a few years and ended when Samuel died. The only object that Samuel ever acquired that would have been worth anything was the Golden Fleece when he sailed with the *Smyrna* and he was allowed to leave the ship to explore the Black Sea coast around Batumi. However, as Max explained to you last month, Samuel died of typhus before he could sell it. His family was unaware he even possessed it."

"And it remains right where it was when he died!" said Khatia, more hyper than ever. "All we need to do is find that figurehead."

"And how can you be sure it's here? That theft occurred almost two hundred years ago."

214

"Because Samuel wrote that the figurehead was in the form of a mermaid!" cried Khatia. She was losing control of herself. "Fred told us he had such a figurehead in his house and he was painting it. It can't be a coincidence!"

"Well, that's wrong," I said quickly. "I can assure you there is no such figurehead in this house."

"I don't believe you!" cried Khatia. "I'm going to take a look." She dashed out of the room.

"Stop, Khatia!" cried Garber, starting out of the room. "Don't do this."

"Forget it," I said, looking at my watch as if I were bored. "Let her go. There's no such figurehead in this house. She'll find that out soon enough. I'll give her ten minutes if it'll get you all out of my hair for good. After that, get her the hell out of here. And if I ever catch any of you on my property again, I'm calling the police. I should have done so already."

"This isn't how I wanted it," he said shaking his head. "There was a way for us to legitimately collaborate. I told Max that long ago, but he wouldn't listen, and it alienated your uncle permanently."

"I don't buy the good cop bad cop routine, Garber. If you are not out in nine minutes, I call the police. Oh, and don't forget to check the studio out back. That's where Fred painted and where this alleged mermaid model would have been if it ever existed. Go ahead. Knock yourself out. You've got eight minutes."

With that he went out the door and into the studio. In a few minutes he came back.

"Nothing there, right?" I said.

"Oh, but there is," he said. "Those sketches hanging on the wall are interesting. I saw the one of the mermaid figurehead. It was on your uncle's mind. There's something here if we could only put our heads together."

"Too late for that," I said. "Never going to happen. You've got one minute. I suggest you go find her. She'll never leave on her own. I'm serious about calling the police."

With a look of resignation, he walked upstairs calling out her name. When he found her, they both came downstairs. They were arguing.

"This place is too big!" she was yelling. "We need more than ten minutes. Why are you doing this, Sidney?" Bette Davis had now become Tony Perkins playing his crazed mother in drag in *Psycho*. Garber had to literally drag her out.

After they left, I locked the door and breathed a sigh of relief. Luckily, I had moved the mermaid figurehead out of the studio and over to the art complex for restoration only a few days previously. It seemed that object was the focal point of their search. I'd want to take a second look at that thing now that I knew more about its history.

And while I was glad that I had frustrated them in their search, I was worried that this little scene would repeat itself in the future. But it turned out I needn't have worried. I never saw the Trevanians or Garber again.

* * * * *

Everything with the Trevanians unraveled very quickly thereafter. The next day, I was sitting in the studio looking at the sketches when I noticed some commotion at the Trevanian house. I had a good view from up there and could see several men carrying boxes and crates from the house onto a truck. I thought no more of it.

Three days later I arrived home from running some errands and saw a half dozen police cars in front of the Trevanian house. Observing from the street were the Tsais and Spauldings. I walked over to them.

"What's going on?" I asked. "This doesn't look like a block party."

"Seems like our neighbors are in trouble with the law," said Tommy Tsai. "Dude was mixed up in some bad shit it seems."

"What kind of bad shit?"

"Not exactly sure," said Paula. "No one is saying. But it must be serious. Both the FBI and Homeland Security are on the scene."

"I don't see the Trevanians anywhere," said Ed Spaulding. "I wonder where they might be."

"I saw some men loading some boxes onto a truck the other day," I said. "I wonder if there's a connection."

"Could be," said Paula. "If I put my writer's cap on, I'd say they knew they were in trouble, made one last attempt to get some of their ill-gotten gains out of that house, then flew the coup."

Her suspicion was confirmed the next day when the news broke that Max and Khatia Trevanian had been accused of selling illegally obtained art both in the US and abroad. "Criminal redistribution of stolen property" was the official name for it, and they had been under investigation for some time by the FBI Art Theft Unit. They were thought to be back in their residence in Geneva. Swiss and US authorities were working together. Their colleague Sidney Garber of Boston was being questioned by police.

That's all anybody knew, but for me that was already plenty to digest.

Chapter 21

MR. PARKER OF *THE GLOBE*

The next day I got an email from Sheila Compton asking if we could meet up. She wanted to talk about the Trevanians. I had resisted her attempts to meet for weeks now. Her interest in me was based on her suspicion that my uncle's death was not all that it seemed and that I could help shed light on what had really happened. I, on the other hand, had only hunches up to this point and did not want to name names or spread any rumors based on guess work. After all, I really didn't know her well, and so I had been putting her off.

But this time I accepted her invitation. I was more than happy to talk to her about the Trevanians. I was hoping she might have some information to give me on what had happened to them. And I was now very willing to share any suspicions I had about them. They had long been on my suspect list. Their names were already in the news, and I no longer saw a reason to protect their reputation if, in fact, they had committed crimes. We had moved beyond the spreading gossip stage—with them, at least. I had another topic I wanted to talk about with her too.

I had offered to meet her at the *Messenger* office, but she said she'd rather meet me at my house if possible.

"I'm interested in getting to know the neighborhood better," she emailed back. "Their house is part of the story."

When she arrived, I took her up to the artist studio where we had a good vantage point to see the Trevanian house.

"Finally, we meet again!" she said. "I was beginning to think you were avoiding me."

"I kind of have been, to be honest with you. I haven't been sure I've uncovered anything worth sharing, but that may have now changed. But you go first. What's on your mind?"

218

"Fair enough. This situation with the Trevanians is a pretty big news item in Boston and in the art world. Have you seen the coverage in The *Globe*?"

"No. I don't subscribe yet."

"Here's their coverage this morning. Read it when you can." She gave me a copy of today's paper. On the front page below the fold was an article with the following headline

DUXBURY COUPLE SOUGHT FOR TRAFFICKING IN STOLEN ART

"Wow," I said. "Front page no less. I'm anxious to know more."

"Me too. All I know so far is what has been written in this article. I'm in touch with an ex-colleague I have on the paper to see if I can learn more. At this point, what I know is that the authorities in Boston and Switzerland have become aware of certain dealings of the Trevanians that are very probably major crimes. They have sold artworks to various museums in the US and abroad of very questionable provenance. Their gallery in Cambridge has been involved too. They've been under investigation secretly for some time now. They seem to have been taken totally by surprise—but with enough time to flee the country and get to their home in Geneva. The Swiss have different privacy laws and protections for people operating in a shadow world like the Trevanians apparently have been."

"So how can I help?"

"The *Messenger* has got to give this some coverage. It's a big story. But I'm not here as an investigative reporter. That's not what we do. Other media will do that. It's more from a human interest story—the local angle. What kind of neighbors were they? How well did you know them? Was there anything odd about their behavior? What can you tell me?"

"What I can tell you on the record is that they were hardly ever home. In my time living here, I only met Max once and his wife twice. I was in their house one time. It was filled with statues and ancient artifacts. Their gallery manager Sidney Garber was there doing some business, but he left shortly after I arrived. There's their house over there." I pointed to the sprawling modern structure through the trees.

"My God," she said looking out the window. "That's the most un-Duxbury house I've ever seen."

"These two were different cats. Anyhow, the place was full of artwork and objects they'd collected from around the world. They also told me about their life in Georgia and how they met there. But that's about it. The other neighbors have been here longer and may have better perspective."

"You mentioned they had lots of art. Did they talk about it at all?"

We had now entered a delicate area. How much should I tell her about my clash with them? I had rehearsed how I wanted to say this.

"They did mention one particular piece of art. In fact, Khatia and Garber came here to my house not long ago to discuss it again. But I won't talk about it on the record."

"Why not?"

"Because it may have something to do with what happened to my uncle. I know you're interested in that. But I don't want my suspicions circulating just yet on that score. I will tell you something off the record, though. I think you may be able to help me. If you can play it my way for a bit longer, then I'll tell you more."

"Okay," she sighed, closing the notebook she'd been feverishly writing down my comments in. "I said I didn't come here as an investigative reporter, and I'll stick to that. What do you know?"

"The short version is that the Trevanians approached Fred with a proposition involving a specific artifact. He told them repeatedly that he was not interested in the proposition, but they continued to pester him. They became frustrated and even trespassed on his property on Clark's Island. I believe he had grown worried over their aggressive behavior toward him. I think he might have even talked to his lawyer about them. In my brief exposure to them, I can see how he might have felt troubled about them. They were very eccentric and mysterious people."

"What was the artifact?"

"I don't want to say. What it is may or may not be relevant. The key point is this. You approached me two months ago with what you called leads that might shed light on my uncle's death. I pursued all of them, and I discovered a lot of interesting things, none of which I am comfortable sharing yet. But what I can share is that, bottom line, if foul play was involved, the Trevanians would be my top suspects. They had motive. There was definitely bad blood there. That may or may not be true with some other people who disagreed with him, but it was definitely true here."

"Do you want to go to the police?"

"No, not yet. I want to explore a couple more things first. And this is where I could use your help. I recently discovered a list of appointments my uncle had made just before and after his death. One of them was to be with you on May 4, the day after his death."

"Yes. Of course I remember. I mentioned it to you the first time we met. He said it was urgent. It's one of the things that made me want to dig deeper into his death."

"Did he tell you what he wanted to talk to you about?"

"No."

"I think I know. He noted he wanted to get information from you on a *Globe* reporter named Derek Parker. Do you know him?"

She looked at me, her eyes wide open, a look of surprise on her face.

"I don't know him personally. He joined The *Globe* after I left there. But I know of him."

"What do you know?"

"I know he wrote the article on the Trevanians that you're holding in your hands."

I looked at it. There was the byline: Derek Parker.

We both stared at each other. The implication was clear.

"Do you think Fred wanted to talk to Parker about the Trevanians?" I asked.

"I'm not sure."

"Fred had made a note about a week before he died that someone had emailed him a newspaper article. I wonder if it could be connected. Any idea what article he was referencing?"

"No, your uncle hadn't explained why he wanted to see me. We can look at the newspaper's archives to see if there's anything related. Or you can ask Parker yourself. I'll see if my friend at The *Globe* can put you in contact with him"

"Thanks."

"Do you have access to your uncle's computer? You might be able to locate the article faster."

"I'm afraid not. Of all the things here in this house, his computer is not one of them."

"That seems odd," she said thoughtfully. "I'll see what I can do to get you in touch with Parker. And I'd appreciate it if you updated me now and then on what you find. I'll respect your privacy."

She left without me making her any promises on that score. But I had a feeling she could be a resource for me going forward, and so I said I'd stay in touch.

* * * * *

After I got Derek Parker's contact information, I emailed him saying I was a neighbor of the Trevanians, that I'd seen his article on them, and I'd like to talk. He was anxious to do so, and he even offered to meet me at my house.

He was a tall African American man in his fifties with greying temples. We sat on my deck, and he asked me what I knew about the Trevanians. I told him what I told Sheila, except this time I included the part about Max claiming he'd found evidence that my uncle had unknowing possession of a valuable artifact of gold that had been removed from Georgia two hundred years ago.

"Hmm," he said. "That's interesting. Nothing like that has been mentioned that I know of. Who was your uncle?"

"His name was Fred Peterson. He lived in this house."

He closed his eyes, deep in thought.

"You know. That name sounds vaguely familiar. But I can't place it."

"In his appointment ledger, he wrote he was going to ask a former reporter of The *Globe* to try to connect him to you. There's also a note that he'd received an article from a friend—I'm wondering if it may have been something you wrote, hence the connection. But he died before he got your contact information."

"Too bad. I wonder what the story was that he read."

"Could it have been the Trevanian story?"

"It's possible, but it could have been a number of others. I'm part of what The *Globe* calls Spotlight, which is its investigative reporting platform. Everyone in Spotlight often collaborates on big stories. For example, I'm a co-lead in investigating art theft. The other leader is a *Globe* Fine Arts reporter. I'm on the team because I started out as a business journalist with the *Wall Street Journal* and art theft is a big and growing global business. Lots going on in Boston going back to the famous theft at the Isabella Stuart Gardner Museum years ago. It's still the largest unsolved art theft in the world. And the MFA and other local museums have had to return works they purchased that turned out to be taken illegally out of their country of origin. Greece, Italy, Egypt, Turkey, and other countries have been very active in tracking down these items, demanding restitution. Turns out the Trevanians were an active party in this sort of activity."

"But nothing about a golden artifact from Georgia?"

"Absolutely not. I'd remember that."

"Odds are that's why he wanted to talk to you, though."

"Probably. But the funny thing is the name Peterson sounds familiar, and I don't know why. It might have come up in some other story I worked on. It's a common enough name, though."

"If you figure out a connection, please give me a call. I'd love to know why he might have wanted to talk to you."

"Me too. Let me look at some of the articles I've recently written on other Spotlight teams. If I can connect any dots, I'll let you know."

He then went into reporter mode, asking me more questions and jotting down my replies. When he was finished, he shook my hand and said he'd send me a preview of the article for my approval.

Chapter 22
PROCESS OF ELIMINATION

The next week three things happened in short order that significantly impacted my view of the circumstances surrounding my uncle's death.

The first was an email I got from Colin Peterson, my long-lost cousin. He had been on my mind because he apparently had met with my uncle shortly before his death. Fred's entry on his calendar was:

May 1
Colin—out of the blue!
Dinner at Saraceno in Boston
Very surprising.
Need to reevaluate things

Colin's email to me said he was flying up to Boston from his home in Philadelphia and wanted to see me. We met at a restaurant in the Seaport District. I had arrived first and had been seated at a table. It had been many years since we had seen each other, but he recognized me when he arrived and came right over.

"You look the same," he said as we shook hands.

"You too," I replied.

That was a lie. I never would have recognized him. I remembered him as having the pampered look of a preppie—or yuppie as it was called then—which had fit his personality perfectly. Now he looked older than his years, balding with lines on his face. The voice I develop for a character is largely based on looks. If I had to do the voice of the man who sat across from me, I'd have modeled it after a low-keyed slightly past his prime Bob Newhart.

He took a seat and the waitress came over to take our drink order.

"How long has it been?" he said after she'd left. "Twenty-five years?"

225

"At least. I've lost track of where you were. How'd you find me?"

"From my father. He told me he'd seen you at your mother's funeral My condolences. I remember her as a nice woman. My father was very unkind to her. As was my mother."

The directness of this comment made barely a minute into our first meeting in decades surprised me. But he didn't stop there. It soon became obvious that he had an agenda in wanting to meet me.

"Let me say something up front," he said. "As I got older, the shortcomings of my parents became very apparent to me. A lot of it was driven by my mother. She grew up with money and looked down her nose at those who didn't have any. My father came to think that way too."

"Which certainly included my parents," I said.

"Uncle Fred too, at least when he was young. When he married a poor Polish girl like Aunt Mary, my parents both wanted nothing to do with her. They said some downright insulting things to her. It infuriated Uncle Fred and he stopped talking to my father. I don't blame him. When Fred became so successful, my parents got jealous. The rift grew even wider."

"I remember Aunt Mary as really sweet. Fred loved her deeply."

"My parents were worse than snobs, though. I couldn't see what they were when I was young. Then I went to college and met Dionne. I said I wanted to marry her, which I did despite their protests. My mother resented it to her dying day. My father did too until only recently."

"Why?"

"Because Dionne is black. My mother was a racist, and my father never called her on it. He and I only started talking again a couple of years ago. Better late than never I guess."

The waitress returned with our drinks and took our dinner order. It gave me a few minutes to reflect on what was happening. I was finding this a remarkable conversation. Little Lord Fontelroy had become an actual human being, and one that I think I liked a lot. His honesty was refreshing and had the effect of quickly breaking the ice of what I thought was going to be an awkward meeting. It was nothing of the sort.

We then began catching up. He was a primary care physician and lived outside of Philadelphia. He and Dionne had three children. He was a deacon in his church. His sister Beth was a teacher and had married an accountant. They had two children and lived in New Jersey. Their mother was dead and their father, Uncle Mike, was alone in St. Louis living very modestly. The demise of the family business had reduced his financial status considerably.

I told him about myself. Although he didn't know much about my life over the last thirty years, he was well aware of my inheriting our uncle's property. He hit that head on too.

"My father told me Fred had called him recently," he said.

"I'd heard. What was that all about?"

"He told him that he was leaving his property to you. He wanted to be fully transparent in his old age. He said he wanted to keep the house in the family, and he felt closest to you of anyone."

"How did your father react?"

"My father is a tired old man. Not much fight left in him. He said it didn't matter to him, but he wanted to tell me. He thought I should know."

"I had no idea I was getting this property. I didn't even know it existed. Were you upset?"

"Not in the least. None of us had treated Fred fairly, including me. I was like any impressionable kid. I knew there was bad blood in the family, and I automatically took my parents' side. But that changed as I began to realize who was really at fault. In fact, when I learned he planned to leave you the house and Beth and me nothing, I actually sought him out. I came up to Boston just to have dinner with him. I'm glad I did. Timing's everything. It was just a few days before he died."

So that accounts for the *note on Fred's calendar*, I thought. I didn't reference that I knew they'd met. I initially thought it might have been a confrontation based on his being left out of the will. Now I wasn't so sure. I was curious to see where this was going, so I just nodded.

"I wanted to tell him how sorry I was my parents had mistreated him and Aunt Mary. He got quite emotional. I told him I knew he'd left you his property and that I thought he'd made the right choice. I also said I wanted to reconnect with you and bury the hatchet. The evening ended with us saying we'd get together again."

"And now you never will."

"No. He died a few days later but not before he did something."

"What did he do?"

"That very night he wrote both Beth and me very big checks. He sent me a note saying he didn't want to change his will yet again but wanted to leave us something. Our meeting had made him reevaluate things. He wanted a full restoration of family ties."

"What did your father say?"

"I haven't told him yet. Fred said not to. He wanted to tell him himself and why he did it. I'm going to tell him now, but I wanted you to know first. My father and I are still working out some things between us. He really was nasty to Dionne for years. I'm still trying to come to grips with that."

The evening ended with us vowing to stay in regular contact. The dinner had been a success beyond my wildest imagination. There was now peace in what was left of the family.

But there was one other thing. I now realized I no longer had any reason to suspect that my uncle had died as some outgrowth of a family feud. A tired, stoop-shouldered old man who had lost his fight and a soft-spoken physician who looked like Bob Newhart and was a deacon in his church were unlikely to have had a role in Fred's death.

It meant two less suspects.

* * * * *

Now for my second vignette.

The day after Jocko got back to Toledo from Indonesia, he turned around and flew to Boston. He said he wanted to rest up from his long trip in Duxbury with me. I thought this a fine idea, but I had no illusions about his true motivation. This was confirmed when, after barely twenty-four hours with me, he casually informed me he was going to drive up to Vermont with Olivia the next day and spend a few days with her and her mother who now lived in Stowe.

"Nice way to rest up," I kidded him. "You make a punishing thirty-two hour door-to-door return from Jakarta to Toledo, then the next day you fly to Boston and show up looking like a rumpled unshaven Bill Murray in *Lost in Translation*, then the next day you drive up to near the Canadian border. Sounds like a good R&R plan to me."

"I can relax when I'm in Stowe, Dad," he said with a faint blush. "Olivia says it's a nice place to just hang out. Her mother's place is up in the mountains. Very peaceful."

"It's pretty peaceful here—as long as you don't have any kayaking mishaps."

Ignoring my little bit of playful teasing, he said, "Besides I want to make a connection up there regarding my dissertation."

"Right. Mountain Lion fecal coffee beans are big in Vermont I assume?"

"You're laughing at me," he said very seriously. "I know you think I'm wasting my time with this dissertation."

I felt terrible at this. Jocko and I share many things, from a love of baseball to a respect for authenticity to a live-and-let-live philosophy towards others. However, he does not share my sense of humor, which is true for vast swathes of humanity as well. I'm usually sensitive to this, but I hadn't been this time. I could tell he was offended.

"I have total confidence in you," I apologized. "I've got a strain of silliness in me that I sometimes can't control. I'm very sorry."

"I'm going to have the last laugh on this, Dad. Wait and see."

"I have no doubt, son," I said, although in my heart of hearts I had nothing but doubts.

Five days later, Jocko returned to Duxbury with two interesting pieces of information. First, aside from resting up, he had actually made a worthwhile connection on his dissertation. Stowe is the original home of one of the bigger coffee businesses in the entire country. He'd been able to get an appointment with one of their VPs and had explained his upcoming research into what he was now euphemistically calling "value-added exotic coffee." This executive was wildly enthusiastic and immediately connected Jocko to a key executive at the company's corporate headquarters just outside of Boston. He had an appointment there the following week.

"The company has been wanting to get into the premium coffee segment for a while," he said. "If I can get them to participate in some testing, it'll be huge for my dissertation. More money too."

I was thrilled, as you might imagine. Besides the pragmatism this exhibited, I loved his enthusiasm. The best thing I ever did was to take a chance on working in an offbeat profession where success was highly uncertain. But I love the work, and I'm the happiest person I know in what I do. Follow your passion is my credo. And for the first time in my life, I saw professional passion in Jocko.

But he had other news of an entirely different sort. He had met two members of Olivia's family.

"Her mother is as sweet as Olivia is," he said. "Moving to Vermont was a good decision. And Stowe is a great place. I could see living there. Laid back, outdoorsy, and people doing interesting things. Lots of microbreweries, farm to table restaurants, a big ski business. I even found two connections to Duxbury."

"Way up there?"

"Yes. One of the rivers where we kayaked cut through a town called Duxbury. There are only a few places named Duxbury in the world, and I've now seen two of them. And the other connection is in Stowe at the Von Trapp Hotel and Resort. Have you ever seen the musical The *Sound of Music*?"

"Of course. In my film critic days, I once wrote a column on the ten most 'un-noir' movies of all time. That was one of them."

"Well, this is the same family that owns the resort. Olivia told me the von Trapps lived in Duxbury, Massachusetts for a few months after escaping Austria and before buying land in Stowe. It is one of Olivia's favorite movies."

That's another actress Olivia resembles, I thought. *A young Julie Andrews.*

But he had met another family member: Olivia's troubled brother Don, the one who had cursed Fred and the house.

"Olivia says he's pulled himself together since moving up to Stowe with his mother. He's settled down and works in one of the microbreweries. He's basically a good guy, very sorry for his conduct toward Uncle Fred. He's very likable. Totally different than I thought. Doesn't look like he could hurt a fly. He'd do anything for Olivia. She has complete faith in him."

This didn't let Don totally off the hook as someone who might have harmed my uncle, but it didn't sound likely that he had. Anyone who Julie Andrews swears by is probably okay.

* * * * *

One of my favorite comedians is Mel Brooks, and one of his best routines is him playing a 2000-year-old man having a conversation with his wingman Carl Reiner. The routine goes like this:

Reiner: Tell us a little-known fact about some historical figure you personally knew.

2000-year-old man: Genghis Khan. That wasn't his real name.

Reiner: What was it really?

2000-year-old man: Genghis Cohen.

Reiner: Why did he change his name?

231

2000-year-old man: Business purposes. Wrote a lot of checks. Killed a lot of Czechs.

Reiner: What's the secret to a long life?

2000-year-old man: Two things. Never leave the house when it's raining—there may be tough guys out there. And take care of every body part as if it were your own.

My last little episode from this period starts with me conversing with a mere youngster—a man only four hundred years old.

It started with the following email invitation from the other and (at least to me) more interesting Julie—the one in Duxbury:

My sister Nancy mentioned to you that anyone who does impressions would enjoy going to the Plimoth Pilgrim village and watching some of the reenactors in action. We are taking some of the Camp Wing kids there this weekend, and you're invited to join us if you are interested.

To say I was interested is an understatement. Where else could I have a conversation with a Mayflower Pilgrim—or at least a reasonable facsimile thereof?

The visit was unlike anything I'd ever experienced. In this outdoor museum village, the reenactors are highly skilled individuals who study up extensively on the biographies of the Pilgrim they are portraying and adopt the vocabulary and accent of that period. They never break character, even though many tourists try to make them. Ask them about Duxbury and they say they never heard of the place even if you point out the Myles Standish monument clearly visible across the bay. If they see your wristwatch, they ask "wot be that strange device on yer wrist, fair sir?" Time stands still in the 1620s. It's good fun, and I figured it was worth my while to hang out there in my quest to adopt some speech patterns that I could integrate into my Milo Sarducci character. Marrying up a credible "forsooth" or "verily" with an impassioned "ciao bella" complete with hand gestures can be tricky.

232

As I was wandering around the village, I inquired of one Pilgrim woman if George Soule was there, and she said he was out hunting. But she introduced me to her husband, John Alden, who was in a little house with a thatched roof, resting. I was having a fine conversation with him when Julie came upon us. She was with three of the Camp Wing kids.

"I see Milo has hit it off with one of the locals," she said.

"I was just asking him in my best fake Italian if he heard that there was a stowaway from Palermo on board the *Mayflower*. He used some salty language, and he told me he'd explain to me if I wanted to meet him after hours. I'm gonna take him up on it."

One of the Camp Wing kids who was standing there said to me in a very pleasant voice, "I loved your routine, sir. It's the first time I've ever been interested in a Pilgrim. I want to ask you for a favor."

It was Billy Tidrow Jr. He had the same look on his face as he did when I'd met him the first time. What I had thought was a glare was nothing of the sort now that I was talking to him. He was very polite and even wanted to shake my hand. I couldn't envision this boy being a problem.

"Sure," I said. "What is it?"

"I'd like to do the kind of work you do, or something like it. My dad doesn't want me to. He wants me to go into business like him. Can you talk to him and explain how your business works? It might help him understand me better."

The father was on my "suspect" list and meeting him under these circumstances seemed a good, unobtrusive way to get a read on him, so I said, "If you think it'll help, I'm happy to."

The day concluded with me having dinner at a waterfront restaurant in Plymouth with Julie and two Camp Wing directors. We sat at an outdoor table. It was a beautiful, clear, early August evening. The moon was full and the company delightful. I felt younger than I had in quite some time. It was like one of those nights with Melanie when we'd first met a lifetime ago. And it was unlike any evening I'd ever spent with

Gloria, which gave me much food for thought.

My conversation with Bill Tidrow, Sr. a couple of days later did too. The result was that I thought it was time to reconnect with Paula to reassess the puzzling death of Fred Peterson.

* * * * *

We sat in the studio looking at the sketches.

"Have you made any progress?" Paula asked.

"Yes, if you call eliminating suspects progress."

"Sure it is. Tell me more."

"Last we talked, you said if this were one of your novels, there were five suspects who might have a motive for killing my uncle. The first is PJ Parsons for jealousy and anger over a broken promise to the historical society regarding the disposition of the house. Second, Don Phipps for the loss of the house he grew up in. Then there was Mr. X who was angry over a failed partnership with my uncle. And finally, two oystermen—Misters Y and Z who were upset because of Fred's actions in the oyster business."

"So who have you eliminated?"

"Nobody 100%. How can I be sure? But my son Jocko met Don Phipps and said he was a nice guy who apologized for getting upset with Fred. And just yesterday I met one of the two oystermen at the request of his son who is a nice kid who likes my act. We had a friendly conversation and the father admitted he was wrong to have faulted my uncle. I'd already been told the other oysterman was the less belligerent of the two, so Misters Y and Z seem longshots, just like Don Phipps."

"As for PJ, I've known him a long time," said Paula. "Yes, he's petty and his marriage isn't in the best of shape. But do I really think he's a murderer? Hard to believe. I think Coco would have sensed it too."

"So that leaves Mr. X, the one who couldn't convince Fred to make a deal to become a partner."

"You mean Trevanian, right?" she said with a grin.

"You knew who it was then?"

"Of course. It was obvious. You said the argument involved a man who said Fred possessed a very valuable golden object pirated out of a foreign country by a son of Josiah Osborne. I knew that Trevanian dealt in such items, and the fact that we now know that he was a looter himself fits right in."

"I've since learned more of how the Trevanians operate."

"Do tell," she said, leaning in.

I told her about Max and Garber's behavior on Clark's Island and Khatia and Garber searching my house.

"So they seem the most likely suspects?"

"Yes. I just didn't feel comfortable mentioning names without any proof."

"And you still don't have any. Something may come out in the police investigation though. It's more likely to if you tell the police. The Trevanians are already under investigation, and you're not in danger of ruining their reputations anymore. They are already ruined. But there's one big unanswered question here with them. While they might have a motive, how could they possibly have performed such an action physically? Can you see Max or Khatia climbing on that oyster shed and killing anybody?"

"Not in the least. It kind of makes me laugh to picture them out there scuffling. They look to be two of the least fit people I know."

"Maybe Garber did it?"

"Maybe. But he seemed to be the calmest one of the lot."

"Sometimes they are the most dangerous," she said. "But we'll see. Anyone else?"

I hadn't told her my suspicions of my Uncle Mike and Colin to begin with, so I didn't feel the need to tell her that they were now off my list.

"No. I'll tell the police what I know about the trouble between the Trevanians and my uncle and see what happens. If nothing comes up there, then maybe I'll have to conclude he just did slip on that oyster shed and died that way."

235

"I agree. Just don't take those sketches down yet though," she said as she glanced toward them. "There still may be something there we've missed."

"Are you speaking as a mystery writer or psychiatrist?"

"Psychiatrist. Your uncle seems to have been keeping some things within him, and he was trying to work through something in his head. We may be missing something. If Fred was murdered, I can't figure out how it happened out there on that shed. Who knows? The answer may come out of left field. It often does in real life."

Something did come out shortly thereafter, but it wasn't out of left field. In retrospect I should have seen it coming. My uncle had indeed been trying to figure something out with his sketches. The two of the *Smyrna*—one in particular—ended up holding the key.

Chapter 23
ADMINISTRATIVE ASSISTANCE

The mystery of Fred's death began to unravel with an email I got from Derek Parker.

I finally remembered where I heard your uncle's name and the *article of mine he might have read. Best to talk in person. Your place or mine?*

I said he could come down here, and the next day we were on my deck talking.

"Fred's name was mentioned in a series I'm working on for Spotlight," he said. "It's about addiction to pain killers and the role various pharmaceutical companies are playing, sometimes willingly. An article appeared in The *Globe* in April under my byline that three of us contributed to. I have a copy with me. I'll leave it behind for you to read."

"My uncle's name is in here?" I said, taking the article. I was surprised.

"Only in passing. That's why it didn't register with me. One of my colleagues was doing research for the article on the pharmaceutical companies involved. One of them is a Boston company called Upsala. They make a pain medication called Prezalix. At one time, Upsala was owned by a private equity firm called LFP Capital. Ring a bell?"

"Was that my uncle's firm?"

"Yes. It stands for Lancaster, Franklin, and Peterson. In his research, my colleague discovered that LFP bought Upsala from the founders a few years back. Part of the deal was that LFP replaced the Upsala executive team and put in one of their own. They made Garrett Lancaster CEO."

"Who's he?"

"Son of Kenneth Lancaster, the current CEO of LFP. It's not unusual for a PE firm to buy out the executive team of a company they acquire.

The company usually isn't doing well, and the acquirer wants new blood to shake things up."

"How did my uncle's name come up?"

"Purely as an aside. In the article, my colleague has a paragraph in there giving a little of the background on Upsala. It was one of those fast-growing biotech companies you see in Boston these days. They had great initial success, then stagnated, LFP bought them, and their drug pipeline suddenly improved. They did an IPO and LFP made huge money. Then came the news that the FDA had complaints about Prezalix and was going to investigate it. My colleague simply wrote that one of the LFP partners at the time of acquisition was Fred Peterson, now retired. That's it. He's been totally out of the picture since the acquisition. The IPO happened after he'd retired. He was never the lead partner in that deal anyhow. Kenneth Lancaster took that on himself. His son is still CEO and now lives in Boston."

"Good thing my uncle kept his distance. Sounds like Upsala might have some problems."

"Yes. I tried to talk to both Kenneth and Garrett Lancaster, but they wouldn't return my calls. All I got was no comment from the company spokesperson."

"I see. I'll read this article more fully. Thanks for alerting me."

"What interests me is that you said you saw on your uncle's calendar that he was trying to find a way to contact me. I bet it was this one on Upsala since his name was mentioned in it. Do you have any idea?"

"None. My uncle and I weren't close. I'm just learning about all the things he was involved in."

"No papers? No leftover notes?"

"Just some sketches which may or may not mean anything. And his calendar of appointments that mentions you. I'll look again."

"Please do. There may be something there."

* * * * *

From that point on, I no longer tried to kid myself. I was now committed to getting to the bottom of what had happened to my uncle. No more half-hearted attempts. No more waiting for information to come to me. Now that art smuggling, drugs, and investigative reporting had become a part of my daily routine, it was a logical next step for me to fully embrace the role of detective.

To that end, the next day I examined yet again Fred's calendar of appointments. I continued to think they were key. The entries that now interested me most were:

April 25
Emma called me
Emailed me newspaper article
Very concerned

April 26
Called Garrett (stonewalling me)
Left message for Ken to call me. No response yet.
Probably need to fly down to meet

May 4
Meet Sheila Compton. Ask her to connect me to Derek Parker of The Globe *regarding* the *article I read.*

May 5
Delta flight 4 Boston to JFK

May 6
Delta flight 43 JFK to Boston

May 8
Meet Danforth in person. *Show him documents and get his reaction!*

Based on my meeting with Parker, I was able to fill in a few blanks now. Fred clearly had wanted Sheila to connect him to Parker because of the Upsala article where he was mentioned as a retired partner in LFP. Someone named Emma had apparently alerted him to the article.

Parker had told me that "Ken" was Ken Lancaster, Fred's former partner at LFP, and "Garrett" was Garrett Lancaster, Ken's son and current CEO of Upsala. Fred had tried unsuccessfully to talk to both Garrett and Ken because, I guessed, of the article.

On April 26, Fred had noted that he might need to "fly down" to meet someone. And he had booked roundtrip flights to and from JFK for May 5 and 6. New York is where LFP's main office is and where Ken worked. Was he flying "down there" to see his old partner on this? It seemed likely. Or maybe it was to see this Emma person. Maybe it was neither—or both.

There was only one way to find out. I searched online for the phone number of LFP's main office in New York and called it. I asked to be connected to Ken Lancaster. A few seconds later a woman's voice said, "Mr. Lancaster's office."

"May I speak to him please?" I said, offering no explanation.

"He's not in. Can I take a message?"

"Yes. My name is Jake Pavlik, and I need to urgently talk to him."

"About what please?"

"Upsala."

There was a moment of silence.

"Can I ask who you are Mr. Pavlik?"

"Yes. I'm the nephew of his former partner Fred Peterson. I'm his heir, and I'm tying up some loose ends."

There was another even longer silence. Then she said, "I'll talk to him later today. I'll let you know."

The next day she called me back.

"He doesn't want to talk to you on Upsala. He said talk to Garrett."

"I'll bet he won't talk to me either."

"You may be right. But I think you should come to New York anyhow. I'm the one you should talk to before you do anything else."

"Who are you?"

"I'm Emma Roberts. I was your uncle's administrative assistant for many years. I've been looking for someone to talk to ever since he died. I think you may be the right person."

The next day I flew to JFK and met her at the restaurant in lower Manhattan she'd suggested since meeting in the office, she had said, was out of the question.

She was an older woman and seemed nervous. We exchanged awkward greetings. We sat at a table, and she looked at me very intently. She was trying to size me up. I was doing the same of her.

"Okay, I'll go first," I said. "I want to know what my uncle was concerned about regarding Upsala. Was he in trouble?"

"No. Let me give you the background so you'll understand. Did you know him well?"

"No. Hardly at all."

"He was a wonderful man. Kind. Principled. I worked for him for many years. When he became inactive in the business a few years ago and started spending more of his time in Boston, I went to work for Ken. He's very different. Very formal. All business."

"Did the two of them get along?"

"Mostly. They divided up the business. Fred managed his portfolio, Ken his."

"Who was Franklin?"

"George Franklin founded the firm. He died years ago. Fred and Ken bought him out before he died. Ken did the same a few years ago with Fred. Ken has run the whole thing since, but he is all but retired now. Garrett will move back from Boston soon and run LFP with his brother Brendon. That's when I will quit, if not sooner."

She said this very forcefully.

"Why may I ask?"

"Because things are much different here since your uncle left."

"In what way?"

"Some very disturbing actions by the firm. Troubling leadership. Upsala is a case in point."

"Tell me more."

"Understand I'm taking a risk with you. I don't know you. I'm hoping you are like your uncle and want to do the right thing. I haven't decided who to go to. I hope you'll do what I know your uncle would have done had he the chance."

"What's that?"

"Go to the proper authorities."

"And tell them what?"

"That a crime has been committed."

"By whom?"

"I think I know, but I need help."

"How about getting help within LFP?"

"That may be where the problem is."

We sat there staring at each other. She was trying to remain calm, but I could see it was an effort.

"The media is going to get involved," she finally said. "I want to be on the right side of this."

"I do too. What do I need to know?"

"A couple of months ago we got a call from a reporter in Boston who wanted to talk to Ken about one of our former companies, Upsala. His paper was running a story about drug addiction and a potential problem with one of Upsala's drugs came up and he wanted some information. I told Ken, and he said he wasn't going to talk to the press. Our spokesperson said no comment. Three days later the reporter emailed me the story. It didn't say much, only that the paper was going to run a series of articles on pain medications and addiction, and one of Upsala's drugs was being investigated. LFP had been mentioned as well as Fred's name. I emailed him the article, and he became quite concerned."

"I met the reporter who wrote that article. He said he didn't think Fred was involved."

"That's basically correct. He was already semi-retired when Upsala got on LFP's radar, and although he came into the office here on occasion, Fred was starting to spend more and more of his time at the place he bought south of Boston."

"Which is where I now live. He left it to me in his will."

"Really? I wasn't aware of that."

"It apparently was a last-minute decision."

"At any rate, Ken followed the pharmaceutical sector and thought Upsala had untapped potential. Since the company was in Boston and Fred had begun spending a lot of time there, Ken asked him to take a look at the company and give his opinion. Which he did."

"Which was?"

"Don't buy it. He didn't see the potential upside. They hadn't launched a successful new drug in a while, and he thought the price to acquire was too high. He wasn't crazy about the management team either. But Ken went ahead anyway. He said they would replace the management team and there were a couple of potential blockbuster drugs in the pipeline, the most promising of which was in the final stages of clinicals. That was Prezalix."

"And LFP did buy Upsala—along with its problems."

"True. But it's important to be clear on the sequence of events. It was three years ago when Upsala was still independent when Prezalix was developed and passed clinicals. Largely because of Prezalix, LFP bought Upsala and brought it to market. It has sold incredibly well for the last two years. Then came the IPO, and Upsala was independent again."

"And some people made a lot of money with that IPO I assume."

"Yes. A LOT of money. Then about six months ago, Upsala started getting complaints from consumers about addiction with side effects such as change of personality, depression, and suicidal tendencies. An article was written in a British medical journal saying the marketplace outcomes for Prezalix were not matching clinical test results. In April the FDA voiced their concern to Upsala and us. No probe, just concern."

"So what did LFP do?"

"Nothing. We said Upsala was now independent. Go ask them. Legal convinced Garrett that all he had to do was change his marketing to better explain side effects."

"You mean to include all that fast double talk at the end of TV commercials for drugs that nobody listens too?"

"Exactly. But then The *Globe* article came out on the FDA investigation, and that changed the discussion around here.

"In what way?"

"First you have to remember I'm just an administrative assistant. I don't know everything—just what trickles down to me. But I do have unusual access to information. Ken is in his eighties and has become disconnected. He's in the process of turning things over to his sons. He has two email addresses, one personal and one business. He asks me to screen his business emails. I don't understand everything I see. But I get the general idea if something is important, and I let him know. In April after The *Globe* article appeared, I began to see emails that bothered me."

"From who?"

"From Garrett mainly. He said he'd started digging into the history of Prezalix, and Upsala's head of Research and Development Dr. Ashook Sarma had discovered some irregularities in the clinical trials. Dr. Sarma had been brought in to head R&D after LFP had acquired Upsala. His predecessor, Dr. Sergei Karin, was the one who had overseen the clinicals for Upsala."

"What do you mean by irregularities?"

"I can't follow it all. I'd seen a number of emails from Dr. Sarma to Ken that some data was either withheld or doctored in some way."

"Has the previous head of R&D Karin been approached?"

"That's another troubling thing. He's moved back to Russia where he still has citizenship. No one knows exactly where he is."

"And no one else from the old management team knows anything?"

"I'm not sure. I just know two things. First, Dr. Sarma is very well respected and, based on his probings, Ken and Garrett are worried. Second, I think Ken and Garrett don't agree yet on what to do."

"You've seen emails on that?"

"I've seen a few. But they do most of their correspondence on Ken's private email account that I don't see. I do know that Garrett has been up here a couple of times recently and they've exchanged harsh words. They got into a shouting match about Upsala in Ken's office a few weeks ago. I overheard a bit before they closed the door. It was enough to know that it was about Prezalix."

"How much of this did my uncle know?"

"I felt he should know his name had crept into the media. He hadn't seen the article in The *Globe*. He called me and I told him what I knew. At his request, I even forwarded him a couple of the emails Sarma had sent Ken about his suspicions that key data on Prezalix had been falsified. I asked Fred to leave me out of this—that he needed to talk to Ken and Garrett because it looked like the media was going to start digging into this."

"So now what? Do you think my uncle would have blown the whistle?"

"Absolutely. He clearly wanted to talk to Ken and Garrett about it, but I'm not aware that he had a chance before he died. From what I can tell, they refused to talk to him since he was out of the firm. But I am certain he wanted to get to the bottom of this. Here read this. This is an email he sent me two days after I sent him the article. I printed it out."

I took the paper and read:

Emma

I've thought about our discussion for a couple of days now and I've decided what I want to do. There has been a cover up regarding Prezalix that needs to be exposed. People's lives have been damaged. Some have even died and will continue to do so, and I think sudden action must be taken. The question is how to do this? I've concluded that LFP and Upsala will try to circle the wagons and keep this internal. Too many people have made too much money on this deal, and they stand to lose it all—and their reputations—if Prezalix gets investigated. No one who profited by this deal will talk to me, and so I'm going to contact The *Globe myself. I will not get you involved. But I will suggest* they *talk to* the *head of R&D Dr. Sarma and one* other—*someone who I suspect I have greatly misjudged. That's all I'll say for now. No one I know* either *personally, professionally, or legally will know what I am going to do.* They *would discourage me from meddling in something like this in my old age, and* the *law may even bog things down at this stage. But how can I in conscience let information like this not be known? Problems with drugs have struck too close to home with me in* the *past. I'll take it from here in my own way. Thanks for doing* the *right thing.*

"That's pretty clear," I said. "His next step was to tell what he knew to the reporter from The *Globe.*"

"And that's what you'll do now?"

"Let me think about it."

"Let me also give you these," she said, handing me a thick folder. "These are hard copies of some of the email exchanges between Ken and a couple of other individuals. I was told to delete all files referring to Upsala and to turn my computer in for inspection. Before I did, I printed out the ones I thought someone would eventually want to see. As I said, I want to be on the right side of this."

I got on the plane back to Boston that afternoon, debating what to do. I wanted to do something but wasn't sure what. I continued to think about it all the next day. I had four options as I saw it, and I even wrote them on a sheet of paper (for once, I felt I needed to be organized):

1. Do nothing. Let it all play out naturally.
2. Confide in someone who already knows about Fred's suspicious death. That means either Paula or Sheila. But is Upsala even related to his death? Very questionable.
3. Talk to Danforth. He says he knew everything about Fred's dealings at the time of his death. What does he know about this? Maybe nothing. He never mentioned it. And Fred

pointedly wrote to Emma that he was not going to involve the law yet since "It would bog things down."

4. Talk to the media. Fred indicated he was going to do that.

In the end, I decided I'd talk to Danforth first. Despite my uncle's warning about lawyers slowing things down, I wanted to get his take on this—both legally and with regard to my uncle's mindset at the end. But when I called Danforth's office, his assistant told me he and his wife were on a Greek Island cruise for the next two weeks. I dimly remembered he had alerted me that he would be out of pocket for half of August to celebrate his thirty-fifth wedding anniversary.

I took another day to think about it, then made a fateful choice. Rather than wait another two weeks and then getting mired in legalese with Danforth, I decided to play it the way my uncle had wanted to. I called Derek Parker. A combination of his digging and some other information I'd found in the emails Emma had printed out for me produced results that were almost immediate and much more far-reaching than I could ever have imagined.

Chapter 24
A MISJUDGMENT

Parker answered my email request to meet with him regarding Upsala by driving down to my house the very next day. Sensing his story was about to get hotter, he was eager to hear what I had to say.

I repeated what Emma Roberts had said.

"I've seen that negative article in the British medical journal about Prezalix," he said. "It's a red flag."

I also shared with him hard copies of several of the emails Emma had given me. One was from Dr. Sarma to Ken Lancaster, citing suspicions he had over the clinical results gathered by his predecessor. It was dated April 25.

I now suspect that proper protocols were not followed in the Prezalix clinical trials. My predecessor Sergei Karin is no longer in the country and many of his staff took buyout packages when LFP acquired Upsala, so it's difficult to get to the bottom of what happened. Two remaining staff members told me they pointed out that sample groups were improperly recruited and were not reflective of the likely user population. Also, analysis of key data was incomplete and, it appears, intentionally misleading. Some results were incorrectly attributed to placebo groups which masked true risk factors. Karin asked for all data to be submitted to him. He worked closely with Upsala legal counsel to create the final presentation made to FDA for approval.

"Looks like there might be a smoking gun here," said Parker after he had read the email. "Where did you get this?"

"The person does not want to be identified."

"This Dr. Sarma is the key. Since neither of the Lancasters will talk to me, I'm going to go straight to him. I see his email address is on this hard copy. Let me start with him and see if he will talk. We might get lucky."

"I'm told he's a real straight shooter."

"And this didn't happen on his watch either, so he has no incentive to not cooperate."

"Unless LFP tells him not to."

"They may have been duped too. I'll keep you informed."

Two days later, Parker emailed me to alert me to an article that would appear the next day in The *Globe* as part of the Spotlight series on illicit drug practices. A segment of it was devoted to Prezalix. The head of R&D had been willing to be quoted. Parker had attached the article.

Pain medication Prezalix, which is manufactured by the Boston based biotech company Upsala, has recently been undergoing FDA scrutiny. A recent article in The *Manchester Journal of Medicine has raised questions on the validity of the clinical trials that led to the drug's approval several years ago. Since it appeared on the market, there have been seven suicides and elevated rates of depression and addiction among users. While company spokesman Melissa Thomas attributed any problems to improper usage, Dr. Ashook Sarma, head of R&D, has hinted that further investigation is necessary.*

"We are examining all of the protocols that Upsala followed prior to our acquisition of the company. We will cooperate with all authorities. If any irregularities were committed in the past, we will share those details."

Spotlight contacted Upsala CEO Garrett Lancaster as well as his father Kenneth, the CEO of LFP Capital in New York, the former owner of Upsala. Neither would comment.

I called Parker to congratulate him.

"Getting someone on the inside to talk is important," he said. "It might open the floodgates. I appreciate you giving me that lead. If you stumble on anyone else, let me know."

This was the time for my next big reveal.

"As a matter of fact, I do have someone else. I've been going through the emails my source gave me, and I was very surprised to see that someone else was very involved in this, and not in a good way."

"Great. Who is it?"

I gave him the name and the email address. I was certain this was the person my uncle had said he had misjudged.

"Tell me what you find," I said. "I'm interested for a couple of reasons."

* * * * *

A week went by, and I was occupied with normal everyday activities. Danforth returned home from his cruise and sent me an urgent email to call him. I decided to wait a bit. I suspected I knew why he'd emailed me, and I wanted to avoid him for a bit longer. Finally, Parker sent me an email, which contained information that I'd been hoping for.

"Attached is an article that will appear in The *Globe* tomorrow. Thanks for your help."

UPSALA UNDER FEDERAL INVESTGATION FOR FRAUD

Upsala, the *Boston based pharmaceutical company, is under investigation by* the *FBI for falsifying data used in clinical trials related to its pain medication Prezalix.*

The *Globe came into possession of certain emails between Upsala executives and former parent company LPF that indicate a conspiracy to bring a dangerous drug to market. The emails were obtained by* The *Globe from a source that wishes to remain anonymous.* The *Globe* then *turned* the *emails over to* the *authorities for further investigation.*

The *emails reveal that Dr. Sergei Karin, former head of Research and Development for Upsala, falsified data and presented misleading information to* the *FDA in order to obtain approval for Prezalix. Karin is now living somewhere in his native Russia. His successor, Dr. Ashook Sarma, is cooperating fully with authorities. Sarma had no knowledge of* the *conspiracy. He has found more documentation of a cover up and has given that information to authorities.*

The *conspiracy dates back prior to LFP's acquisition of Upsala. Evidence shows that Karin, based on* the *guidance of Upsala's legal department, ignored all recognized protocols to recruit valid test cohorts and systemically altered test results to gain approval for a drug* the *company desperately needed to complete an acquisition that would reward executives at both Upsala and LFP with eight figure payouts.*

Emails obtained by The *Globe indicate that* the *two prime movers in* the *conspiracy were Karin and chief legal counsel of Upsala prior to its LFP acquisition Lyle Danforth of Hingham, Massachusetts. Danforth's office on Commonwealth Avenue in Boston was raided three days ago by* the *FBI, and his computer was seized and scrubbed for information. Many of* the *facts of* the *alleged coverup were discovered as a result. Danforth was out of* the *country at* the *time. He is back now and being questioned by authorities.*

I immediately called Parker.

"Congratulations on the story," I said. "It looks like Danforth is going to pay the price."

"Yes. Those emails you gave me opened the door. Once I saw those between Sarma and Ken Lancaster, I contacted Sarma, and he was very willing to talk on the record. Garrett Lancaster had authorized him to."

"Wow. Suddenly everyone is willing to talk."

"The Lancasters had tried to put a lid on this and buy some time to figure out what to do. They were totally blindsided by the doctored clinical trials. But, ultimately, when they knew this was going to leak out to the public, they thought they'd get out ahead of it. After all, the bad stuff didn't happen on their watch. They inherited it. They do stand to lose a lot of money, though, and they wanted to manage the narrative. But that's out of their control now."

"What was Sarma's attitude when you talked to him?"

"He was very upset and had begun his own investigation. He found serious problems with the data Upsala provided to the FDA. When he probed the two Upsala researchers who had not taken buyout packages, both recalled that the conclusions they'd reached on the data from the clinicals did not match the conclusions Upsala submitted to the FDA. They challenged Karin on this, but he said they had misinterpreted some data sets, and he had reached different conclusions. Further challenges were met with warnings and reprimands not just from Karin but from Lyle Danforth in legal. I contacted two researchers who had taken buyout packages and they reported the same. They had become uncomfortable with Upsala's management and were happy to take the packages and leave."

"And then I see from your story the FBI seized Danforth's computer."

"That blew the lid completely off the case. We contacted the police, and there was enough probable cause to issue a search warrant. With Danforth being out of the country, his administrative assistant turned over files and Danforth's computer. It was a treasure trove of information that clearly implicated Karin and Danforth as the ringleaders in the fraud. Although Karin is out of reach, Danforth is going to take the fall. He may not be alone if anyone else at Upsala participated."

"Anybody at LFP?"

"Probably not. The Lancasters don't seem to have known anything about this. It happened before the acquisition. Their problem was they made a bad business decision to buy Upsala in the first place. They hadn't done their due diligence."

"Just like my uncle had warned. He had sized up the situation perfectly from the start."

"And once he learned from your source what had happened, he clearly wanted to see justice done."

Indeed. Emma Roberts, the source that would be forever unknown to all but me, had triggered the whole series of events and had motivated my uncle to come out of retirement to fix it.

I had one final question for Parker.

"Were there any communications found between my uncle and Danforth on this?"

"I don't know. I haven't seen the materials the FBI seized when they raided Danforth's office. It's still an active investigation, and they have their rules on what to release. It'll all come out over time. But, rest assured, there's enough here to throw the book at Danforth. LFP will lose money too. They will undoubtedly have to pay some damages. Based on what I know, it's all but a closed case."

But Parker was wrong there. It was not a closed case by any means— at least for me. My original interest was in finding out the truth about my uncle's death. In the process of doing so, I'd inadvertently helped to uncover one hell of a drug scandal, and that was great. In the grand scheme of things, that was probably the most important outcome. I was proud to have played a role.

Still, there was the matter of Fred's dead body in the oyster shed. Why and how had it happened? Was it related to the drug scandal? To the Trevanians and the art smuggling? Or something else? I needed to get to the bottom of that.

I had a hunch there would be a final twist to all this. I was right. And it didn't take long for it to turn up.

Chapter 25
THE FACE WITH THE QUESTION MARK

Jocko had continued to stay with me after his return from Vermont. He had already completed his classes to get his PhD, and now he needed to complete his dissertation. Although he could do much of that anywhere, he did need to occasionally meet with the three-person faculty team evaluating his work back on campus. That hadn't gone particularly well in the past, but with his newfound focus, he was getting optimistic. His next meeting was in early September, and he'd have to return to Toledo for that. But until then, he could stay in Duxbury which, given that's where Olivia was, suited him just fine.

The two of them were at my house watching TV one night when I casually mentioned I should get out to the Gurnet and arrange for that rusty shed to be repaired.

"Your uncle had told me he did some of his sketching out there," Olivia said. "Can I come when you go out next time? I'd love to see where he worked."

"Are you available Saturday?" I asked. "We can ride out together."

"I'll come too," said Jocko. The poor kid was acting like a lovestruck teenager these days.

When Saturday came, we drove out rather than take my boat. The weather was a bit iffy. There was talk of a Nor'easter coming in that evening. It was fine now, but I didn't want to get caught on the water if some weather came in suddenly. So we banged our way through fifteen minutes of potholes until we reached Gurnet Point.

We entered the shack and looked around. There was Fred's chair where he used to sit and sketch, the table where his books and appointment calendar had been, the bed and kitchenette. I hadn't been there since I'd removed the mermaid figurehead and the sketches from the wall weeks ago. Everything looked the same.

"You're right," said Olivia, wrinkling her nose as she surveyed the room. "Not much here. Not very inspirational for an artist I wouldn't think."

Jocko said they should walk over to the lighthouse, which left me alone. I then went to the shed and looked inside. I saw a big difference from last time. It had been filled haphazardly with junk but had now been cleaned up and the floor was swept. It was still filled with stuff, but it looked like there had been an attempt to organize it.

"What the hell?" I muttered. "I don't understand."

As I stood outside looking in, I heard a voice from next door. A man came up to me.

"Hi," he said. "Are you the new owner?"

"Yes, I am."

"I live next door. I'm Nick DeLorenzo."

"Hi. I'm Jake Pavlik. I inherited this from my uncle."

"First time out here?"

"Third. I was here last month. I met the man who watches your house off season."

"You met Zack?"

"No. It was a big young guy named Joe. Tattoos all over his arms."

"Zack's my house watcher. He's a small older man. Must have been someone else."

"He said he did odd jobs around the Gurnet. He said my uncle wanted him to rebuild his shed."

"Oh, I know who you must mean. I saw him here a couple of weeks ago. He was in your shed doing some work. Looked like he was cleaning up. I assumed he'd been hired to do some work."

"Not by me. I guess I should get a lock for that shed."

"The guy looked familiar, and then I remembered who he was. He had done a little work around here a few years ago. Your uncle had hired him to watch his place off season, but he ended up firing him. He accused him of stealing. He hasn't been seen here since, until a month or two ago.

Zack said he saw a big stranger just kind of hanging around. He looked like a tough guy with an attitude. It was probably the same guy I saw cleaning your shed. Zack questioned him, and the guy just laughed at him and walked away. Zack was concerned enough to mention it to me."

"Did you ever see my uncle out here?"

"Yes. A few times last summer. He came out to paint and think, he told me. I knew he wanted to fix the place up too. I heard he died. Are you going to keep it?"

"I don't know. I don't see that I'll ever use it. I'm not a painter. But do me a favor. Let me know if you see this big stranger out here again, okay? I don't like the sound of him."

"Me neither. I'll let you know."

I gave him my cell number and took one last look at the shack and shed. Someone clearly had been in the shed moving things around. It led me to an inescapable conclusion. The big stranger who had called himself Mr. Fixit had been out here snooping around.

When Olivia and Jocko returned, we headed back to Powder Point. We decided we'd get "grab and go" dinners from Brothers and bring them back to the house. As we drove down Washington Street over the Bluefish River Bridge, I saw a strange sight. About a half dozen oyster sheds had been towed by skiffs from their moorings in the bay and all the way down river until they literally abutted the bridge. They were packed in tight there.

"What's this?" Jocko asked.

"I can see this is your first Nor'easter," Olivia laughed. "In a storm, the sheds get pushed into a protected place. It's either here or in Eagle's Nest Bay by the Marshall Street Bridge. If they stayed in the bay, they'd get destroyed by the wind. Lots of damage can be done by these gales that spiral in eastward from the Atlantic. Flooding, power outages, trees down. It's our biggest nightmare since we jut out right into the water. The only thing that saves us is the barrier beach. Without that, there wouldn't be a Duxbury as we know it."

"Seriously?" I said. "That sounds ominous."

"Yes, seriously. But we do have the barrier, so we'll be all right. I've got to go. We all need to batten down the hatches."

Her warning was prophetic. At about 10:00 that night, the wind began to howl and our power went out. I didn't know what hatches were or how to batten them down even if I did. Being the klutzes that both Jocko and I are, we didn't even know how to fire up the back-up generator. We just went to bed in total darkness to ride it out.

As I lay there with the house rattling in the gale, I was a bit unnerved by the thought that I was as exposed to the elements as all the Soules, Petersons, and Osbornes had been in the centuries before me. Mother Nature was still boss. But what was most on my mind was the Gurnet and the big stranger who had been out there inside the shed. I wondered what it was that Mr. Fixit thought needed fixing.

* * * * *

There were now two investigations under way. The Trevanians were in Geneva, under indictment by both the US and Swiss governments. Their possessions in their Duxbury house had been confiscated by the authorities and were being examined. I would love to have gotten my hands on what Max had claimed was Samuel Osborne's logbook of the voyage of the *Smyrna*. I phoned Caroline Hawksmoor at the historical society office and told her what Trevanian said it revealed. She was very surprised.

"I never heard of such a logbook," she said. "The Osbornes were very minor figures. This could change everything."

"If that book is authentic, it would be of real historic value then?"

"Absolutely. I don't know if I believe the whole Golden Fleece thing. And it's pretty wild that it could be somewhere on your property even if it does exist. That aside, if it's true that Osborne was smuggling opium into the country, that would be a major discovery. It would add a new dimension to our understanding of the opium wars."

"Do you think the historical society could request the logbook be given to it to examine or even keep? I'd love to see it."

"I don't know. If the Trevanians are proven guilty, maybe. I'm going to ask around and see what is allowed in a case like this. Thanks for the tip."

The other investigation that impacted me of course was Danforth's role in the Upsala affair. His computer and files were being combed over by the authorities and Parker said a "treasure trove of information" was discovered. I would have loved to know if any of it mentioned my uncle's involvement but didn't know who to ask. If Parker couldn't access the information directly, how could I? I figured I'd have to wait a considerable period to find out.

But I didn't have to wait for long. As it turned out, I didn't need to call the police. They called me. They told me to get down to the station. An FBI agent wanted to talk to me there.

The next day I met the agent.

"I'm Agent Higgins," a man said. He had short hair, was middle aged, and had the neck of a linebacker. He looked like Lee J. Cobb—tough and all business. I was quite nervous. I'd never been remotely in this situation. My only frame of reference were various noirs where the "feds" sprang into action to confront the bad guys. Did they think I was one? His first sentence to me didn't immediately assuage my fears.

"We've been investigating the activities of your uncle's lawyer Lyle Danforth. We established probable cause and carried out a search and seizure on his and his assistant's computers. I want to talk to you because your name and your uncle's appear on some emails. You know Danforth, correct?"

"He handled my uncle's estate, and I met him several times regarding that. I assume that's how my name has come up?"

"Actually, it was in another context. That's what I am interested in. Do you know about the Upsala case?"

From the way he phrased the question, it was obvious that Parker had fully protected my anonymity with the authorities. No one knew that his *Globe* article was partially based on crucial information I had provided him. I, like Emma, was an anonymous source at this point.

"Yes, I've read about it."

"You are mentioned in an email exchange between Danforth and an individual we don't know. Take a look. Read this one first." He handed me a printout of an email to Danforth dated May 4.

The sender was a "Gurnetmrfixit." It simply said: *It was way trickier than I thought, but your buddy won't be giving you any more trouble. Mission accomplished.*

Danforth had replied: *What??? Call me to explain.*

"I don't understand," I said. "How does this involve me?"

"By itself, it doesn't make much sense. Look at this other one."

Again it was to Danforth and the sender was "Gurnetmrfixit." It was dated June 8: *I met your buddy's nephew out here today. I saw him take some stuff out of the house and shed. What should I do?*

Danforth's reply: *Clean up that place ASAP!!! Call me at once!*

"Okay. I guess I see the connection now," I said. "My uncle is obviously the buddy and I'm the nephew."

"Did you go out to the Gurnet around the date of that email?"

"Yes. I don't remember the exact date, but I went there for the first time in early June. I'd only been in town a couple of weeks."

"Did you talk to anyone?"

"Yes. A big muscular young man with tattoos on his arms. He said his name was Joe, and he said he watched after my uncle's and the neighbor's houses in the off season. I recently met the neighbor, and he said that's not true. The neighbor said the stranger looked familiar—like someone who had done a few odd jobs around there a few years ago and hadn't been seen since. What do you make of all this?"

"No idea at this point. We're just checking out best we can every email and phone call Danforth made in the last few months because of Upsala. He's in a lot of trouble. Everything we have found is fitting together nicely. The problem is he recently deleted everything. Luckily, we've been able to retrieve a lot of it."

"That's possible?"

"Yes. After thirty days it becomes tough. But, luckily, Danforth didn't know his assistant had the computer set up to automatically back up everything on his computer on the Cloud. The deleted emails are still there, and we were successful in subpoenaing them from the internet provider. At any rate, everything we've found fits together—except these few emails to Gurnetmrfixit. We'd love to know who he is and what his relationship was to your uncle."

"Me too. In fact, when I met him, he told me his name is Joey Fixit, and he gave me his number. It's in my contacts." I pulled it up and the agent copied the information.

"Thank you. This may be a fake number, but we'll check it out. If anything comes to mind, let us know. Upsala is a very big case."

By this time, I did have something else in mind. The question was should I tell the FBI now what was in my head, or should I wait a little longer to think through everything? I decided to wait because there still was something that made no sense to me. I left and drove home.

The sun was out as I drove up Washington Street. I passed a group of kids jumping off the Bluefish River Bridge. How different the scene was from the other day when the sheds were packed tight.

A lightbulb suddenly went off in my head. I spent the next couple of days collecting my thoughts, unsure of what to do. Then two pieces of information came my way. One was a weather report, the other was a phone call from Olivia. Why wait any longer? I called Higgins and the next day he was at my house.

"I have a suggestion," I said.

"Which is?"

"Go to the Gurnet and dust my shack and shed for fingerprints and search for any blood stains."

"Why?"

"Because it'll tell you who Mr. Gurnetmrfixit is. I think you'll find that he killed my uncle."

"What makes you think that?"

"Have a seat, Mr. Higgins. Let me tell you my theory of the case."

Chapter 26
THE THEORY EXPLAINED

It took a few weeks for it all to play out. August had turned to September when the news came out that Lyle Danforth was indicted for the murder of Fred Peterson. Derek Parker's article broke the story with a headline that said it all:

FORMER UPSALA LAWYER INDICTED FOR MURDER
KILLS CLIENT TO SILENCE HIM

The headline the next day turned a few heads too.

FBI CREDITS NEPHEW FOR SOLVING
MURDER OF HIS UNCLE

My role in it had come out—and I was just fine with that. I owed it to my uncle to get this right, and I had.

Now that my role was public, people were approaching me to congratulate me, to compliment me, or to ask for a fuller explanation of how and when I'd figured it all out. Paula Spaulding wanted to do all three. She was the very first person I sought out after Danforth's guilt was announced in The *Globe*. I went over to her house that same day to offer her my thanks for her help.

"I could not have done this without you," I said. "You taught me how to think through this from the start."

"You just needed somebody to talk to," she smiled. "I want to understand your thought process."

"Do you know who first said Fred's death seemed suspicious? I don't think I ever told you."

"No, you didn't."

"Sheila Compton of the *Messenger*. I owe her a big thank you too. She gave me my first few leads. I was very reluctant to follow them, but in my own way I did. Caroline Hawksmoor, Coco Parsons, Olivia Phipps. Sheila encouraged me to talk to all of them. I got a little bit of information from each one. That's when I first came to you for advice."

"It was just a case of organizing your thoughts at that point."

"Then I found those sketches. They seemed important, but I didn't know what to make of them. Your background in psychiatry helped me. Getting inside Fred's head at the end of his life became important, and you showed me that those sketches were key."

"The description of your uncle as a visual storyteller is perfect. Even though we called it an evidence wall, it really wasn't. There was no evidence in those sketches. I was kind of playing along with you on that, frankly. They were Fred's way of telling us what was on his mind at the time of his death. We can see in hindsight that the history of the house, the legacy he wanted to leave, his experiences in the town with oysters, Coco, and the Trevanians are all clearly reflected in those sketches."

"But I was still kind of lost," I said. "Those sketches seemed to be based on local squabbles. As much as I wanted to believe we were getting at something, I still felt deep inside that nobody we mentioned was a likely murderer. Coco's husband, the oystermen, Don Osborne. The more I got to know about them, the less I believed they had committed murder."

"You never know when someone will snap—it's often a trivial thing. But in this case, yes. It seemed a longshot that anything Fred was involved with here in town would have put him in danger—particularly since he was always the innocent party in all of these grudges against him."

"But then there were the Trevanians," I continued. "The first time I met them is when they invited me to their house for lunch. I thought they were very strange but not dangerous. I wrote them off as eccentric. But then when Khatia and Garber barged into my house demanding access, I began to get concerned. She, in particular, seemed unhinged. Then there were the two incidents on Clark's Island where Max and Garber were caught on video secretly digging. I began to see the whole lot of them as being fully capable of criminal behavior."

"Which has now been proven."

"Art criminals, yes. But were they murderers? It was hard for me to see them as such. How could they have gotten out to that shed on the bay? That was the first time I thought that whoever did this might have had an accomplice—someone fit enough to commit a crime that would have involved a certain physicality. In this case I thought of Garber. Again, my thinking was evolving. And then I met Derek Parker and everything changed again."

"How did you meet him?"

"He was covering the Trevanian case for The *Globe*. When I mentioned my uncle was Fred Peterson and had been looking to connect, Parker said the name rang a bell. It turned out Fred's name was mentioned in passing in another story he was covering—the Upsala case. He gave me some information that led me to a woman whistleblower with my uncle's old firm in New York connected to Upsala. Danforth's name appeared on emails that implicated him in a coverup with the pain medication Prezalix. I brought the emails to Parker and he started digging. He developed a key source within Upsala, a scientist named Sarma, who turned up more information incriminating Danforth. Parker ultimately alerted the police and FBI. They seized Danforth's computer, and it contained enough information to have him indicted for mail and securities fraud. Parker was key. He really should be given most of the credit for exposing Danforth."

"Reporters are often the best assets in exposing criminals. Almost all writers of whodunnits have a detective as the protagonist. I sometimes use an investigative reporter as the lead. It freshens things up."

"Like Jimmy Stewart in *Call Northside 777*, right?"

"Hey, here's a thought. How about I use a guy who does cartoon voices as my lead investigator for my next book? That'll really shake the genre up!"

"I'll expect royalties."

She laughed. "Okay, back to your theory of the case. So Danforth commits fraud with Upsala. That doesn't connect him to killing your uncle though."

"True. This is when I decided I was the best one to quietly take the lead in the investigation. I was the one suspicious of my uncle's death. The thought that Fred Peterson was murdered hadn't even crossed the minds of Parker or the FBI. They were investigating a drug conspiracy led by Danforth and a Russian emigre. Their work was done, or so they thought. But I knew more than they did."

"Like what?"

"I was the one who had a previous relationship with Danforth, and I began to completely reevaluate him once I knew he'd already committed one crime. He had seemed so open and helpful to me. But was he really? First, I remembered Coco's comment that Fred had told her he deeply regretted a business deal in which he badly misjudged somebody. Since he had just recently learned of the Upsala conspiracy and Danforth's role in it, I guessed that was what he was referring to."

"A nationwide drug scandal would have disturbed him a lot more than a little infighting over a couple of small oyster farms."

"My thought too. And he said he had badly misjudged some person in the process. Who was that person? Then I caught Danforth in some lies to me personally, and I wondered if he was the one."

"What lies?"

"A couple of small things at first. He had consistently portrayed my uncle as old and frail while everyone else described him as energetic. You even used the word robust as I recall."

"He was. He did slip on the ice last winter and had a concussion. But that had nothing to do with his being frail. This place can be pretty brutal in winter. I know Tommy Tsai slipped on the ice too. They don't de-ice the roads well enough in town if you ask me."

"So why, I wondered, had Danforth wanted me to think Fred was so shaky?"

"Because it would make it more plausible for people and the police to believe that Fred's slipping and falling on the oyster platform was an accident?"

"That's what crossed my mind too. I even began to question why Danforth wanted to receive all the mail from 3 Spyglass even after Fred's death. At first, I thought he was trying to be helpful. But then I began to wonder if he wanted to screen it first. He didn't want me to get anything that I might find suspicious."

"Come to think of it, the last thing he'd have wanted was a family member to inherit that house. Who knows what they may have discovered later—which is basically what ended up happening."

"I've thought a lot about that too. From the very first time we met when he went over the will, Danforth said he strongly disagreed with the terms of it. He said that he'd advised Fred to give the house to the historical society outright and leave me cash instead. That's the only honest thing Danforth ever told me. But he didn't tell me his real motive. He said it was to avoid complexity. It was really to get me the hell completely out of the picture. He didn't want any family member to ever move to Duxbury."

"So even a clueless outsider from Toledo was a threat to him, even if a small one?" she smiled.

"You could say that. But then I discovered Danforth's most telling lie. It's the one that made me pretty certain he was a murderer."

"What was that?"

"He had told me he had never been out to the Gurnet and had no knowledge of what Fred did out there. But then the FBI seized Danforth's computer and showed me some puzzling emails between Danforth and a certain Gurnetmrfixit. I recognized this nickname because I had met an individual prowling around the Gurnet shack who called himself Mr. Fixit. From the emails I saw, it was obvious Danforth was well aware of the place and was somehow connected to this guy. There was one email that was dated May 4, the day after my uncle died. It was from Gurnetmrfixit and said that although it had been trickier than he thought, Danforth's "buddy" wouldn't be causing him any more problems, that it was "Mission accomplished." Other emails I saw indicated that "buddy" referred to my uncle. And what mission had Mr. Fixit accomplished?"

"That's an ominous statement."

"The FBI found another email from Gurnetmrfixit that was sent the day after I had met him at the Gurnet in early June. He told Danforth that I had taken some things out of the shack and shed. This seemed to alarm Danforth, and he told him to "clean up the place ASAP" and delete all emails to him. I happened to go out to the Gurnet with my son and Olivia soon after, and I met a neighbor for the first time. He said he had recently seen an individual cleaning up the shed. The door has no lock. The neighbor said it was a big guy with tattoos who looked vaguely familiar. It was clearly Gurnetmrfixit, and I knew this guy was trouble."

"We're approaching a smoking gun here."

"I was missing one more piece. If Gurnetmrfixit had been hired to kill my uncle, how could he have done it? A dead body with a fractured skull on a highly visible oyster shed in the middle of a busy bay was far more likely to have been the result of a tragic accident rather than a murder. No one could remember seeing anybody on that shed that morning."

"You'd have thought the murderer could have found a more secluded spot."

"It turns out he had. It all came to light for me when I was driving home before the Nor'easter last month and saw all the sheds had been moved and packed in tight against the Bluefish River Bridge."

"Hmmm. I think I see where you are going."

"It had dawned on me if those sheds were so mobile, then a murder could occur anywhere. The body could then have been put in the shed when it was near the Bluefish River Bridge, then towed back by a skiff to its mooring in the bay only to be discovered later. The first thing I did was check the weather report for early May."

"And you found…"

"That there was a storm warning the evening before my uncle died."

"So the sheds would have been moved to the bridge."

"It turns out most were not, but a couple were. The storm never fully materialized. Some rain and wind but no Nor'easter. The next morning it all ended, and whatever sheds had been moved would have been towed back to their moorings. Bobby Atkinson's shed was one of them."

"So your theory was somebody killed your uncle somewhere and was able to put the body into the shed in a storm?"

"Yes. Those sheds literally touch the Bluefish River Bridge. There's a parking lot right there. Somebody would have had to carry my uncle's body only ten feet from a car to a shed. And Fred was not a big man. He probably weighed about one hundred sixty pounds. A strong man could easily have done it."

"And so the next day the owner of the shed or one of his crew goes to work and finds the body inside?"

"Yes. The body was mostly inside the shed and the door was half closed."

"So whoever towed it out there was the murderer?"

"Not necessarily. Whoever towed it out there in the half-darkness of the morning could have done so very innocently and been totally unaware that there was a body inside. In fact, that's exactly what happened."

"What made you think that?"

"Because I had developed a strong hunch of who the murderer was and where he had committed it. That's where Olivia comes in. The day after I'd talked to the FBI, she called me and said to come to the art complex. She had something to show me."

"A painting?"

"No. When I had gone out to the Gurnet shack the first time and saw Mr. Fixit, I had seen a wooden statue that intrigued me. It was actually a ship's figurehead in the form of a mermaid. It was very old and damaged.

It looked like Fred had been using it as a model for a painting of his."

"Ah, yes. The crying mermaid. I remember you mentioned you had brought the figurehead back when you first showed me the twelve sketches."

"Yes. It was missing its right arm, which I found in the shed by the shack. I thought it would be interesting to bring both pieces back home and have the figurehead restored. By the way, it turns out it was carved by Josiah Osborne himself and has some historic value."

"So you brought it back?"

"Yes. The big piece was seven or eight feet long, but it was a lot lighter than it looked, and I was able to maneuver it into my SUV. I had just loaded the pieces back into my car when I met Mr. Fixit. He'd seen what I'd been doing."

"And did you ever reconstruct the figurehead?"

"That's where Olivia comes in. I had given the two pieces to the art complex. I figured they could find a person to restore it better than I could. The reconstruction had just started when Olivia gave me a call to come in and look at it. I went to the Complex. The two pieces were in an annex. The man doing the restoration had noticed two surprising things about it. First, the entire top half of the figurehead was hollow. That's why it had been so light to carry."

"That's strange."

"Trevanian's man Garber had told me that the old Osbornes were smugglers and used the hollowed out figureheads to stash some of their lootings and bring them back to the U.S. I thought he was nuts, but it turns out he was right."

"And Olivia called you because they had found some loot in it?"

"No. The restorer noticed something even more interesting. The paint on the figurehead was badly faded, in some places totally gone. But on the splintered off right arm he noticed a red stain that was bright. It looked recently made. He looked at it and thought it might be blood. He examined it more closely and saw there was hair on the stain too. It looked suspicious and he stopped work to call it to Olivia's attention. Since I had brought the pieces to her, she wanted me to look at it. I hadn't noticed it before."

"What did you think?"

"That's when I finally got in touch with the FBI. I told them I suspected that the stain might be my uncle's blood. I said my theory was that Fred had discovered Danforth's role in the Prezalix conspiracy and Danforth had wanted to silence him. I told them everything I've just told you, and they thought it was enough to get a DNA read on the stain as well as dust for fingerprints on it. The analysis of the blood showed that it was Fred's. There were fingerprints on the wood that matched those of a Joe Fallon, a drifter originally from Dorchester who had done jail time for assault. He had been living on and off in Plymouth doing odd jobs, including a few months as a part-timer on an oyster farm in Duxbury. The FBI located him in a place he was renting in Plymouth and seized his computer and cell phone. They found plenty of communication between him and Danforth. Also, his bank account showed several huge deposits from a bank account that was traced back to Danforth."

"So a writer of whodunnits would now say that you had established that Danforth had the motive, opportunity, and means to kill Fred. The motive was to silence Fred from telling the authorities what he knew about Danforth's involvement in Prezalix."

"The FBI believes there's no question of Danforth's guilt and that Fred had the information that would have helped prove the case beyond any doubt."

"Okay," she said. "So Danforth's hit man Fallon could have killed Fred anywhere and put the body in the shed afterwards."

"And the theory was the place where he had done it likely was the Gurnet where the figurehead had been. Sure enough, the FBI found traces of Fred's blood in the purple shack. When Fred's death was immediately ruled an accident from a fall on the oyster platform and the body cremated—something Danforth arranged—neither Fallon nor

269

Danforth felt they had anything to worry about. Fallon carelessly tidied up the Gurnet shed a bit but felt no sense of urgency to do more than that. He left more than a few traces of Fred's blood in that shed. His fingerprints and traces of Fred's blood were found in the car too. One of the things that had made Sheila Compton suspicious was that surprisingly little blood was found by Fred's body in the oyster shed. Now we know why. He was killed somewhere else."

"And, finally, the means. I gather that Fallon used the mermaid figurehead to deliver the blow?"

"Yes. The smaller part that had slivered off—the right arm—served as a club. It was the size of a baseball bat. Although much of the interior of the figurehead was hollow, this arm was solid wood. He had tossed it into the shed with the other junk after he had killed my uncle."

"I must say that's quite the theory."

"Look, the authorities have only been looking into this for a short time. Undoubtedly more will come out. And, rest assured, Danforth is going to fight this. Already he's trying to make Fallon the fall guy. And Fallon is very willing to testify against Danforth."

"I'll bet he's looking for a plea bargain of some sort. Each will try to throw the other under the bus. It will take a while to sort out."

"Yes. There are unanswered questions. A big one is why did Fallon put the body in the shed as opposed to leaving it somewhere else? He hasn't said anything about that. He hasn't even fully admitted his guilt yet. That'll come out later."

"This will be a doozy of a trial. Danforth sounds like the kind of person who will fight this to the end. He's a very clever lawyer who will find the best representation and look for any loophole."

"Clever and evil."

"Don't hold your breath waiting for a quick judgment on this."

Chapter 27

WITNESS FOR THE PROSECUTION

There were two major trials that occurred over the next twelve months. The first was the Prezalix case which was tried in federal court. Danforth tried to paint the picture that the Russian, Karin, was the guilty party and that he was just an attorney trying to represent his client based on the information he was given. He argued that Karin was the scientist and drug expert, not him.

Yet there was a mountain of evidence against him. Testimony from Sarma and a couple of researchers proved that Danforth was not only fully aware of the fraud but had devised the strategy to deceive the FDA. The fact that he knowingly continued the cover up even after people had died weighed heavily against him. He was found guilty on charges of mail fraud due to falsification of clinical drug trial data, securities fraud for profiting from his deception, and manslaughter because his intentional deception resulted in deaths. He was sentenced to a significant prison term and a huge financial penalty. He was immediately imprisoned pending appeal.

The murder case, which was to be tried in state court, was more complicated. Two grand juries were convened—one to hear the evidence against Danforth, the other against Fallon. Both Danforth and Fallon were indicted.

The evidence against Fallon was overwhelming. Fred's blood and Fallon's fingerprints were found at the scene of the murder (the purple shack on the Gurnet), as well as on the murder weapon (a club found in the rusty Gurnet shed), and in Fred's car (which Fallon had driven from the Gurnet back into town with the corpse in the trunk). This evidence plus incriminating emails and phone messages convinced Fallon's attorneys that the best strategy was to fully cooperate with the prosecution and plea bargain for a reduced sentence.

The prosecution was amenable to this. The big story for them revolved around a world class criminal like Danforth, not a cheap thug like Fallon. The lawyer had committed a crime with Prezalix that had led to the deaths of a number of people and ruined the lives of many more. Therefore, his hiring of Fallon to commit murder—though horrific in its own right—was connected to an even greater evil, namely the Prezalix conspiracy. The prosecution wanted all the elements of that conspiracy fully exposed. If Fallon could help shine a light on the extent of Danforth's criminality, they'd consider a reduction in his sentence. So Fallon became a witness for the prosecution in the case against Danforth.

The trial dragged on for weeks. Danforth's defense kept shifting strategies. They first claimed Fallon had acted on his own, then that Karin was the prime mover in the plot to kill my uncle. They asserted that Danforth had been duped himself until the very end. Yet the emails on Fallon's computer showed complete complicity on Danforth's part. Testimony that Fred knew of Danforth's role in the Prezalix scandal and was going to reveal what he knew gave Danforth a clear motive. Most crucially of all, it was discovered that two huge crypto deposits had been made into Fallon's bank account from an offshore shell company that was traced back to Danforth.

Then Fallon took the stand and, in his long, rambling testimony, he explained how the killing had happened. He often was inarticulate and was asked repeatedly by the prosecution and judge to clarify various responses. Almost all of what he said corroborated the prosecution's theory of the case which, frankly, was the theory I had given them. It filled in some important blanks too.

He had first met Danforth several years prior. Danforth was out on the Gurnet with Fred soon after Fred had bought the property. Fallon had been doing some odd jobs out there and asked if Fred needed any help. Fred hired him to caretake the shack off season but ended up firing him after only a few months because my uncle suspected him of stealing some things. Years later, when Danforth needed to have Fred silenced, he remembered Fallon as an unprincipled tough guy capable of doing anything. He contacted him.

"But he was very cagey," testified Fallon. "When he called me, he said he was going to connect me to somebody he knew that needed a dirty job done. He said that he didn't want his name involved in any way and that I should deal directly with this other guy. But I knew Danforth was totally involved."

The prosecution asked who this other person was.

"I never met him," he said. "We only talked on the phone. He had a heavy foreign accent. Lyle Danforth said something later that made me believe he was Russian."

This was obviously Karin. With him now safely in Russia forever, he would not be refuting any testimony against him.

"And what did this foreigner tell you he wanted?"

"Me to kill an old man who had a place on the Gurnet. When he told me who, I remembered I had met him once with Danforth and had even done some work for him before he fired me. I had no love lost for the guy."

Even though Danforth had said he didn't want to be associated with this "dirty deal" with Fallon, he eventually took the risk of telephoning him. He was worried that Fred was on the verge of going to the authorities and couldn't wait any longer.

Fallon testified Danforth had yelled at him, "Obey the goddamn orders that Russian gave you for Christ's sake!. Now!"

The Russian had given Fallon no orders on how and where to commit the crime. And Danforth had already told him he wanted to keep his distance. So Fallon was on his own to plan this.

He decided to kill Fred on the Gurnet. From their previous interactions, he knew that my uncle went out there a lot to sketch. Best of all, the area was remote.

"There's never anybody around at that time of year except an occasional work crew or caretaker," he explained. "I wanted to make it look like an accident, and there's a good spot for that near the Gurnet lighthouse."

As Fallon talked, the prosecution repeatedly alluded to the maps of the area it had prepared so that the jury could follow along. The people of Duxbury were particularly interested to learn of Fallon's explanation of how he had committed the murder. How could such a brutal murder have been committed in familiar places in the town they knew so well? They were fascinated by the logistics. (Note: I was able to get copies of these maps in order to explain it all later to Uncle Mike, Colin, Beth, and the Kaplers. Those maps, plus one of the many sketches Fred did of Gurnet Light that I later discovered among his papers, are included at the end of this chapter for reference).

Fallon described the lighthouse as standing on the edge of a cliff that has been badly eroded. In fact, it's so bad that, in a monumental engineering undertaking, the lighthouse had to be moved further back a few years ago so it wouldn't fall over the side.

"My plan was to subdue him in the shack and dump him over the cliff. I figured it would be considered an accident. An old man gets too close to the edge and poof…"

The way he dismissively snapped his fingers at the word "poof" showed a cruelty that didn't go unnoticed by the jury. But he'd already made his plea bargain arrangement, and he went on.

"So I had to find a way to be there when he would be. I'd been trying to get a handle on his movements, and I knew he went there once or twice a week by car. I considered driving my own out there, but I was afraid of being noticed by somebody."

He had good reason to worry about that because the Duxbury Beach Reservation, which is the nonprofit that operates the beach, has a security vehicle stationed just over the Powder Point Bridge on the beach side inspecting traffic that heads out on the Gurnet Road. Access beyond that point requires a vehicular sticker issued by the town. And then, once you finally arrive at the little community of houses by the Gurnet lighthouse, there is another security checkpoint. Only Gurnet and Saquish residents are allowed to enter. Fallon needed to avoid that level of potential scrutiny.

"So no car for me. I decided I'd take a boat across the bay. I don't have a motorboat, and I couldn't get one without getting somebody else involved. That's the last thing I wanted to do. So I decided to go out by kayak. You can paddle out there from the beach off Shipyard Lane. I'd done it a few times in my clam digging days."

He didn't own a kayak either, but it was easy to find one. Many owners just leave them randomly stacked up at the Shipyard Lane beach after they are done with their paddle. It is a lot easier than hoisting it onto a roof rack atop a car and hauling it back home.

"There's always at least twenty of them just lying there year-round. Nobody worries about theft. All I'd need to do is buy a paddle, park my car in a little parking area near the Shipyard beach, take a kayak, paddle out to the cove by the Gurnet, and drag it ashore into the beach shrubs. I would then wait for the old guy to arrive at his shack, knock him out there, then take him to the cliff in the back of the lighthouse and toss him over. I would then paddle back to Shipyard, get in my car and that would be that."

The way he said "that would be that" implied a disturbing casualness—like this was a day at the office. But there was nothing casual about his attention to detail.

"When I got out to the Gurnet, I didn't wait for him too close to the shack because I didn't want anybody to see me hanging out around there. So I walked to the lighthouse hill and looked at the shack in the distance through my binoculars to see if his car was there. It's only a couple of hundred yards away."

The first couple of days Fred didn't come, so it was back across the bay to the Shipyard beach, put the kayak back among the others, and try again the next day.

"I said to myself I'd try it once or twice more, and if he didn't show, maybe I'd have to change my plans."

But on the third day, he saw Fred's car pull into his driveway . It's only a three minute walk from the lighthouse to the shack, and Fallon rushed down. The door was unlocked and Fred was just arranging himself to sketch.

"My plan was to catch him totally by surprise, overpower him, tie him up, take him to the cliff, untie him, and throw him over. I didn't want any trace of it looking like he was killed in advance. This had to look like an accidental fall. I figured I was strong enough to handle an 80-year-old man and pull this off with my bare hands. All I brought in with me was a rope to tie him up."

But it didn't work out that way. When Fallon barged through the door, a startled Fred had time enough to start to reach into his pocket.

"I panicked. I thought he was reaching for a gun. I looked quickly around, and I saw this piece of wood right next to him. I grabbed it and swatted at his head. I connected and he fell over unconscious.

"This wasn't how I planned it. But I could still make it work. I just had to get him to the cliff. With the long fall to the rocks below, the body would be so banged up it would still look like an accidental fall. All along I'd planned to get him to the cliff by using his car. There's a road that ends right near the lighthouse, so I searched him to find his keys in his pocket. As I searched him, I saw he really did have a pistol on him. Anyway, I walked outside to open the trunk before carrying the body out."

As he made his way to the car, he was horrified to see a man standing in front of the neighboring house. It was Nick DeLorenzo's house watcher Zack. He had testified previously that he checked up on the house twice a week and was just leaving. Fallon was sure this other man had seen his face.

"I went back in the shack in a panic. Now somebody could place me on the Gurnet that day. If a dead body was found at the bottom of the nearby cliff the next day, it might now come out that a stranger had been seen in the old man's shack at the same time Fred's car was there.

Although I hadn't done any work out there for several years, I was afraid this guy who saw me might remember who I was if he was questioned. I had to change my plan and get that body and car off the Gurnet. It had to look like he had left there with no problem."

Fallon explained that he'd stayed in the shack with the body on the floor, his head spinning. He peaked out the window constantly, hoping the other man would leave the neighbor's house. He was so nervous he vomited into the toilet. Finally, he saw the other man get into a car and drive away. It was getting dark. It was now safe to carry the body out of the house and into the trunk.

He quickly cleaned up the blood as best he could. Luckily, there wasn't much. He threw the wood into the shed in the pile of junk that was in there. He didn't spend a lot of time covering his tracks. He figured once he got the body off the Gurnet and it was found elsewhere, this remote place would never be examined as a murder scene.

"I loaded the old guy's body into the car. It was fully dark by then. There wasn't a soul around."

As he drove, he debated what to do with the corpse. Getting it out of town and dumping it in the water or a field somewhere seemed like a good bet. But where? Maybe somewhere in Rhode Island or New Hampshire? The state lines for each were only an hour away.

By the time he crossed over the Powder Point Bridge, it was now completely dark and a light rain started to fall. He knew bad weather was forecast, and he was afraid it might become difficult to drive if things got worse. Also, a new worry hit him. If he drove very far, it would mean leaving his car at Shipyard Lane overnight. Police cruise through the town's beach parking lots every now and then after hours. Beach vandalism has been on the rise. A car left overnight in any of these lots— or even just into the wee small hours—would definitely be noticed and probably even made note of. Maybe he should transfer the body into his own car. But maybe that was too complicated. He had no idea what to do.

277

As he passed back through Powder Point and reached Washington street, he saw something that stopped him dead in his tracks: two oyster sheds had been moved against the Bluefish River bridge for protection against the storm. This was his chance. He could dump the body in one, drive Fred's car back to his house on Spyglass less than a mile away, and run back to his own car in the Shipyard Lane parking lot. He would be out of town within the hour.

"I recognized one of the sheds that was owned by Bobby Atkinson of Bayside Oysters," he testified. "I had done some parttime work for him a couple years ago. I lifted the body into the shed and closed the door halfway so nobody would easily see it from the outside. I was hoping it wouldn't be noticed until the morning when it was back in position in the middle of the bay. That way, the death could be considered caused by an accidental fall, which had been my idea all along. It would just have been in an oyster shed, not at the bottom of a cliff."

Sure enough, a skiff operated by an employee of Bayside Oysters towed the shed back to its mooring at 5:30 the next morning after the storm had passed.

"I was barely awake and it was not even totally light yet," testified the employee. "The shed door was half closed too. I didn't notice any body inside it."

Fallon concluded his testimony by explaining that after he carried the body into the oyster shed, he drove Fred's car back to the house on Spyglass and left it in the driveway as if it had been there all day. He then went out back to the pier and cut loose Fred's kayak. There was a brisk wind and the tide was really rolling in, pushing the kayak further into the harbor area. Then he ran back up Washington Street to the Shipyard Lane parking lot where he'd left his car and was gone.

The impromptu plan worked beautifully. Bobby Atkinson found the body the next day when he took his skiff out to the shed to begin his daily work and discovered the body and notified the harbormaster at once.

Fred's kayak was found floating in the middle of the bay. The police concluded that The Wall Street Oysterman, a familiar face to all Duxbury oystermen and known to visit them regularly on the water wearing his usual windbreaker, old khakis, and sneakers, had paddled out to the shed in the morning and had fallen forward into it. The door, they reasoned, was partially open either because Fred was in the process of opening it, or because it had not been closed tightly enough the night before (those doors have no locks and have been known to become ajar in rocky water if not closed properly). Then he had fallen head first into the shed by either slipping on the wet platform or tripping over one of the oyster crates that were found scattered about near the shed door. Just an old guy with a history of falling taking one final tragic one.

"The storm kind of fizzled out before it got here," said Harbormaster Chip Gallagher. "I wasn't even aware any sheds had been moved. I guess Bob Atkinson and one or two others did as it turned out."

"I lost a shed in a storm last year," Atkinson later explained. "Now I'm super cautious. I have a standing order with my team. If there's any doubt, just move it out. As it happened, they didn't need to. I wasn't even aware that they had. But my guy was just following instructions."

The jury was mesmerized by this story. The trial was held in Boston. None of the jury members were from Duxbury, so all of the maps, photos, and videos provided by the prosecution were very helpful in understanding the logistics. Fallon was very credible and, because of the plea bargain, he was convicted of second-degree murder. This carried a sentence of life in prison, but with the possibility of parole in fifteen to twenty years. He'd be fifty-five when he got out and would have many years left in him.

Things turned out worse for Danforth. Some wondered if he would go for a plea bargain himself. But he did not. Even a plea would have meant a lengthy prison sentence on top of the one he had received in the Prezalix trial. At his age, he would spend the rest of his life in jail even with a plea, so he elected to continue with the trial. It was all or nothing for him. Although his attorney was successful in casting suspicion onto Karin as a likely co-conspirator, it had no impact on the case against Danforth. The jury found him guilty of murder in the first degree. This meant life in prison with no possibility of parole. He started to appeal the verdict but then backed off. He was already ruined and in prison over Prezalix. He was penniless, his wife had left him, his two children abandoned him. So he decided to take the easy way out. He was able to find someone to slip him some cyanide, and he took his own life.

Nearly two years after my move to Duxbury, the inquiry into Fred Peterson's death had finally ended.

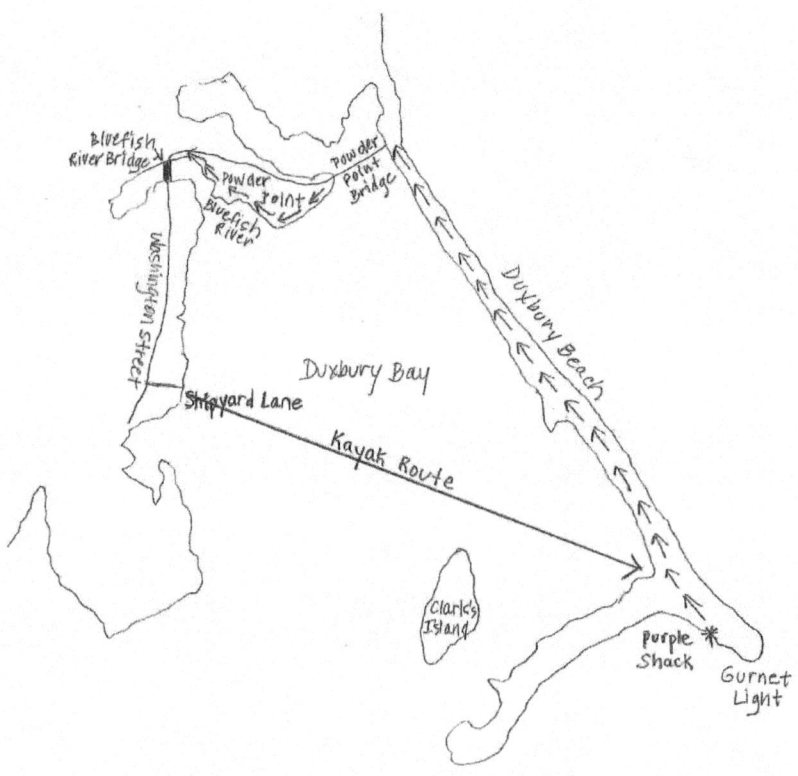

FALLON'S MURDER ROUTE

Bluefish River Bridge

Powder Point

Powder Point Bridge

Bluefish River

Washington Street

Duxbury Beach

Duxbury Bay

Shipyard Lane

Kayak Route

Clark's Island

Purple Shack

Gurnet Light

→ Fallon takes kayak from Shipyard Lane Beach, paddles to Gurnet. Kills Peterson in Purple Shack.

- - -→ Puts body in Peterson's car by Purple Shack and drives along Duxbury Beach Road, then across Powder Point, Dumps body in Oyster Shed parked against Bluefish River Bridge.

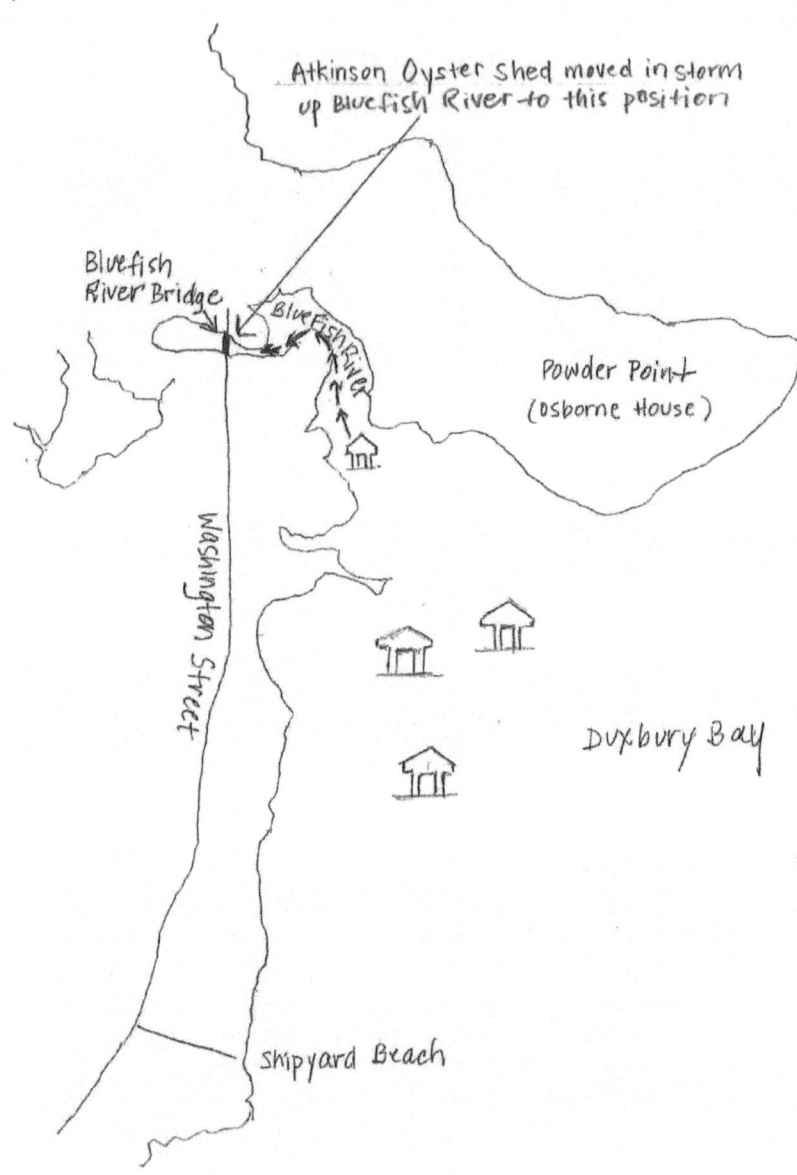

Atkinson Oyster shed moved in storm up Bluefish River to this position

Bluefish River Bridge

Bluefish River

Powder Point (Osborne House)

Washington Street

Duxbury Bay

Shipyard Beach

Clark's Island

Purple Shack

Gurnet Lighthouse

Epilogue

A year has now gone by since the death of Danforth. It has been a time of reflection and decision for me.

First the reflections. I've thought a lot about Fred. He's the real protagonist of this story, and I wish I had known him better. I'm not certain I've portrayed his personality and motivations fully here. But honestly, how realistic is it to think that I could? After all, I hadn't spent any time with him for over thirty years. Some of all this is guesswork on my part, relying as I must on what other people who knew him have told me. I've spent a good amount of time discussing him with those that he confided in most (Paula, Coco and Olivia) and others in town and elsewhere with whom he associated. Importantly, I continue to look at his sketches and paintings. They might be the closest I'll ever get to knowing who he was and what was on his mind. Taking everything into consideration, here's what I've concluded.

In general, he was extremely popular and admired for his generosity. He gave his time and money to many groups in town. He also donated a lot of money to other causes and institutions around the country. In essence, except for giving his house to me and some money to Beth and Colin, he gave away every penny he had ever made to those in need. And he made a lot.

Yes, there was some friction between him and a few people in town, but in the grand scheme of things the squabbles were very petty and none of them were his fault. Even with those few who openly resented him, he is now remembered in a positive way. He was probably dismissive of—or, at most, merely irritated with—the behavior of the two oyster farmers and probably even Trevanian.

I want to think of him as happy in Duxbury, and in general I believe he was. But there is no question that at the very end of his life he was having moments of real sadness. It bothered him greatly that he was going to die without leaving a legacy, either personal or professional.

The key figure in all this was Danforth. I was never quite clear on the exact circumstances under which he had become my uncle's lawyer. Danforth had told me they met when he was chief legal counsel for a company that was trying to negotiate a deal with Fred's company LFP. When Danforth left corporate law and went into private practice focusing on high-net-worth executives, my uncle had approached him. Fred's long-time lawyer in New York had just retired, and he wanted someone near him in Boston. Danforth's administrative assistant, with whom I've had several illuminating conversations in the last year, confirmed all that was true.

What I didn't know was that the company Danforth had worked for was Upsala, something he would not have necessarily thought was worth mentioning. Although Fred didn't like the deal to acquire the company, he had been impressed with Danforth. Fred was long gone from LFP by then, and it wasn't till the very end—probably only a few days before his death—that he fully realized what a snake Danforth was. Hiring him as his lawyer was the biggest mistake he had ever made, and it cost him his life. I was surprised that a successful businessman like Fred could have made such a misjudgment. When Danforth's assistant was asked about that during the trial, she said:

"Lyle began to say that as he got older, Mr. Peterson had lost his fastball. That's the term he used. He always laughed when he said that, like he was happy about it."

Maybe that was it. Although Fred was okay physically, it was very possible his mental state had declined, and Danforth took advantage of it. Or maybe Danforth was so diabolically clever that he would have fooled anybody. I've known people like that. Clearly it was Danforth he was depicting in the bizarre sketch of the face with a question mark. It was somebody that had fooled him, and the title of the sketch The *Face of Evil* leaves no ambiguity about how he ended up feeling about Danforth and what he had done.

One day about three months after the trial, I was looking at the box of things I'd brought back from the Gurnet. For what seemed the umpteenth time, I read the note on that sketch.

Title: The *Face of Evil*
Note: scene of bustling harbormaster area, boats (sail and motor), three oyster floaters. A human face hovering in sky above it all (a question mark where features should be), menacing. Who is this and how to depict? As The *Hangman?* The *Merchant?* The *Fool?*

I had a question on something else I saw in that box, and I asked Paula about it.

"I've pretty much accounted for all the things I found in the Gurnet shack," I said. "The mermaid is being restored at the art complex, and I think I understand the sketches as much as I'm ever going to. All of his calendar notes have pretty much clarified themselves over time—except for one. I never thought it was significant, but who knows? Maybe you will understand."

"What is it?"

"Take a look." I showed her a piece of paper onto which I'd written down the entry in question.

April 15
Noir class
Séance on a Wet Afternoon
Hits close to home. Painfully relevant

"Did you and Fred see this movie in your noir class?"

"Yes. It's a British movie. It's excellent. I'd never seen it before."

"Me neither. What's it about?"

"It's quite offbeat. It's about a very disturbed medium who channels a baby boy she gave birth to that died shortly afterward. It kind of made her crazy. Trying to communicate with the baby kept her going. Why do you ask?"

"I'm wondering what he means about it hitting close to home and being painfully relevant. Any idea why he'd say that?"

"No idea. Fred never said much in that class. He wasn't like you and me with the movies. He liked them but didn't love them."

So the note remained a mystery. What on earth was going on with him?

Then I learned something significant from my Uncle Mike that offered a possible clue. Because our family was now fully reconciled, he was eager to talk about the past, and he told me something I had never heard before. Only he and my mother had known it. I, of course, knew that Fred and Mary had had no children. What I didn't know was that she had taken a fertility drug and had given birth to a full-term child with severe birth defects that lived for a week. It was a boy that they had named Fred Jr.

It got even worse, said Mike. The fertility drug produced side effects that made further pregnancy difficult. It was ultimately taken off the market. But the damage had been done to Fred and Mary. She was never able to get pregnant again, and the experience had scarred both of them for life. Mary died of breast cancer several years after that, and Fred lived out his grief alone. This raised a question in my mind, and I thought Coco was the right person to ask for perspective. We met about once a month, and Fred would always come up.

"Was Fred religious?" I asked her over lunch one day.

"He did talk in a kind of spirituality toward the end," she said. "Why?"

"I found some tarot cards in his possession when he died. Paula told me a while back that she thought those cards were inspiring his last sketches, and I think that's true. It always struck me as a strange source of inspiration, though. Kind of mystical for a man who seemed very pragmatic. She also told me that he was interested in a movie about a medium who channeled her dead child. He said it 'hit close to home.' Those were his exact words. Then I recently learned that Mary had given birth to a baby boy that had died within a week. Did you know that?"

"Yes. I knew. He didn't want to talk much about it, though. It was too painful. I did know that he had come to believe in an afterlife and that he'd be reunited with Mary and the baby. Have you seen the epitaph on his grave?"

"Yes, a couple of times. It says he is now reunited with Mary."

"He had told me he was having her ashes moved from the cemetery in Toledo to be buried with him here someday. And did you notice the Latin phrase also?"

"Yes, but I never translated it."

"He explained it to me. It's *Ut omnes unum sint*. It means *that* they *all may be one*. I am sure *all* includes their baby too."

"Did he follow any organized religion?"

"Not that I know of. But he did have an interest in transcendentalism. Do you know anything about it?"

"Very little."

"It was a nineteenth-century philosophical movement centered in New England. It emphasized instinct and nature rather than logic and reason. He made several trips to Concord where the thought leaders like Thoreau and Emerson had lived. I know he had some books on the subject. You might check out his bookcase in his study. That's all I know."

Tarot cards, communing with spirits, and being reunited with a dead child, a belief in instinct over logic. These were all on Fred's mind at the end of his life. It felt like he had been struggling to make sense out of all that had happened to him in his long life, and he had turned toward a sort of mysticism. So some ill-defined "otherworldliness" must be added into the jumble of contradictions that made this enigmatic man who he was.

But now that I knew more of his backstory, there was nothing enigmatic about how he felt about drugs being on the market that could cause harm. One had wrecked his little family. It was easy to see why he was so upset that his former company had played an enabling role with another one, Prezalix, even if they had done so unknowingly. He was on a mission to see that justice was done.

His personal experience certainly shed more light on the sketch of the *Smyrna* unloading illicit cargo and the reference to "Unfortunate Partnerships." The courts granted the Duxbury Rural and Historical Society's request to keep Samuel Osborne's logbook that the Trevanians had claimed to have found (as it turned out, there really was one). Caroline let me look at it and, sure enough, Trevanian had been telling the truth. Samuel had written that he'd obtained a valuable golden object from Georgia. He never clearly identified what it was—it was the Trevanians with their knowledge of the Black Sea coast and its history who had come to the conclusion it was the fleece of the Argonaut story. No such golden object—fleece or otherwise—has been found, at least not yet.

But far more importantly, Samuel's notes made clear that he and his father Josiah had formed a partnership with a couple of customs officials at the docks in East Boston to illegally offload Turkish opium into the country. My uncle had learned of this at the same time he'd discovered the Prezalix scandal. His sketch of the *Smyrna*'s mysterious cargo and his notes alluding to "unfortunate partnerships" seemed to be a reference to two drug scandals two centuries apart: the Osbornes and the customs officials with opium and Upsala and LFP with Prezalix. That third banner in the final painting was going to be a reference to the latter, I felt sure. To him, it was a case of the past and present blurring together. He was obsessed with that theme and it was one of the reasons why he, as a descendant of the Petersons and Soules, so closely identified himself with the land, the house on it, and its history.

Adding it all up, I have to admit Fred remains an elusive figure to me. He was a very benevolent, highly successful, and extremely principled man—but one with deep secrets who was fighting some past demons.

I know one thing for certain, though: against all odds, he had reached back into his past and put his faith in a fondly remembered nephew and son of his best friend to carry out his legacy. And in doing so, he had changed my life completely.

So much for my reflections. Now for the decisions.

* * * * *

As the months went by, it had become obvious that Gloria and I had no future together. I'd gone to Toledo a couple of times and she to Duxbury. Something was missing, and we both finally admitted it. Our split was friendly. I even asked her if she would still do my taxes. She politely refused, saying it was better I find somebody in Boston. I didn't push the issue, but there was another reason.

Julie and I had seen more and more of each other, often by chance, around town. I don't even remember asking her out on a date—we were too old for that. Everything developed organically you might say. We just always seemed to be running into each other and deciding to do something together last minute. I found her attractive, bright, and empathetic. She says she found me very funny and thought I had a nice way with people.

"I knew from the start you were the type of guy she needed," Nancy confided in me. "You make her smile. She hadn't done that in years."

One day a couple of months ago, we were having dinner at The Shipyard Inn and talking about the future. By the time dessert came, we'd agreed we should get married. A month later we tied the knot at a very small ceremony at my house. I knew that Colin was a deacon in his church, and so I thought it would be a nice touch to have him perform the ceremony and keep it all in the family. Bennie Kapler was my best man (again).

"Get it right this time, Snake" was his rather inelegant toast to me (I later overheard Judy giving him a good tongue-lashing).

There had been one other significant development too. Jocko and Olivia announced their engagement. They are going to get married in the fall up in Vermont where her mother and brother live. Donald will be the best man and a colleague of Julie's at the art complex will be the maid of honor. The wedding will be a pretty big affair and held at the Trapp Family Lodge in Stowe. Aside from Stowe being important to the latter day Osborne family, the lodge is a wonderful place. It's connection to Duxbury (distant though it be) adds to its appeal too. There will be many joyful sounds of music there this autumn.

The other big thing in Jocko's life is he is finally finishing up his dissertation at the University of Toledo. Even better, he has actually been offered a job at the large Boston coffee company in their product supply department. They love the guy. I do too, and I love that he's going to have a paycheck.

This made us all question where to live, and I threw out an idea that surprised everyone. Nancy had moved into the apartment near the bakery in the center of town and was managing very well there. Julie had been living alone in their house near Camp Wing ever since. She loved the place, and I liked it too. It was plenty big enough for our needs. I asked her if she'd be okay for us to live there.

"Of course!" she said. "Spyglass is beautiful, but it's so big. The two of us would get lost in there."

"I agree. Then there are the neighbors. The Trevanians are still fighting extradition from Geneva to the U.S., but one thing is for certain. They will never return to this country. So their house was just sold to a young guy with two kids who works in crypto. He and Tommy are already calling themselves bros. And the Spauldings are going to finally downsize and move to a retirement community. Probably somebody young who works as an influencer or something like that will buy it. Milo Sarducci and his Algebra-teacher wife won't fit in. A younger growing family should live there."

"Got anybody in mind?" she smiled.

"I do. I think a young up-and-coming man in the animal waste supply chain coffee bean business whose wife is a curator in an art museum would fit right in, particularly since they say they'd like to have a few kids. That place is big and needs to be filled."

"Makes sense to me."

It did to me too, and for another reason I didn't mention. It seemed embarrassing to share it—sentimental, superstitious, emotional, all of the above. Jocko and Olivia living there would mean that the descendants of the original owners of the property, the Soules and Petersons, would be united with the descendants of the Osbornes who, somewhere in the shadowy recesses of time, had gotten ahold of the land and built a house there where a family had lived for two hundred years. No more drama. No more curses. Just a straight line across four hundred years of American history connecting the past with the present (and future). An appropriate ending, I thought.

Surely this was the best legacy my uncle Fred could ever have dreamed of. With all the happiness he had provided me, I was honored to give him something in return.

ACKNOWLEDGEMENTS

The saying "it takes a village" could not be more appropriate—both literally and figuratively—with regard to the writing of this book. It is no exaggeration to say that I could never have written it without the extraordinary help of some people who know our little village of Duxbury far better than I can ever hope to.

I would like to acknowledge several people above all, starting with Carolyn Ravenscroft, archivist and historian of the Duxbury Rural and Historical Society. When I emailed her out of the blue and told her about my project, she was happy to help. I showed up at her office on St. George Street unannounced a number of times and would sheepishly say, "I have just one more question." She routinely would drop everything and dig out one dusty tome or another from the Drew Archives that would answer my question. Among other things, she gave me the story of the *Smyrna* and its Black Sea voyage. I'd never heard of it and knew immediately I wanted to use it. She is a true scholar.

Many New England towns have great history, but few have a group as dedicated and knowledgeable as the Duxbury Rural and Historical Society to present it to the public. Headed by Executive Director Sabrina Kaplan, the DRHS staff and trustees do a fabulous job of maintaining a number of historic properties around town and offering informative and well-researched talks and events throughout the year. Here's to the next 400 years! Needless to say no one in this book is based on any member of the DRHS in even the slightest way.

Similarly, Tony Kelso, Duxbury town historian and program coordinator for Duxbury Senior Center, provided crucial information and perspective. He supplied me with documents that helped me understand the overall history of Powder Point and the evolution of property rights there. While the Osborne family is fictitious, as is Spyglass Lane, his insights helped me construct what I hope is an accurate historical context for such a family and place to have plausibly existed there. An engaging speaker as well as historian, he, like Carolyn, is an extraordinary resource for the town.

And a very special thanks to Charles Weyerhaeuser and Peter Mello for allowing me to use the wonderful Art Complex Museum as a key element of this book. Founded and created in 1971 by Carl and Edith Weyerhaeuser, it is an incredible institution and resource not just for Duxbury, but for the entire region. Charlie was the Director of the Museum for fifty years and is something of an institution himself in town. Under the leadership of current Executive Director Peter Mello, the Museum is poised for another generation of success and strong community engagement. Thanks, gentlemen. And Olivia Phipps is, of course, completely fictional.

I had a fantastic conversation with Terry Vose. I had asked Tony if there were any "real" Petersons still living in town (my characters with that name are all fictitious save the original John Peterson and his in-laws the Soules). He immediately connected me to Terry, whose mother was a Peterson. Terry told me a bit about his own history on Powder Point living in a "real" Peterson house and his memories of the area going back over seventy years. It was fascinating, and I told him he should write his own book. Go for it, Terry! And thanks.

I want to thank Andre Martecchini for offering me his encouragement and support. A former member of the Selectboard, world class sailor (no exaggeration—South Africa to Australia in a sailboat? Wow!), and friend, Andre helped me understand a few of the basics about how a small New England town operates. He pointed me in the right direction a couple of times.

Most notably, he connected me to Joe Grady. Joe has had a long and illustrious career in Duxbury governance in land conservation and other endeavors, including his current ownership of an oyster farm. Joe was nice enough to take me out to his oyster farm in the bay. After furnishing me with the requisite oysterman gear (waders, overalls, oyster sacks, etc.), I ventured into the water to try my hand at oyster farming for a morning. He then let me climb onto his oyster shed where I proceeded to lie down spreadeagle trying to simulate a dead body. God knows what was running through his head when I gave him my phone and asked him to take my picture (see Outtakes). Whatever he was thinking, he was gentleman enough to keep it to himself.

I got additional key information on the oyster industry from Duxbury Harbormaster Jake Emerson. All of the oyster farms and farmers mentioned in the book are totally fictitious other than Island Creek, but I tried to get the basics of the industry right. Jake is a busy guy, but he graciously took the time on a couple of different occasions to answer some of my rookie questions. Thanks, Jake.

On a couple of occasions, I launched my kayak out of Shipyard Lane and paddled out to some oyster sheds. Trying to get an appreciation of life in the industry, I had several ad hoc conversations with oyster farmers (I'm sorry I never got their names). I learned what a great group of people work in this industry—committed, energetic, collegial. Any of the events portrayed in the book regarding the oyster industry are 100% the product of my imagination. Any errors I've made regarding the industry are totally my own and are unintentional.

Many thanks to Preston Tice, Assistant Director of Fleet, Campus, Safety for the Duxbury Bay Maritime School. He took me out in his boat to tour the bay one fine June morning, pointing out many elements of it I would have otherwise missed. Importantly, he took me to Clark's Island where he gave me a little tour (first time I ever discussed Plato in a motorboat). I also appreciate his willingness to help with some photos. DBMS is a great town asset. My California-based granddaughter Vivian Snyder has spent several summers now participating in various excellent DBMS programs. Thanks to that, she now knows there's a pretty great seacoast on this side of the country too!

This is my third book, and in each one I find Carl Meier's Lifelong Learning film noir class creeping into it one way or another. I'm pretty sure he'd deem most of the many film references in this book appropriate to a tale that does have noirish elements to it (I'm guessing the lone exceptions would be The *Sound of Music* and Don Knotts in The *Incredible Mr. Limpet*). Keep it up, Carl. I may want to write another book, and I need your material…

Al Bangert has been a key resource in two books I've written. He is an engineer and has spent his career in manufacturing and supply chain management. My last book *Secrets Among Friends* is narrated by an engineer that has more than a few things in common with Al (including a couple of similar career moves and a wife named Donna!). In this book, I was looking for a profession that a free-spirited guy like Jocko could finally get excited about. One day Al and I were in his kitchen having a general discussion on offbeat supply chains and whether a whole book might be written on this subject. We began discussing exotic coffee, and I immediately knew that Jocko had finally found employment. Thanks, Al!

Then there were the chance meetings with interesting people while poking around doing "research." On a visit to the Pilgrim's Hall Museum in Plymouth (America's oldest museum by the way), I met Kathleen Wall, Visitor Services and Public Program Manager. I discovered that she has been a reenactor at Plimoth Pawtuxet Museum over the years (Mary Soule no less!). She not only told me a bit about the Soules, but also how the Plimoth Pawtuxet reenactors research and master those great Elizabethan-era accents that they skillfully adopt for their character. Milo Sarducci was the (il)logical next step. And Ruby Schiller, Executive Assistant to the Executive Director of the Duxbury Art Complex Museum, was kind enough to show me around the impressive campus one afternoon when I wandered into a mosaic class by accident. The museum was closed that day, but she opened it up to give me a little tour.

Besides the oyster business, I wanted to include another contemporary local business into the book. Because I love the store, I chose Brothers Market (the parent company is Roche Brothers). Thanks

296

to Kevin Barner (CEO), Roger Bowles (COO), and, in particular, Russ Blais (the great store manager of Brothers in Duxbury) for being good sports in allowing mention of their business in this novel. I was tempted to make one of them into a murder suspect but thought they wouldn't consider that a good marketing idea for a local, community-minded grocery store.

A very loud and sincere thanks to Stephanie Blackman of Riverhaven! Her editorial skills and advice were of tremendous value. I wanted to keep every aspect of this book as local as possible, and I'm so glad to have worked with Riverhaven and a real pro like Stephanie.

Shout outs to three family members. First, my sister-in-law Kathleen Keeney. She helped me with the legal aspects of this book. She answered every one of my questions in great detail. (I shudder to think how much time she devoted to this—perhaps it was a way to keep her mind off of the travails of her beloved New York Mets?) She's one sharp lady who really knows her law. She's another one who could—and should—write a book.

Secondly, there's my son-in-law Dana Snyder in LA. My narrator Jake makes a living doing cartoon voices. So does Dana. I kind of looked to Dana as a bit of inspiration in creating Jake. Not from a biographical standpoint—there is no resemblance there at all between the two (other than that both are very successful, have done work for Disney and The Cartoon Network, and like "old-time humor"). But I always thought that Dana's profession was an interesting one, and I thought it would be fun to integrate it into the story. Snippets of what I've learned from Dana about the animation world are sprinkled into this story.

The year this book was published saw a couple of wonderful births. The first were twins—twin towns that is. Duxbury and the very real town of Dorking, England agreed to be "twinned" based on a shared history. About thirty miles south of London, Dorking was the birthplace of two Mayflower Pilgrims: Peter Browne and Priscilla Mullins. She later became the wife of John Alden and was immortalized in Longfellow's poem. The Mullins house in Dorking still stands and is the last remaining original house of a Pilgrim in the UK today. Aside from these two real people, Dorking was also the birthplace of an "unreal" one—Benjamin Peterson, a fictitious descendent of the original Duxbury Peterson, John. According to my narrative, Benjamin emigrates from Dorking to Toledo and establishes a branch of the family there.

The second birth was June Liberato, daughter of Michelle and Chris. Welcome to Planet Earth, Junie! The world needs you!

Finally there's my wonderful wife Eileen. Once again she's helped me out with some great sketches. As an artist, Fred Peterson has nothing on her! Thanks, Sweetie. What a journey we've had together!

OUTTAKES

An oyster shed moved up the Bluefish River
to the Washington Street Bridge before a storm

Acting out a murder scene: No Academy Award here.

A "landlubber" trying to learn the oyster business

Kayaks piled up at Shipyard Lane Beach.
Clark's Island and Gurnet Point in the distance

47506CB00004B/1012

9 781951 854508